WIDOW
~1881~

FLATS JUNCTION SERIES
BOOK 2

SARA DAHMEN

WIDOW 1881

Promontory Press
www.promontorypress.com

ISBN: 9781773740393

Cover designed by Edge of Water Design
Typeset by Spica Book Design
Printed in Canada

0 9 8 7 6 5 4 3 2 1

To Katie and Heather,
always my first editors
and for always reading

and my husband John,
who allows me to disappear for weeks
in the crazed writing silence that comes out of the blue.

Contents

Rockport. 1

Dakota Territory 9

Gloucester 299

Notes for the Reader 409

Acknowledgements 412

Historical References. 413

Book Club Questions 415

SITUATIONS WANTED

THE MILITARY

ALL VOLUNTEERS WHO DES
ire to receive the highest bound-
ies paid cash down in hand should
apply to CAPTAIN & CO., 300
Broadway, room 12.

ALIENS - ENGLISH, SCOTCH,
Irish, German and all foreigners
wishing to volunteer are guaranteed
the highest bounties, cash in hand.
Apply early. CAPTAIN & CO.,
300 Broadway, room 12.

A NUMBER OF WELL RECOM
mended Irish females want situations as cooks, chambermaids,
nurses, girls for general housework
&c., at Mrs. KELLY'S Home &
Orphanage, No. 20 Dartmouth.

A NURSE, THOROUGHLY
trained and competent to take the
entire care of an infant or two small
children wishes a situation; is a
Protestant and a good seamstress.
Superior references. Call at 31
Bridge Street *no good*

A WOMAN WISHES TO TAKE
in a gentleman or family's washing
at her own residence. Call at 45
Gray St.

A COOK WANTS A SITUATION
understands English and American
cooking; is an experience baker;
good city reference given. Can
be seen for two days at No. 4 W.
Canton.

WANTED: 20 4-OX TEAMS and
10 Wagons for Freighting from
New York to the Black Hills. For
particulars, address Smith & Parker,
New York.

SITUATIONS WANTED

A YOUNG ENGLISH GIRL
wishes a situation as nurse and plain
sewer; willing to make herself useful;
good city references. Call at 5 Med-
ford Qt.

A SITUATION WANTED - TO TAKE
care of children to do plain sewing or
light chamberwork. Call for two days
at 11 Yarouth St.

A RESPECTABLE GIRL WISHES A
situation as a plain cook, washer and
ironer; has good city reference. Call at
Waltham St. in the candy store.

A SITUATION WANTED - AS WAIT-
ress; no objection to chamberwork and
waiting. City references. Call at 202
East St. Botolph.

A YOUNG WOMAN WISHES A
situation - to take care of growing children and do sewing or chamberwork
and waiting; wages not so much an
object as a quiet home. Appointments
at Chester Sq.

WANTED: BY HOLLAND GIRL-
chamberwork five days a week. No
English. Room 3, South St

HOUSEWORK, WANTED, A WO
an for general housework in the western territories. Must be sturdy. Send
word Box 30.

WANTED PROTESTANT PLAIN
cook, washer and ironer; inquire
through Lewis Law.

THE ADVERTISER (WHO HAS JUST
lost her baby) and has a full breast of
milk wishes a situation as wet nurse.
Can be seen at 8 Oxford Pl. between
Oxford & Harrison Ave. *perhaps!*

SITUATIONS WANTED

WANTED - COOK, GENTLEWOM
an elderly preferred. Write to Box 48,
care Hampton Law.

if only...
IN RETURN FOR PASSAGE TO AU
stralia, refined young lady will render
services as Companion, Secretary or
Nanny. Expert stenographer. Highest
references. Box 16, care Surry & Associates.

HONORABLE AMERICAN, 30,
with some means and hiw own office,
desires acquaintance of sincere, affe-
cate, Protestant girl; object matrimony;
correspondence onfidential. Box 98,
Boston. *already tried this...*

HOUSEWORK, WANTED, A WOM
an for housework in the country. Ital-
ian or French. Apply through Box 16,
care Surry & Associates.

HELP WANTED IMMEDIATELY:
Cook laundress and housekeeper for
Great House. Apply in person 170
Pemberton Sq. References required.

HOUSEWORK - MIDDLE-AGED
woman for housework: plain cooking.
Possibly could use woman with small
child. Boston. Apply 67 Chauncy
Ave.

MAID, WHITE, WANTED FOR GEN
eral housework; reference required.
Call at 11 Chatham St.

WANTED - A MIDDLE-AGED OR
elderly woman to assist in general
housework and plain cooking. Inquire
Box 59.

Box 30
February 3, 1881

Dear Sir or Madam,

    I am writing in regards to the notice in the Boston Advertiser for a housekeeper. Until my husband's passing, I managed our household, some plain cooking, and general nursing for him. My husband's affairs are nearly in order, and I would be available to take the train to the Territories as soon as 1 March.

    It appears $6 per week is the expected rate in Boston for a housekeeper, but I am very willing to take a reduced wage if room and board are included and to account for any discrepancies between the city and the west. My recommendations and references are few, but we might arrange a meeting if it will facilitate this opportunity further.

    The west has always garnered some particular fascination for me, and I look forward to an opportunity to experience it. As for my sturdiness, I assure you I am not lacking.

    You may contact me through my late husband's offices. I appreciate your consideration.

    Sincerely,
    Mrs. Jane Weber
    c/o Ward & Weber Shipping
    Boston

To   Dr. P. Kinney

Received at _____

5 February   188 1

Ad results 2 candidates. One claims nursing and hardiness.

$3/wk wage. Tara can assess.   Weather?

R. McH

Blank No. 1.

The Western Union Telegraph Company.

Dated _____ *Feb 10* • _188 1_

Received at BOSTON PROPER OFFICE

READ THE NOTICE AT THE TOP.

To: Dr. R. MacHugh

Capable, hardy nurse?
Is sufficient $2/week, rm/board.
Check ability. Regards to Tara —

Weather terrible. Hskeepr wait 'til March.
—Paddy

Mrs. Jane Weber
c/o Ward & Weber Shipping
Boston
February 15

Madam,

Please excuse my delay as I required some weeks to telegram west. I write on behalf of my colleague, Doctor Patrick Kinney, who works in Flats Junction, Dakota Territory and requires a housekeeper and cook. The winter has been especially difficult in the Territories this year, and I have had to wait to receive his response.

The death of his elderly relation has left him without means to manage his house and he has asked me to solicit someone as soon as possible. We believe your background in simple nurse duties will be helpful as Doctor Kinney handles all manner of illness and issue—both man and beast—and any assistance would be beneficial.

My wife, Tara, will meet you this Wednesday at the Tremont to disclose all the particularities of your arrangement and to receive any of your references. While you seem very eager to begin your adventure, the weather in the Territories will likely keep you in Boston until later in March.

Please plan to be at the Tremont in three days at noon. I have also enclosed the correspondence between Doctor Kinney and me pertaining to your employment.

Sincerely,
Dr. Robert MacHugh

Box 30
Boston
February 18, 1881

Dear Dr. R. MacHugh,

Please extend my deepest regards to your wife for her time and company at the Tremont earlier this week. Mrs. MacHugh led me to believe the position is mine to take, and I hope to reassure you with this note that I am ready as soon as spring allows for better travel.

The reduced wage, while lower than I had hoped, will suffice with room and board included, and I look forward to confirming the appointment with your colleague in the Dakotas. In truth, I am relieved my lack of references did not meet with more resistance. As Mrs. MacHugh may have mentioned, I have little to keep me in Boston with my husband's passing in December, and I would like to find some way to busy myself away from society. It seems Providence certainly has a hand in this situation.

I received your additional note regarding which train lines to take out from Boston, and which to switch to in Chicago and Milwaukee. I will plan to go through Vermillion and Yankton to Flats Junction, and I will await further instructions with anticipation.

Sincerely,
Mrs. Jane Weber

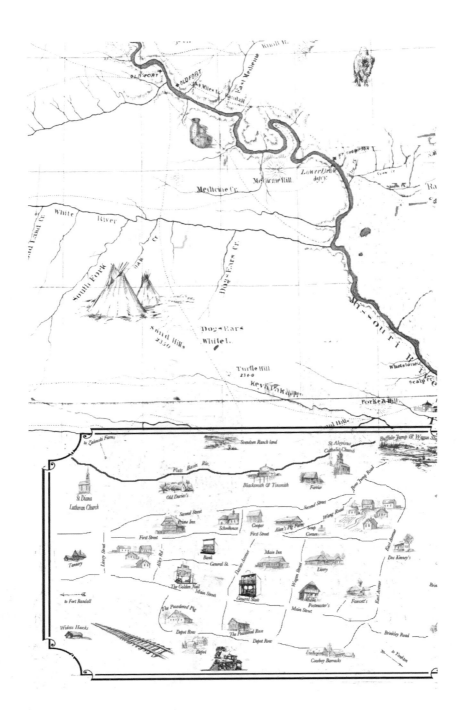

RICE'S
SECTIONAL MAP OF
DAKOTA
TERRITORY.
DRAUGHTED BY FRED STURNEGK.
Published by the St. Paul Lithog. & Eng. Co.
1872
ST. PAUL, MINNESOTA.

Widow 1881

Flats Junction Series

Rockport

12 March 1881

Black is proper.

Black covers my closets and my body, drowning me in the rules, expectations, and pity that come with it. I know all the rules, and I've followed them as precisely as I should. Well, except for the one week when I didn't, and now I must suffer those consequences. I suppose there is many a good reason a woman in black shouldn't follow temptation or allow her curiosity to take over in the absence of a sturdy husband.

Smoothing the fine black wool skirt over my knees, I gaze out of Mother's parlor window and absently pet the frail china vase she sets out for visitors to see from the street. Fear, despair, and something like exhilaration battle in my mind and chase around my chest as the heaviness of Mother's borrowed jet brooch weighs me down. I'll have to return it when my mourning is over.

The tinkle of a tea tray heralds her entry, and she drifts in behind the maid. I wait for Mother to sit and shoo Mary away before taking my old childhood seat to her right.

"Will you pour, Jane?"

I take the silver pot, testing the weight of it as I lift and pour into the elegant cups set out for the occasion. She watches quietly, adding a lump of sugar and a sliver of lemon with the small pewter fork. I stare at her soft white hands and the gleam of the tea set and note the nutmeg dusted across the top of the bread. Will spice be easy to find in the Dakotas? Will I be able to use half the recipes I know?

"Are you sure, Jane, that you want to do this?" Mother asks. Her eyebrows are high, and the slim fingers holding her tea cup grip hard and tight as her knuckles quiver. "Your father and I have room here."

Mother's voice is cultured and gentle. She means it would be the appropriate next step. Without a home or children, or even my late husband's business to keep me in Boston, a proper, well-bred widow woman would do her job best by fading into obscurity, letting the blacks of her gown fade to purple and violet and grey. She assumes I am what I have long strived to be since I married: decorous, respectable, and amiable. She doesn't know I am running from her as well as everyone else; that this dash to the West is more than a fanciful, grief-stricken whim. Like my father and sister, Anne, Mother thinks I have once again read far too much than is good for me, and that I have been taken with the claims of Western adventure. Anne expects me back within a month. I hope I prove her wrong. I'll *have* to prove her wrong.

I don't bother to answer my mother's hidden request. There's nothing more to say. The train leaves Rockport in roughly an hour. Though the tea cools quickly in the china, I drink slowly and with care, savoring the sugar and the lemon I've added. My research didn't need to be deep to understand how lemons will likely be hard to find in the Territories.

Will I ever taste a lemon again?

What will it be like? How will I fit in? I know my place in Massachusetts. First the daughter of a businessman, and then the wife of one. I understand my place as a widow too, and perhaps I would have succumbed to it had I not been free with my curiosity after my husband passed. I will be hired help in the West, and not much more. But it is the safest course given the research I've gleaned in the hidden corners of the Boylston Street Public Library. I will have a better chance in the West—for everything.

"Mother, I'll miss you," I say suddenly, heading off the next round of indirect pleading she is certain to try. "But you know me."

Her mouth goes slack and pulls down, revealing the wrinkles she tries so hard to hide with powder and ointment. She's still beautiful to me, though, and I reach to grasp her hand.

"I gave up adventuring when I was a child. I have a chance now, and the funds to do it. When else will I have such a choice? But I'll still miss you."

She sighs and smiles lightly. "I suppose I should not be surprised. If Anne had done this, that would be far more extraordinary. But it will be an experience, I'm sure."

Likely there will be so many experiences I'll be light-headed and spinning in short order. But it will be research of its own kind, and I believe I can manage that. If there is anything good that comes from widowhood, it is that I can make up my own mind without asking anyone else to sanction it.

The mantel clock chimes and I stand, clearing the skinny creases of the wool and shifting the layers of fine petticoats underneath. Mother floats to her feet too, looking stricken and defeated.

When I embrace her, she feels oddly frail and small. The lace on her bodice is crisp and sharp and pointy under my chin, and the swish of her satin gown sounds overloud in the foyer. Father has had the wagon brought to the front and he waits next to it, looking gruff, grizzled, and severe as always. I climb in, the sea wind tickling the edges of my black crepe bonnet, and the heavy salt air soaking into my wilting gloves. Will I wear gloves in the Dakotas? Does anyone?

Yanking hard on the long seam of the left-handed glove, I rip it out so the string dangles, rendering the entire piece useless. It feels strangely vindicating.

Mother waves with her edged hanky, eyes bright. She won't cry in public—I know this just as sure as I know I have no wish to bring any shame on her, or Father, or even my sister. It's yet another reason I'm leaving. Father jerks the horse's reins and clicks his teeth and we're off, my small carpet bag and trunk bouncing along the cobbled roads.

"Seems a bit dramatic, Jane," Father comments. "Not that I will try to dissuade you."

I twist in surprise. "You think I can manage?"

"Well, you've handled Henry's house for the past few years without any mishap." Father guides the horse around the edge of town, hugging the ocean before we turn toward the train station. "If you can keep house in Boston, I suppose you can in the West. Might be a bit rougher, but you'll be paid."

Father doesn't know how little I'll make, nor the hazy expectations of my ability to help with patients. Distress and uncertainty have strangled most of the excitement I've harbored. Without many photographs or reliable sources other than the few sensational dime novels I've secretly scoured, I have had no way to really prepare for this journey. I only know there will not be teas or fancy service or maids. And I am sure there will not be china or silks or lace, and I can only hope there's some way to get food from a nearby general mercantile. Will I be expected to grow and store the food? Will I butcher my own meat? I hold back a shudder, feeling the shivery shot of panic pull up, and then convince myself once more that Flats Junction is a sound choice. The town can support a full-fledged doctor! It must have some sort of civility and be more than just a shanty-town.

At the train depot, Father helps me out of the wagon and carries my bags stiffly, but purposefully. His back almost creaks with the effort, but he will not have any of his women do such heavy labor. I watch the other men loading trunks and boxes while the women flutter fans and hats and scarves against the chilly breeze whisking through from the water. I tighten my own wraps and wait for Father to handle all the particularities of finding me a seat for the first jump of a tangled journey. It has been odd to be home these past few weeks after the sale of the Boston house, waiting for the weather to clear in the Territories, and getting a sharp taste of widowhood under the roof of my parents. It is almost as if I had never left.

I wait on the cushioned bench at the depot, smashing my hands inside the black fabric of my skirts. Civilization bubbles up suddenly: a waft of the nearby perfumery, the buttery brown puffs from the bakery, and the sounds of hooves on stone-paved roads. The smooth tones of the passing ladies dances over my ears, the clip of their shoes light and neat.

"You're settled," Father tells me as he steps from the dusty stair of the train car. The engine huffs its impatience and the fresh paint on the front car gleams black and red and yellow.

"Thank you, Father," I tell him, hoping to convey more in my tone than I feel I can tell him outright. He takes my hand and presses it, squeezes it, and then releases it. His mouth is tight under the whiskers, and yet he has no air of despair or urgency. He might expect to see me home too, just like Anne does. "I will try to write. And goodbye."

He nods gravely and rocks back on his heels, hiding his hands behind his waist, and I smile, wishing I could embrace him for all he'd bluster.

It is my own urgency pulling me into the train, my own hope to escape. I find my trunk and hold tightly to my carpet bag. When the locomotive starts, I feel the ties of my life—a curated, careful life—start to fray. I'm not sure if that is frightening or freeing.

Dakota Territory

CHAPTER 1
20 March 1881

"Madam." The gruff whisper wakes me.

I blink in the dusky morning. The pasty, round face of the conductor peers down at me. The hard seat, itchy unwashed flannel, and spongy unending smell of wet wool wraps itself around me once again. Why couldn't he just let me doze? It's the ticket agent's job to be polite. What kind of politeness wakes a woman in the middle of a long journey?

"It's your stop, Madam."

My head clears as much as it can from sleep. We've arrived! Finally!

"Flats Junction?" I ask.

He nods sympathetically, glancing down at the circle of gold on my finger. My ring tells a story of its own, and it has bought some protection on this journey into the West: either I have lost a husband, or I go to this wasteland to stay with one. Neither is easy, just like this horrifically long train ride. They say a person can reach coast to coast on the railroad in less than a week, but my journey from Boston to the Dakotas has been almost nine days. Reports I'd read must not have accounted for the changing of trains, or the occasional worn rail that breaks, or the fact that the weather has been abnormally difficult this year.

I glance outside and shudder as I gather up my smaller bag. It looks like it's still bitingly cold. I grip my coat tighter around my neck and follow the narrow, dirty path out of the train. I'd been lucky enough to secure a lower berth in the center of the car, and I spent most of the journey escaping the jar of wheels and opening doors, but I am still eager to escape the scents and fumes and choke of smoke and coal. Besides, I am beyond anxious and excited to see my new home. I *hope* it will be home.

The platform of Flats Junction is brittle and weathered. The creak of planks, boots, and wheels is still subdued. The train groans behind me as the steam billows under my skirts, stuffing more black smoke under my petticoats.

It is a rather large town with a mud-packed main street intersected by a few other wide, rutted dirt roads. I am surprised to see so many houses. I had thought the Territories were sparsely populated. What makes this town so special? Was the train junction here first, or was it the town and then the train? While it is unexpected, I am pleased with the number of families Flats Junction sustains. Perhaps it will not be so desolate here. I pretend I don't see the raggedy edges of all the buildings, the leftover drifts of snow melting slowly under the ropes strung or broken between homes. As I pause, a tiny Chinese man walks past and whacks a large pig on the bottom with a hard stick. He ignores me completely and hobbles away, shouting a completely indecipherable language and continuing to thwack the sow heartily. He is so small I am not sure the pig can even feel his attack.

I hear the thump of my small trunk, and the conductor tips his fingers at me as he drops it unceremoniously at my side. How is it I have sat on a train for eight days and yet do not know the names of any of my companions, nor the different ticket agents and conductors? I would like to know his name to thank him warmly, but propriety and expected train travel etiquette chains my tongue. The rules are quite clear: no singing, whistling or loud discussion at the depots or on the train; no taking a hack between stations; no drinking; no elaborate clothing or jewels. The last is laughable. I have never had any jewels.

Other people come off the train behind me. Their rising excitement chatters and clips into the cold spring air as they walk over to a dining hall across the street. It's so early the sun is not fully awake, but the lights at the hall blaze and the smell of bacon and grease hang heavily in my nose. It is too much. Adjusting my satchel, I pick up the small trunk in my other hand, wondering if I should carry it or not in my condition. Ridiculous! There is no reason or good end to fretting over myself. I've headed West for the chance at continuing a respectable reputation and to give myself the opportunity to make my own choices. I must be strong and physical and be able to carry loads. I must show the doctor that he will have no reason to send me back home. Fear skitters through me and pools in my stomach, but I push it off as I hoist the end of the trunk in my free hand. The luggage is Henry's and very manly with stained oak sides, thick leather bands, and battered brass trim. It is heavy—too heavy. I suppose I will have to drag it.

13

I walk carefully beyond the depot, past the dining hall and a dilapidated saloon where a sand-whipped sign reads *The Powdered Pig,* and slide by several shacks and a very old abandoned livery building. Across the street is the general mercantile. Goods cram the barrels along the windows and a woman is hanging a lantern at the door as she opens for the day. Two figures already are on the porch, poised to follow her inside out of the cold. She jiggles the door of the lantern shut while the two older men scurry indoors. Their faces—one long and pale and the other fleshy and white—appear as wobbly ovals in the front glass window, gazing outside with obvious interest. My eyes slant away. Are they staring at me? Surely new people come to Flats Junction all the time.

I cross the crusted paths between buildings before the grocer can disappear into the darkness of the store. As I move, the chill of the spring morning hits my cheeks and hands and chaps them at once. My trunk hits a bump. The earth is still mostly frozen, and the bit of ground scoured clear by the wind is littered with animal dung. A particularly large, old pile of horse apples has caught the edge of my luggage and I tug it free, my arms already aching and my bones protesting the cold.

Winter is not far gone, that much is plain. I know Flats Junction is far enough north of the Missouri River to have few worries of the flooding they predicted as the train went through Yankton, and perhaps there will be more blizzards yet this season. Everyone west of Iowa speaks of them with such reverence. They cannot be as terrible as the northeasterly storms that crash upon the shores of Massachusetts, can they? Is it true that this past winter was longer and

14

colder than any in memory? I look at the leftover snowbanks. With some imagination, I can see that the drifts could reach some rooftops. Shivering, I move on. I hope it's all just an exaggeration.

"Excuse me," I call to the grocer woman as I breathlessly mount the mercantile stairs. My Eastern accent betrays me immediately, and she turns to me with a frown that stops my smile halfway. Already I may have made a bad impression, and I rush to placate her obvious annoyance. "I am so sorry, please, but if you could tell me which way Doctor Kinney's practice is, I'd be obliged."

"What do you want with the doctor?" She stands over me, strong hands in fists on her hips. Her eyes narrow and she looks me over, taking in the lapels and plain cuffs of my grey coat, the new polish on my black shoes. I am not ashamed of my clothes or my body, though her scrutiny makes me pause. Do I look very dilapidated and travel worn? She is still frowning slightly as she takes in my hair and hands. Then suddenly her face softens, like butter and oil in a pan, melting and betraying her inordinate beauty. It is an immediate transformation.

"You're his new housekeeper?"

I nod.

"His place is two streets over easterly, the house with the blue shutters." She smiles at me with a new warmth in her eyes.

"I am thankful," I say as I start down the stairs.

"He won't be awake yet; don't bother heading over there," she calls. "Last night Alice Brinkley had her babe and he was up all hours. Doesn't pay to make a bear of him by waking him earlier than he ought. Come in for a cup."

15

I pause, uncertain if it is done to be so familiar with a new acquaintance, but I realize the sense in her generous words. I do not wish to start my employment on a bad footing, so I turn and follow her into the store. It smells of warm grain, rusty metal, and aging molasses. Shapes loom everywhere. Most of the mysterious bumps and heaps display their rugged, shaggy appearance once my new acquaintance lights a few lamps to ward off the last of the early morning shadows. Plows, straw hats hanging in sunny cascades by a wall stuffed with shelves of fabric, and spools of lace are stacked high along the window sill. There are two steps to a curtained door behind the counter, and she turns to me, beckoning toward it.

"Pour some drink and sit behind the curtain a spell. I'll join you shortly. Always a bit of a rush when the five o'clock train pulls in."

She disappears behind a large pile of seed stacks, and I am left to drag my small trunk and bang my carpet bag through the congested paths of the store before peering around the faded calico curtain. A large, blue-flecked urn is steaming.

"New?"

"Staying awhile, then?"

I spin around and hit my shin on the brass corner of my trunk. Jerking with a decidedly unbecoming grunt, my eyes settle on the two older men lounging in decrepit rocking chairs at the main window, a half-finished checkers game on a barrel between them. Both are still bundled in layers of flannel shirts of varying degrees of faded and fraying, and the rotund one has not removed his hat even indoors. I am transfixed with it, sitting on the tufts of curling, yellow-grey hair, before remembering my manners.

16

"Good morning."

They glance at one another at my formal greeting, and the wizened, skeletal one rubs his hands together and leans toward me.

"Heard the doc was gettin' himself a housekeeper from out East." Beady green eyes narrow at me, my clothing and then my shoes. He spits into a battered tin at his elbow on the window sill. "Must be yourself, then."

I straighten and ignore the throb of pain in my leg. "I'm Mrs. Henry Weber, of Boston."

"Boston, is it?" The man's skinny arm shoots out and thwacks the pudgier man on the bicep. "She's from Boston-way, same as our Doc Kinney is. All citified up, ain't she?"

"Yup." The bigger man is far less interested in me than he is the game of checkers.

"Though perhaps not so much a sawbones as the doc, do you think?"

"No."

"I'm Horeb Harvey, and this is Gilroy."

"Greenman."

"Gilroy Greenman, if you please him."

I dig my heels harder into the edges of my shoe soles and smile as benignly as I can into Horeb's scrutiny. The man is leering at me as if he is close to my twenty-eight years and not with one foot in the grave, but his partner is using the distraction to invest in a bit of devilry on the checkerboard.

"Well, Mr. Greenman and Mr.—"

"Oh, it's Mister and sir, is it?"

"Horeb! Leave her be!" The grocer swerves around a stack of precariously balanced tins of *Borden's* condensed milk with a sack on her shoulder. There's a chatter of unintelligible language as two tittering Chinese women peer around the front door. The woman glances at them, then me, and then frowns at Horeb Harvey. "Go on back, ma'am, there's the brew still hot. Coming, coming." The woman is gone as quick as she'd appeared, heaving the load out to the porch and down the stairs, followed by the Chinese pair.

I nod stiffly at the two elderly men, and Mr. Greenman's suspender twangs with a snappy satisfaction as they return to their game.

Tugging my trunk up to the two steps along the back doorway, I take my satchel and step into the woman's proffered sanctuary, just as a squawk fills the air.

"Goddamn you, Gil—you hellish mule! You moved my reds!"

"Ain't."

"You did—I'm sure of it!"

"Ain't."

After almost two weeks on a horrendously noisy train car, I shake my head at the strident arguing, at least on Mr. Harvey's part, and ignore the sounds of the escalating quarrel.

There are mugs hanging on hooks over the black stove. I take one and pour myself a cup, absently sipping it before I realize what I took for tea is actually strong coffee. It is thick and muddy, and I cough a bit, glad the woman is not here to see my face after I try her concoction.

This is obviously her private space. There is a short plank table with a few stools and a bench gathered around it next to the stove. The crockery and pans are piled up haphazardly on a shelf over the stovepipe. I can see she is just as disorderly here as she is in her store. The rugs are fraying and fuzzy with use, but the bed is neat and made precisely. Curtains are nothing more than long rags hiding the blinding sun as it finally rises. There are no photographs or portraits on the walls, no artwork hanging or decorative vases on the table. She is spartan, a bit like me. I am eager to learn more of her. Perhaps she can be my first friend here.

More people enter the store. The slam and jingle of the door gives way to stomping. I hear men's voices flowing fast and loud, though I do not trouble myself to eavesdrop any longer. Instead I pace the room. It feels good to move after being so many days on a train, and my legs still have a bit of wobble and weakness. I just want a bath, and a clean dress. Scratching my neck, I shudder. Suppose I've picked up nits? Lice? The idea makes me want to rip my clothing off and scrub at my skin until it's red. My breath comes fast and hard, suddenly and without warning. My boiling fears and choking half-truths threaten to overwhelm me. What if there is no bathtub? Have I given everything up for good? Was it worth it?

Pointless. It is pointless to worry so! I'm here.

The voices are loud again, tempered by the womanly voice of the grocer. She has a tinkling laugh, a booming sales pitch, and a flippant way to send the customers out the door. Glancing around again, I wonder if she is like me: widowed and alone. The bed along the wall in the far corner is a single one. If she was once married, she has adjusted well to being alone.

I haven't. If anything, losing Henry has made me far too rash and foolish. Why couldn't I just have kept my mouth shut, my inquisitiveness buried, and pretended I didn't want to try something extraordinary? I could be adventuring in my widowhood, surely, but perhaps on a civilized steamboat tour, not as a housekeeper with an incredible amount of bone-weary work ahead of me.

It's at least forty minutes before the grocer enters the back room and sloshes coffee in a mug, and my personal reverie is lost. She perches on her seat across the table as she guzzles the horrible liquid and continues to scrutinize me, although I am sure I am not much more interesting than any other woman. She is the opposite of me: tall, straight, with high cheeks and a straight nose. Her hair is pinned up, but it's obviously thick and is glossy black with glints of red. I am fascinated with her hands: long-fingered, strong-nailed, and dry. She wears no wedding band. What is her life story? Will I ever have the nerve to ask?

I am worried I have imposed on her, but she immediately starts to question me, familiarly and nosily.

"So, you've come to keep house for the doc?" she asks again.

I nod, twisting the mug in my hands.

"Sit down and join me. Sit!"

I comply and answer her at the same time. "I am. He answered my letter in response to his ad." I hope she offers something I don't know yet. I have so few particulars about my new employer, only that he is, by complete lack of option, doctor, midwife, dentist, vet, and chemist in this town.

She dives into the subject without further prompting, to my relief.

"His former housekeeper died a few months before the holidays, same as many this long winter. She was his great-aunt. I've been stopping by when I have the time to try to keep his place tidy, but he's used to the charity of others for a hot meal, and he's rarely home." She pauses for a moment and then looks at me squarely. "My name is Katherine. Kate."

I nod at her and smile encouragingly. My formal name slips out, though I do not mean it to do so, nor to sound so stiff. Habits are hard to change.

"I'm Mrs. Henry Weber."

While she nods in return, more questions crowd my mind. A rooster crows nearby. It is the third cock to sound since I entered her kitchen, and she stirs in her seat. How late in the morning is it now?

"He'll be getting up soon if he isn't yet. You best be on your way if he's expecting you."

The doctor can't be sure of my exact date, especially with the trains running so abnormally slow with the snow and particular coldness this year. But I am eager to get out of the musty room and breathe the cold, fresh air outside, even if it means fighting the wind. The train whistle blasts as it departs Flats Junction, and the faint echo of its steam hisses through the boards of the store.

I bite down on my tongue. It is done, then. I'm here, and ready to live the life I've reconstructed and planned. It will be enough.

I stand and take my emptied cup to the washbowl. "Thank you for your hospitality. I am incredibly grateful."

"You looked like you needed it. Your man must be down on his luck for you to hire yourself out for home work," she states, but I know there is hidden meaning in her comment.

I look down and gather a solemn expression. Guilt erupts through me in a whirling, confusing storm. I should mourn Henry more fully. I should have kept my curiosity hidden as I have schooled myself to do and stayed within the confines of society. Instead, I gave in to that same inquisitiveness and allowed myself far too much freedom. But here, all anyone must know is that I am a widow.

So, I sigh and say to Kate, "My husband, Henry, is recently deceased. I need to make my own way now. You said Doctor Kinney is two streets over? The house with the blue shutters?"

As I look up at her for confirmation, her face once again darkens, but she tries to mask her scowl and gives a tight "yes." I take my satchel and turn my back to her. I'll figure out her moods later, as I hope to stay in Flats Junction for a while, allowing my past to filter away as much as it can, for however long I am allowed to stay.

The two men are still at their checkerboard. They seem to have put aside their differences for appreciation of the game.

"To the doc's, then, is it?" Mr. Harvey says smartly.

"Yes." The trunk hits the back of my knee. Dare I try to carry it? As I scrape it out the door, wood protests against wood and suddenly, the burly Mr. Greenman swoops to pick up my luggage.

"Why thank you, Mr. Greenman," I say, and raise my eyebrows at the amazement spreading on the skinny man's face as he watches his friend stomp out the doorway. "And good day to you, sir."

Mr. Harvey's mouth twitches at the 'sir,' and he spits noisily as I walk out.

The roads are bumpy and the ground is dark and brown where the snow is gone or scraped away by the wind, and I find it easiest to keep my mind on my feet as I pick my way around the wagon ruts, horse prints, and dung. I try not to think of the cobbled streets I left, and the swept front porches and painted wood of the homes. Here everything is grey and brown and russet and not a bit of green or color to be seen. And oh heavens! It's so very, very cold!

The handful of buildings I've seen so far are shabbier than I expected of a fresh, young Western territory town, but perhaps those are just the less expensive ones near the rumble and dirt of the tracks. We squeeze past the post office. Ahead is a crossing where an inn and a small school stand sentinel. There are bits of white paint still clinging to the broad, planked wood of the inn, and a creaking sign of decorative wrought iron declares it to be the *Prime Inn*. The school is empty. Has it been too cold? Does school stop all winter long?

"First Street," intones Mr. Greenman as we turn right and head east through town.

The blocks are long, and the houses still a mix of mean and shabby shanties with occasional well-kept two-story buildings. I want to stare more, but everything is barren, and the cold eats at my fingers and feet. As we hit yet another crossroads, the eye-watering blast of pig manure chokes me. A frenzied shout barely gives warning as a horse tries to make a run for it from the open door of the livery. Mr. Greenman doesn't break his stride at the commotion, but I feel my heart give way to another round of apprehension, and I berate myself severely.

Don't look at the shabbiness!

Ignore the sign above that one decorative house—did it say *"free women"* on it?

23

Stop thinking about the smells, the meanness of the houses!

Focus on what you must do to keep this job and find a place for yourself. Be wise, Jane. Remember your choices. This was the best one.

But I forget to hedge my natural interest for gleaning information. My voice ripples in the cold air. "How many bordellos are there in Flats Junction?"

"One."

"But that sign . . ."

"One official. The rest, less so."

Where am I? The cold pricks my eyes and I brush away salty tears. I'm not really weeping. It's more the chill. I try to think of nothing negative or scary and watch Mr. Greenman's sausage fingers on my trunk as he carries it easily along First Street toward the very easternmost part of town. It is simpler here. And there are supposed to be less strings, less society, less need to care about whether things are proper or not. I hope the simplicity of Western living will allow the town to accept me, though I am inconvenienced with an unexpected remnant of my past life.

When the doctor's home looms in front of me, it is cast in morning glow that is extra bright from the nearby snow. The shutters are blue as Kate promised, though I can see the chips and scratches in the paint with the starkness of sunlight on them. Mr. Greenman goes ahead of me and drops my trunk without ceremony so one of the brass ends inherits another gash. He turns abruptly to the road again.

"Thank you, Mr. Greenman."

"Gilroy." His voice is a throaty grumble.

"Thank you, Gilroy."

And then he is off, huddled against the late winter breeze. After I watch him for a moment, I take the few stairs to the door. Oddly, it is open slightly, even with the cold spring morning, and a makeshift screen stands between me and the dark dimness of the interior. My knock echoes, though my knuckles barely feel it.

Doctor Kinney must be rustling in his back rooms. There is a muttering and a short curse after my knock. I look at the neighbors' houses with interest and a bit of trepidation. Who are they? Will they be kind?

There is a short wait, and then a clambering from the rear of the house brings a shadow into my sight.

He is not as tall as I expected and not nearly as old as I assumed. Though there are lines along his mouth and wrinkles in the slants of his eyes, they are more from fatigue than age. I guess him to be five years my senior, perhaps ten if I am careful in my opinion. He pauses, and we stare at each other from both sides of the screen.

I find my voice. "I'm Mrs. Weber. Here to keep house for you, Doctor."

CHAPTER 2
20 March 1881

There is a long moment as the doctor measures me, considering. I don't typically mind waiting, and do not fidget, but I'm now aching with cold. He finally opens the door and stands aside.

"Come in. My study."

His voice has an Irish lilt with a cadence of something more, and I bite back an impulse to comment. My roots are in Massachusetts, and many neighborhoods are filled with Irish voices. I step inside, and he pulls my trunk in behind us almost as an afterthought.

His office is tiny. A narrow wooden desk is covered in files and papers. Boxes stack on the floor while bits of paper haphazardly sprinkle through his overloaded bookshelves. The chaos reminds me of Kate's general store, and the flood of memories from this morning alone crowd into my head.

He stands behind the desk and I perch on the only other seat available: a worn straight chair with a spindle back. It is not very comfortable. His blue eyes peer at me in the watery light; only a small window brings in the morning sun. And while his hair is quite dark, like Kate's, the sun tips it with the barest trace of red. I suppose I should expect a little of that for the Irish in him. Should I mention that I am used to his culture? That in Boston some of my neighbors were Irish? Or perhaps he, like me, tries to leave the East in his past, and I would do well to keep from reminding him of it.

I so dislike not knowing my footing! Everything had once been arranged, organized, and curated. Damn Henry, and damn the doctors who couldn't heal him, and damn my own inability to do nothing about it!

"Mrs. Weber." Doctor Kinney says my name slowly. "I'm glad you're here."

"Yes," I say guardedly. "Thank you for agreeing to take me on. I am grateful for the work." It is all I can say. I am more than grateful. This work will give me a purpose and save me from the quiet fading of widowhood. Better yet, the distance of Flats Junction from Boston is enough for me to pass along the story that the babe I carry is Henry's.

He sits down so we are more at eye level, but he is quiet for a long moment. I glance around the room again and see the corners are filled with grey and black dust. The smell of old cooking oil, sour milk, and a pungent, overarching odor of sanitation acid and iodine settle on my already trav-el-weary clothes. I want to scratch my skin raw of grime and then wash everything again the minute I think of my dirty petticoats. I wonder if my stays are caked with black dust.

The doctor sighs and looks away from my face, then dives into the subject with a straightforward manner.

"I'm sorry for your loss. You must miss Mr. Weber very much."

I give a small nod, not trusting myself to answer. I am often afraid the truth will come out, and it would be so very improper and unbecoming. I should be glad that I had had a husband at all, and I should mourn him better than I do. I owe him that much.

"We need to go over the particulars of your duties. But first, there is the matter of your room and board."

"Oh?" I panic inwardly. My correspondence about this position with the MacHughs in Boston had been plain about the larger points of the arrangement, and I feel discomfited to discuss funds already. I do not have enough saved to pay for a room at an inn every day, and he certainly isn't paying me enough to manage it. We had confirmed that I would stay in his previous housekeeper's room. Or did the MacHughs tell me falsely?

"Yes," he pauses again, then meets my eyes. "You are younger than I supposed, and it would not do to have you stay in my auntie's old rooms upstairs as I'd planned."

His words deflate and embarrass me further. He's right. I know acutely that my status comes with its own stigma. Now that I know he's in his middle thirties, the revelation of my condition might be mistaken by the town and I will have lost all I gain with coming West. The old panic rises and tastes like yellow bile.

But I still cannot afford the inn, and I voice as much, though I say so with apology and embarrassment. He waves it away with a large, bunched hand.

"I'm not goin' to have you stay at the inn, Mrs. Weber. But the only other place I can think of is boardin' you with old Widow Hawks."

"That sounds fine," I say soothingly, trying to be as easy and amiable as possible. All at once, I recognize why his accent is unusual. Doctor Kinney is an Irishman, but his brogue is faintly Scots.

"Widow Hawks is Sioux." The statement is almost defiant, and it brings me from my thoughts.

Sioux?! There is a large part of me that hesitates and recoils. A Sioux! I thought all the Indians were gone—living in the obscurely named Indian Territory or on a reservation. The shock of his suggestion sinks in further, and only bare threads of dignity keep me from protesting outright.

Live with an Indian? I don't want to! I can't! I'm worried that she is, by definition, an outcast. If I stay with her, I will be shunned immediately among the townsfolk. If that is the case, then why did I bother to leave Boston? I could have stayed and been an outcast there as well. If I admit it fully, I'm afraid of living with an Indian. Everything I've ever read in the papers back East paints them as fearsome, heathen, and uncivilized. My mother would be beside herself, and my sister, Anne, would leave on the next train if this was her only option for a room. Then again, I've never been much like Anne.

But I look at the doctor and realize he seems oddly anxious himself. Does he expect me to scream and refuse? I suppose he might. He would not offer this unless he thought it was safe. I must trust someone, and why not my new employer, even if he *is* a doctor? If he does not doubt the widow, I have no reason to do so either. This rationale is all I can muster, and I keep my gaze on his face. If I close my eyes, I'll likely grow dizzy with the swirl of numbness, fatigue, and distress raging in my chest.

"If she is a fair landlady, I have no objections," I manage to say evenly, and he relaxes slightly, then leans into the worn wood of his chair and looks me over. I take the time to take in his stocky shoulders, the round muscles of his arms, the holes in his shirt, and the patches in his leather vest, shiny from wear. He has curls in his dark hair, and he is newly shaved. At least there is some tiny semblance of civility here!

He nods slowly, as if he is still mulling what we have already decided.

"Yes. She's like family to me, and I know you'll be treated well. It is best." His eyes watch me. I do not know if he is just observing or if he is creating opinions already. I scramble to make an excuse for my dilapidated appearance.

"I've only just arrived … haven't had a chance to straighten myself or put on anything fresh."

He sighs. "I'm sorry again for your recent loss, Mrs. Weber. I know you are in mournin', but the work here is hard. You'll be advised to cast off the blacks and greys soon and wear more suitable clothing anyway."

His pragmatic attitude is a balm to my need for order and logic. I do not like being fussed over, and mourning Henry has been chafing enough, but I feel I must make a point to respectability.

"My period of mourning is not to be over for another twenty months."

His voice is hard all at once. "That is for the East and city livin'. There is no time for mournin' like that here, and the fabric of your gown will be in tatters in short order."

The words are harsh, and my hands clench hard in the folds of my skirts. And yet, to cast aside the obviousness of my widowhood would be freeing. To do so now, mere months after Henry's passing, seems to be one of the best ideas I've heard in a long time. There is also the need for a second dress. A loose one.

I'm nodding and agreeing all at once. "I have enough saved to make what is needed. I would think Kate can steer me in the right direction on cloth."

The doctor's head comes up. "You've met Kate already?" His voice is softer.

"Yes. She was kind enough to offer me coffee when I arrived on the train. We spoke briefly."

He smiles for the first time since we've met, and I like the way the lines bunch on his face and how his blue eyes squeeze to half-moons. My body settles further into the uncomfortable wooden chair with something like relief. I think he will be a kind employer. I *hope* he will be! And fair. And reasonable, when the time comes.

We fall into discussion about my duties: cook, clean, organize, mend, care for the garden and home, and generally do wifely duties without being his wife. This is good. I feel I have a purpose again, and thankfully, it does not come with the strings attached as my marriage had. I have vowed not to tie myself to another union that is so detached, and I am glad I can hide myself in this new role for decades should everything be acceptable here. I've miscalculated once and have no wish to do so again.

As we reach the part of the discussion pertaining to the use of patient files, there is a knock on the door. It is a young cowboy, covered in dust and clapping a hat to his thigh as he pushes through and turns directly into the office. There is little privacy here, I note.

"Doc! Hank's horse ain't getting from the far side of the pasture this morn. We've tried everything short of force. He thinks something's wrong with him." As an afterthought, the boy looks at me. "How do, ma'am."

The doctor sighs and stands. I notice he does not bother to tidy any of his clothing. His slightly disheveled state must be a standard. He glances at me, frowning slightly.

"I'll be back for midday dinner, I'd think, Mrs. Weber. If you could manage to fix up a bite, we'll head to Widow Hawks' place later to get you settled. Alright then, Manny."

As they amble out, I see the doctor grab a well-worn Stetson from a hook behind the door, and a large, worn, leather hunting frock coat. The door and screen slam behind them, echoing across the street. I'm left in semi-silence. I am surprised to hear a drip of a spigot somewhere deeper in the house. Around me, dust settles across the beams of watery sunlight, trailing slowly down to one of the piles and piles of patient folders on the floor and desk. I blow out the lantern in his study and suddenly have a pang at the loss of the easy gaslight in Henry's office. I look once more into the gloom of the small room and want to sit back down and sleep. And I'd like to read through the books and papers on the man's desk. There's a copy of a map of the Dakota Territory on the wall, a sketch of the town, and one of the books on the top pile on the floor has a florid name: *The Pharmacopoeia of the United States of America, by the Authority of The General Convention for the Formation of the American Pharmacopoeia, Held in 1830; Second Edition.* Dear heaven. Why did I tell him I knew something about nursing?

I only know what it takes to ask doctors very particular questions without sounding too smart, and how to read a few medical journals. And I can make a patient comfortable, as I did for Henry. Somehow, I doubt now that will be enough to suffice. What am I doing? What have I done? I want to curse Henry for leaving me, and to damn my sister and her husband for their little party. And most of all, I want to curse myself. All my years of planning and organizing, lining up a respectable husband and then restraining my nature so I was the proper wife, all of that, gone, with no thanks to my own damnable curiosity.

Ignoring the pull and call of the rest of the books, I step out of the small room to set my wrinkled satchel on the scuffed plank floor.

As I walk down the narrow hall, I glance briefly inside each door. Next to his study is the surgery. The instruments are a dull silver that gleams in the half-light. The walls are whitewashed, and a nail holds a thin, wood-framed certification. There is a large black cabinet with wide beveled glass doors. Through the glass I see bandages piled neatly, beakers arranged according to size, and other utensils I don't understand. His surgery is the opposite of his study; neat, tidy, and precise. The dripping comes from a soft brass and silver spigot. I didn't expect something so fine in a simple house in the West. The spring-loaded piece must be attached to an outdoor water pump and cistern. Will he let me use this for cooking, or will I still have to haul water from outside?

There is a staircase to my right. I assume the bedrooms are up there. At the end of the hallway the kitchen yawns open before me. The room is wide and the stove is large, double the size of Kate's, and the unsoiled pans and pots are still hanging on hooks. Perhaps his great-aunt had kept a good fire going, keeping the meals hot and ready. Shelves

33

line another wall, where a few plates and knives sit in a line. The rest are all dirty in a nearby wash or still sitting holding half-eaten food on the wide slab table in the center of the room. There are a few chairs around it and one long bench. There is even natural light slanting in from the eastern windows, and a back kitchen door is shut tight against the cold. I will be spending much of my time here and I find myself well-pleased.

I do not know how long it will take Doctor Kinney to do his veterinary services, so I decide to mix up a batter of flapjacks if the ingredients are in the pantry. Surprisingly, the place is rather stocked, as if he didn't know what to do with the dry goods. I was not so well off, when married to Henry, to have a cook, although I did have a weekly maid to help with the heavier cleaning. The chemistry of the kitchen comes natural to me. It is one of my few talents. I step around the kitchen, cleaning bowls and spoons as I need them, and stoke the stove and heat the griddle pan so it's hot for when Doctor Kinney returns. The cast iron is black and smooth with age and use. His auntie must have cooked often.

Flapjacks are not really lunch, but they are all I can think to do without knowing his schedule. Perhaps in the future, I will learn his methods so as to properly guess the lengths of his work. I hope I do right by his expectations. There was so little time to discuss his demands in detail, and I must keep this job.

While I wait for him to return, I decide to start working at the mess of the kitchen. I am only halfway through the suds of the dishes when I hear him racketing into the house, slamming the door. Strangely, I think of the babe in my womb, and how I might ask the good doctor to not slam the door when he or she is sleeping. When I think of the baby, the uncertainty of my position is a solid choke, and I barely catch up the dry, heaving sob in time.

But he doesn't come right in. Instead, I hear water and realize he is at the tap in the surgery. I am grateful he at least thinks to wash his hands.

He walks into the kitchen with a sturdy stride, and I give him a small smile and motion wordlessly to the place I have set at the table. I pour him a cup of my own coffee brew. I make it differently than Kate, though I am, myself, used to tea. My coffee is strong, but not thick, without the grains floating in it. I use the old trick of adding eggshells to settle the grounds before pouring. It tastes rather good. Henry used to compliment me on it often. I wait for the doctor's reaction, or a word of approval, but none comes. He is fidgeting behind me. When I finally turn with a plate of golden jacks, his face falls blank. I am immediately worried. I need this work for my own sanity, for protection, to keep my practiced and careful life of respectability intact. Worst of all, I had thought to do a good job from the start. I see now he is frustrated instead of pleased.

He tucks into the flapjacks so fast, I move to make more immediately. This time when I turn around, he is just finishing the food so he is not watching me, and I am saved from the disapproval on his face. I make more, hoping I have enough batter to fill his stomach as he eats nimbly, quickly. The next batch he seems to eat slower, for when they are finished, I put the next fresh ones on a plate near his elbow so he can take them when he is ready.

I put the rest on the slab and sit across from him. I twist the mug in my own hands nervously, staring at my fingers so as not to watch him. My hands are not a true lady's hands. There are burn scars from my oven back in Boston, blunt fingernails, and a few small callouses. My veins are blue and visible. They are not long-fingered hands, nor very powerful, but they are capable and strong. I always thought they'd be strong enough for anything, but now I'm not nearly so sure.

Finally, I sense him shift, and I glance up to see him leaning back in the chair, looking content. He sips his coffee, piercing me over the rim.

"Were they good?" I ask the trite question to fill the silence.

A smile flits its way across the craggy features. "Delicious, Mrs. Weber."

"Thank heaven," I cannot help but murmur. "Then you won't fire me right off?"

He sets the mug down hard on the table; it had been halfway to his mouth again. "Why ever would you think that?"

"You were so displeased with me, I thought, when you first came in?" My voice is quiet and low, but he hears me and gives his unruly head a small shake.

"Don't take it so personal, Mrs. Weber, I beg you. I was starvin' hungry from the late-night birth, and annoyed with Hank, who has no business bein' a cowboy. He keeps draggin' me out to handle his horse ... which has nothin' wrong with it."

"Oh."

There is another pause. He sips his coffee again, then mentions off-handed, "But if you wanted the full of it, I was a wee bit amazed you had the food all ready. Did me a bit of a shock."

"Ah. I was wondering!" I cannot help but lean toward him, earnest to placate.

He makes a dismissive noise.

"The flapjacks I'll take over what my old auntie would have done: had a cold sandwich on the sideboard for me to pick at whenever I showed back up. I couldn't complain on her, though. I don't have the leisure or time to manage the house or yard or make food for myself. But your hot food beats cold any day."

I press my lips together, then offer tentatively, "Is there a way, perhaps, to guess at when you might be home so I can manage hot food more often than cold? I can see … I mean, if your schedule is never ending, then it could be difficult sometimes, but perhaps you could always send word along? The town doesn't seem so large that it'd be difficult."

He gives me a shrewd look, and I wonder if this conversation had not already happened between him and his aunt. Am I only showing how completely naïve I am about the West?

"That is not a bad idea, Mrs. Weber." His voice is thoughtful instead of mocking, so if he has had this notion already, he hides it well. "We can try it out and see how it goes?" He does not condescend to me, so I take a bit of heart. Maybe I will be able to appease him or find a rhythm to his daily work after all.

He leaves me then, and I hear him rustling in the surgery before he sticks his head around the door, giving me a bit of a lopsided grin.

"I need to do my rounds, but before I do so, shall I walk you over to Widow Hawks?"

I glance around the kitchen. Now there are the dirty dishes from lunch as well as the earlier mess. I give him a small smile.

"Perhaps I had better stay here. Clean up a bit. And if you'd be so kind to let Widow Hawks know to expect me after dinner? Will you be back then?"

He gives a shrug as he tugs a medical bag from the room. "If I'm not, I'll try to send word."

The door slams, followed by the softer echo of the screen. I gaze around the kitchen, and then do not pause to think further and concentrate entirely on my chores. If I stop, I'll want to fall asleep. If I look around, I'll cry at all the work. There are no gaslights, no electricity, and no running water. I'd thought of this when I looked to go West, but I didn't realize how horrifically primitive it would be, even in a doctor's house. Part of me is aghast that there has been no time for me to settle in, to even wash my face. How mussed do I look? How disheveled? My dress is dark, but I can smell the old sweat and smoke residue in the creases of my bodice. If I felt more familiar with my employer, I might try to find a washroom and tidy up, but then again, why bother? I will only get dirty again as I clean up his kitchen.

And thank heaven for the mind-numbing work!

The kitchen takes up the remainder of my day. Usually I'd be ravenous in the morning, but I've gone all day with barely a bite and have hardly noticed. Everything is nearly too much. Besides, should I make myself a meal whenever I am hungry? There must be rules, but I don't know them yet.

I find the well in the backyard and am thankful it is not completely frozen over. After hauling water in, I try to clean the floor twice and the benches and tables thrice to remove the grime that has built up all winter. The water and dust make the edges of my nails grey and leave huge wet spots against my skirt.

Tomorrow I will black the stove and hang up the pots and pans in an order to my liking. The shelves must be restocked with the cutlery, but I want to try to reorganize the pantry. I find I like having a home to tend to again. I muse that by tending to the doctor, I will be helping those who are sick as well, just as I had tended to Henry amid all the conflicting advice from the doctors back East. Maybe I won't have to do much in terms of real nursing.

When I clear the bottom of the pantry and shift the bag of flour, a grey shadow sprints out, and the dash and squeak of a mouse shoots by my foot. I scream shortly before slamming a hand over my mouth. What will the neighbors think?

The mouse has gone toward the stove, but finding it hot, scampers hesitantly toward the table. My fingers are trembling as I reach for the roughly hewn broom. How can the doctor have a mouse in his house? Shouldn't he be fastidious and careful about such things?

I inch toward the animal, and the tiny black eyes glare balefully up at me, challenging my speed and my effectiveness. Lunging at once, I miss, and it takes off toward the hallway. No! I can't let it leave the kitchen. I dash, and the swish of my skirts deters it at the last minute, where it scurries back toward the flour. Launching the broom and missing again, I grab a tin mug and toss it desperately and foolishly. It misses and hits the stove. A short, ridiculously pitiful ping rings through the room and the mug falls to the floor, freezing the mouse and exposing a deep dent in the base of the cup.

Grabbing the broom tighter, I move toward the animal again, but it jumps behind the flour sacks once more. My breath is fast, and I feel hot and sweaty and frustrated, and more than a little shaky. I've never had to chase a mouse before and they're far faster than I would have bargained.

But now I'm angry and feeling more like a failure. If I can't protect the food in the larder from even a mouse, what kind of housekeeper will I be? I take down the heaviest skillet I can see and raise it high before ripping back the flour sack with a fast kick of my foot.

"Aha!" I yell at the same time I bring the pan down, my hair escaping out of my knot and my knee hitting the edge of the stove as I bend swiftly and crush the mouse with a horrible, meaty crunch. At once, I feel my mouth fill with spit as I realize I now need to clean up the skillet as well as the splatter of the mouse. More wiggling catches my eye and I shift and raise the skillet once more.

But it's not another mouse. It's a nest of baby mice! I close my eyes and inhale, willing my stomach to settle, and a knock pounds on the back door.

Who—? I push back my hair and try to twist it up with a pin using my free hand as I move to open the door.

It's an older woman with a heavy shawl: tall and spindle-framed and sour.

"Heard a scream. Didn't know why the doc might have someone screaming over here," she sniffs, peering into the kitchen suspiciously. "And didn't know he had a woman here." She looks me up and down with obvious skepticism.

"I'm Mrs. Weber, the new housekeeper."

"Are you, now?" She eyes my skillet. Too late, I realize I'm still holding it sideways, and the crushed, pulpy remains

40

of the mouse are muddled and oozing on it. "I see you've been busy."

"Will you come in?" I'm not sure I should be entertaining anyone, especially someone I don't know. But she says she heard my scream. Likely she is a neighbor, then.

She hesitates, looking a little nervous, then steps in out of the cold while leaving on her shawl and cocks her head at my cookware.

"You might want to clean that off."

I glance at it and shudder. "I . . . how?"

"Good heavens." She impatiently grabs it in her narrow, tough hands and turns to the door. She leans into the snowbank nearby and hits the iron against the ice. Bright red rivers of mouse blood match the bits of fur and are left in the circular imprint against the white. Turning back to me, she hands me the skillet. "You wash it off with lye and water, same as everything else."

"Thank you," I say, trying to muster any dignity I can, but I cannot help but glance at the flour corner.

She follows my gaze. "More mice?"

"There's a nest of little ones," I admit, thinking of the mouse's remains and gagging. "What do I do with that?"

The woman's neck pulses forward like a chicken's and she gapes at me. "You're to be the housekeeper for the doc, are you?"

"Yes."

She sniffs, stalks over to the corner and picks up the pile of baby mice, nest and all, goes to the door, and flings the whole handful out into the cold. Wiping her fingers on her apron, she bobs her head again in that strange forward-backward rock.

"I'm the neighbor to your north. Emma Molhurst."

"It's ... nice to meet you. I look forward to getting to know you as the weather warms," I offer, and she gives an exaggerated sigh.

"Sure, sure. You've got enough money for a ticket back East, have you though?"

I gape slightly and then nod without speaking.

She jerks her head to the side. "That's good then."

Without another word, she yanks open the door and disappears into the afternoon. The sun is already setting. I find myself standing at the stove, placidly swirling a thin soup. There were navy beans in the larder, some cured ham, and a few old beets. I am glad there are spices enough to make the soup edible. It is just spring and the snow is still heavy, so there is not much in the garden for eating. I'll have to find seeds from Kate to plant. Can the doctor afford them?

Just as I wonder if he will send word that he is to be late, I hear him springing back into the house. He is loud and clattery, even for a man, and I wonder that his patients are not immediately overwhelmed with the racket he makes coming into a place.

"Smells good, Mrs. Weber!" He strides into the room. I glance up at him, glad he is joining me for another meal. I have so many questions, though I am not sure he will have the interest or the time to answer them.

"Set yourself down. I have tea ready."

He nods absently as he leaves again, and I hear the water splash. Cleanliness does indeed seem to be important to him. Once he is back in the kitchen, I hand him a mug of tea. He sips while staring out the window, where shadows grow long.

"I sent word to Widow Hawks. She'll expect us at dusk," he says without looking at me.

"I thank you for your thoughtfulness. It sounds like it was a busy day. Would you care to tell me over supper?" I turn to the table to ladle the soup. He catches me mid-movement and swiftly takes the hot ironware out of my hands and deftly places it on the table. I am unsure about his helpfulness. Is this his nature, or is he simply being kind this first day? Henry never helped in the home.

"You wouldn't know anyone I speak of," he says, sitting down on the bench as I bring over the spoons. He is not looking at me now, but his eyes are traveling over the surfaces and along the walls where the newly washed dishes are standing up straight and proud. He glances at me as I sit across from him and ladle out the soup. "Besides, I don't want to bore you."

I smile at him tentatively. "I should learn, somehow, to know my neighbors and the town."

His face breaks into the same lined smile, and he gestures for me to fill my plate. I sit across from him and we share the salt before he dives into the day's rounds.

"First, of course, there was the check on the Brinkley newborn and Alice. It's her first, so I knew she'd be nervous to start, and her husband, Mitch, is worse. Her milk hasn't quite come in yet, so I had her set to suckle the boy they call Pete. The longer he goes, the quicker her milk."

I set my spoon down to listen closely to this. It is new for me to hear these earthy matters. I will be a mother soon, and these stories have a bittersweetness I yearn to hear. The doctor continues, stabbing at his stew with vigor.

"Mitch is set to stay with her though it's spring plantin'. Most of the family'll be too busy to care for her much."

This need for help is something I understand, and I am quick to jump in. "I could make overlarge portions these days and take the leftovers to them."

This makes him look up at me squarely. "They won't take to charity. None do here, really."

"Who does?" I counter rhetorically. "They'd be doing us a favor, taking off leftovers that would soon go to spoil with only two to eat them."

He laughs heartily at this reasoning, leaning back from the table. I am pleased with his laughter. It is free and large and fits his size, and it fills the space briefly.

"Very good, Mrs. Weber. Very good."

His hands are immediately busy again with the stew as he outlines his other calls: a crone with arthritis, a few broken bones on the cowboys, a case of infected saddle sores, and one sickly, early spring foal in a rancher's stables.

We finish the stew over the story of the foal. I think I should have made a dessert, but there was not much time, and I hadn't thought so far ahead. He settles this worry for me by standing and looking outside.

"We'd best get over to Widow Hawks' soon enough."

I stand, too, and stack the cutlery, chiding as I move. "I'll not go until the dishes are done. You've gone too long without a clean place, and I can't finish my first day with a dirty kitchen."

After lighting the lantern on the table, I move quickly to the washbin to wash up the bowls and forks. The sun must set soon, and I do not know if nights are safe outside.

44

There is movement next to me; the doctor has taken a rag and is drying dishes as I finish them. This makes me pause. Surely the ease with which he deftly dries and replaces on the shelves comes with practice. Did he help his old aunt with home chores? I find myself voicing this wonderment without thinking, and he nods.

"Yes. When I'm at home, I like to be involved with the upkeep. It's a nice change from the daily work."

"May I ask … were you close with your aunt?"

He shrugs, but I find myself doubting his lack of feeling. "She was family. Who doesn't care for their family?"

"You must miss her."

The doctor is quiet. He places another dish on top of the first, carefully and with additional precision, the tin clinking.

"She was all I had left."

I think perhaps I should say he has time to marry and have a family of his own, but these words choke me. I should not be so quick to prescribe marriage as an answer. I thought it was, and I was proven wrong.

"I am so sorry, Doctor. Truly, I am. I did not know her, but she must have been someone incredibly hardy to handle the work here."

He looks down at me. The Irish eyes are not twinkling now, but I sense he is glad to discuss this quietly, even though I am a stranger.

"She was. Thank you."

We stand there for another moment looking at each other, until our hands reclaim the washing, and I finally reach the last pot. The copper gleams in the lantern light, though I see a crack along the cramp seam of the bottom.

Will it be my task to have it repaired? I suppose so—just as it was in Boston. As he puts away the last bit of cutlery, the doctor pauses and inspects the mug I've dented already, but he says nothing and simply puts it in its place. Relief fills me. I don't know if I could handle another reprimand today.

Dusk settles. We put on coats to leave for Widow Hawks' home just as a horse skitters out of the gloaming from the main street, stopping in front of the doctor's home. The rider doesn't even bother to dismount.

"Doc Kinney! Tate's leg is swellin' up something fierce, just like you said it might …!"

He doesn't finish before the doctor is swinging out of the house and heading for the hitching post out front where his horse waits, patient and calm, munching on its dinner.

"Infection. Got to watch for gangrene. I must go, Mrs. Weber. Head straight over to Widow Hawks: down Main, across the rail tracks, last house on your left. Be back tomorrow. Seven sharp."

I have no wish to walk alone any more than I have to, so I head out immediately with my satchel and trunk. The night sky is navy ink, but there are no stars. A tremor ripples through me as I step into the cold. Tugging the handle of my luggage with a sore arm, I greet the dark with deep trepidation.

Thankfully, the main street is peppered with homes. A large building, its sign swinging with the words *The Powdered Rose,* blazes with lanterns, rising against the darkness in the south. The general store and a few other buildings—the post office, the Main Inn, and a small hobby farm—huddle against the cold, but still have tin and copper lanterns lit in windows and inside animal shacks. The spaces between the wooden structures are black holes in the night. I pass a huge saloon called *The Golden Nail*, and the music, laughter, and shouts filtering through the cracks in the planks are rowdy enough that I catch the song.

> *He's a snorter and a snoozer,*
> *He's the great trunk line abuser.*
> *He's the man who puts the sleeper on the rail.*
> *I'm the double-jawed hyena from the East!*
> *I'm the blazing bloody blizzard of the States!*
> *I'm the celebrated slugger; I'm the Beast!*
> *I can snatch a man bald-headed while he waits!*

Why isn't everyone home? It's so very, very cold! I shudder and drag the trunk past a few more haggard shacks and a couple larger homes, and then the smell of the tannery hits my nose, and I want to lose my supper. My arm is numb with the weight of the trunk, and the back of my shin must be bruised twenty times over as the edge bangs against me. I've dragged it clear across town. What did the doctor think, leaving me to fend completely for myself? Perhaps my hope for civility here is nothing but an illusion.

The main street is long and wide, but the presence of buildings disappears abruptly as the road becomes a track. The chunky, leftover snowdrifts between houses give way to smooth, wind-scoured prairie. It seems few people have a desire to be near the tannery. Where am I supposed to go? The night is darker on the edge of Flats Junction, and the wind snakes across the brittle land. Dark shapes seem to quiver along the far end of my vision, and I start to lose my breath as a freezing panic sets in again. Is it buffalo? Wolves? Oh, dear God!

Dear God!

Where do I go from here?

The rail tracks stretch out ahead of me. One end leads to the depot and back to Yankton, and the other vanishes into the night. As I look from one part of the line to the other, my eyes stop seeing flickers of phantom animals. Focusing against the dark, I see a low structure. Doctor Kinney was correct, in a way. In the daytime, Widow Hawks' home would be hard to miss.

Set quite a few paces away from the last building, and the only structure on the far side of the tracks, her place is a long, rambling house. As I get closer and step in between the rail ties, I notice a few hides airing out, and a blackened fire pit in the front yard. My trunk catches on the last tie and I pull, my stomach twisting with the effort.

As I come closer yet, a bone-plated lit lantern reveals that I have arrived at Widow Hawks' place. I notice the strange, native artwork roughly painted on the door as I approach. She must be home, since warm light glows softly from two tiny windows. Apprehension coils through my bones, and a shiver threatens to knock my breath out. Will she be wild and fierce, and chant alien words over me? Will she be angry I am to stay with her? Perhaps Doctor Kinney misjudged her nature, perhaps she will use me to set an example to other whites in Flats Junction, and I'll wake to find her wielding a tomahawk over my bed.

Why did I say yes to this idea? I should have taken rooms at the inn! Either of the two in town, regardless of how shabby and worn they look, would be better than this!

Not for the first time in my long, cold, hard journey west have I wished desperately that I was barren, as I'd thought all these years. Why couldn't I just mourn Henry in peace? Why must I carry this child ... and because of it, lose everything I had planned and expected for my widowhood?

I know the answer. It is one my sister uses to condemn me, even though she's stopped saying the words: *You're too curious, Jane!*

She is right, in so many ways.

I knock before I have a moment to fully compose myself, barely finishing when the door swings open wide. In my mind's eye, I had expected her to be a stooped, hardened, tiny little woman. Instead, she is straight and towering, a tall, black silhouette against the fire in the hearth behind her. I sense her eyes on me as she silently moves aside with a dancer's step. It is my invitation to enter, and I do so tentatively, still swallowing my fear.

The fire is ablaze and crackling, but the one long room is dark in the corners so that I cannot see much around me. Thankfully, it's toasty and cozy and warm. A whiff of burning sage and hot meat curls into my nose. I leave my battered trunk and satchel near the door and curl my hands into my coat. What does one say to an Indian? I stand, uncertain, for a long moment before I realize she is not going to offer my ideas of expected social norms for visitors.

She glides silently in her mix of soft deer hides and skirts, and fluidly squats near the fire where pieces of straw are half-braided. Her hair is bound in one long plait, and in the firelight, I can see it is mostly a steel-grey.

When I kneel on the floor next to her, she does not look up. Her hands are busy, nimbly braiding and weaving. I think to help her, but I doubt my prowess in making the pieces tight and proper enough for her purpose, whatever that may be. I only wish to do something—anything—with my hands, but there's nothing but the grass, dried and crackly, and my inadequacy taunts me.

What a fool I am.

I should never have let my carefully composed personality slip at my sister Anne's winter party. I am a widow! I'm supposed to wear black, and mourn a dead husband, keeping my head down and my mind blank. Instead I found delight in speaking with my brother-in-law's cousin, and I played completely to the stereotype of wanton widow. Theodore looked like an older, yet more robust version of my sister's husband. He was fascinated with my old research, gleaned from medical journals and newspapers for Henry's illness, and I truly believe his interest in my mind was genuine. I had recalled Anne's old taunts: *No one will care about the atlas you read, and it's unbecoming to peek at the news over Father's shoulder. No man will want your opinion, not even your husband. You just wait and see!* She had been right, but Theodore was different from Henry. He hadn't scoffed at me.

And the affair? It was nothing like the chilly, careful intercourse of my marriage. It was new and fresh, and I actually found a small spark of pleasure in his arms, which was a far cry better than the times Henry had come to my bed. Theodore was a kind lover, our attraction was mutual and a bit breathless, and we did not share any false statements of love or affection. It was an expression of defiance on my part: I wanted to break away from the stilted, orderly terms of my reality that Henry and I had crafted together, and to see what it would be to choose someone for the attraction I felt instead of the partnership it offered. And Theodore understood. He gave me the chance to be free and wanton, and after a week of brief, orchestrated meetings, we decided it was best to stop.

And then he was gone to Europe, and I was left with the discovery of the child in my womb. Theodore's child. Not Henry's.

I'd spent four days staring into the fire of my sitting room.

What to do? Where to go? How to hide it?

I couldn't give in to the expectation of the loose and wild widow woman, and I couldn't let the shell of my social respectability crumble once everyone saw I was pregnant with a child that could not possibly belong to a man deceased. What would become of me? I would be ruined! Too many medical journals and articles read during Henry's illness, and my long battle with doctors made me far too wary to try an abortion. I felt my age and my strength gave me a better chance to keep the child. But where to go? How to hide?

And it was by the fire of my parlor that I read the ads, one of which brought me here, to this small town in the Territories, halfway between Yankton and Fort Randall, where no one has a need to know my true story. Least of all, this odd native woman who is quiet and strange.

As the silence stretches in the cabin, I wonder how I will live like this. How will I work twelve or fourteen hours for the doctor, never knowing his true schedule or his needs, to mind his whole household, only to come stay every night and wake every morning with this peculiar woman who does not speak to me? Nor do I know how I am to repay her for this kindness. The questions pile into my mind without end. Do I owe her rent? Do I owe her service? I am a stranger. An Easterner. A white woman. I know nothing about her people or her ways.

It's too much.

Too many unknowns.

Too many bizarre and shocking things, too many new buildings and faces, but the icy weather inching into my blood overrides it all.

Though it is early in the evening, I feel I should sit up with her, as might be proper, though my eyes close on their own. Suddenly, she lifts herself and walks to a dark wall. Not knowing what else to do, I stand and watch her. In the shadows, she gestures, so I approach to find a small cot simply prepared and covered in a hide of an animal I do not recognize in the night.

This is to be my bed. *Hides?* I had never dreamed of such a bed! She walks away before I can murmur my thanks, even though I don't mean it. It is a far cry from anything I had prepared to handle. I had thought the bedding would be stuffed with straw, but I'd planned on cotton sheets, at the very least. It is yet one more thing that makes me want to give up on this first day.

But it is not worth a fuss. Not now. Nothing will change my circumstances now.

She returns to the fire, and I assume she will not take kindly to a request for privacy in this wide-open room, or my hope for even the slightest bit of clean water for washing. It is her home, after all. Maybe Indians don't wash up each night and morning. I must abide her rules, whatever they may be, and my mind churns with the uncertainty. Turning my back to her, I unbutton my well-traveled dress, stained further now with oil and grease along one sleeve, and strip to my undergarments. A simple nightgown, an unadorned nightcap, and I am ready for sleep, save for washing up.

Widow Hawks does not move, and I am too embarrassed to disturb her. At this point, I am not entirely sure she speaks any English. I turn the hides and blankets back, crawl in, and face the wall. Normally, I would expect to spend most of a night wondering and counting all the worries I hold about my new job, the doctor, and the Indian woman with whom I live, but instead, I fall into a deep sleep immediately.

CHAPTER 3
21 March 1881

I wake with her as she rises early. I can barely see the sunrise through the cracks in the hides and faded calico over the windows. She is stirring the fire embers and generally making a racket, which I did not expect from her. My body protests the earliness of the hour, but I get up and pull the cap from my head. Oh, dear heaven. I can barely move! My arms are stiff, and my feet are sore, the toes refusing to bend. There is a deep ache in my hips, and I have several cracks ready to burst into bleeding seams along my thumbs and palms.

How will I work with such pains?

How will I do this every day?

As I rub my head to wake better, my hair feels waxy and slick. I absolutely must wash up today, so I tentatively step toward Widow Hawks, and she swings to look at me. She is not quite as tall as I remember from last night, but she is still many inches above me. Her face is inscrutable and strikingly foreign.

I gesture along with my words. "Do you have a cup and water I might use, please?"

She looks at me a long moment, then walks out of the house. I wait, hopeful she understood me. There is a sloshing, and the door bangs open to show her wrestling a good-size washbin into the room. It is full of water and chunks of ice, and my eyes widen.

"Widow Hawks, I thank you. But this is too much trouble. I will gladly wash my hands and face outside tomorrow."

Her back bends effortlessly to put the bin by the fire. She does not acknowledge me and turns to the hearth. I watch her, spellbound and uncertain for a minute. It is then that I notice she has no clocks.

This thought rouses me, and I step, barefoot, naked, and shivering, into the chilly water. It makes me gasp. Will all my baths be so frigid here? Though it is not nearly as lovely as a full sitting bath, I try to discreetly weed out the dirt in the cracks of my knees and under my arms. The water bites as I wring my hair out and the rivulets snake down my body. It's not long before the water is filmy with dusty grime from the long train travel, not to mention yesterday's labors in Doctor Kinney's kitchen. After pulling on my other mourning dress, I lace up my shoes, noting they will need to be replaced with the sturdy kind I saw Kate wearing. Widow Hawks wears soft leather shoes, native made, and decorated with paints long faded. Are they comfortable? Half her clothing is almost exactly what I have been told the Indians wear: primal, savage clothing, but it does not seem out of place, nor threatening now that I see it all put together.

Plaiting my hair up neatly and coiling it with pins, I am ready without much fuss. There! I allow myself a private smile to think of the ladies at home with their finery and needs. I am thankful I did not require a maid to dress me out East, or I would be lost today. At least it is one solid thing from my past that will help me here!

The widow is sorting cans of dry goods when I go to the door. My instinct would be to touch a person after the offer of a bed, but she's not my usual type of acquaintance. So, I pull myself back from placing a hand on the older woman's shoulder. Instead, I use my voice as warmly as I might to mask the quiver of uncertainty behind my tone.

"The doctor said you would be a fair landlady, Widow Hawks. I see you are. And I thank you. I know I am a disruption. Please let me know how I might ... offer my thanks to you."

She does not turn or move during my speech, so I press on, anxious to make at least one decent impression.

"I am ... I'm a widow, too, like you. I ..." My words stifle me because I know nothing of her marriage, and I cannot make more out of mine than what it was.

It seems she still will not speak, so I leave the house and walk briskly in the soft morning light toward the doctor's house. I wish I could ignore the unsettled nerves that rise with her silence. What is wrong with saying good morning? Good day? Anything to put me at ease! Or is she so cold and quiet because she dislikes white people? If so, why is she here in Flats Junction?

The air is not quite as brutally cold as yesterday, so I slow my steps. I want to take the time to look about the town.

The land is flat and easy to read, yet there is a rise to the land toward the east, careening sharply up to the milky

56

sky. There are more hills in the distance, dotted with a smat-
tering of trees, though most of the landscape is prairie. The
road and the railroad cut a scar across the pale soil peeking
through the windswept snow, and I step across the rail ties
and enter the town proper, passing the main street to try
another road. The grid of the town seems practical: three
main streets with a handful of short lanes to connect them.
A neat parish on the west end of First Street bears a proud
sign across the brick declaring it to be St. Diana's Lutheran
Church. Second Street curves upward from the corner of First
and Livery, which I can just decipher from scratched, wooden
sign posts. At least someone here has tried to give the town
some semblance of order! I choose Second Street. I'm almost
sure every road empties along East Avenue, which runs by
the doctor's front door. Flats Junction cobbles together, with
closely packed homes, shacks, and shanties in varying degrees
of care and decay, though one ostentatious, multi-story house
has filigree and painted trim. Lanterns are lit in several windows, and I realize a woman at the back of the Prime Inn
is actually waving at me. I wave back, and the gesture does
much to warm my heart.

The school is empty today. Across an alley a cooper's sign swings, and across the street, along the edge
of a frozen, narrow river, the town blacksmith is already
at work, obvious from the early ringing of hammer and
belch and blow of the bellows behind a broad, closed door.
Nearby is the farrier.

At the next crossing, I smell the pigs and their manure
just as I hear an inordinate amount of screeching and yam-
mering from a small group of tiny shacks built in a circle.
As I pass by, two Chinamen stagger out of one of the hovels,

arguing continuously. They are carrying an enormous cast iron kettle between them toward the black fire pit in the middle of the hovels. The two tiny Chinese women I remember from the general store yesterday follow them. One notices me and gives a miniscule, half-hidden jerk of her hands. It is so small I'm not sure if it's a wave at all.

The packed dirt and crusty snow under my feet crunch loudly. When I reach the doctor's home, the silence of my pause at the front door is disconcerting save for the sudden, unexpected clang of the church bell behind me. It is piercing and sharp and metallic, and rings from the other church in town: a broad, white, clapboard structure with *St. Aloysius Catholic Church* painted in black across the doorway.

Should I enter through the front or the back? Will he keep the back locked? I face the day with some level of worry and trepidation. His house is quiet, so I let myself in and take care for the screen door to close with barely a squeak. But then, I notice a soft glow in the kitchen and realize he is already awake. Is it after seven? He has a lantern lit on the table though he is nowhere to be seen. His puttering upstairs shuffles on the floorboards over my head.

For a moment, I am suspended. My house in Boston was not much bigger than this one, and I could always hear Henry wherever he was rummaging even if he was sifting files in his generous office. It's almost as though he has not died, and I am only imagining the shimmering grass outside. I might blink and see my beloved ocean instead. Henry was dark-haired, well-dressed, and kindly. I found him dull and yet, appropriately attentive. Our courtship was brief; he wished for a bride and I wanted to run a household of my own, and our match was what I'd hoped to find: calculated, simple, and refined. We were not often without the ears of a chaperone, and the stilted conversation that began our relationship continued throughout the marriage. Once our vows were spoken, he came to my rooms as required, and did not demand much of me even when it became apparent a child would not come easily for us.

I was not happy, but I was content to be married, and I had liked the common chores that came with managing a kitchen, a suite of rooms, and the occasional dinner party. It was not a good life to be a spinster, living with family forever, only to end up alone in the lateness of age. I knowingly took a wooden marriage with all its expectations over a quiet grey retirement.

Here, I'll be able to keep my dignity, carry on with the courteous shell I've created for so long against my nature, and no one will question my respectability, my rashness, or my choices. No one will know what a single, seven-day slip of decorum has cost me. It will be worth the harder work—and I hope I can keep up. Although I am outrageously nervous about this choice to come West, and the fears surrounding my slowly unfurling pregnancy, I feel a freedom I haven't known since my childhood.

I am my own woman here, and I can make my life again.

This seeps into my bones with certainty as I look about the doctor's kitchen.

Putting on the kettle, I move to the pantry and think a good hot breakfast of eggs and bread would do him well. As I finish up the coffee and heat the pans, he enters and breathes out loudly so I need to turn to acknowledge him.

"Good morning, Doctor Kinney."

He nods in response but gives nothing else. I pour him a cup and turn back to the eggs, mentioning off-handedly, "Widow Hawks has no clock, so I hope I am on time."

He comes to stand next to me, watching me beat the eggs, then takes the bread and slices four thick slabs.

"You are on time. In fact, you are early, Mrs. Weber." His voice is contrite. I stop beating the eggs, and the kitchen is suddenly silent. He is not smiling at all, and fear wells in me. Have I displeased him already, again?

His lips press tightly together. "I am sorry you had to go alone last night. It is embarrassin' to me. To ask Widow Hawks to take a boarder is easy. She is a good woman and we'd do anythin' for each other. But to ask you to go alone, without introduction … it was inexcusable."

I look down at the sticky eggs resting in the bowl cradled in my arm. It would not do to be truthful with him now, to tell him that I was scared with the dusky night walk through town, nor that Widow Hawks does not speak to me. Not that I am sure I can be so forthright to my employer anyway, regardless of how kind he is.

"You would feel better if I forgave you, then?" I ask.

"Please, yes."

"Then you are forgiven. Though I don't think it's necessary," I add as I continue whisking and spinning the eggs. He stands next to me for another moment, as if words are trembling on his lips, but he says no more. I should have expected him to be a gentleman, but his worries are still touching, nonetheless.

It means I do not have to fear a short temper from him, or unfair accusations. This is hopeful and good, as I have other anxieties, such as the babe I carry. At this thought,

60

I am stabbed with guilt. I should be honest and tell him about this coming issue, but my words are stuck. As I muse, I know the answer for my silence: it does not seem real that I carry a baby. There is much irony in this pregnancy. Henry would not give me a child, and I did not know I could even conceive. And Theodore himself does not know of it. Likely, and logically, he'd ask me to take care of it—to rid myself of the result of our few, fleeting moments together.

But I know what I will tell the doctor, and anyone else who asks, and even the child when it is born. I will say that somehow, in one of those last, strangely sterile moments together, Henry had finally fathered a child.

Doctor Kinney and I eat companionably. I appreciate the meal as I suddenly realize that I am hungrier than ever, and quietly hope he leaves some eggs in the pan so that I might have a little extra. Unfortunately, he leaves nothing to spare, but he praises my cooking. As he finishes his coffee, he leans back.

"How did you find Widow Hawks?"

Swallowing my own mouthful, I answer carefully, unable to meet his eyes.

"She was accommodating. Thank you for arranging a bed."

He stares at me, as if measuring a response, and gives a slight nod while he sets down the empty mug.

"I'll work in the study a wee bit until I start rounds. Thank you for the breakfast, Mrs. Weber."

He leaves the kitchen. I am still hungry, and I decide to make a bit more during dinner and supper to allow me seconds, and still have leftovers for the Brinkley family. I haven't forgotten the plan to see one of the doctor's patients today.

The day is overcast, so I decide to take a peek at the slowly unfreezing garden once the dishes are finished. It is nice to not have the sun beat down on my hair and back as I chip around the soil to see if I can figure what—if any-thing—is planted. I worry the spring will get on faster than I realize. It's a sore project, though, and I give up trying to decipher the garden to tackle the scrubbing of the kitchen's ironware and skillets crusted with rings and blooms of rust.

I kneel outside in the yard with my coat flung over my back, and my hands turn rusty and brown, and my fingers go numb with the sloshing, cold water. I mull over the schedule of the days and try to find a rhythm. I will make breakfast, and we will eat. Then he will do paperwork, and I will do chores. He will visit morning patients, arrive for lunch, and then head back to rounds until dinner. We will have dinner, and I will clean and return to my silent rooming partner on the far end of town. It is full and busy, and it will not be an idle existence. More than anything, I'm grateful that I have a house to keep and someone to feed, and a job far from Boston.

One of the small iron pots turns over in my palms. I crack off a particularly dense piece of rust and spill the spoiled water onto the ground. The chalkiness of the dirt here reminds me of Henry's dry skin, and the way his body, always slim, seemed to break apart from within as his sick-ness grew. He'd been told by numerous doctors of a wasting illness they could not fix. It seemed to wax and wane without warning. Some had thought the sickness lived in his blood and needed to be drained. Other doctors wanted to treat him with horrible medicines that made him feel worse. Conse-quently, I did not know which doctors to believe. To remedy this, I spent many long months reading pamphlets and the occasional medical journal, to no avail.

For a time, I had wondered if it was his marriage to me that had caused him sadness and his odd apathy. There was no love between us, so I found I could not throw myself into cheering him, and I had begun to think I was an unsound wife. Perhaps, I had reasoned, it was no wonder he did not smile much at me, for I hadn't tried to charm him. This guilt drove me to try to find a cure, no matter how unbecoming Henry thought me as I chased articles and pamphlets on healing. As the doctors trickled in and out of our door, he finally gave up asking me to stop learning and instead, begged that I not tell the doctors my opinions and to keep my research to myself. He once muttered that he had no idea he'd married such an inquisitive woman. I do not think, even now, that he meant it as a compliment.

But as our marriage tripped along slowly, we became closer, friends even. And later, I was his advocate and his nursemaid. Eventually, even that was not enough. My Henry, husband, lover, and kind friend had succumbed to the disease, and I wore the black veil of the widow. The gowns in my closet are still ash and grey and black.

As I think of the bleak colors of my dresses, the sun breaks through the clouds and hits my hair and the back of my neck, heat soaking into the dark fabric of my mourning clothes. I do not realize how exhausted I am until I stand up and immediately feel dizzy, falling to my knees to keep from fainting.

"Mrs. Weber!" There is a call from the house. Doctor Kinney has stuck his head out of the window. I did not realize that he could watch me from his office. "Are you alright?"

I nod, feeling my heart pump hot blood through my head. His head disappears back inside. Picking up the cleaned skillet and kettle pot, I carry them in and dry the last of the dirty wares in the kitchen while staring outside the window. There is much solace in making a schedule. It makes me forget where I am and keeps me from screaming aloud against the trail of my life, which meanders so opposite to the vision I'd had.

The garden needs seeds, and I wonder what I should plant. I do not have much of a green thumb, and I have no understanding of what grows well in the soil out here. A few wealthy acquaintances back East kept greenhouses, though I did not have that luxury. But I want—likely will *need*—fresh vegetables for cooking. Well, that's yet another question needing an answer.

I wipe my hands on my apron, and head back into the cooler shade of the hallway. The doctor is taking his hat from the peg by the door, and his coat is already on, but he stops and looks at me with concern.

"I have two patients to visit this mornin'. Don't trouble much for luncheon."

I wave away his worry. "It's no matter. I'll have something small."

He shakes his head, plops the hat back on the peg, and marches into the kitchen, calling to me over his shoulder. "You should feel free to wash up in the surgery whenever you like, Mrs. Weber. If you're keepin' clean, I have no issue with you usin' it."

I enter the laboratory with some hesitation. It has pale, whitewashed walls, and shiny glass and silver instruments arrayed on a side table. In the cabinet, vials are carefully

64

labeled and organized. The tap is moist with soft condensation from the room's warmth. I pour some water out on my hands and clean the rust from under my nails.

Turning, I see him standing in the doorway watching me blandly, a tumbler of lukewarm water in his hand.

"You're a bit pale. Have enough to eat after your long journey yesterday? Still recoverin' a bit from the trip, I shouldn't wonder," he explains, then hands me the glass before heading back to the door.

"Thank you," I call, belatedly, as he walks out. I am not sure he hears me. I have forgotten to ask him how long he will be. Guessing that two patients in town might take an hour or so, I calculate. Likely I have time to dust the house before I make the midday meal.

I do not touch the lab. I don't know how to sterilize his equipment properly, so I dust around the piles of paperwork and mounds of books in his office. The map on the wall pulls me in, and I look at the dotted lines, the railroad names, and the long, wispy feathers of rivers, creeks, and streams. It is only a partial map of the Territories, but Flats Junction is marked as Flats Town, with the "Town" crossed off and "Junction" written in by hand. I suppose when the rails came through and crisscrossed here, the town saw fit to change its name. A large smudge on the top right is labeled as "buffalo jump."

I wipe down the shelves around his books, ignoring the titles as best I can so I don't get distracted, and then debate lining up his files and papers. The top one catches my eye. I recognize the doctor's rather rounded hand, and I'm drawn in before I can stop myself.

Patient - Dell Johnston   J

Address - The Powdered Pig Saloon

Occupation Saloon Owner

Dates	
Jan '75	*Influenza; mild case.*
May 77	*Damaged outer ear - hit with frying pan. Fortuna is unharmed but admits to assault! Minimal damage to inner ear.*
Sep 80	*Saloon brawl. Broken ribs, smashed finger. Set finger with wood and muslin splint, and asked patient to rest on rib injury. Patient agreed to rest for a single night only.*
	Rumor: saloon brawl started with Fortuna's girls arriving and soliciting clients.
	— Must talk to Fortuna.

I glance below Dell Johnston's page and see a large "F" in the corner of the next paper, and I realize it's the mysterious Fortuna's file. Good gracious! I've been at it a day, and I'm already sticking my fingers where they likely do not belong. I know I'm supposed to be some sort of nursing aide to the doctor, but I've been given no leave to inspect patient files.

Leaving the office with my duster, I slip the rag along the shelves on the kitchen before hesitating a moment at the stairs. I wonder if I should intrude on the living level above, but decide that as the housekeeper, I cannot shirk half the house. I walk up the narrow stairs. A few of them protest with pops and squeaks.

There are two bedrooms and a communal washroom. One room is spare, the faded, flowered coverlet the only evidence that the space once was his great-aunt's bedroom. A cross over the bed speaks of their Irish Catholicism, and there is not much to dust other than the bed rails, and tops of the bedside table and bureau. Her bed reminds me of my easy fatigue, but I push the thought away and turn to the washroom. A tin bathtub on planked flooring is shielded by a dark calico curtain. There is a matching curtain strung along the wall, allowing for privacy so a person might bathe while another primped at the wash station. I note the curtains will need a spring clean. The water in the pitcher is low, so I see he has washed out the bin. The floor needs a scrub, and the bathtub, too, but I am pleased the doctor is not sloppy.

Bracing myself, I look in his private room. This, to me, is the doctor's ultimate sanctuary, and it feels deceptive to walk into his bedroom without asking for permission. The bed is made, though there are wrinkles in the thin blanket. His clothes spill about indiscriminately instead of hanging on the hooks. There are a few books on the table by the curtain-less window. I am struck by the fact that he has artwork on the wall. One picture is a small, simply framed portrait of an older woman. I wonder if this is his recently deceased aunt. Another is a wedding picture. A photograph. I think there is resemblance in the man's face to the doctor, but the couple's clothing is old fashioned, and I wonder if they are his parents or his grandparents. I like the woman's eyes.

Stop! I'm prying again! Shaking myself with a stern reprimand, I dust around his things, then head back downstairs into the kitchen. Lunch is a light soup, and I am stirring as he slams the screen door and walks in.

"How were your rounds, Doctor?"

"Good. The calf is doin' fine, and Tate's leg is handlin' my treatment," he says, before disappearing around the corner. I hear the familiar gush of water, and then he is back, and eyeing me as I set the table.

"How are you feelin'?"

I think of the babe in my womb and catch my breath, only managing, "Quite well."

"I should have thought of it—given you time to settle in more than I did. It's no wonder you felt peaked earlier." He considers, then goes to the stoneware jug, pours out more water and wordlessly hands it to me. I am embarrassed that I am already such a bother on my second day of employment.

I say this while we eat, and he shows a half-smile.

"You're not used to the weather, work, and extra needs here. Until you're seasoned, I don't mind helpin' to keep you alive." His voice is lighthearted and I stop worrying for the moment. There is too much to learn and figure. If I really think of all the dangers, the changes, the amount of heavy work I am to do, I will panic. Best bit by bit. It's that or run screaming through the house in a fright, which will likely only bring the wrath of Mrs. Molhurst, the neighbor, which sounds unappealing as well.

Perhaps I should tell the doctor about the babe now, but it seems far too early. I wish to confess my condition to someone, but to tell a man—this stranger—within a day or two of our acquaintance goes against my nature. This entire situation is beyond comprehending. Not only is my widowhood and surprising pregnancy after so many years of barrenness something new, but to be expected to offer the secrets of my life without history or relationship is beyond my ability. The words are nearly impossible. I must adjust, I know, and eventually spit out the details of my health. I just simply cannot. Not yet.

After some silence, I venture, "Where might I find seeds for the garden?"

"Kate," he answers between bites. "And you ought to get your cloth from her, too. Make yourself a serviceable dress or two and a good bonnet."

I nod, then glance about the kitchen. "Where do we get milk and cheese?"

"The Brinkleys. We trade services and goods. It's how they're payin' for my help with the new babby, but otherwise, they're the family that supplies most of us 'round here with dairy."

"That reminds me, I've made enough food for us and them. Might I take some over today for their supper tonight?" I ask. He gives me a true smile with his eyes crinkled, half-moons. I smile back despite myself.

"Alice'll be grateful. I'm headin' to them next; why don't you come along and meet them. You can head to the general from there."

I agree, and we companionably clean the dishes together while I ask him what plants he would suggest I try in the garden. His aunt had squashes, cucumbers, dill, herbs, carrots, beans, and potatoes. I wonder about tomatoes, and he approves my idea to try them. I'm heartened by his encouragement.

We walk out together for the Brinkley's place. He courteously opens the screen door for me, and I recall the gentlemanly way Henry had treated me. I am surprised to think of him with such nostalgia. He was not a passionate man, nor a very expressive one, but he had been polite, careful, and respectful of me. He had been very grateful to find a bride he could talk to and could easily take to gatherings. Unlike Doctor Kinney, Henry was not one to remain a bachelor.

"How long were you married, Mrs. Weber?" the doctor asks sociably, and I try not to start. It's as if he is reading my mind.

I want to brush off his questions. They're very forward. But we're not in Boston and, apparently, the months of niceties do not pass here before people move into personal questions. I should not be surprised by this, especially given the prying way Kate asked questions of me yesterday. I'm so wrapped up in organizing my new life, battling the dirt, adjusting to the frightening place I must sleep, and fighting nausea, that I keep forgetting the people are different here.

Was it only yesterday I arrived? How strange. I am more overwhelmed than I realize.

I try to open myself, speak calmly, and answer my employer as truthfully as I can. "I was married almost four years. My mother was glad. She'd started to worry I would be too old to wed. Well, older than most girls out East, that is," I admit, offering up more information than I intend in my fluster.

"No children?"

"No. It was ... difficult ... for Hen ... for us." I pause, then decide to give him a broader picture of my marriage. "Mr. Weber had health issues." I answer without thought, forgetting for a moment that I am pregnant, and by the time I speak, the moment for confessing is gone.

I think he is going to ask more questions of me, but we draw up on the farm, and the doctor turns and hails some of the men in the fields. I should remember to ask him about himself, and of the photographs in his bedroom to repay him his interest in me. Besides, it will be good to understand my employer to properly manage his home.

The Brinkleys are not far from the town. Their farm is the first on the main road east, visible even from the town square. It is pretty, neat, and obviously successful. I count five homes on the property as we make our way there. Each one has a woman's touch of a window box, curtains, and painted doors. I can smell the cows, the sheep, and a muddy aroma of land and snow mixed. These are the scents of peacefulness, a familiarity that feels welcoming.

A few garden plots already sprout tiny green leaves. So, it is possible to start here early! My garden may very well be late by the time the seeds arrive if Kate doesn't keep packets on hand. I'm not sure I should attend any churches to meet the women and get some of their saved seeds either. I'm not Lutheran or Catholic. Will that matter?

As we level up with one of the homes on the Brinkley farm, I hear the tiny, distinctive sound of a newborn's hic-cupping, fussy cry. The doctor gives a brief knock and then, carrying the pot of cooled soup, walks in casually without waiting for anyone to answer the door. I follow him, carrying

71

a basket of condiments. If I had had time, I would have tried to make bread, but there wasn't time—not time for bread, let alone time for me to breathe and settle in.

I glance around for the Brinkley family. It's a home that might once have been tidy, but currently feels completely disorderly. Doctor Kinney moves with purpose to the bedroom. I hear his accent soften with a croon as he addresses the mother and baby. He has put the pot of soup on the stove in his passing, and I move toward it. Food, I know I can do. I hope there are no nursing duties with today's visit; I might fold completely.

A young man comes in from the side door with a pail of milk and an empty washtub under an arm. He stops short at the sight of me.

I smile encouragingly. "Hello, Mr. Brinkley. I'm Doctor Kinney's new housekeeper, Mrs. Weber. We've brought you some dinner." I move to the stove and pull a pot from the sideboard. It needs washing before I can put the soup in for them to reheat later.

He is still staring at me, then remembers himself and sets down the washtub. "You're here with the doc?"

"Yes. He's already in with your wife and the boy."

Mitch sets the milk on the table and brushes past me to the bedroom. He seems an eager father, as if he is willing to learn about his son. I admire this, as well as chuckle at his poor attempts to keep house while Alice recovers. I'm surprised there are so few women from the farm helping her.

I fill the washtub and clean out the pot and a few dishes so the table can be set. Then I pour the soup from Doctor Kinney's crockery into Alice's and set it on the stove. As my hands move around the heavy plates and clay mugs, my wedding band clinks loudly against the rims. It reminds me of life back East. It seems any little thing can do so. The amount of housework I am doing now is not so much new to me, but it is the roughness of it all, the lack of fine things and city amenities that make it far less easy. My arms still ache from yesterday's work, and the soreness hasn't worn off one bit. How long will it take before I feel some strength?

"Mrs. Weber?" The doctor's voice spins me around. I see a small bundle cradled in his arms. He looks strikingly tender, and I feel myself catch. It is an interesting vision. It is not often I would think to see a man holding a newborn.

"Is everything alright?" I ask.

"Can you manage wee Pete while I examine Alice?"

I look past the doctor into the bedroom where the husband is sitting next to his wife on the narrow bed. He does not seem inclined to come out and hold his son. I wipe my hands on my apron and go to get the baby. If this is a nursing duty, I can certainly manage it.

The doctor's hands seem overlarge as he gives over the child, carefully maneuvering his little limbs, and the pass of precious cargo is a delicate moment as we both watch the sleeping babe. The little boy is light, air-like, and smells like sweet, warm skin and powdered bedding. Do all babes smell good? I do not know. I have held so few. I hold him a bit awkwardly at first, but Doctor Kinney puts a hand on my arm, then adjusts the crick of my elbow.

"He won't break so easily, Mrs. Weber. Relax here. Good." With a casual tap, he releases me and walks back into the bedroom and shuts the door. I'm dazed by the baby I hold, and am overtly aware of his pale skin, the blue spidery veins on his temple, and the shell of his ear. He is roundly robust, and his plump lips still have a drop of milk on them. I am suddenly filled with apprehension for my own child. Will it be a boy like this, perfect and little? How shall I care for him? How shall I love him and provide for him? The enormity of the undertaking scares me so absolutely that thinking on it for long makes me feel faint. I am afraid to do the whole experience alone, afraid of the uncertainty, afraid of the birth, afraid of what Theodore has left me as a token of our few stolen moments.

For a moment, I want to rail against Henry. If he hadn't died, everything would still be the same, and I wouldn't be facing either widowhood or motherhood. While Henry was not the husband I had dreamed about in my youth, he was steady and grave. To lose him so early in marriage, before we could build much tenderness or history, leaves me still feeling detached from his memory. I enjoyed being married, but the marriage itself was filled with guarded lovemaking, quiet conversation, and dispassionate expressions. I feel as though I had not fulfilled the potential within me to be a wife, and now I will not fulfill my potential as a mother. Having a child must be very different here, though I expected as much when I made the choice to come West. I doubt there will be such a thing as a formal nursemaid. Besides, I will not be able to afford it. And I have no family in the Territories to help.

But it was this or face everyone I know and tell them I was not proper, and not demure, and not a good mourning widow.

I allowed passion, curiosity, and a fanciful few hours to make a vulgar, lustful woman of me. If my family and acquaintances knew this, they would never forget it. I would live under the ache of shame all my days.

I bend over the baby and will myself not to cry. Without realizing it, I am swaying lightly, holding him nearer so I can press my forehead to his tiny one.

"Mrs. Weber." The doctor is back. I lift my eyes, glad there are no tears. He has a half-smile on his face, but it is almost sad, and he takes the baby without another word. I go back to the stove and finish the rest of the dirty dishes so that the kitchen area, at least, is picked up.

He returns again. "Ready?"

I glance at the bedroom. I have not met Alice, and it seems rude that I've been in her house and managed her dishes without at least introducing myself, but I figure there will be time for that later. I nod and follow him out.

We walk in silence for a minute. The air is warmer than earlier, though I still find the breeze cuttingly cold. To bridge our quiet, I ask, "There is not much help for Alice?"

He understands my question and gives a rueful chuckle.

"Not at the moment. Mitch's family isn't happy with him for takin' a day or so from spring plantin' and farmin' to spend time with his wife and babe. The men figure, if he's so sure to help with the babby, the womenfolk can keep workin' in the fields instead of taking over Alice's household. They'll get over it soon, and Alice'll win them over, too. But in the meantime, thank you for helpin'."

I nod, pleased he notices my work, but continue my questions about Mitch. "He's unique in being so involved in ... women's issues."

"Aye." Doctor Kinney thinks for a moment, then says with bluntness, "I wish more men would be interested. It would be a godsend to some of the women 'round here who do not have family to help them, and it might make it more likely I'm called for a birthin'."

"I can see your point," I say. He touches on a subject I was musing earlier. He gives me an amused sideways smile.

"You don't agree?"

I think. I am rather traditional and, to me, it does not seem a man's place to be with his wife during childbirth, or even after. But then I wonder about myself. What would I wish, if Henry were alive and the child his? Well, I would be too embarrassed to have him near while I screamed in labor, or to hear the diagnosis after I gave birth. But suppose my marriage had been with a man whom I loved, instead of simply held in affection? Suppose our child had been conceived in passion, not the careful, chilly sex I'd known? What if Theodore and I had been madly in love? Then I might wish for more sharing in everything, from childbirth to childcare and beyond.

"I think perhaps some marriages do not make it easy for such openness," I say.

The doctor does not rejoin my comment at first. He nods once or twice. Then he says, unexpectedly, "Do you not have family, Mrs. Weber? Parents?"

I smile with reflection. "Yes. I have a mother and father. They are alive and live in Rockport."

"No siblings?"

"I have a sister who is older than me." I refrain from talking further, hoping he lets it be. I don't wish to speak of my sister especially, nor the man she married.

"Did you not wish to be with them after your husband's untimely death? Forgive me, Mrs. Weber, but family is important out here. When one does not have any, we tend to create our own to survive. But you left yours. Were you not able to return?"

I hug the empty soup pot to my chest, wincing slightly against the tenderness of my bosom. How to answer this truthfully, vaguely, so I can create the story I wish to provide? Well, surely my mother would have let me have my old room. I'd been married a few years, but they had kept my childhood house. My sister would not have welcomed me into her busy life, though had I begged, she would have eventually, unhappily, relented. And I would not have wished such a thing for myself anyway. Imagine seeing her husband James every day! I would certainly be reminded of Theodore—the two look so much alike—and why I'd relented to the affair in the first place.

And no matter what, I could not go to anyone widowed and pregnant with another man's child.

"I could have gone back to family, I suppose," I say, unwilling to dive into my past further than I already am. "But I married late and had enjoyed making my own household. To return would be too ... easy."

"And you are not partial to easiness?" There is surprise in his voice.

"Maybe not. Life has not been difficult for me, nor has it been easy," I explain obscurely. "But that is most lives, is it not, Doctor?"

He shakes his head at my trite comment. "Yes. But when given an easy way out, many would take it. Instead, you embark on a journey, alone, to a place where you know no one. I must say it's a bit gutsy. Here we be."

We've quickly arrived at Kate's mercantile before I can flip the discussion to his own history. I mull on his characterization of my spirit. Do I have a bit of spitfire in me? I think he is mistaken. It was a simple choice for me. Even had I not been pregnant, to return home as if I'd never left would be taking a step backward, ignoring what I'd learned as a wife and lover, and forever succumbing to life as a widow. I'm not a wild woman, nor one who will dramatize life's woes, but I certainly had no intention of fading into obscurity even before I was saddled with a babe.

"Be sure to pick up proper shoes. Kate knows my billin'." And he is off, his easy athletic gait propelling him down the street.

The store is warm, and I wonder how hot it gets in the heat of summer. Perhaps she will open the glass window. It is dusty and smudged, and the same two men are sitting at it in front of their checkers, though they are not playing today. Both creak in their chairs when I enter, and I instinctively cringe as they turn toward me.

"Back, are you then?" Horeb Harvey smirks and rubs his old wrinkly hands together. "Doc say you need to do his shopping for him then, does he?"

"It's just … for me?" I feel foolish to give them my order, and flustered enough to provide far more information than I intend.

"Boots?" Gilroy stares pointedly at my shoes.

"That too." I nod, noting that the two of them seem to be wearing the exact same layers of flannel as yesterday.

Oh heavens! Yesterday! Have I only arrived yesterday!? It feels like it was ages ago.

"Heard you're bunking with the old Widow Hawks," Horeb declares, settling back in his chair and picking at a tooth. "You ain't scared of the Injuns then, are you?"

"Ah ..."

Kate suddenly comes out from behind a shelf with a fraying burlap bag slung over one of her strong shoulders. I have to wonder how she keeps up the store without any men to help her.

"Jane Weber." Her voice is more melodious than I remember, but she does not seem as welcoming today. "What can I get the doctor?"

I hesitate. "It's not for him. For me. I ... I need proper work things, he says."

"Does he now?" There is a forced lightness in her voice. "Well, he's right. Those shoes won't last the summer." She stands before me, drops the heavy bag of dried beans to the floor, and frowns at my light city footwear.

"That's what I said!" Horeb calls.

"Ain't. I did," Gilroy argues.

"Well, I figured the same," Horeb tells Gilroy testily.

Kate ignores their insertions into our discussion, and I try to do the same.

"I would be obliged if you could help me, Kate." I'm surprised to realize that I am pleading. Please let her be a friend to me here. Please let her help me fit in. How else will I have friends? I'm sure most other women here in Flats Junction are all married and have children. She and I must be alike, to be alone and need to survive. "I know nothing of what to do here."

She finally meets my face. How beautiful she is! Why is she unmarried? And why is she so skeptical of me? I wish I were a brave person to ask her these questions, using the casualness Doctor Kinney asks of my own past.

"The shoes are over here." Spinning on her heels, she goes to a table where serviceable shoes pile together. They are all black or dark brown. There are no laces on most of the boots, though a few have metal toe tips. I pick out a few pairs that seem to be my size, and I try them on while Kate heads to the counter. She calls to me over her shoulder.

"You won't be doing much riding out, so you'll need mainly clothes for tending house, I should think. Just one split skirt, an overskirt, and a housedress or two should do you."

"Tell her to pick a pink! None of the gals around here wear pink!" Horeb suggests.

"Fortuna's girls," Gilroy reminds.

"Well, them. But they don't count."

Kate shakes her head and calls across the store. "Likely Jane doesn't want to dress the way the bordello girls do, Horeb."

Heat floods across my forehead, and I bend to try on another pair of boots. I am embarrassed about this expense on the doctor's credit, but do not know if I should express this to Kate. Then again, she is privy to the doctor's accounts. She might tell me what he can afford.

One soft, well-worn pair fits without pinching, and I wear them over to the counter to get a feel for them on my feet. They are immediately more comfortable than my city shoes, and are broken in across the lasts under my feet. I walk to the back of the store and find Kate on a ladder, pulling down fabric materials.

"Kate ..." I start softly, then dive in while she continues to move in silence. I'm too aware of the obvious eavesdropping of Horeb and Gilroy, but there's nothing to do about it. "Kate, I am unsure how to pay for this. The doctor is paying me in board, not much in the way of cash. It will take me some time to save it up to repay the debt."

She pauses for a moment, then comes down to the floor with a stack of cloth. The look on her face is softer. I do not understand the mercurial nature of her moods at all. They are disconcerting, and yet becoming of her, so that I wish to figure out the enigma of her personality. There is a charm about her. Is that why she's been so successful as the general's manager?

"Jane. It's alright. If I know the doctor, he will consider this part of your 'board,' but I can make a note in the accounting so that should you ever wish to pay him back, you would know how much."

"Very well," I agree. "But do not let me choose things that are too expensive, anyway."

"Well, you've done fine on the boots already," she says, peering down at my feet.

I smile tentatively at her, and then browse at what she has spread out. A brown work calico makes sense to match with the leather split skirt she recommends. But I am dissatisfied with the options for a housedress. Kate has brought out mostly dowdy, plain colors. I am not vain, nor am I prone to dress prettily, but I do have an idea of what looks pleasing on me.

"Do you ... I wonder if you might have something in more color?"

"It will fade faster," she remarks a bit sharply. I bite my tongue against a quick reply against her, unconsciously staring at her orange blouse and blue skirt. It looks lovely on her, and it doesn't seem to have faded much unless it is very new, which I doubt.

"Perhaps ... perhaps something in blue ... or even yellow?"

"Pink!" Horeb yells.

"Green!" Gilroy bellows.

"Damnit, Gil, you know she'd look much finer in pink."

"Yellow, please, Kate?" I ask.

She climbs back up with a huff. Is she so easily offended that I did not take to her suggestions?

"You won't need much frill," she reasons from her perch. "No men to dress for here, like out East."

"That ain't true, Kitty. We all will look."

"You boys don't count," she shoots back.

Horeb cackles and Gilroy snorts.

"Boys! She calls us boys yet, is it?" Horeb wheezes. "Kitty, this woman is good for you. Gets you all spiced up. Plus, fine enough to look at, even in mourning." He leans forward and cocks his head appreciatively.

"Pay them no mind," she advises. "It only encourages them to make noise. Anyway, you'll want a plain calico. It's no good to be flashy here." She glowers at the two old men.

I nod sagely, playing along with her irritation and counsel. "You're quite right. Besides, my late husband did not much care for bows and things, so I've forgotten how to really adorn myself."

She seems to relent a bit and comes down with some prettier fabrics. I choose a yellow calico, and then I cannot help myself as I ask her to pull down a lavender with no pattern at all. I simply like the color, and I know my dark brown hair and lighter skin look well in purples. And if I wear purple, I won't be so far off my mourning requirements. I'll still feel slightly proper.

82

"I'm just going to be happy to wear color again, you see," I try to explain to Kate. "The colors of mourning are not suitable here, nor do they look well on anyone."

Kate gives a half-shrug of indifference and goes to cut the bolts for me. I ask her to cut enough to make a bonnet of one or two of the fabrics. I hope my sewing skills are up for this challenge. I've learned, as any woman does, the physics of making clothing, but I am more used to making samplers and cross stitches than actual garments. In Boston, everything could be bought from the local seamstress and dressmakers.

As she cuts, the door swings open, and two women enter the general. One is tiny, wizened, and spry and the other overly tall and big bosomed. They are chattering loudly, only to stop and pay their respects to Gilroy and Horeb.

"It's the Warrens! Missus Elaine. And Toot," Horeb greets. "How goes it at the Golden Nail?"

"Very fine. Bill is getting in an iron juicer so we can have lemonade this summer at the big July Fourth festival."

"Ahhh. Trusty Willy has sent for a new contraption, has he?"

"You all know you want to try my lemonade, just like I made when those fancy railroad men came back in '78." The elderly woman's voice is reedy but strangely cultured.

"Sure do," Gilroy agrees.

She flashes him a smile marked by teeth stained with brown tobacco. Flushing, he abruptly turns to the stale checkerboard. Horeb glances at Gilroy with narrowed eyes, and then looks up happily at the other woman, who looks to be about the same age as Doctor Kinney. Horeb looks pleased. He has an alarmingly close view of the bottom of her bosom and seems very content with it.

"And Missus Elaine. You've had no luck trying to buy out the Prime Inn, so I've heard," he mentions.

She shakes her dark, glossy head and folds her arms over her chest, but that only plumps her breasts higher, and Horeb's eyes gleam. She frowns and then looks around for Kate.

"I need to look over our credit. I want to make sure my figures match," she announces. Kate nods, finishes cutting my fabric, and heads over to the ledger. Horeb watches with open disappointment as Elaine walks away, Toot following. To avoid being his victim again, I wander to the seeds and sift through the small packets. Thankfully, I will not have to order out for them, as Kate has quite enough variety. Each small bag rattles with dryness. While picking out the seeds I had discussed with the doctor, I spy a case of metal goods. I go over to look at them while Kate finishes my parcels and recounts the numbers of the Golden Nail Saloon slowly with Elaine Warren.

My fingers lightly graze the glass top of the case. It is filled with the finer things I would expect to see back home. Gold and silver glint in the sun streaking in from the large front window, glowing on dust that seems suspended in the air. Like me. Suspended in this new reality where I do not know half of what to make of things. Frozen in a body newly taken over by a foreign condition, feigning my reality to everyone I meet.

I block out the barbs Horeb is shooting at Gilroy, the muttering of the ladies at the counter, and glance at the watches. Theodore had had a fine watch, and I remember him taking it off carefully before we'd have relations. The-odore, and his fine chiseled face that so resembled James'.

84

Theodore and his damned kindness. Theodore who thought my mind was unique and interesting. I'm glad I didn't love him, but his presence is constantly with me. I wish I could erase it all. I wish I could be more like my sister Anne, and her easy way in society, her disinterest in learning, and her ability to laugh and charm.

Kate walks silently, even on the rough plank floor, and she scares me when she speaks lowly into my ear, "They are men's watches." The general is quiet again, and I look up and realize the Warren women have left.

"I know." I rap the glass once. "My Henry had one just like that." I point, then turn away.

She adds up the goods carefully in her large, thick, leather-bound book. The accounts fill over half of the yellowy pages.

"How are you getting by with the doctor, then?" she asks as she finishes her numbers with a flourish.

"Well, it's only been two days. Barely. It's all overwhelming. And I have so much to figure out. I'll learn, though, I suppose." I want to be strong and optimistic, even as I doubt my answers.

"Yes," she gives a little snort. "Every woman's dream, to keep house for a man."

"I don't mind having a purpose, whatever it is." I say, and I realize my tone is a bit like a retort. Apparently, her surliness can rub off on me.

She relents slightly. "I don't mean it particularly to you, Jane." She uses my front name comfortably, as if we have been close friends for years. "I mean that it's something I wouldn't want to do. I've too much I want to prove. To this town and to myself." Her declaration seems heartfelt, and from the silence of the two elderly gentlemen, it must be something worth noting and not teasing.

"You're a braver woman than me," I give her. Kate actually smiles at this and I, again, think she is unusually beautiful. It is a good compliment to give her, it seems, for she becomes cheerful.

"Well, then, good luck with your planting. I'm sure I'll have to stop by when I can to see how you're getting on."

And with that, I leave the store, uncertain if she is a friend or not.

CHAPTER 4
4 April 1881

No one seems to mind that I sleep at Widow Hawks' house—
or at least, no one has said a word against me to my face.
Sometimes, I think I see slivers of glances as I hike to her
house across the railroad each evening, but either I'm too new
to bother with directly, or everyone is still holding out on a
final opinion. Perhaps it's obvious that it is my only choice
other than one of the inns. Or they figure it is proper enough
that I am staying anywhere but with the doctor, especially as
I am not an elderly woman keeping house for him.

The hope that I will not be ostracized trickles through
me, though I feel ashamed that I wonder at all. I should be
thankful for the free bed, for her hospitality, however strange
I find it, but I'm still scared sometimes. I don't know her at
all, and she doesn't speak to me. And I do wish the doctor
could have come up with another solution for my board.

I sit next to the fire near Widow Hawks, wrestling with the sewing in my lap. I know this is a peaceful process for some women, but I am too rusty to be able to sew aimlessly and just let my mind wander. I would like to be complacent about the stitches, but instead, I must concentrate.

I cannot believe I have been in Flats Junction for just two weeks. It is still all a blur, and it feels as though eons have passed. I am constantly considering my next step on how to properly keep house for the doctor, how to keep my garden watered now that spring has started in earnest, and soon I'll have to do the laundry.

I'm still confused by the weather as well. The snow has decided to disappear with frightful speed, and there is news of devastating floods all along the Missouri. Fort Randall itself is struggling, Pierre is underwater, and Yankton and Vermillion are nearly washed away. Some craftsmen simply give up on rebuilding in those towns and are moving inland and into Flats Junction. A Jewish shoemaker and his wife arrived earlier this week from Vermillion by wagon, as the railroads are still down, causing a bit of a stir. Not because Isaac and Hannah Horowitz are Jewish, it seems, but because everyone is overtly glad to have someone in town to repair shoes professionally and to make new ones. I hear they have just settled into an abandoned old saloon and are already swimming in orders.

I met Sadie Fawcett when she stopped in for tea, unannounced, with her gaggle of children. She had no qualms telling me that she plans to have more, as her husband prefers a big brood, though I have yet to understand how a woman could *stop* having children anyway. She proudly informed me that her husband, Tom, runs the bank. A tall woman introduced herself to me as Anette Zalenski at the door of St. Aloysius after Mass. She was warm and welcoming and clasped my hands, saying she is glad to see the doctor has a new house-keeper. I liked her immediately, but there was little time to have a chat with her several children running in circles around the church and my need to make the midday meal. It felt com-pletely fraudulent to attend Mass with the doctor, but it felt even odder to not go to a service when nearly everyone appar-ently attends one church or the other. It seems the only person who does not practice a religion is Widow Hawks herself.

I glance down at my hands. So far, I have made a bonnet and the bodice of the yellow dress. I hope it fits. I worry at how I will take it out when my body starts to swell with preg-nancy, and likely, I will need another few yards of cloth for a maternity dress. It is early yet, I know, and there will be many months before I really must take care of my appearance.

Good heaven! I'll be in confinement here! I haven't really looked at the women. No one seems to be hugely preg-nant, so I have no notion of what is considered acceptable and proper here.

I don't know the rules! I have no way to research and learn about the customs other than to fumble my way through them. I want to like it here in Flats Junction. I want to feel at home and at peace, and to scatter the unsettled feeling in my stomach so it disappears completely. If I was a weepy woman, I might feel relief with tears, but I know it will only give me a headache and red eyes.

And it won't fix a thing.

I've already made a mess of things by talking to Dell Johnston of the Powdered Pig Saloon, mentioning how odd it is that there's a place called the Powdered Rose just down the street. He shouted so loud, he turned purple. Everyone on

Main Street had stared, but no one had explained until much later. Sadie Fawcett told me that there is a feud between Dell and Fortuna, the bordello matron, but she didn't elaborate about what.

And someone shot someone else by the livery yesterday, but the doctor didn't give details when he came in from that calamity. He just washed the blood off his hands and sighed very loudly as he cleaned his instruments in the surgery.

Widow Hawks seems content to continue sharing silence tonight. I do not know yet if she understands English completely. She sits amicably next to me and fingers her own weaving and arts. She may not speak English, but I notice articles in her home that do not seem to fit. There is a silver hairbrush, half-hidden by wools in a basket, and a small locket hanging from her neck on a gold chain. But I do not ask questions and try to respect her tranquility. We still do not take any meals together, but sit by the fire for an hour or so in the evenings, and divide the place for sleep.

My mind turns again to my task at hand. My sewing skills are so incredibly poor and take so long. My time of mourning isn't over, but it's already obvious the threads of my smudged grey and black frocks won't hold up. The hems are already ripped to shreds. The doctor has not said anything about my raggedy dresses, but it's just one more thing to make me feel disgusting all the time. I'm thankful for his silence; likely he has forgotten when I was to stop mourning. He even told me I should stop with the Eastern theatrics of mourning for months. The notion is so very improper, but I am unbecomingly eager to give up the black cloth.

The night quickly turns old for me, so I make my way to bed.

CHAPTER 5
5 April 1881

In the early morning, I wake to vivid nausea. It is a constant churn. Waves of it overpower me until I am able to stumble outside and relieve my stomach. I kneel in the earth outside Widow Hawks' home, heedless of the dirt and dust on my nightgown, thankful I did not retch in her home, and hopeful I did not wake her. Strangely, the nausea does not immediately subside, so I wait, a hand to my head, shaking and lightly sweating.

She is silent as a cat. I start when her hand first comes around my forehead. Waiting a beat, she then lifts me up and brings me back inside to the embers of last night's fire. A fat blanket is thrown around my shoulders, and then she bends to wake the flames so any chill I feel is quickly gone with the heat and the coziness of the wool.

There is silence, except for the crackle of new wood thrown on the flames. Widow Hawks comes next to me, crouching. I marvel at her easy gaits and bends at her age, which must be close to fifty. Her coloring makes her appear ageless.

"Does he know?"

Her voice is low, with a melodiousness that is oddly familiar. There is an accent to her words—I hear it immediately—but her English is pure. I want to smile with happiness that she has finally accepted me enough to speak, that I am worthy of her time. She may misinterpret my grin, though, so I bite my lips.

"Henry? No. He didn't know. He ... he died even before I knew myself." The lie comes, practiced in my head, but spoken aloud for the first time. I cannot look at her as I say it.

"I do not speak of your husband. I mean the doctor."

I pause, suddenly realizing that she has appropriately guessed the situation. How could she know so quickly? Weakly, I shake my head negative. She is quiet again, then says, gently, "You ought to tell him, so he knows to give you rest."

"No," I say, disagreeing with her. "I cannot be a bother to him. It's my job to take care of him, his kitchen, and his house. He has to think I am worth keeping on as a housekeeper instead of one that is only an expensive trouble."

"He won't send for another."

"But how will he not? I must work as long as I can, hoping he will be kind enough to keep me after he knows of my condition, and to let me stay after the babe is born. Some homes in Boston don't mind if their cooks have little ones. He will have to put up with a babe in his house all day. I cannot imagine he will be happy with it, bachelor that he is. I must let him see my worth for a while yet. It's too soon to say something."

"I will speak to him," she says, as if that will handle it all.

"Please, don't," I beg.

"Yes," she nods sagely. "And he will be happy to take care of you and the child."

"I don't wish to ask him to do that."

"You won't have to. He will. He is a good man. Now back to bed for you. I will wake you in time."

I try to protest further, but I know my arguments are weak and half-formed and stupid. She does not seem to hear my protestations anyway.

I allow her to tuck me back into bed where I sleep, dreamlessly at first. But then, I am filled with odd, earthy dreams of pregnancy, lifelike and lustful. One dream is Henry, holding the child I carry, and I am confused, for I know he is dead and the babe isn't his. Another dream is of Kate, beautiful and glowing in the sunset. And the last is of the doctor himself, looking down at me. Inscrutable. Displeased?

Widow Hawks wakes me at the last vision, so I leave this morning with the strange thought in my mind. I am almost afraid to walk to the doctor's house and see him, but when I find him, he is his usual jovial self.

As I set him breakfast, I broach the subject of his office. Anything to keep my brain from scattering to the corners of my fears and insecurities, and the gnawing discomfort I feel knowing Widow Hawks is aware of my condition. She even took the lie I gave her.

"As I have most of the house straightened, I was hoping I might help you in your study," I announce, pouring more coffee into my mug.

"How so?" He peers at me over the rim of his own drink.

"Well ... I'm wondering if I might act as secretary a bit? It'd be the thing a nurse does, and you asked me here with that in mind, didn't you? I could put things to rights, the papers in order by last name or family, and have everything easier to find. That way, perhaps, when you are out, I could access things. Only in an emergency, mind you. To help?"

He gives a little chuckle. "You needn't ask so gingerly, Mrs. Weber. It's a grand idea."

"I have some knowledge of the profession with my husband's illness," I continue, encouraged. "We tried many things to cure Henry."

The doctor's eyes narrow. "What kind of treatments? What kind of doc did you see?"

"Oh—everyone we could afford. We tried a homeopath, though they were going out of fashion with their odd ideas of treating symptoms with a drug that will also create the same symptoms."

"I'm aware of what a homeopath does." The doctor waves a hand, leaning forward toward me. "I was apprenticed to an Eclectic who leaned toward the homeopathy, but he was one who tried a bit of everythin'."

That explains some of his diversity. I know that Eclectic doctors use everything from modern advancements to herbal supplements. Henry preferred those types of physicians over the sterile, clinical men of the large hospitals who probed him with speculation instead of care. He also refused to see traditional doctors steeped in the practice of bleeding out a patient. None of it mattered in the end, of course. And none of my research and reading, done in the lamplight of night, and expressed with careful consideration in the face of skeptical, dismissive doctors, helped either. I'd done a poor job of tending my husband in health by not caring for him deeply, and an even worse job trying to keep him healthy in sickness.

"Did you find some relief for Mr. Weber in all the time you nursed him?" he asks with a scientific earnestness, then seems to remember himself. "Ach, I'm sorry, Mrs. Weber. I forget it was recently you lost him. Come on, then, I'll help with the wash-up so we can march into the office mess together."

Upon taking the dry cloth from the peg near me at the washbin, his arm brushes mine, and I keep my eyes on the suds and my hands so that I do not have to look at him. I'm uncertain in his presence today. I wonder if it is the uneasiness of my dreaming last night, or the way he speaks to me of doctoring, as if I am his peer. But there is this, which I'd forgotten: that I can offer help as someone who knows a little bit of the medical trade. I'm confident of what I've read. Perhaps that might help convince him to keep me on when he discovers my pregnancy.

"What nation is Widow Hawks?" I ask, by way of conversation, hoping I'm asking the question properly.

He carefully lines up the clean forks with the others. "She will say she is *Sihasapa*. Folks 'round here call her Lakota Sioux too, or Blackfoot, which is more precise."

"I don't see any other natives around town. I wonder why she stays," I muse aloud, thinking I might eventually be able to ask her that question myself. Now my nights need not be silent as she has decided to speak with me. It is a small step toward acceptance, to be sure, but a good one.

"Eventually, I expect you'll meet others. She has a very interestin' story. If you get her in the right mood, you might hear it one day," he says plainly but with finality, and then finishes the last piece of cutlery. I pour out the water and follow him into the office.

I cannot imagine how he does any work in here. It is so cluttered that I am at a loss where to start, so I sit on the floor and pull a pile of books toward me.

"Perhaps if we clear off the bookshelf and build it back up from scratch before moving to patient files?" I offer.

He stands in the middle of the chaos with his hands on his hips, looking a bit forlorn now that the task is in front of him, and gives a rueful little laugh as he surveys the mess.

"You know, Mrs. Weber, I sit in here every day and generally do not worry about the way it looks. I suppose it doesn't do for patients to see this disarray, and it would make it difficult to have an assistant help out if nothin' can be found. If you are signin' yourself, that is."

"Exactly," I say, and start to sort out the books in front of me by author's last name. He pulls down the rest and makes a pile next to me on the floor.

"Might you want to get the rest from upstairs in your bedroom?" I ask casually, and he stops moving suddenly.

"You've been up there, have you?"

My cheeks flush in embarrassment. "To dust. Clean the floors and scrub up the washroom."

"Oh, aye," he sighs. "I noticed it was all cleaned up and forgot to thank you. Of course, yes. I'll go get them."

I hear his steps above me. In the moments of his absence, I flip through a few more patient files. One catches my eye, and I read through it with speed and a little bit of shyness, and then avid curiosity.

Patient - EvaRose (no last name)   *E (?)*

Address - Fortuna's - the PowderedRose

Occupation (Dancer)   (prostitute)

Dates

Jan '75	Influenza; bad case.
July '75	Attempted suicide. 8 stitches, left arm. Determines it was an accident.
	2 weeks later - "stitches opened by themselves" - likely a second attempt. 10 stitches applied.
Aug '76	Hemorrhoids. Prescribe diluted witch hazel bath and a pause of a all "activities" - Fortuna angry and determines I cannot treat her girls if I ask them to stop working.
May '77	Fortuna requested visit to resolve ER's bruises on her calves. Discovered new ranch hand (J. York) on Svend-sen ranch prefers to tie the girls up.
	Discussed with D. Svendsen before Fortuna found him. J. York dismissed.
Sept '77	Hemorrhoids returned. Prescribe undiluted witch hazel direct on sores, plus asprin.
Mar '78	Patient attempted self abortion with knitting needle; result: infection of uterine lining, perforation, and intense bleeding. Fetus expired, but not dislodged.
	Fever at 103 by the mercury, and discharge is

I'm about to turn the page and hope the riveting diagnosis continues—did this EvaRose survive? What did he do to save her if she did? Fascinated by the story, I glance at the next file, but my moment for snooping is gone, and I hastily return the papers to their place. The doctor

clambers back downstairs loudly, thumping each foot heavily on the stairs with the pile of books in his hands. He sets
them down on the floor before crouching next to me, and
we work in companionable silence again for a few minutes
before my prying and inherent drive to gain information
gets the better of me.

"I couldn't help but notice the portraits in your room
when I dusted. Are they of your family?"

He stops shuffling faded copies of medical journals. I
immediately regret my familiarity. The easy and abrupt way
people ask questions out here is starting to affect my own
judgment of conversation and character. In trying to adjust
and fit in, I am unwittingly becoming a nosy housekeeper. I
should keep my eyes down and my mouth shut!

But then he starts talking, slowly, as if whittling the
tale of his youth from the depths of memory.

"It was the famine. My family, like so many others in
Ireland, was allowed to keep only the potatoes to eat. When
the blight came in the forties and everyone began to starve,
my parents and siblings and I were affected too. I have no
direct memory of this. I was the youngest, and the healthiest.
My great-auntie, a widow at the time of the famine and with
just enough money for passage to America for herself and one
other, came to my parents and asked for one of us to take
along. My father was her favorite nephew as they were close
in age—he the eldest child of her eldest brother, and she the
youngest of ten."

"And your parents chose you?"

He nods, then picks at the thread of his story calmly
and plainly. "They did choose me, as the babby and newly
weaned. I'd grown strong enough on mother's milk even as

the rest began to starve. The potato blight was … it destroyed. You can ask the Salomons, the blacksmiths, they are here because the same potato disease hit Poland. I wonder too if my parents thought I had the best chance of movin' hearts to pity as my auntie traveled, bein' small and young. It was a decision that saved my life."

I want to ask more questions right away, but wait, pulling more books and putting them on piles. Finally, he sighs deeply, and finishes with obvious resignation.

"We often wrote to the village back in Ireland, tryin' to find out what happened to the family. As I grew older, I learned to make different kinds of inquiries. Before I left my apprenticeship—before we left Boston—we finally discovered they'd gotten lost in the workhouses and then mass graves, likely."

I consider his story. It's not entirely unique, and similar to the stories of many who lived in Boston. But now I can understand better his determination to be a doctor in the far reaches of America where there is little help, his desire to save people, and his worry about people like Alice Brinkley having enough to eat. He wishes to give back what had been given to him, for I am sure it was both hard work and luck that brought him as far as he has come. And now I know that he really is alone. The death of his aunt deprived him of the last bit of family to his name.

There is silence, save for the soft pound of book covers thudding against others as we finish sorting and start to shuffle things onto the shelf. He has quite a few worn and patched medical books, several fictions, which surprises me as he doesn't seem a reader, and more scientific books than I can count, on everything from plants to chemistry to animal studies. Some are not in English. Is he far more learned that he lets on? Can he actually read the German? Maybe he will let me read some—the English ones, at least—if I should ever have time on my hands. The notion unfurls in my chest. Maybe ... maybe when he's gone, I can snatch a few words. If he wants me to help him as a nurse, I think I desperately need to know more than I do!

I make us a light lunch, and I realize I am not very hungry after the morning's retching. The doctor does not seem to notice my lack of appetite as he eats as heartily as ever.

When he leaves to make his afternoon rounds, I take it upon myself to continue in his study. There are papers in each folder, and soon I realize he does have a method to his disarray. Sometimes, it becomes a matter of simply writing a person or family name on a file and putting it into alphabetical order. Most of his scribbling is hard to understand, so I could not read about cases if I *were* to become a busybody. Some names I have to put aside to ask him about later, when we have a moment again in his study.

Though I try not to meddle, I cannot help but look back at the study of EvaRose the prostitute. I learn she is one of three girls employed by Fortuna, the madam of the Powdered Rose bordello. She survived her attempted abortion, dated only four months ago. Reading of the intensive care she needed is one more affirmation that I made the right medical choice to bear Theodore's child instead of trying for an abortion myself. If I had tried to rid myself of the babe without a skilled physician, even if I had one I trusted, I likely would not have survived it.

There are many more people here in Flats Junction than I realize, and the names start to blur, though some are familiar. I know William Warren of the Golden Nail Saloon. There is a host of strange Chinese names that makes me pause as I read their occupations and connections. It seems Peng and Yan Yeng operate a tiny noodle and soup shop, which explains the heavy kettle I saw them heaving that first morning walk. They are married to sisters. There are four Wu brothers who are apparently lackluster laborers, good only for odd jobs. This in comparison to the Chen brothers, who are relatively successful farmers and come with a short list of injuries due to their preference for Oriental healing. Doctor Kinney does not seem to hold their medicinal ideas in high esteem based on his notes.

There are a lot of cowboys, most employed by the handful of ranches here, and their names bleed together as manly shorthand: Bernard, Hank, Tate, Thunder, Manny, and Noah. More and more, until I stop counting. I note the Fawcett name and am surprised at the lengthy notes on the children in that family.

But there are absences too. Why are there no files on Horeb or Gilroy, or the blacksmiths? I know the town has a farrier and a tannery and a livery, among other things, and yet there are no files on the tradesmen here. Why not? Surely they get ill and injured.

I take a break from paperwork to wash the clothes. Today the spring air seems warm enough that things might dry quickly. I must come up with a rhythm to my week: certain days for laundry, washing, scrubbing, and cooking, but I have no handle on the weather. I brace myself to enter the doctor's personal space again. It is time for me to tackle his clothing.

101

As I bundle up his clothes, which smell of dust, old sweat, medicine, and of him, I hear the screen door slam shut. I frown. The doctor is not due back until supper. Could it be a patient? I brace myself and head down, hoping it's nothing too urgent. I can soothe a fever if needed, but I can't put together broken bones!

The stairs are steep so I cannot see below, but I nearly run into the doctor himself at the bottom, as he's standing in the narrow hallway with his hands on his hips. I hope I have not displeased him with continuing in his office. I suppose there may be personal papers he wishes to keep private. I cannot think why else he is glowering.

"Mrs. Weber. Give me those," he growls, grabbing the laundry. The surliness is unlike him. I have not seen him cross yet, and it is entirely unnerving. Is he ashamed of his dirty clothes, or does he not want a woman washing them, especially since I am not his kin as his aunt was?

"It's alright, Doctor. I don't mind doing them. It's part of my duties, to keep house, I mean, I thought ..."

He shakes his head, walks out of the house, and dumps the clothes unceremoniously next to the washbin, where I have hot water waiting, and the can of talc nearby. I follow him outside.

Staring at the bin, he asks irritably, "Did you pull this wash yourself? Filled it too?"

I shrug and give a frown. "Yes. How else ..."

"You're to ask *me*!" He swings around and puts his hands back on his hips, then changes his mind and crosses his arms. Agitated yet, he shakes them out and stalks into the house.

Suddenly, I realize what has happened. The doctor

102

must have spoken to Widow Hawks. I feel the heat of embarrassment rush to my cheeks, and I'm sure I look as flushed as I feel. I've seen myself like this often enough in the mirrors back East, and I hide my jaw in my hands, trying to draw the color down.

Suppose it is not real. I have not yet felt the quickening. It is early—too early to really discuss it. For this employer to know, when my lover had not, feels as if I am exposing my private bedroom to a stranger.

Terror shoots into me. I hadn't wanted him to find out. Not so soon and not like this! Damn the widow! I'd asked her not to speak! Now he will send me back home to be a widowed mother alone in the quietness of her parents' house with the sharp stigma of a loose woman. No one back East will truly believe the child is Henry's. They might think I went wild in the West.

I follow him back inside slowly, thankful he has the tact not to yell at me out in the yard, where I am certain the neighbors, especially prim and brisk Mrs. Molhurst, would hear him. I do not want my pregnancy so public yet.

No one knows me here. There is some safety in that, and I must convince him to let me stay. And I must tell him the same lie. There's no other way. Everyone here in Flats Junction must think I was as married and settled as I say. And the doctor, too. What would he think, having hired such a disreputable woman? The shame of my brief desire for Theodore, and the self-loathing I carry rises up and tries to suffocate me.

My heart batters in my chest. Will I faint? Will I be able to hold my head to his and beg him? Can I spit out the story and will he believe it?

The doctor walks into his study, fuming and vibrating with anger, and I feel I must follow him to hear my fate. He stands with his back to me, surveying my work. Already there is some order, and it's easier to move about the small space. I can see by the bend of his head that he is still angry, still thinking of what to say to me. I fear my dismissal with a rushing, blinding wave and grip the door frame with intensity, a sliver of wood working its way into my thumb.

"How far along?"

His voice has softened a bit, and I try to relax, and try to think of the numbers I've created.

"I ... I am not quite sure. I think perhaps sixteen weeks now? It is still early."

"Does your family know?"

"No. I ... Henry didn't even know. I myself didn't realize it until we'd already settled on the date of my arrival here."

Finally, he turns to look at me. I cannot read his face. It is blank of any emotion. Is he still angry? Frustrated? I try to hide my shaking hands, and my intense fear of termination, and my worry that he will disbelieve my honor. He is suddenly completely in charge of my future. Will he condemn me? Send me home?

"You didn't think to say anythin'?"

"It did not seem fitting to bring it up at our first meeting, and life has ..." I shrug in anguish. "It has been busy. It still does not seem possible I could finally ... that Henry had ..." I cannot bear to finish. To discuss sex, and my husband's difficulty conceiving, if not my own as well, is too much to say. And it's all false anyway. How much

104

should I say? And will I remember it perfectly? It does not matter that he is a doctor, and he is accustomed to these discussions. He is not my doctor, does not give me exams, and is not my confidant.

"Mrs. Weber." He steps closer and lightly puts a hand on my shoulder. "I am not a bad man, I like to think. I am tolerant. I have always vowed to be so. I am not angry about this comin' baby, only that you were too afraid to speak up."

"Please … you will let me keep working?"

"Within reason."

I start to protest, but he shakes his head and puts his second hand on my other shoulder. The weight of his arms is heavy, yoke-like. He pins me, serious and determined to have me meet his eyes.

"You will let me do the heavy liftin', Mrs. Weber. You must. You forget I like to help around the house when I can. And you must just tell me what you need before I leave. I don't mind."

He gives my shoulders a quick squeeze before releasing me and turning to his office desk, shaking his head. I am surprised at how light his voice is as he comments, "It is shapin' up quite nicely. Now, back to my rounds. Supper in a few hours, Mrs. Weber?"

"I'll be sure to have enough for the Brinkleys, as well," I respond weakly as he brushes past, as if nothing out of the ordinary has happened. He grabs his hat, bounds outside, and swings onto his horse. From the screen door, I watch him spin the mount around and canter off, his body swaying easily with the jaunt of the animal's gait.

Once he is out of sight, I sink to the floor and breathe a long sigh. The choke of tears presses upward and into my throat. Thank heaven he did not see it fit to send me back on the next train out! A small tremor passes through me. What would I tell my folks if I had to return? They still do not know I am pregnant. They'd think I'd turned loose here, never imagining it all started much earlier. I shudder to think of such a response from my loved ones, and I am mercifully thankful of the doctor's tolerance.

CHAPTER 6
26 April 1881

Widow Hawks sews my dresses for me. She insists that she can do it deftly, faster. That she cannot bear another night sitting next to me and watching me labor over each stitch. And, of course, she is right. Within three weeks, both house-dresses are finished, with neat patterning and easy seams. I have a purple bonnet to match the lavender dress and my brown calico is set with the split skirt so that I might start to ride easily, like the way I saw Kate do when she traveled with some of the cowboys to visit Yankton to see how the town was faring after the flooding. While I am afraid to go on horseback with the babe in my womb, I know it is some-thing I must eventually master.

There are funny whispers about childbearing that I overhear even without meaning to. Tales of sighting a deformed calf sent Julie Bailey, the farrier's wife, into a tizzy. Apparently, she is of the belief that such a view when pregnant might mark the unborn baby and produce a hermaphrodite. And a woman in the family way should never touch her face after thinking about out-of-season food. That particular bit of nonsense was discussed after Mass this past weekend, as that too can mark the babe. I think I will keep this pregnancy quiet as long as possible, if only to avoid such types of advice!

I am beside myself with happiness at the companionship of Widow Hawks. She hums, now, in the morning and night, native songs that resonate throughout the room. I'm surprised to realize I'm glad to have a child who will listen to such lovely, haunting melodies. When I tell her this, she smiles fully, and I am always struck by her serene beauty. Her teeth are white against the dark cinnamon of her skin, and the creases of her eyes remind me of the doctor's when he grins, and of Kate's when she smiles, though that is rarer still. I do not know how Widow Hawks makes her way, how she comes by groceries or dry goods. Like everyone here, she has a garden out back. Sprawling squash vines reach out beyond the borders of the garden, while beans curl around poles, and potato plants nod gently. But I do not see how she survives on her own. It is, like many things yet, a mystery.

We still do not share meals, nor much else other than silence or quiet chatter in the night. I have not accused her of approaching the doctor about my pregnancy. It feels ill-placed to do it, as she has been a constant nursemaid when I've been ill in the mornings. And she is my advocate with the doctor if I am too shy to ask for anything, though that is slowly changing. I find him eager to help however he may, and he is even professional about my occasional bouts of nausea, which, thankfully, are lessening considerably. I wonder at this, but then I remember he has no living relations. He may be glad for any babe to be part of his life, if only to have someone to care for in the way of family. Already I can see how one easily cleaves to others when alone out here. It is easily done. I'm doing it myself.

Today, I wear the new yellow calico. There is no need for me to dress for riding, so I think the serviceable brown will be good for days when much work is to be done, particularly outside.

Widow Hawks fits it to me, making a final tug or two.

"How did you learn to sew so prettily?" I ask. She has made an attractive bodice, and a full skirt, with plenty to let out when I grow bigger with child. Her own clothing is usually a mismatched combination of traditional deer and rabbit hides, and English skirts with calico shirts, so I do not see how creating a ladies' dress is possible for her.

"I learned how for my daughter's sake," she says quietly. It is an answer I do not expect. "And for my husband, for he wished me to wear your English dresses sometimes."

"Well, I thank you. I finally feel a woman," I say, and I take her hand and squeeze it. So, she has a daughter. I feel relief. I might be able to ask childrearing questions of her. She hangs on to my fingers a moment longer but says no more.

When I walk to the doctor's house, I pass the two usual townsfolk who watch me. One is a grandfatherly figure who is always out to watch the sunrise on the porch of his daughter's family home. George Ofsberger has aged rapidly even since I've been in town. His son, Douglas, is the town postman. I wave, and he tilts his head in his usual response.

The other is a cowboy who is always up brushing his horse at the livery, as if the stallion is the most important thing in the world. And I suppose it *is* the most important thing, or being, he owns in the world, so I cannot blame his obsessiveness. Today he stops brushing to give me a second look.

"Good day, Missus Weber," he says and tips his hat. I nod silently in return.

As I turn onto First Street, a huge coyote sprints across my path, ducking opportunistically into the trash outside the pig farm and causing the sows in the crowded barn to shriek and squeal.

I let out a scream of my own, and the cowboy comes springing toward me from the livery stables, his hand holding nothing but the horse brush, raised high.

"Mrs. Weber! You alright? What is it?"

I put a hand to my chest and heave a short breath. The cowboy looks around in consternation, and then notices the big wooly animal near the sty. He marches toward it without fear, and I follow him only because I don't know what else to do. The pigs are still causing quite a ruckus, and Alan Lampton, the purveyor of the pig and pork trade, runs out without anything on but his faded, stained long underwear, brandishing what looks to be a stove poker.

The coyote, suddenly noticing it is cornered on both sides, bares its teeth, pricks its long ears even higher and then rushes off toward the north, sprinting up the wide path called Bone Jump Road. Alan and the cowboy stop and look at one another, then the pigs, and then me. I smile, suddenly feeling foolish, and shrug, trying to hide the quivering of my chin. The animal had been huge! Suppose it had tried to attack?

"He's gone." Alan grunts. "Did he eat one?"

"No," I say, feeling confident in that, at least, and my voice cracks. "Just wanted whatever you have in the slop piles."

I gesture to the huge, disgusting compost of food and table bits spilling out of the troughs, and the rotting wooden bins by the side of the fence. Alan nods, looking satisfied.

The cowboy turns to go back to the livery, and I don't know what to say to either of the men. Do I thank them? Did they save me, or was I never in danger? But neither give me any mind as they separate, so I take the last bit of road to the doctor's. My heart is still throbbing from the excitement, and my blood pumps so tightly behind my eyes, it's a wonder I can see straight.

It is quiet as I let myself in. He must still be abed or not quite ready yet.

As I make the coffee, I think again on Widow Hawks' words about dressmaking. I wonder where her daughter is, or if she, too, has died as the husband has. With my increasing ability to ask personal questions, I still do not go about asking the important ones, it seems. I've spent too many years shielding my inclination to research and learn about everyone and everything. It's a shame. Had I come out here when I was younger, before I'd come out to society and then married, I might never have learned to shut off my nature.

"Mornin'." The doctor speaks as he rounds the corner, but stops up so quickly, I turn to make sure he did not trip. Instead, I see him taking me in, a shrewd look in his eye.

"Yes?" I do not understand his look.

"It's ... the coffee smells delicious."

I lift an eyebrow at his stilted comment but say nothing. We eat the toast and cheese in relative silence. Today I am helping in his study again to go over the updates to his files. I look forward to a morning inside and to be seated, as

111

I am quite tired. It is much better than scrubbing the floors, which is my duty tomorrow.

"Mrs. Weber," he says slowly as we finish eating. I do not look up until his hand reaches across the slab table and taps the back of my own so I will meet his face. "The new dress is very fine on you."

"Oh!" I exclaim, and I try not to laugh. He does indeed have an eye to color, then. It is not what I expected of his character. "I ... thank you."

He nods, as if the compliment is sufficient and normal enough to say, and then finishes his coffee. We do the dishes together, as we have started to do when he is not called away by patients. I still think it's a bit odd of him to help with such womanly chores, but it is his house and his kitchen, after all.

"Widow Hawks mentioned she had a daughter," I say, feeling the statement is awkward, but not sure how to bring up the topic. I glance at him and am surprised again to see his face look tender, soft, and a bit wistful.

"Yes, she does."

"Does? Is she around here? I hope I have not deprived her of a bed and place at her mother's home."

"Oh, no, that you have most certainly not done. Widow Hawks' daughter is quite independent." There is affection in his voice.

Since he does not immediately offer up more, I drop the subject, and try to come up with other conversation, but it all escapes me. I hope I get to meet Widow Hawks' daughter.

I spend an amicable morning doing patient paperwork with the doctor, and then polishing instruments in the afternoon as he does rounds. It's another nursing duty that falls

112

on me now, and I hope to figure out the name of each tool eventually.

But then he mentions over supper that I ought to have my sidesaddle clothing on hand, so that I might dress for patient visits some days.

"I could use your nursing skills," he says. "Not for the very difficult cases, but when it would help to have a second pair of hands again."

"Did your aunt help you, too?"

"Yes, she did, sometimes," he admits. "It did help to have a woman's face around, even if just for the families. And it might help again to have a woman available for those who don't want me."

"Why wouldn't they?"

He looks a bit dismayed, and rubs a hand along his neck roughly. "Well ... Doc Gunnarsen before me was ... he wasn't very ... effective."

"What does that have to do with you?"

"Ah ... you know that old adage about sins of the father?"

"But you're not related to the old doctor, are you?"

"Oh no!" he exclaims, scraping his knife along a dark stain on his tin plate. "No. I stayed because Percy and Widow Hawks asked me to stay. And I was lookin' for a place to set down roots after wanderin' the Territories to find a town that could have me, support my practice. I'd almost given up, to be truthful. And the Indians ... well, I came here on a bad day for Flats Junction and ended up havin' lots of patients from the first day. Treated the Sioux too. And I was lucky, what with Doc Gunnarsen dyin' earlier in the year. Well, it worked for me, anyway. My Aunt Bonnie and I had enough

113

work to keep us busy. So aye, I'll take a nurse again, however you can manage it."

"Alright then." I agree, though I am uncertain what I have just agreed to do. I have no true nursing training, only how to make an ill patient a bit more comfortable, as I did for Henry. I suppose I know some about how doctors like to work, and I am at ease at the side of a sickbed. I absently spin the wedding band around my finger, and then suddenly wonder when it will be proper for me to stop wearing it.

"Now then, we've finished up a mite early for the evenin'. What do you say, Mrs. Weber, to a bit of readin' on the porch?" It is a tradition we do now that the light lasts longer, and when we can manage it.

"Of course," I say. I set about finishing up the kitchen and put away my apron.

We read a bit of *The Conduct of Life*, and I like to hear the doctor take a turn with Emerson's words, as his lilt is soothing. I try not to drift to sleep. Even a day without hard physical labor leaves me exhausted at times.

"What I cannot understand, Mrs. Weber, is why you waited so long to be married." At first, I do not realize he has stopped reading. "You're a decent lookin' woman, you know. Did you pine for your husband before he married you? Wait for him to have enough money?"

Goodness! I am now not drowsy at all! The doctor is asking very detailed questions provoked by our reading material. I am shocked my employer wishes to know these things about my past. What could come of it? How dare he presume to pry?

"Why ... I mean ... that is to say ..." I trail off, then gather my courage to be frank, molding the words as best I

114

can, allowing my past to filter through me, and giving in to the private pleasure of sharing information and knowledge.

"I was, soon after I was introduced to society, sometimes asked by young men to dance or to be called upon. My sister was a celebrated beauty and married young to … to James."

After all the years and my marriage to Henry, I can finally say my brother-in-law's name dispassionately and without feeling heat feather through my skin. He had been the first young man to catch my eye, the only one I would have considered marrying. Except he'd been captivated by my older sister, and he had chosen to formally court her instead. It had felt like a betrayal, though he'd never given me any indication that he held me in affection. It still had made family gatherings difficult.

In a way, Henry rescued me from that. And then I dove back in the minute Henry was a month in his grave, enjoying the attentions of a man who looked very much like James.

"But I did not really find most of the men I met to be interesting," I say instead. "I knew my duty, to find a proper gentleman and be settled, but I was careful in my choice."

"And Mr. Weber was proper?"

I nod briefly, twisting my hands into my skirts. "Yes. And by the time I met him, I'd rather scared off the handsome young bachelors who were interested at all in marrying me. I was known for being a bit … earnest. I found research to be interesting and the newspapers a topic for discussion. Such qualities are not very attractive or desirable in a wife. Henry liked how I would listen to his thoughts and sometimes add my own. We were a very intellectual match. I was older and wished to settle down or risk spinsterhood. He wished for

115

a wife to aid him in society for his work and to keep him company. It was a decent arrangement."

"It sounds proper." The doctor watches my face as I talk, leaning forward with the book closed between his fingers. It is a bit refreshing to unwind my marriage, to see it dispassionately, and without emotion in the retelling. I cannot complain. Henry had been true, had not stepped out, nor held any horrible faults. I cannot blame him, even in death, for a lack of desire that had been missing from the start.

There's a shuffle and snort, and our heads snap up at the intrusion. The sun is starting to set, and a horse and rider detach from the long dark grey shadows along the homes.

"Speaking of proper. Begging pardon, Doc and Missus."

"What is it, Bern?" The doctor is on his feet, expecting an emergency, though I do not detect that in the languid manner of the man. He slides down, grabbing the reins of his mount, and walks up to the porch. It is the cowboy from this morning, who had attempted to rescue me from the coyote. He is a bit dashing, with dark hair, and eyes that squint at the corners. I hadn't noticed that earlier.

"It's getting a bit late, and I was going to offer Mrs. Weber a walk to her quarters."

From the astounded silence in the yard, I cannot tell who is more stunned by his proposition, the doctor or myself. Is this how it is done? Without proper introductions to this man who goes by Bern?

"Well, I ..." I glance at the doctor. He has a strange, half-bemused smile on his face and gives me a small nod.

I am to take my leave with this man I do not know?

116

"Go ahead, Mrs. Weber. I'll see you in the mornin'. Thanks, Bern."

I press my lips together. This is most unexpected, and I feel befuddled from dissembling to the doctor and not quite willing to handle a new introduction. I am familiar with this cowboy only by his willingness to come to my aid when I shrieked. Yes, he is polite to me, saying hello, smiling, tipping his hat, but that is all I really know of him. He has not shown interest in me before, but I can only guess that this walk home is a prelude to romance, and I am nervous about this notion. It still seems so early in my arrival. I have been in Flats Junction for mere weeks.

What would he think if he knew I was with child?

"Mrs. Weber." He tips his hat to me, waiting. I gather my things, bid the doctor good night, and we begin the walk down East Avenue and onto Main Street toward Widow Hawks' house. "Bernard Masson, at your service. Folks around here call me Bern. I like that better than Bernie, myself."

I nod, smile, and decide to offer him my own front name as is common here.

"You seem to already know I am Mrs. Weber. Please call me Jane."

We are silent until we are nearly to Widow Hawks' house, and I am halfway relieved but also confused. Why has this Bern decided to escort me home today? Does he think I need the help as I'm so obviously skittish? If I cannot handle the sighting of a single coyote, maybe he pities me.

"You're kind to walk me," I venture.

"It's no trouble at all, Jane," he returns, and tips his hat to me at the edge of the railroad. He then mounts his horse and rides off without a word.

117

"Well, I'll be!" I say under my breath. This interlude, and my chatting with the doctor today, has given me new voice, a new strength. I decide I will ask Widow Hawks about her daughter tonight.

I stop short as I turn to the house. I see a mound of animal carcasses next to the doorway, half rotted and black with flies. Thankfully, it does not make me vomit, but I am shocked that Widow Hawks has left this. It is unlike her.

Going in, I see her methodically making the fire. The smoke is pungent, filled with sage and other acrid fumes. Without a word, Widow Hawks walks outside, likely to fetch water as usual.

I go to my bed and see my dresses all fitted out and ready, but I cannot enjoy them. I am too riled and discomfited by the stack of rotting remains I'd witnessed.

I go to find her outside. She's digging a hole in the ground. It is not very deep or wide.

"May I help?" I approach her. She wipes a bead of sweat from her brow. Though the sun is nearly set and the light is fading fast, it is still quite warm.

"Get you inside. I'll be in soon." Her voice is hard and firm.

"Please let me help."

She sighs very softly, then juts her chin. "Fetch me that bag there, then, but take care not to touch anything but the corners."

I go to the bag nearby, but recoil when I realize it is filled with the animal parts and carcasses from the doorway. Widow Hawks is still digging the hole, humming a tune that sounds like a dirge. Holding my breath, I find the courage to pick up the sack and bring it to her. There are strange native symbols written on the cloth. I feel quite out of my element.

She continues her song for another long moment, eyes half closed in the rhythm of the digging, and then hauls herself out of the hole. Picking up the bag reverently, she starts to chant softly in her native tongue. I watch, fascinated, and a bit fearful, as she carefully places the bundled bodies into the opened ground, sprinkling them with dried herbs. Rocking on her heels, she tilts her head to the sky, where evening glows with its first stars.

She finishes the chant and begins to scoop the earth back into the shallow hole. I begin to think of it as a grave and say as much as I start to help her, using my hands as a shovel.

"Weasel. Otter. They are sacred animals and should be given high reverence," she says softly, sadly, as if mourning.

I stop moving dirt. "These animals are sacred to your people?"

She nods.

"Then why take their fur and leave their poor bodies to rot?" I try to keep any negative emotion from my voice. I truly do wish to understand her culture, as it is fascinating in small doses. It is nothing like what the papers back East say about Indian life. It only proves to me that I cannot always accept what I hear and read—research must sometimes accompany information.

Her head snaps up and for the first time I see what she might be like if angered.

"You must not think I did this! These animals were left on the doorstep as you saw them. It was meant as an insult."

119

My heart sinks. There is a stigma, then, toward Widow Hawks. She seems kind and has not caused trouble since I have been in Flats Junction, and she seems assimilated enough that I did not think anyone minded her. No one has spoken out to me about her, but then I have not been in public with her. And perhaps I am so new that no one will tell me any truths.

We finish the burial in silence and go back inside. I know tonight I will not ask Widow Hawks any personal questions. Feeling exhaustion wash over me, wiping away any niggling worries, I decide to just go to bed.

CHAPTER 7
25 May 1881

It has been a month since the incident, but I find myself thinking about it often. There is a spookiness, an anger to the action, as well as cowardice. It is worse because the actions are not discussed around town. Do people know who perpetuates such crimes? Are they even aware of it? Or is it an understanding, unspoken and slightly condoned, that leaves people silent? Perhaps they do not want to know who is so cruel to their neighbor, though it is obviously someone who has some sort of knowledge about native preferences.

I tell Kate about the animals when I am at the general store. She frowns darkly when I give her the details, and then she mutters, "It is not the first time, nor the last, that the cowboys will play a mean trick on her. There are some in this town who want Widow Hawks gone."

"Is it the cowboys, certainly? But why? She does not cause trouble."

121

Kate gives a snort. "She doesn't have to. She's Indian. And she has done enough to warrant trouble. Were she to live her life in vindication, I still don't think everyone would forgive her."

I pause, wondering if I should ask the question, then decide I want to. I want to be a bit nosy. Perhaps my housemate would prefer I talk to her openly, but I feel that Kate is easier to speak to, and I wish to share confidences with her anyway.

"Kate, will you tell me? About Widow Hawks?"

She presses her lips together and looks at the bag of buttons we are sorting through. I wonder what it matters that she relays this story. She is always full of town news short of malicious gossip, and I find Kate to be a good source of information about anyone the doctor is treating, or anyone who has an ailment unspoken.

"Come back with me."

I follow, dreading her coffee concoction. She pours the sludge into two mugs for us and I stir mine while she guzzles down the first half of hers. She sits next to me, one eye on the door through the half-opened curtain.

"Widow Hawks was the mistress of the town's late banker, Percival Davies."

I am struck silent at this declaration. It is not what I expect to hear, so I absently take a gulp of the coffee and wish immediately I had not. I sputter, but Kate thinks it is because I am so shocked. She nods shortly, peevishly.

"I know. Exactly. There was a tribe of Blackfoot who camped nearby in the western hills by their old buffalo jump during the summer months, before their movements were more restricted. He saw her walking with them. Let's just say, he was … *smitten*."

122

"He didn't marry her?"

She gives an indignant laugh, as if she is invested in this dead man's story.

"He was already married. To a woman who lived back East and refused to join her husband in the rough and tumble of the Territories. She was happy with the money he sent back but preferred her parlor in North Carolina."

I digest this. "Widow Hawks chose him, then? I mean, it was a love match? He couldn't keep her by force, I should think ..." I know nothing of the natives, nothing of their way of life, only that a few short years ago, a great war had torn the Territories apart, and that the natives had experienced the loss of it. They had been subdued, and I could only expect they would have required some sort of retribution if one of their women had been taken without consent.

Kate tosses her head, and a few black tendrils escape. "No, she wanted to be with him, too, I guess. They did love one another; that was always obvious. So, she left her people and stayed with him in town. He was the banker, powerful and arrogant in his own way, and the catalyst for most big things happening here in Flats Junction. And regardless of the tongues wagging, and the anger of most of the men, he kept with her. They had two children. Eventually his wife died, and he was able to legally marry Widow Hawks. They were only wed a short time before he died."

The story sputters to a halt. I bite my lip and try to picture the older woman I know as sure-footed, strongly silent, steely, and stately. She was once a lovestruck girl, brave enough to leave her people and resist the scorn of the towns-folk to stay with the man she loved. What kind of love is that, so resilient and true that it spans nations and manners of living? I cannot imagine it. It is not surprising to me now that she has such fluent English, that many of her habits are familiar to me and not savage. She was gentrified by her lover-husband and now straddles both worlds. Strangely, this raises my opinion of her.

"And the town? They grew used to her?"

"Oh some, like Doc Kinney. He was an outsider, too, when he and his aunt arrived. Driven out of Boston by those who hated the Irish, and unable to find a place that could support his work. He wanted to practice medicine, you know, regardless of his youth at the time. And old Davies took him under his wing, knowing the town needed a good doctor. The doc respects Widow Hawks from that time staying with them, and for what Percival did. And because he understands what it is to be an outcast."

I am astounded at Kate's astute read of the situation, and marvel at her practical approach to such a wild retelling. So, Doctor Kinney had left Boston because of his heritage. Did people really not trust him? Here? In Boston? I want to believe it's not true. I want to trust him in the way I've never done with others of his profession. But it seems that same mistrust runs deep here as well.

"Thank you for telling me this story," I murmur, as it is the only thing I can think to say. I think Kate is becoming a friend indeed, though I cannot truly tell whether the information she has given today will help me shape a picture of both of these characters with whom I interact daily. Still ... it is research, isn't it? It's not gossip! It's not much different from gleaning bits of knowledge from pamphlets, just as I did when Henry was sick. It's just collecting wisdom.

124

"Well then." She shrugs and stands, finishing her coffee. I guiltily stare into my cup. I have not touched mine since the first gulp. "Let's finish up your shopping and get you back so your beau can walk you home." She gives me a wink.

Ever since the first time Bern Masson walked me to Widow Hawks' from the doctor's, he has been by nightly. Sometimes on his horse, and sometimes walking, he strolls from door to door with me. Such a thing is noticed. Kate is shrewd, and she has started to tease me about having a sweetheart. She does not seem to recognize that I am not blushing about this, for I am not certain about having a suitor at my age and with my situation. But with Bern doting on me, Kate does as well, as if now that I am being courted, I am more fun to have around.

"That will be all, then, on the doc's account?" she asks, writing in her ledger carefully. "The buttons, the pickled fish, and paper?"

I nod. She finishes wrapping the parcels and ties a string so that they are easily carried. As we turn to the door, the doctor himself walks in, and Horeb and Gilroy swing with delight at someone new to pester.

"It's the old sawbones! Come to gather up your housekeeper, is it?" Horeb cackles.

"Sure is," Gilroy agrees.

"And all merry today, is it? Get to chop off an arm or a leg?"

"What if I told you it was somethin' else entirely?" The doctor turns on the two older men abruptly and wiggles his finger. "What if it's an entirely new operation includin' a lot of whiskey on the man, but afterwards he's not much of a man. If you catch my meanin'."

125

This seems to stun Horeb momentarily, but Gilroy looks nonplussed.

"Ain't a thing."

"You don't mean that, Doc," Horeb says uncomfortably. "You're teasing is all."

"Care to find out?"

"Ain't."

"I'm sure you're dandy, Gil, but maybe Horeb here would like to see how well I wield a knife. I'm even better with it than the saw."

Horeb crosses his hands low over his belt, half-hiding the manly parts Doctor Kinney is threatening.

"We all know you're fine with anything sharp, Doc, no need to prove it again."

"If you say so." The doctor turns, and then notices us. His eyes are twinkling, and he doesn't seem a bit uncomfortable that he's had such a lewd discussion in front of women. "Mrs. Weber! Kate, hello. How are you?" he asks jovially. He has had a lighter load of patients now with the warming weather, and it puts him in good spirits.

"Just finishing up," I comment, and take my packages, but he scoops them up and away from me before fixing his blue gaze on Kate.

"Will you be organizin' the usual festivities for the Independence Day celebrations?" He looks at her directly and she gives him one of her rare, full smiles.

"Of course. I have not had a chance yet to fully ask Mrs. Weber for help, but with her assistance, I'm sure it will be the best to date."

He glances at me briefly. "I'm sure then, too. The men have been buzzin' about nothin' else, though it's more than a month away. Let me or Mrs. Weber know what you need, then, will you?"

"Yes, Pat. I will."

As we walk out, I try to keep my eyes downward so Kate does not give me her sarcastic, arched brow at my shock. Kate called Doctor Kinney by his front name. No one else I have met calls him so familiarly. She must do it to continue to stun me, especially based on the conversation we just had.

"Did you have a nice visit?" the doctor asks conversationally. I glance up at him and nod, so he continues. "I'm glad you're gettin' on with Kate. She could use a good woman friend."

"She's been very kind to me, as most here are."

"And you're feelin' alright these days?"

I give him a smile. "I am, thank you, Doctor. Most of the ills have passed."

"Good. I'm surprised you've still been feelin' them. You'll let me know when you start to get too tired, though, won't you?" His voice betrays his worry, as if my earlier omission leaves him uncertain of me, and I regret my silence once again. But how could I have known he would not reject me? So many employers would have been appalled. I am learning that he takes ideas of family and tolerance quite seriously, whether it's blood or not. I am starting to think he sees me as a sisterly figure, and I do not mind that. It is comforting.

"I will. I promise," I swear earnestly.

He walks slowly in deference to my condition, and I start to piece together Kate's story with what I know of Flats Junction.

"Doctor, how long have you lived here? In Flats Junction?"

127

I ask this without looking to see if he is annoyed with my question, but he answers readily enough.

"Oh, let's see. I arrived in '74, I think it was. So it's been about seven years now. Long enough to make a difference, but certainly not long enough for half of Flats Junction."

"What do you mean?"

He sighs. "I've still got to prove my mettle, Mrs. Weber. Half the people here hesitate to call on me for any-thin'. They weren't impressed with me when I first came to town, and they certainly didn't trust the doc before me to do much more than offer bad medicine or bleed them, and he was typically drunk when he did, so why should they trust any doctors?"

"But you truly wish to help them," I say indignantly, remembering the files on each patient in his office. His details are meticulous and touch on more than just illness. Are the missing town names, such as Horeb's or Gilroy's, because they don't trust him? Is it because he's Irish, or because they don't trust his profession? Or did he do something so awful early on that half the town won't forgive him?

We arrive at his house, and he lets me go ahead of him as a gentleman will, hanging up his hat before shrugging into the conversation with a final shake of his head.

"Many here don't think they need my help. And they don't care about the science behind the work. To them, any new idea sounds more like some Indian snake oil, and folks around here certainly aren't keen on Indian methods, no matter if they'd help or no."

The evening meal is cold sandwiches and a fresh salad of new lettuce. My garden is a slow success. We eat in the backyard by pulling the kitchen bench out and spend the meal overlooking the land to the east without obstruction. The late afternoon shadows are a deep grey, but the sun's rays last even longer now that it's almost June. I lift my face to the light; it is a soft, pale gold, reflecting off the dusty prairie grasses. There is the low scissoring of insects as I look out at the green in the distance. One can smell the earth here, and hear the brushing of leaves and plants. I think about Widow Hawks, coming out from the trees that huddle near the old buffalo jump, and meeting Percival Davies. What was their first meeting like? Had they fallen in love instantly?

"Mrs. Weber," the doctor breaks into my reverie. "Have you ..." He stops short, gives a small sound, then alters his voice oddly. "Do you know that the color of your eyes is very unusual?"

I give him a little frown. What an odd thing to say. I recall my eyes as being generally brown, same as my hair, though a lighter shade. I say as much to him, but he gives a shake of his dark head, still looking at my face in the sun.

"They're brown, aye, but then they give way to green and blue and grey. I could not name a color to them."

"Well, and your eyes are blue," I say stoutly. "In case you were wondering."

He starts to laugh at this, loud enough that I wonder if Mrs. Molhurst will come to see the jest, but he quiets down and resumes eating. I look at him, thinking about how he must have known Widow Hawks and Percy Davies before and after their marriage, and how he says he will do anything for her. I admire his loyalty and his acceptance of them. I wonder if his aunt was the same. I suppose I will never know unless I ask. He must owe the widow and the former banker a great deal for the stake they gave him in Flats Junction.

"In any way, will you be helpin' with the Independence Day plans?" he asks around a mouthful.

"Kate has not mentioned anything to me yet. She organizes it all?"

"Sure. Some years there are fireworks if a peddler comes through in time. But mostly it's the cowboys racin' and displayin' their husbandry skills with the cows, all the womenfolk makin' a good spread of vittles, and there is generally a bit of a fair with the games and all. Some of the Army boys from Fort Randall will ride in for the girls and the dancin'. We are not part of the union yet, out here, but we like to act as if our joinin' were around the corner."

I think of the grand and stately affairs of the Eastern cities, with people attending them in their Sunday finery, cannons blasting, bands playing, candy, and the sweet cold tang of lemonade. And at the end of the hot day, a walk along the seashore. This will be very different, but I look forward to showing the town my cooking skills, which have been progressing well as I become more attuned to the kitchen and the potbelly stove's particularities. And Toot Warren of The Golden Nail is said to be quite a cook, plus she's making lemonade. Maybe there will be a taste of the city after all.

"Is there a dish you'd like me to make?"

"Can you do a pie?" he asks.

I laugh. "With what fruit?"

"Ach, there's a point. I suppose there's no use in tryin' to make somethin' from nothin'. Well, then, do the cold chicken you made the other week. That was delicious. Pick up one at the Brinkley's next time you're out for milk and eggs. And whatever else Kate needs for the celebration."

130

"Alright." I give him a little smile and begin to clear our plates and wipe the table. The doctor joins me, as is his preference, and dries almost as fast as I wash.

"I've been thinkin' of doin' the herbal remedy for the Zalenski young'un," he mentions off-handedly. He is speaking of a child we saw together yesterday, and I recall the mother, Anette, and her strained eyes under sleek blonde hair. "It's a spring cold to be sure, but I don't like the sound of the cough. You know what I mean?"

"You mentioned a poultice?"

"Aye. Nothin' so fancy as you are used to in the cities, I know, but I'll know if I need to be more aggressive in treatin' the child if the onions and herbs don't work."

I nod. "Of course. Just tell me the specifics, and I can go over to their house while you're on rounds in the morning."

He grins. "Now see, that's luck to have you here. You can do the medicinals some of the time."

As I finish the suds, there is a knock on the door. The doctor turns from his drying to the front of the house.

"Right out!" he shouts through the hallway. Turning to me, he has a smile on his face, half teasing. "Your beau is here, m'lady."

I swat at him with my apron, which he catches and tugs, pulling me along. My face is close to his, and the smirk leaves his mouth. Suddenly, he is serious, intense, and asks lowly, "You are sure you wish to walk with him?"

"What else should I do?" I ask quietly, as I release the apron so it hangs limply from his hand, and walk out of the kitchen. This exchange unnerves me, but I brush it aside and give Bern a small smile as he waits for me off the porch. He does not have his horse today.

131

"Everything okay?" he questions easily. I look at him, surprised he is sensitive enough to notice the slight change in my manner, and realize I cannot speak my mind, that I do not know him enough to be honest. Perhaps there is something about him the doctor knows and wishes to warn me. Perhaps it is best to find out more about this so-called beau, and not hear the news secondhand, the way I have learned about others today.

"Yes. Everything is fine. Thank you," I say. On the way home, he tells me about his family, his parents in Minnesota, and his brothers who both work a few villages down the rail line. He speaks of them fondly, and of his riding and love of horses. I know nothing about the quality, value, or work of livestock, so I am interested. He is open, talkative, more so than ever, so we stand outside Widow Hawks' door for a spell before his stories end. Then he tips his Stetson and leaves.

Widow Hawks is waiting for me when I walk in. She is standing, watching the door open. She looks a bit anxious.

"Is he going to court you in earnest?"

"I don't know. Does it matter?"

She gives a small shrug and motions aimlessly with her hand. "Not now, no."

I see my opening and pounce. I go to sit next to her as she kneels and picks up her stitching. She is making a bunting for the baby. She figures I will be due in the fall, but I know it will be later than that. I plan to tell everyone how mathematics and my cycle are never very precise.

"Well, it's not always so passionate, is it?" I reason. "It wasn't so with Henry, why should it be any different now with Bern if he is interested in me? You were married. Were you happy?" I mean more than happiness, but I do not know how to put the words just right.

132

Her hands still, and she bends her head. I see the sparkling silver hairs sprinkled in her dark grey braids. Finally, she looks up at me. The long lines framing her mouth are noticeable in the waning light, her black eyes are soft with melancholy.

"I was very happy. Happier than I could have imagined. It was not always easy, and there were difficult weeks and months, but we had one another always. Not doubting his love was beautiful in itself."

So, there *was* passion between her and Percival Davies.

I wish I had met him. I wish I had seen them together, so I could read what a good marriage, a good, strong partnership, looked like. I could have modeled my own fate along those lines, and I would know if a future with Bern had much to recommend it, or if I truly am trapping myself again, slowly, into another loveless union.

"He sounds very kind," I say instead, and she smiles into the distance.

"He was incredibly so. Kindness with a backbone of strength. I rarely see such a combination. Patrick has it, though not nearly so tough as my husband. Likely that is why we took Pat in when he and his aunt came to town. Until they built up the house. Because we saw a bit of ourselves in him."

It takes me a minute to remember the doctor's front name. We are quiet together again. The fire crackles as it eats the new logs, and I inhale the sage leftover in the air. My comfort with Widow Hawks comes so much from our companionable silences. So many times, I was quiet in my life and my marriage, and while I accepted it, it always felt forced. The silence here is comfortable. Even tonight, when I wonder about Widow Hawks' past, and my mind is whirling with implications, I don't feel the need to speak.

She gives the softest of sighs and moves to begin her evening rituals. I go to my bed, stripping down before putting my hands on my belly. Nothing is quite showing yet, though perhaps my waist is slightly thicker. If I were truly pregnant with Henry's child, how much bigger would I be?

I do not turn when I ask, "Why do you suppose that cowboy, Bern, walks me home?"

"Because you are an available widow woman. And you're not afraid of hard work." Her answer is bald and bold and unexpected.

"When shall I tell him about the baby?"

"When you are showing, I should think," comes her response. "When the babe quickens."

I do not like to think of that conversation; it will be intensely uncomfortable. I worry about what the handsome cowboy will think of me. It almost bothers me to think that he will stop courting me, and I am surprised to realize that I enjoy his attentions. It is heady, and it is a bit intoxicating to think I could make him do many a thing to win my full favor. And yes, I'm grateful for his interest because it means the other cowboys don't ogle at me quite as openly as they used to.

When I was first out in society, there were suitors interested in both my sister, Anne, and me. Anne had a particular idea of what she had wanted in a husband, and I did not. So, when I was introduced to James Miller, I had been shocked with my response to him—to his wit, his smile, and his charm. I'd thought I'd finally found a match. One who would listen to me, to my notions, and understand that under all the practiced calm and steadiness of my actions, lived a woman with a deep, inquisitive sensibility. But then, Anne had noticed James, too. And then it had been over, for no one could withstand her charisma and her laughter and brilliant eyes.

I had thought my spinsterhood was all but certain until Henry had attended one of the parties in Rockport, where he often pulled shipments of granite and lime. We had found ourselves standing along the edge of the dance floor, and it only took one song length for us to realize we had mutual hopes for our lives. I wonder now if that will be the way of it with Bern. I wonder if he simply wishes a wife to cook and clean for him, or if his affection for me borders on passion.

I don't know him well enough yet to feel fully in control of the situation. If—*when*—he discovers I am pregnant, will he leave me alone? Will he believe me when I say it is the child of my dead husband? A widow is often thought of as a bit of a temptress who knows the pleasures of the bedroom and is not willing to forgo them, and who will do anything to entice a man to the sheets. Could I work here with such an unwarranted stigma on my head? Would the doctor want such a woman working for him, one who is so shunned by his town?

I'm petrified of my pregnancy and all its shortcomings. I don't want to lose this odd freedom in Flats Junction. I don't want anyone to think poorly of me, especially Widow Hawks and my employer, and even a few of the women who send me tentative overtures of friendship: Sadie Fawcett, Anette Zalenski, and Alice.

But this child will make me risk it all, from the loss of a handsome man's attentions to, possibly, my employment. I wish I could have come here without such a heavy burden in my belly.

CHAPTER 8

3 July 1881

Independence Day celebrations come up quickly. I am mostly just grateful, as it means a break from the usual workload, and I am especially intrigued about what the doctor will say about my cooking. His challenge for a pie had me cull the earliest of the tomatoes, all green and unripe, and soften them, cook them, and spice them. I taste as I go along and I think I might pass the pies off for apple, which are nearly impossible to come by out here. I do the cold chicken as well, as we'd discussed, just in case the pies don't turn out.

Kate has me in charge of the ladies' contributions while she is busy decorating the general store, post office, bank, and other public buildings with new bunting she's had delivered. I'm glad to help her, and I wonder if it means we're truly friends.

Bern has asked me to watch him at the races, and I have said I will try to do so amid the food preparations. The cowboys have several specialties they like to show off for the townsfolk's entertainment. Since telling me in detail about his protective and loving parents, and his competitive, but earnest brothers, Bern speaks more freely each evening, though he rarely asks about me. I do not mind, as I do not have any colorful stories to share and much to keep quiet. His lack of probing reminds me of the gentlemen back home, who did not pry with personal questions so quickly.

I finish the pies in the morning and put them off to cool while I go about my scrubbing. The kitchen and surgery wipe up easily, but the hallway, stairs, and especially the washroom take a good long time, as the wood seems to soak up soap and dirt more readily there. One could call the wood stoic, solid, and give it human characteristics that one would wish for oneself. I mull along these lines as I scrub. Today I'm trying lye instead of vinegar, which I found in the doctor's surgery, and the mixture seems to be working a bit better, though my hands are itching with the concoction, and my eyes burn.

As I take the dirty bucket of water down the stairs, the doctor comes in from his early rounds and catches me at it. He frowns a little, and brushes travel dust absently from his shiny vest. Then he sighs and hikes up the stairs, his mouth twisted in a weary grimace.

"Mrs. Weber, really!" he admonishes, meeting me halfway up. "Stop liftin' things!"

"How am I to get any work done, then?" I ask him a bit irritably, as I relinquish the bucket. He pauses on the step, wavering.

"Use smaller buckets. Anythin' like that," he says, a bit deflated. "Confound it, Mrs. Weber. I don't want you or the wee babby hurt."

137

I am heartened at his worry, but what woman does not like a little pamper now and then? I meekly follow him down the stairs.

He sniffs suddenly and stops, peers into the bucket, then at me suspiciously.

"Lye?"

I lift my shoulders. "I wanted things very clean."

He frowns, and then grabs my hand, flipping it over to see the palm. The flesh is red, and I resist the urge to scratch it. "You used lye water? Did you know the right mixture?"

"What mix?" I glance at my skin. The itching is giving way to pain. It's as though the lye has burned my nose as well, the odor lifting like an invisible powder to sizzle away any ability to smell.

"Don't you know how to use lye properly?" He drops the bucket and my hand and strides into the surgery.

I follow him, wiping my fingers briskly on my apron, and then notice that the fabric seems to be disintegrating in large patches, and parts of my skirt as well. What on earth?!

He turns to me and settles a basin on the operating table. "Put your hands over this. It's goin' to hurt for a bit."

"What?" I hide them behind my back.

"I've got to stop the lye from diggin' into your skin and burnin' you worse than it is. Cold water, lots of scrubbin', and then I'll put on a bit of salve."

I hesitate, the typical questioning bubbling up. "How do you know just water will work?"

He looks indignant. "I'm a doctor."

"But—"

"Mrs. Weber, don't be foolish. You've already shown

me you have no understandin' on lye water, and you've ruined your new housedress. Now is not the time to argue."

Embarrassment charges through me, and I bite my lips against the sting of his reprimand. He's perfectly correct, and I am not sure if I feel more ashamed or upset. And the dress! I hadn't thought of the dress! What a waste! Widow Hawks just made it, and now it'll be patched and ragged from the start.

I let him pour cold, clear water from his copper water cistern over my hands and the splash makes me cry out. He apologizes abruptly, then puts more water over them.

"Too late," he says mournfully, inspecting the skin. "Burns for sure."

Snatching a hand back, I look over the palm and am surprised to see that my stinging skin looks completely raised with puffy, red blisters. Good heaven! What have I done?

The doctor is rummaging around his glass bottles and canisters, and the clinking is loud in the sterile space. When he turns back, he still looks completely befuddled.

"I can't believe … you mean to tell me you had no notion of how to work with lye? Why didn't you clean with a simple water and vinegar?"

I press my lips tighter and scrape my fingers together, wincing with pain, which is building higher, and hotter, as each moment ticks along.

"I … I didn't know."

"What did you clean with back in Boston?"

I hesitate, meet his steady, blue gaze briefly, and then look down at my bubbling hands.

"I didn't clean much. Not like this."

The doctor gives a short, angry huff and takes my hands back in his, laying them palm up on the operating table and leaning over them. Then he opens a creamy salve and starts to daub it on with delicate circles, his frown deepening as he goes.

"It's goin' to hurt for a bit," he states. "And you'll need to patch your clothes when you next wash them out. Or the lye will keep eatin' them."

I nod, watching, and mesmerized by the curls of cream he continues to swirl into my flesh. He adds another layer, blending it in slowly, the wide pads of his fingers tracing the lines of my hands, and the raised welts of the lye. I can almost forget my foolishness in the sensuality of having someone take care of my needs. When was the last time someone managed for me? Henry? Before he took to his bed?

"Did you have a maid, Mrs. Weber?" he asks quietly, startling me out of my memories.

"A maid?"

"To clean your house in Boston."

"I ..." I close my eyes briefly, wishing I could have a better answer. "I had a maid once a week, yes. But I did my own cooking."

"Well, that part I can figure," he says wryly. "And likely had a garden of sorts as you've managed to plant the vegetables without too much trouble."

"I would dust," I tell him, salvaging what dignity I can. "But it wasn't proper for a businessman's wife to be on hands and knees in the privy or on the kitchen floor, scouring."

He raises his head to meet my eyes directly. "I see."

Does he? Does he understand what he's been asking of me? I've put aside my pride to clean, I've stumbled through most of the steps of keeping a full house in shape. And I've done it all without real knowledge of what I would find in the Territories. I've had to make it up every day, hoping I do right.

Winding clean bandages around my hands, he tightens them briskly and then removes the bin of water now full of lye.

"You'll need to wash down the rest of the stairs, and wherever you've cleaned, with plain water, so it doesn't stay as a dusty white coverin' over everythin'. Just splash it down and get the lye off the floorboards and sweep it out onto the porch so you don't muddy your hands."

I nod wordlessly, thankful that he doesn't seem angry anymore. Why is he so kind? What else should I say?

"I'm sorry."

The words are abrupt, but soft, and I don't actually mean to say them aloud. He spins around as he wipes his hands with a cloth.

"Sorry?"

"I didn't have the experience you might have expected."

He's silent for a moment, and then looks up at me, his face relaxing as he shakes his head. "You never overpromised, I suppose. You just said you could be a housekeeper. And you've done well enough. It's a shame about your new skirts, though. And your hands'll hurt for a good while."

Hurt? They throb so hard, tightening and blistering even under the cream that I want to scream.

"Did you do your own laundry?"

I pause again, wishing I could offer a rosier response. "I did, yes, though some of it we sent out for laundering."

He sighs, and then shakes his head. "Anythin' else?"

If I ever were to give in and tell him about my pregnancy's truth, now would be the time. Should I press further, and ask him what kind of expectations he has for my nursing abilities? He cannot be so displeased that he's thinking of dismissing me, and now that I've spent enough weeks here, I realize there's little reason for him to fire me for anything other than theft, or my complete inability to keep up. And even though I've revealed exactly how stupidly inexperienced I am, he doesn't seem inclined to worry on it further.

Is it fortune, or is he simply very good at burying his disapproval and disappointment?

Well, there's nothing left to do now but feed him lunch and hope that I can spill enough water to wash out the lye on the floor later. He follows me into the kitchen, still mumbling about my mistake. I grab the kettle of yesterday's soup, something that doesn't require me to do much with my hands. I try to ignore the tatters of my apron or the holes in my skirts. I hope they will be an easy fix. Will Widow Hawks be exasperated? Upset? Will she just quietly take in the holes? Might I fix the holes myself? It's just a work dress. I cannot be the only person who has ruined a dress.

To put aside my embarrassment, I ask about patients as I heat the soup. "How did the poultice work with Anette Zalenski's youngest?"

"Well. She's mendin'," he says comfortably, sitting down and grabbing the bread from under a cloth, where it is hiding with the butter.

"I'm glad to hear it. I saw her the other day in the general," I respond. "But she was busy with her mother and I didn't get a moment to ask about it. Speaking of ... I have been wondering why Anette's mother is always at the blacksmiths. Does she keep their house?"

"Oh, that." Doctor Kinney wipes his mouth with a fast swipe. "Anette's mother, Berit, married Walter Salomon, the elder blacksmith, back in the sixties. Before my time. I hear it was a love match many thought endearin'."

"Why so?" I wonder, watching the bubbles pop in the broth. I love to hear the stories that make Flats Junction unfold yet again for me, coloring the spaces of each person I meet.

"They were older. Both widowed. I suppose when one marries late like that, it's only if you love one another instead of as a necessity."

The idea is sweet indeed. A marriage of passion instead of bland acceptance or need. I suppose that is my own thought now. I suppose it is why I am waiting for my stomach to twist with joy and fluttering when I think of Bern, so I know I am not repeating my old life once more.

Then the doctor spies the pies cooling and exclaims in delight.

"Where did you find fruit?"

I laugh. "It's green tomatoes. Hope they are good. I've made three."

He stands and goes to peer at them, then gives me a halfway hopeful, and devilish, grin.

"I could try one to make sure."

"Doctor Kinney!" I smile. "Wait for tomorrow."

"Barely," he chuckles. In a bout of lightness, he grabs me and does a quick two-step about the kitchen. I cannot decide what has made him so silly, the July heat, or the coming celebrations. His arm comes around my waist, his large hand grabbing my bandaged one carefully as he spins us around the table. I laugh at him, at his sudden freeness, and also with a bit of weepy relief. He stops us in front of the stove. At first, he does not release me, but holds me lightly, searching my eyes. I do not understand his intensity, but I am surprised to find I enjoyed our little jig, and the masculinity of his embrace.

"You'll dance with Bern, I suppose," he says, loosening his arms. "There was your practice, then."

"If he asks me," I shrug indifferently, and turn to the stove.

"I'm sure he will," he mutters, before setting out the plates. His murmur strikes me as odd, almost possessive, but I dismiss it. The doctor may like my casual female companionship, but he is one of the most courteous men in Flats Junction. I have no reason to expect him to step outside the perimeters of propriety.

Stirring the soup, I notice the tin on the edge wears thin along the copper pot. I will make a stop at the smithy soon. I've not had a reason yet, and have not met either smith in town as they keep to themselves.

I think on my day. After lunch, he will be off to afternoon rounds while I circle the neighborhood to check in on some of the women to make sure all is set for tomorrow's festivities. But first I must dash the floor with water. And go change my dress. It will certainly not do for me to go calling on the women in the ruined mess I'm wearing. I may have gotten used to harder labor and difficult chores, and now I don't scream very loudly when I find a mouse in the house, but I won't let rough living change some of my civilized niceties.

We eat in easy companionship. The soup has a meaty flavor thanks to the handful of beets and turnips. We discuss

144

his cases and my upcoming jaunt around town to confirm the foodstuffs.

"Don't approach Sadie Fawcett head on, you know. She knows what she is supposed to make this year. And when Kate asked for casseroles from Clara Henderssen, she bent Sadie's nose, or so I was told when I was there checkin' on Sadie's youngest's broken arm. Go about that one gently and use lots of praise, or you'll have burnt puddin's for the town."

I file away the information.

"And please wear a bonnet. And take water when you visit." He finishes up the meal with reminders. "No faintin' in the heat."

"Yes, Doctor," I say, and move to take the dirty dishes to sit in the washbin with the knives. He gets his bag and hat. He's so busy this week that he does not have as much time to spend with me in the kitchen. I miss our banters when I wash and he dries the crockery, but I say nothing as I know his work is far more important than my company. And truthfully, I am getting busy as well with the summer needs of the garden, and my own slowly mounting duties as his assistant, filing papers and delivering medicines.

He pauses in the doorway. "Mrs. Weber."

I glance back at him.

He gives me a little smile. "Save me a dance tomorrow, will you?"

"Of course." I am pleased he asks me. It is nice to know he wishes to spend some time with me socially.

CHAPTER 9
3 July 1881

I make my own rounds in the afternoon after pouring water over the floor and sweeping it out, leaving the planks to dry and changing into my yellow calico. Widow Hawks is not home, and I know I will admit to my mistake about the brown dress tonight. I don't look forward to telling her my foolishness, but there's going to be relief in being done with the mishap.

It is hot. The sweat trickles down my back and under my collar, and I wear my wide-brimmed hat against the sun. Sadie Fawcett responds well to my flattery, as the doctor predicted. She has that tongue for gossip, too, so my stay is long at her table before I can make an excuse to leave, knowing everyone will hear the story of my mess with the lye and my blistered hands.

Still, the break in the coolness of her kitchen gives me the strength to make the longer walk out to the Brinkley farms. Alice Brinkley and her family will bring a roast cow, and I want to be sure they have no issues providing the main meat for the gathering, but I notice it is already on a spit when I stop in to see Alice. Nancy Ofsberger, the postman's wife, will be cooking a huge batch of potatoes. Between all the other women in town, there will be a good spread.

I swing by the doctor's to pick up the copperware to drop at the smith's and stop at Kate's general store on the way to the tin shop. She is finishing the decorations. Her porch will be where the awards are to be given for the winners of the races—both foot and horse.

"All set?" She glances up, a pin poking out of the corner of her mouth.

"I think so. And Bern has promised to set up trestle boards for the tables before the racing."

"Your man is becoming quite a helper," she teases me and I have enough understanding to blush.

"Well, do you need anything else today? Otherwise I'm off to drop off some copper for repairs."

She eyes the pot under my arm. "You're going to have Marie do your work?"

I raise my eyebrows. "I thought I'd have the tinner do it. Isn't that Thaddeus Salomon?"

"He's the blacksmith," Kate smirks. "You'll be wanting Marie. She does the copper and tin work around here."

"Oh." I hide my surprise and wonder why no one has mentioned that the tin shop is run by a woman. I've only heard talk of 'the tinsmith' or 'the blacksmith.' Is it because everyone has accepted a woman in that role, or because no one approves? "Well, do you want anything from them for the festivities while I'm there?"

"No." She turns back to the bunting, but not before I see how uncomfortable she is suddenly. "The smiths don't always come anyway, as neither of them likes a good dance, and Marie is not exactly a good cook. Still, if Thad's father's wife is there—Berit. See if she might bring some of her potato dumplings. She does the best in town."

Kate's dark hair has completely fallen out of the heavy bun she wears. It is a glossy black and picks up the ruddy light of the setting sun. I think she is the loveliest woman I have ever seen. I am always a little in awe of her, and I feel I must always be working toward her approval, to confirm I'm a proper woman worth her respect. It taints my aid for the celebration preparations with a sort of desperation.

She is busy though, and does not have time to chat with me long. I tell her I need to get back to make dinner.

"Jane!" she calls as I slowly walk back down the stairs. "What happened to your hands?"

"Lye. I'll tell you later," I say, and am glad neither Gilroy or Horeb are in the general today to bother me further. Likely I'll get an earful soon enough, as they'll hear the tale from Sadie.

"Well, thanks for your help." She graces me with a full smile. "It was very nice to have a friend to do this with, this year."

I smile back, and head north to the tin shop, filled with a small sense of triumph. As I go up Davies Avenue toward the north end of town, I hear my name.

"Mrs. Weber!"

Doctor Kinney is the only one in town who calls me so formally, so I turn and wait for him to join me. He carries his medical bag in one hand and a large sack of flour in the other—likely the payment from one of his patients today.

"Where are you goin'?"

"I know it's late." I show him the pot. "I was just going to drop this off at the smiths for repairs. Dinner will be easy and fast. It's much too hot to cook."

He searches my brow with a clinical eye. "You've been keepin' cool enough, I hope?"

"I have. No fainting spells, honestly."

"Well, then, let me walk with you and we'll make off for home together."

We arrive at the smithy soon enough. It's on the edge of town, where the skinny Flats Basin River—more a creek than an actual river—winds and trips. Thaddeus Salomon, a giant of a man, is pounding hard on a hunk of iron, building what looks to be part of a wheel. He is looming and intimidating even as he concentrates on his metal. His apprentice stands to the side, pumping the bellows at intervals, and one of the blacksmith's own sons is nearby, watching with alert eyes.

"Don't interrupt his rhythm," Doctor Kinney murmurs to me. "And besides, you need to go through to the coppersmith."

We pass by the ringing hammer into an adjoining room through a wide, double door. A strong woman bends over a broad wooden table filled with shimmering white tin and rose-gold copper scraps. She is not as old as I expect, and she has two young girls at a nearby table scribbling on tin with scribes. One looks to be actually forming work.

Her dark head straightens, and she looks at me over the counter briefly.

"I'll be there in a moment."

149

We wait as she carefully finishes a circular cut, the fat scissors shearing through the copper as if it was butter. I see her hands are terribly scarred along the back, crisscrossed with healed cuts on every finger.

"What can I do for you?" Her voice is neutral.

"I need this repaired, please." I offer up the piece. She takes it from me, her dark eyes immediately drawn to the worn tin and spotty copper.

"Well, then," she considers, twisting the crockery into the light. "I've a bit of a backlog. It'll be several weeks."

"I can manage. There's no rush," I tell her, feeling as though I must placate her. The shop suddenly feels strangely quiet, and it's only after I hear the shift of boots on the dirt that I realize the blacksmith has stopped his banging and is standing on the threshold staring at us, his fists resting on wide hips.

Doctor Kinney nods at the man, but doesn't offer his usual warm chatter, which immediately puts me on edge. The blacksmith barely nods back.

"Fine. I'll send one of my children when it's finished. Or stop in by the middle of August, I'd expect," Marie decides, then moves the copper off the counter and starts to scratch into her ledger. The margins of the paper are covered in artistic doodles. She slams the cover shut and raises her eyebrows at us.

"No need to pay until the work is finished and satisfactory."

It's obvious we are dismissed without a single piece of gossip or small talk. I edge out, but the blacksmith hardly moves out of the way. Doctor Kinney ambles behind me, still calm, his own bulk as reassuring as my shadow.

150

"Thank you," I say, looking up at the hulking smith.

He frowns. "Don't be thanking me. It's her what's doing your repairs."

Glancing over my shoulder, I hedge, uncertain if I should offer a second thanks to the woman smith, but Doctor Kinney is fairly pushing me out, and Marie isn't looking at us, but at the blacksmith.

As we make our way back into the street, her voice echoes through the rooms. "Really, Tadeusz, after all these years?"

The man's response is a muttering rumble, and I look up at Doctor Kinney. He keeps his eyes straight ahead. It's only after we leave that I realize I forgot to ask for Berit Salomon to make potato dumplings as is her usual.

"What was all that about?" I ask frankly.

He swallows and glances down at me. He's silent for so long, I wonder if he won't answer. Have I asked a personal question that is too sore?

"Remember how I've mentioned that I have only been here for seven years?"

"Yes."

"Well, the day I arrived in Flats Junction, there was an Indian raid. The Crow were fightin' Widow Hawks' people, who were campin' up the hill by the old buffalo jump as they do every year. It was before most of the Indians were required to stay on the reservations. And the Crow came into town and started creatin' havoc, butcherin' and shootin' arrows just to make mischief, to cause bad blood between the whites and the Blackfoot Sioux. Before that, the people in Flats Junction generally didn't mind the passin' of the Sioux in the warm months. But ever since ..."

151

"How does that ... forgive me." I pause. "It's just they were so short with you. Us."

He nods. "That's on me. They don't like me much. The first time Thad Salomon met me, I was in the middle of rescuin' people from that raid, choppin' off a leg or an arm if there was no savin' it. He wasn't too happy about that—some still begrudge me that particular day. And the Salomons didn't trust old Doc Gunnarsen before me, so they don't feel they need to give me a chance either."

He shrugs as he finishes. "I can see their point, though I'm not pleased. I hope they'd call me if they felt it was an emergency."

"How many years do you think it will take before people will trust you? All the people?"

"Ten? Twenty?" He gives a laugh as we reach his porch, but it's a sad sort of laugh, and the vulnerability in it surprises me. "Maybe never. How long did it take you to trust a doc with Mr. Weber's health?"

I walk into the coolness of his hallway, considering his question. As he takes off his hat and rubs a hand through his damp hair, I look him in the eye, choosing truth.

"Never. I didn't trust any of the doctors. They all differed so much. That's why I started to read up myself, as much as I could. Not that it mattered. Nothing saved him in the end."

He looks at me keenly. "Do you miss him so very much?"

Pressing my mouth tight, I wonder whether to tell him *how* I miss Henry. I don't, not in the way he means. I never loved him. I appreciated him, and I thought him kind. But how can I miss someone who never stirred me? Who was simply a means to an end?

152

He seems to realize I will not—or *cannot*—answer, and goes silently into his office. I move to the kitchen and slice up cold vegetables, a bit of cheese, and hearty bread, fumbling with the knife. We'll have new bread today, for I've discovered a knack for baking.

I think on Kate as I try to push the afternoon's uncomfortable encounters away. I wonder how she came about, as a single woman, to run the general store in town. Without a man to help her with funds, or around the shop, I am continually impressed with her hard work and ambition. She is something of a leader in this town, respected by the women from what I can tell, though she does hit them rather hard around the head with tactlessness sometimes. And the men all seem to give her a wide berth, as if she is not a woman to court, even with her exotic beauty. Did she put them all off, like I did before I married Henry? I will have to ask the doctor.

As I muse on this, he walks into the kitchen, whistling.

"You're in a good mood," I comment, thankful he's moved on from the pensive way we ended the conversation earlier. He gives me a grin before glancing over at the pies. "And don't even think about it. There had better be three whole pies here tomorrow when I come to fetch them."

"You have my word," he vows, and sets himself comfortably at the table, reaching for some hard cheese. "Though I want to be first in line to try them."

"There will be other sweets, too, in case they are a flop," I say. "And my chicken."

"Sounds like it will be quite the day tomorrow," he says, eyes glinting. I have a feeling the doctor likes a good party.

"Will you be partaking in the activities and all?" I ask.

"Just the dancin' and the minglin', I'm afraid. I'm not one for ridin' my animals as fast as those cowboys. I am on hand for when anyone, horse or rider, gets hurt, though."

We start to eat, and then I carefully ask, keeping my tone neutral, as I hope what I am about to ask is not gossip, but common knowledge.

"I have been wondering, and I keep forgetting to ask Kate ... how is it she is running the general? It is unusual for a woman to go at it alone, isn't it?"

The doctor shrugs and grabs carrots from the platter. "Maybe. Many a widow has made it work in the town's I've seen. Vermillion had three generals before this spring's floods, and one was run by a woman alone as well. Kate hasn't married, so she's had to learn a bit on her feet. But she was lucky. The old owner stayed around and helped her learn the books and orderin' before he died."

"He took her on, like an apprentice?" I ask, uncertain on how the social structure works here in unconventional situations. For instance, how did a woman become a tinsmith in Flats Junction?

He gives a little laugh. "Oh no! Kate bought the store out from under him. Harry was a good man, but his health failed shortly after I came to town."

"Kate must have had a good inheritance."

"Some, yes. Her father was livin' at the time, and he helped her buy it. She wanted to be independent. She always was. A regular spitfire." His voice goes tender as he talks about her, and he gets a small smile on his face that I do not often see.

It dawns on me that the doctor is soft on Kate. If that is so, I wonder if she knows.

154

"You've known her long?"

"Since I arrived in Flats Junction with my Aunt Bonnie. Yes."

I test my newly formed theory. "You should dance with her tomorrow."

His head comes up, the blue eyes guarded.

"What makes you say that? I doubt Kate has any wish to dance with anyone. She's never been one for a spin."

"Ask her," I prompt, feeling a bit of a matchmaker. "She might say yes." I think about how she calls him by his first name, and I smile a little, too. "I think she would, indeed."

He leans back, a faraway look on his face. I wonder if he's ever shown his affection toward her. He is Irish, and while I see his passion in his work, he does not seem overtly romantic.

"You think so, do you?" He smiles a little sheepishly when he catches me observing him. He covers quickly. "You'll be sure to dance once around with me, then, won't you, Mrs. Weber?"

"I gave you my word," I say lightheartedly. I feel my entire day has dashed me up and down. Fear, worry, and enjoyment are all tangled together in my gut. I just want to go to sleep, but I know when I get back to Widow Hawks' house, I will have to explain my ruined dress.

We begin to wash up the dishes together by discussing the happy news that fireworks will be set off tomorrow evening, and the doctor re-wraps my hands after the bandages are soaked through. The sting seems to have disappeared, and the swelling is down considerably, for which I'm very grateful.

155

Bern walks me home. He is bursting with bravado and excitement for the Independence Day races. He is an able cowboy, though I have not heard him spoken about town with reverence. I do not think he will take the races by storm as he says he might, but I listen and nod. It's possible I lead him on with my amiable evening strolls. He may abandon me when he learns of my delicate condition. But for now, I will bask in his manly attention.

Without Kate's bidding, I asked Widow Hawks to make a cornbread for tomorrow, and I smell it in the fire when I walk in. The corn has a sweet and earthy scent. I know it will crumble perfectly in my mouth, and that it will be seasoned with one or two herbs. She is chanting lightly. I smile as I listen and watch her finish the bread and unwrap it to cool.

"You ought to wear the lavender dress for the festivities. You haven't worn it yet and we need to see if it still fits you," she says by way of greeting.

"I ruined the brown," I respond, gesturing to my bed, where the dress from my morning mishap droops across the furs. "It seems I have no notion how to use lye for cleaning."

She nods. "I noticed the damage. I can patch it."

"I'm so sorry. All your work," I sigh. "I should be the one patching it.

"Do you know how?" She eyes me up, but not unkindly.

"I think so. I'd like to try," I say.

"Good. Then I'll pull out the scraps for you. Now, let's get on the lavender."

She is very kind to think of my fashions, as if I was her own kin to fuss over. Everyone in town is making such a commotion about Independence Day and I feel like I must do something special, too, so I don't mind the trouble of trying on the dress tonight. With her help, I slip into the fresh cloth, and we find we need to take out the waist seams an inch right along the edge of the hips. It's an easy fix for her talented fingers.

"You're small for how far along you are," she observes as she fits the lavender dress around me. "That is nice, and a little unusual. Most of the women here have babies that are very big."

"How big?" I ask nervously.

"Oh, twelve pounds or so at least, is what I recall hearing."

I gulp and clutch my belly tightly. The round curve of my womb is there, but it doesn't seem to be getting too big too fast. I'm glad of it, and yet nervous too. I'm planning to tell everyone how Henry and I conceived at Christmas, right at the end of his illness, so the dalliance with Theodore five weeks later won't be too far off the mark. If I don't start looking more pregnant soon, will it be obvious that my timeline is very off? I press on my flesh and will it to spring back bigger and rounder than before.

"I'll need to say something to Bern soon," I admit. She doesn't say anything in response. Since she has had children, I rely on her for leadership on the proper way to do things, and I hope she will give me direct answers on how best to tell people I am pregnant. Will she know what words I should use so I do not create a stigma on myself? Will she give me an idea on how to gracefully keep a beau I may want to have around?

"Widow Hawks," I start as she unbuttons my outer dress again. "Why did you marry a white man?"

"I wasn't long married to him before he died. Have you learned the truth?" I blush as she looks at me directly and nods, answering her own question. "Ah, I see you have. But I think you are really asking why I left my people, to live where I was not well-liked or often respected?" She pauses, then says decisively, "Because I am a strong woman, and I know what I want. I wanted Percy, and he me, and we never doubted one another. We had beautiful children, and when we could, we married in the white man's way. And we did not waste much time being without each other. Life is too short."

"Why haven't you gone to live on the reservation then? After he passed?" I think of the one in the West, the one I hear mentioned in passing conversations.

"Because I want to be near my only family living."

"Your son? Daughter." I recall. "You have a daughter." I watch her spin the needle and start to pick at the seams of my dress. I want to learn the tricks, do as she does them, as I will soon have enough sewing of my own with the baby.

"My son died in childhood, but my daughter lives. You know her. My Katherine, though she goes by Kate."

CHAPTER 10
4 July 1881

I cannot believe how early the town rises on the Fourth of July. Everyone meets in the center of town, at the crossing of Main and Davies streets, where the general store and the Golden Nail Saloon stand as sentinels to the festivities. Handsome Joe Greenman of the Prime Inn, and Robert Brewer, the owner of the Main Inn, bring barrels of rainwater to the general's shadow, and sweeten them with sugar. Toot Warren has her son, Trusty Willy, carry out a gigantic barrel of her lemonade from the Golden Nail, with Elaine planning to demonstrate the use of the new juicer. Gilroy and Horeb move their seats to the general's porch so they can watch, jeer, and taunt everyone who walks by, as the races will take place on the west end of Main Street, circle around on Depot Row and return back in front of the post office. Tables up Davies Street display wares for sale from the cooper and the tannery. David Fawcett has old rifles for trade, while Jarle Henderssen is hawking his wheels. Kate plans to feed everyone along

General Street between the bank and the Golden Nail. The town feels swollen with bodies and shouts and good humor.

Fortuna, the owner of the Powdered Rose bordello, has had her girls decorate all their windows with ribbons, and I hear several of the Brinkley wives discussing how distasteful the display is. Dell Johnston is quick to pick up on it, and he heckles the girls whenever he passes to his own saloon—the Powdered Pig—shouting up into the open windows that they'd best use those ribbons wisely and cover themselves up. Fortuna takes to rushing out with her biggest frying pan whenever she sees him, and Horeb takes bets from anyone who walks into the general on what hour of the day Fortuna will finally get a whack on Dell's head.

Alan Lampton has provided a pig roast, and the smell of it makes one forgive the disgusting scent of pig urine that usually billows around his buildings. The Yang brothers have set up a table across the street with a well-seasoned noodle soup, sold by the cup to whoever wanders by with an empty tin, though many are waiting for the free dinner provided by the women of Flats Junction.

I see the newcomers, Isaac and Hannah Horowitz, wandering about with interest early in the morning before they hustle to set up a display of used, discounted shoes Isaac has had stashed away. Sadie Fawcett immediately asks them to save a pair of ivory heeled boots, as Miss Harriet Lindsey, the schoolteacher, watches with envy and dismay. Joseph Greenman has paid the peddler for the fireworks, and he has an array of the unfired shots on display in front of the Prime Inn. The livery is full of horses and wagons brought in from farmers and their families in the neighboring area. I wave to solemn Danny Svendsen as he rides in with a large group of his cowboy hands fresh in from the ranch, Bern among them.

The town echoes with shouts and laughter and horses whinnying. Already, it feels like it will be a hot day, but no one seems to mind. I head to the doctor's house to pick up my foodstuffs.

Still stunned by last night's revelation, it rolls over and over in my mind. Kate is the daughter of Widow Hawks and Percival Davies! And that means Doctor Kinney knows her from his time spent in the Davies home when he first arrived. His affection for her must go back years. I wonder why he has not courted her. Or is he too shy to ask, without a parlor to sit in or a father to recommend it? Or am I wrong about his heart, and he merely sees her as a woman he's known a long time? Does he have no romance in his bones? It doesn't seem so, otherwise I'd have to believe he might try romancing me sometimes with his kindness. I wonder if I'll get an answer to my hunch today.

My reverie is broken by the doctor himself, who meets me at the door in clean shirtsleeves and pants, still attaching his suspenders.

"Mrs. Weber!" He waits for me as I walk in, shutting the screen door without letting it slam and follows me into the kitchen to watch me make the coffee. I wonder at his loitering, his hovering about me, so I turn around and see that he has grown serious.

"You will please to remember you must drink water all day. It will be hot, and the womenfolk can faint on us enough as it is. I don't want one of them to be you."

I brush it off. "You're too kind to worry." He shakes his head and crosses his arms. I know the stance. It is a bit argumentative.

"I mean it, Mrs. Weber."

I nod in return and pour his coffee, which he takes into his study. I do hope he dances with Kate today. I'd like to see them together and to finally make a match of it. If he's going to be properly married, raise his standing in Flats Junction, and find happiness, it seems she's the best option in town. Single, unhindered, and beautiful. Why wouldn't he want her? He'd certainly be far better off with Kate. Otherwise there are few other single women for him in Flats Junction, myself among them. I don't think I could handle such a scandal should he show such interest! No—he ought to court her. Woo her. They'd make a handsome pair.

Grabbing up my pies, I notice an amber bottle on the corner of the stove glinting in the sun. The doctor's scrawl lists sideways on the label:

Mrs. Weber –

Use daily, morning and night until skin recovers.

R⨯. Equal parts glycerine, yolk and butter

Warm regards –

Doctor P. Kinney

How kind of him! Sweet, nearly. The thoughtfulness tickles my sensibility, and I tuck the bottle into the pocket of my apron for safekeeping.

162

When I arrive at the food tables set up on General Street before midday, the women trickle in with their delicacies. Alice Brinkley finds me, her little Pete strapped to her back for the walk into town. He is only a few months old, but already the birth seems eons ago.

"I've seen the men bringing the beef on the wagon before the games begin. Mitch's mother is bringing tarts and some cheese."

"Thank you, Alice." I smile wholeheartedly at her, and it strikes me that I might be able to ask her womanly questions as my time grows near, and that she would answer them. The thought brings me comfort. In truth, she is more a friend to me than Kate is, though I see Alice less than I would prefer.

"And here are the puddings!" Sadie Fawcett announces, with a trio of children behind her. Each little one is balancing a bowl carefully in their plump arms.

"Bravo!" I turn to her, winking at Alice over Sadie's head.

The women are all in a good competitive spirit, and I hear the chatter of cooking secrets and childrearing advice patter through the small gathering. It is a clear, refreshing sort of simplicity. Everyone is familiar with each other and offers their thoughts and personal opinions freely. Most call me Jane, and I like how I know most of them by sight, if not name, from my walks around town and my attempts at trying to fit in during the Catholic Mass. While I still miss the smell of salt air, and the pattern and ease of my life in Boston, I like the people out here more than the ones I knew in the careful society of Henry's circle.

"Jane Weber!" Anette Zalenski is at my elbow. "I've heard you are a big part of the festivities this year."

I smile up at her. Anette's wheat-blonde hair coils in gleaming, thick braids and the cornflower blue of her calico dress matches her laughing eyes.

"I'm trying to make a go of it."

"Oh! And I've brought along mother's *klubb*—the potato dumplings—her usual."

Her stout husband, who is several inches shorter than Anette, holds a large pot in his wide hands. Kate motions him to the end of a table, and Anette grins at me again.

"You haven't met my mother formally yet, have you? She used to convince old Walter to get out for the dancing, but don't expect Marie or Thad. And I won't stay long. I told my Jacob I want to be home early. Perhaps to do the usual."

I'm not at all able to follow her train of thought, and she winks cheekily.

"You know. Making another babe." My mouth drops open, and Anette laughs outright. "You blush as much as Marie does when I tease her about the earthier parts of life."

Still chuckling, she turns to scoop up the youngest one by her skirts, and walks away, her husband, Jacob, shooting me a half-sheepish smile at his wife's antics before following her toward the huge group gathering near the edge of the school house. Judging by their tall blondness, I would guess they are Anette's siblings and family. I only know one of them: Jorge. He works at the tannery. He's here with his lanky wife and several tow-headed children.

"The races are starting!" Shouts rise from the gathering crowd.

164

Alice is at my elbow again. She knows, like everyone else, that Bern has been courting me, and she leads us through the growing throng so I might be able to get a good view. At first, I cannot spot him, but then I see his horse and then himself.

Bern is striking in his way. He's lean and a few inches taller than most of the other men. His dark brown hair is longish along the back of his neck, and it is swiped along his forehead under his hat. I'm quite sure he's around my age, or thirty at the most. Like the others, he's dressed in rumpled and dusty clothes, with worn patches along the insides of the pant legs from always being on horseback. He seems very sure of himself, as do most of the cowboys lining up. I think perhaps I should be anxious for him, but I find I am just merely interested.

At the gun, the horses are off, down Main Street, to the Tannery on the west end, and then back around, racing through Depot Row and squeezing past the old abandoned livery building. They circle north, then, and climb the hill to the ancient Sioux buffalo jump, where old Henry Brinkley is waiting to make sure every one of the horses zig-zags through the tall pines. Crossing Flats Basin River at its deepest, they then skirt south on Second Avenue, sopping wet and yelling. I watch in silence, while Alice cheers loudly next to me. I smile and try to care more than I do, but it is mostly just grass and dust and prairie once the riders head up the path-like Buffalo Jump Road. Ivar Henderssen is helping Henry Brinkley with the judging, shouting disqualified riders from his perch on Tommy Winters' house whenever Henry waves. His decrepit father, Morten, gives a running commentary through black teeth in his thick Nordic accent: "And there's Hank, straight from Texas, surprised he's still awake, you hear he slept at every meal last week—ah, and Thunder, of course, still alive and keeping Chrissy guessing when he will marry h—oh, and the ginger. What's his name? Tate, yah, Tate, sun still burning him as bad as ever. And there goes Noah. He was telling those bad Catholic jokes again, Lara O'Donnell's sure he's going to hell …"

Bern somehow escapes Morten's comments, careening toward the finish line, his face tight and set as he leans over his horse. He slaps his reins, leaning over the saddle with intensity. For a moment, I think he might collide with grizzled Thunder, who is just ahead of him, but he pulls back just in time.

"Oh yeeee!" Alice shouts and waves as the last riders bolt past us. She turns to me, wide-eyed and flushed. "Your Bern took fourth. That is very good!"

"Is it?" I ask. "And he's not *my* Bern, you know."

Alice stops short and gives me a curious once-over. "Do you wish he wasn't?"

I look away from her, at the horses and riders who have finished, Bern among them. I suppose many women might call him dashing, same as I think. But I do not feel myself especially drawn to him, and he is more a convenience than a love. I realize this at the same time I know that I should not dismiss him so outright. That my affection for him ought to grow.

"There you are!" Bern swaggers toward us, sweat and dust mingling on his face and clothes. He grins widely. "Did you see the finish?"

"We did," Alice puts forth quickly. "It was exciting!" She is so much more vivacious than me, and quick to smile back at anyone. Somehow, her joy translates to an infectious

166

happiness that fills the air around her. We're almost exactly the same age, but she's not burdened by secrets, by the need for properness, or the strange draw to learn and inspect and doubt. I wish I could be like her.

"Yes," I intone instead. "Very much so."

"Jane! Time to get ready for lunch." Kate beckons me through the crowds, and I feel as though she is rescuing me. Alice and I follow her to the long tables groaning with food, and we unwrap the last few cheeses from the Brinkley farm. Bern follows us to eye the spread and gives an appreciative whistle.

"If this is lunch, I cannot wait to see when it's time to sup."

"Mrs. Weber made pies." All of us turn to see Doctor Kinney standing nearby, his shirtsleeves rolled up in the heat. "And I know Kate is always good with puttin' on a better celebration than the previous year. She outdoes herself every time."

"Go off, you." She waves him away teasingly.

I watch their banter. I do not know if I can read anything between them that is particularly flirtatious, though they are certainly animated with one another.

Widow Hawks approaches, the cornbread in her hands wrapped in smooth brown paper.

"What is she doing here?" Kate mutters. I am surprised at her sudden rancor.

"Well, you put me in charge of the food, and I thought all the women who wished to do so were contributing," I say, stumbling for an answer.

"Not her." Kate is seething mad. It's so obvious and palpable I could choke on it. I know I am the cause of her fast, dark mood, though I do not understand why.

"But she—"

"Tell her it's not wanted. I don't want her eating here!" She turns on her heel and marches away. I glance at the people who have overheard. Bern looks bemused and unshakable, as if he has heard this exchange before. Does he agree with Kate? Alice studies the ground, trying not to notice the row, and the doctor is a bit awry, as if the exchange befuddles him. It certainly does me. Even though I only found out last night that Widow Hawks and Kate are mother and daughter, I would have still asked the widow to help. Her simplicity, and how kind she has been to me from the start, weighs more on me than Kate's fickle temper. I go to Widow Hawks and move aside some of the dishes.

"Good," I tell her. "Thank you for bringing this over. It smells wonderful."

She gives a nod, and says almost sheepishly, "Well, I've never had the chance to do much for the celebrations. I'm happy to help."

There is more to this comment, I think. She is always trying to be well-liked, to be included in this town, though I feel that she does not help to break the stigma by wearing native adornments and clothing. Still, I know her cornbread to be delicious, and I thank her profusely.

Doctor Kinney appears at my side, looking excited.

"Your cornbread! I haven't had it in years!" He sneaks a piece out from the wrappings before I can swat his hand away. Widow Hawks laughs with delight.

Mitch Brinkley arrives, looking for Alice and his son, and his eyes light up at the cornbread, too. "Authentic native food? Let me try it!" He also grabs a piece.

Before long, a line forms, and we women stand aside so the menfolk can fill their stomachs. I watch Bern go through. He has washed up a bit after the first round of games. I try to tell myself that he is a good man, and I should be lucky to be doted upon. He fills his plate high as the rest, but he deliberately skips the cornbread, just as Kate walks over, steps through the line of people, and deftly pulls the plate off the table, leaving an empty space on the boards.

"Oh, but—!" I cannot help objecting. Alice quickly places her hand on my arm, tight and careful in warning, so I bite my tongue and stay quiet. The shame of my silence is choking, too.

Kate carries the remainder of the cornbread into the general store. Gilroy and Horeb let her pass without a single tease, but then again, they are both elbow deep in pig grease as they eat noisily. I can only imagine that Kate will toss it to the birds. I am utterly bewildered at her actions. It seems so unlike her. Out of the corner of my eye, I see Widow Hawks hover on the edge of the celebrations. She watches her daughter with a bowed head, resigned, as if this has happened before. Is she not the strong woman I think she is?

CHAPTER 11
4 July 1881

The games are charming. Children race in three-legged heats for the prize of a nickel, and the adults laugh over charades. Little ones dodge between legs, tripping many dancers, and babies fall asleep in the drowsy heat of the July afternoon. There is no true rest for many of the ladies, as we all hustle in the background to ensure the evening meal is laid out in plenty, though I do find time to watch some of the charades. Old Henry Brinkley, Mitch's father, offers a lively impression of a cowboy on a bucking bronco to the delight of the group. Thunder, a grizzled enigma and the oldest cowboy at the Svendsen ranch, manages to mime carrying off a blushing bride. Bern takes his turn as well, and makes everyone laugh with his example of a child who has lost his sweet in the dirt. I think, through my chuckles, that he is not so bad if he is willing to be silly like this.

"Drink." I turn to see the doctor holding a glass of sugared rainwater. I detect a bit of ale on him and squint.

"Have you been at one of the saloons, Doctor?"

"Ah, no, but it is a celebration after all, and some of the men have brought out their homemade beers and whiskeys. I don't mind a bit o' samplin'."

"Maybe you need that more than I," I tell him seriously, jerking my head at the water.

"Nonsense. You've a wee—"

"Hush!" I snap, and he has the grace to look about with guilt. I may have to keep an eye on him. He is Irish, after all, and Irishmen love their whiskey.

I watch him carefully during supper, and I catch his wink when he helps himself to an overlarge slice of my pie. He does not seem to be in any danger of being drunk, and I decide I may not need to worry about him after all. Bern, I notice, does not touch any liquor, which I find interesting. The rest of the Svendsen ranch hands are certainly enjoying the alcohol.

As evening falls, Kate lights lanterns around the perimeter of the makeshift dancing space in the middle of Main Street in front of her store. I help clean the tables with the women to the sound of the musicians warming up fiddles, jaw harps, and a banjo. The chords of song snippets echo around corners of buildings. It will be fun to do some dances. I think back to when the doctor spun me around the kitchen, and I cannot decide if I look forward to a dance with him, or Bern, or either of them at all. One is brotherly, the other eager for my attention, but I shouldn't be overtly partial to either in the case of romance. I think I've had my fill of such notions, as the child in my belly can attest.

I take off my apron and fold it onto the stairs leading up to the general.

"It went well, Jane. Thank you again," Kate says, as she passes me to take the last of her crockery up onto a table on the store's porch. Because I have angered her, I am not sure she will welcome my assistance next year, though I would so like to continue to be included in her plans. Once she had disposed of the cornbread, it seems Kate went back to being amiable for the rest of the afternoon. Widow Hawks has kept to the very periphery of the festivities. My heart still aches: I did not know there is bad blood between Kate and her mother.

"My pleasure. I hope to help again," I say, trying to keep any plead from my voice.

"Oh, most definitely I'll use your help," Kate agrees, as she comes back down the stairs. "I'll be glad for all the help I can get."

"Sure she will. So long as she don't have to talk much to the womenfolk, what with you doin' that for her," Horeb ribs, leaning comfortably in his chair, hands folded over his skinny belly. Where did he pack away that heaping mound of food?

"Sure," Gilroy agrees.

"Kitty."

I swing around, surprised at the nickname, but not surprised to see the doctor standing next to me, staring up at her.

"What?"

"Will you dance with me?" He holds out his hand, and I look at his open face, the lines nearly gone in his anxiety, and then at her, where she stands above us at the top of the steps. As I really look at her, I realize Kate does not look much like her mother. She looks down at him, and I think she seems much pleased with his request.

172

"Why, Pat," she says, almost coy as she takes his hand. "I thought you'd never ask me."

They walk, hand in hand, to join the other couples nearby, who are forming circles. I smile as I watch them. Even if I'm not an extremely talented housekeeper, I might be decent at matchmaking. I hope it makes him happy.

Toot Warren materializes out of the gathering dusk, and peers up at the gloom of the porch. "Gilroy Greenman, you may as well get your body down here to dance with me. I'm old as you, and we both of us might be dead this time next year. No use in waiting."

Horeb snorts, but there's a creak of a chair leg as Gilroy obediently follows Toot into the group of dancers. They bump into Trusty Willy and Elaine, where they tower over the majority of the people. Alan Lampton is cleaning off his pig spit, but his eyes are glued to Harriet Lindsey, who tries very hard to ignore him and maintain her patina of stiff schoolteacher properness. But her high color betrays her, and I'm not surprised when Alan asks her to dance the next song. She agrees, and as they waltz past, Alan's voice drifts up: "… my favorite pig, Mrs. Purty. The blasted Chinese …"

"You know, Toot's a good woman," Horeb confides to me, as we watch the couples come together. "Kept the Crow out of the liquor back in the '74 raid by putting all her cayenne pepper in it. Worked a charm."

I cannot help but giggle, forgetting myself, and Horeb looks pleased with my reaction to his gossip.

"Ah, and have you seen old Shen ride his pig around town yet?"

I shake my head. "I haven't. Yet."

Bern detaches from the other cowboys and waves, making a beeline toward us. When he reaches the general, he swings me around to the dancing with abandon. He is bursting with joy. Cowboys do not often get a day off like this. We mesh between the townsfolk and the handful of Army men in from Fort Randall. When the band plays the slower tunes, Bern holds me loosely and easily.

"I saw you at charades," I tell him.

He laughs a little. "I hope you don't think I'm too much of an idiot."

"On the contrary. It was quite endearing," I say truthfully. He gives me a happy grin and holds me a bit tighter.

"Your hands are fine? I didn't have a chance to ask you, but Anette and Sadie both said you'd burned yourself with lye water."

"An accident," I agree.

Looking away from Bern, I see Widow Hawks watching the dance, her dark eyes catching the lamplight and her deep skin glowing. I hesitate, then finally decide I must speak to Bern about her, and my misstep earlier in the day, if I am to consider any kind of future with him.

"I have embarrassed myself," I admit, and he looks down at me inquiringly. "I thought it was appropriate to have Widow Hawks make baked goods too, like all the other women. I didn't know she and Kate didn't get on."

I look up and see a slight frown on his face. He doesn't answer right away. At first, I think he will be the type who clams up, instead of discussing a displeasing subject.

Finally, he speaks. "I know you must stay with her, for proper's sake, but most of us don't like that she stays, now that old Davies is gone. She belongs with her people and she'd do right to leave her daughter alone, to give Kate the chance to make a life of her own without fuss."

"But she is Kate's own mother."

Bern sighs. "Let's not harp on this subject on such a fine night, Jane."

We finish out the song without more discussion, and I am not sure why I am disappointed.

The musicians take a break, so everyone finds a drink or refreshes their stomachs with the food still sitting out. I see Kate and the doctor talking animatedly, as if they are reconnecting for the first time, and I smile a bit to myself. Bern leaves to get us cold drinks. I'm so tired, but the night is still young.

"Jane. Don't weary yourself." Widow Hawks is at my elbow, gently steering me to a seat.

"I am so sorry about the cornbread," I half-whisper. "I didn't know!"

"It is all fine. It is not surprising to me. I did it for you. And to see if anything has changed. It has not. And that is what it is," she states pragmatically.

As we speak, I notice Bern standing across the dance floor, holding two cups. He watches us, and hesitates for the longest time, before turning away to talk to someone behind him. I frown, but before I can say anything, Doctor Kinney presents himself.

"Time for our dance, Mrs. Weber!" he exclaims, and takes my hand. The music players are back in place, grabbing up their instruments with gusto.

I look up at Widow Hawks, but she just smiles and murmurs in her native language, then English. "*Wačhíye!* You dance, Jane."

175

The doctor and I join the other couples swaying to the tune. He whirls me into his arms, holding me easily, as he did in the kitchen. I enjoy his embrace a bit more than Bern's, but I think it is only because I know the doctor better.

"Are you havin' a good time?" he asks me, his eyes twinkling with fun and, I suspect by the smell, a bit more whiskey.

"Well, I am, I suppose. And you are, too, I hope?"

He glances over my head, where I am sure Kate is waiting. "Aye. It has been good to talk freely with Kate today. We don't often have the time."

"You have a long history with her," I prompt, and he gives me a surprised look, but the drink seems to have loosened his tongue.

"I have known her a long time, Mrs. Weber. She was a beautiful girl when I first came here, and she has grown into a fascinatin' woman."

I nod silently to this and change the subject to discuss the day's activities. We enjoy our chat so much that we take the next dance, too. Bern eventually cuts in, and the doctor graciously relinquishes me halfway through our conversation. He does not look at Bern when he does so, but he gives me a small wink without a glimmer of a smile.

"The doc's dancing a lot with Kate," Bern mentions, nodding his head to them as they join the group again. "That's something to see."

"It is?"

"Most men don't dance with Kate, much. She doesn't encourage it, and besides, she's ..." He stops, and then gives me a little grin as the music picks up. "And here we be again!" We are swept away with the dancers.

But his words have me utterly confused. What is it about Kate that everyone seems to know, but no one wants to say?

Another break in the music finds me seated next to Alice, who looks wearier than I feel. I suppose she is tired from a long day in the heat, cooking, and minding little Pete. He is tucked into a basket nearby, as are several other infants, sleeping soundly regardless of the revelry around them. She tucks a corner of his blanket absently, and gives me a smile.

"You're having fun?" she asks.

"I am. It is good to be without the daily chores. Gives one time for socializing," I say.

"And Kate is too, for once." Alice nods across the night, where Kate still talks with the doctor. She is aglow with conversation, waving her hands animatedly. Was their friendship so diminished until tonight?

My own fatigue makes me less careful about my questions, and I fall into the habit of others in Flats Junction by asking almost tactlessly, "What is it about Kate that makes her so difficult?"

Alice gives a sideways glance. "You're her close confidante, aren't you?"

I shrug. "In a way. But I feel I do not know her at all. I hear of her history from others, really."

"I shouldn't. It's gossip."

"Of course. I don't mean for you to speak poorly of her. I only wondered. I like to find answers to questions. A bad habit," I admit.

I feel Alice give in before I hear her sigh. Relief breaks through the tension in my chest.

Finally, will another little town riddle be solved?

177

"With Kate being an ... well, she is illegitimate, and a half-breed to go with it. It is not a good combination even out here, even before the war," Alice says, laying bare the deep double stigma against Kate. She alludes to the heavy skirmishes between the Sioux and the white settlers, fought not even fifteen years ago, and the reference chaffs me. I desperately wish there was a way to learn more of the actual story of the Territories, beyond the snippets I recall from partial stories in the newspapers back East. I'd love to hear from men who fought, and women who lived through the fear.

Alice continues with Kate's story instead, lulling me into a smaller version of history.

"So, she was ignored at the best of times. Ostracized, taunted, and teased. When her brother died so young, she was left utterly alone."

"And her parents did nothing?"

"They ... had eyes for one another to be sure. And old Davies did what he could to curb what he heard. Nothing was ever really done to her outright, of course, out of respect for him and his station in town. He had a way of ... *bending* people to his will. Especially if they owed the bank money. Or if Mr. Davies made a deal with them. You understand? But what Kate endured must have been more than enough. From childhood on, I think she always felt she had to prove her worth, her legitimacy, her intelligence."

"So, she bought the general? To force everyone to work with her and respect her?"

Alice nods and shrugs at the same time, and looks down at her lap, fiddling with her skirt folds. "My belief is that she was able to overcome her pride and ... maybe her ...

178

strong dislike of her father to allow him to help her buy the general. Maybe she felt it was the least he could do. I don't believe she'd ever really forgiven him."

"I still don't see why she couldn't forgive her own mother." As I say the words, I am struck by my own relationships. I get along well enough with my mother, and should she ask for anything I would do my best to oblige. Perhaps my sense of duty toward her is because we now live a country apart. Mayhap I lived down the street from my parents, as Kate does, and there was past anger between us, I might not think so kind-heartedly if they meddled in my life.

The look Alice gives me is one of incredulousness, as if I am too dense and naive to understand. And she is right. I grew up with restricted lessons, a lack of daily newspapers until I was much older, and nothing in my own experiences compares to the way of life out here. I have had no pre-conceived notions, by fortune or providence. To have severe prejudice against the natives is not an immediate, nor truthful, response. I understand, of course, some in Flats Junction judge Widow Hawks, but she is nearly English in habit, regardless of her past misdeeds with Percival Davies. What is the harm of her? Unless ... Kate prohibits it, intent on some sort of backlash against her mother? Forcing her mother to ... what had she said once? That if Widow Hawks lived the rest of her life in vindication, it would not be enough. I see now her point, even if I do not agree with it completely.

Any further gossiping is cut short. Mitch and Bern present themselves as the music picks up again. Regardless of our tiredness, Alice and I smile at one another, sharing the warmth of womanly understanding, and stand to take the hands of our menfolk.

Doctor Kinney cuts back into my twirling after the fireworks. This time, he is obviously drunk, and I do not understand where he finds the liquor. I know he does not keep any in the house, so I can only suspect that more alcohol is served elsewhere, though very few other gentlemen are stumbling. I can only see three or four of the cowboys still dancing who are suspect. As I sway with the doctor, I look around, noticing several of the young lads languishing along the edge of the lantern light, hiccupping and red-faced.

"You danced with Bern nearly all night." It is more an accusation than a statement, and I try to shush him. His skin is flushed in the soft yellow lantern lights, and, like all of us, he is sweating in the night heat, though it smells more like booze than anything natural.

"He is the only one who asks much," I say, placating and reasonable. The doctor gives an annoyed shrug.

"He's not who I would have chosen as your beau."

That he has an opinion at all is slightly surprising, though I suppose the doctor would take an interest in the man who might steal away his new housekeeper.

"I wanted to thank you for the salve for my hands," I redirect his thoughts. "I'm sure it will help."

"Oh, you found that, did you?" He smiles absently. "Good, good."

I'd like to say how I found his thoughtfulness especially touching, and how his little label buries itself in my mind, but he grouses again about the heat and the lack of sweets at the food tables, and his attitude breaks the moment.

Thankfully, our dance is short, and I am in Bern's arms again for the last three songs. I watch the doctor out of the corner of my eye. He dances once more with Kate, then joins the cowboys still tipping back the jugs.

The music stops a bit after ten o'clock. Mitch Brinkley appears at my elbow.

"Pardon, Mrs. Weber. The doc's done his annual enjoyment of the whiskey. I'll help you take him home."

I follow his glance, and I am dismayed. The doctor sprawls with the worst of them. He looks in no shape to walk the short distance home without aid. I doubt he can even stand. The cowboys are singing a silly tune now that the musicians have stopped the music, and I blush when I hear the nature of the song. It includes a lady's skirt, and something about her bosom. One of the Army officers seems to be the leader of the bawdy ballad, his arm rotating in lazy circles a step behind the beat.

"That's enough, then." Bern takes charge at my silence. He and Mitch extract the doctor from the group. Slinging one arm around each of their shoulders and sandwiched between them, the doctor stumbles and starts toward his house.

I follow, uncertain what to do. I feel it is my place to see him settled. A shadow steps next to me. It is Widow Hawks.

"Every year he does this," she says quietly. "I am usually the nursemaid."

"I'll do it this time," I say.

She gives her head a little shake.

"I can do it," I insist. "I'm not too tired."

"It's not that, Jane," she says gently. "I'm only thinking of your reputation."

"My—" I stop. My pregnancy might not show, but it will not do to spend a night alone in the doctor's house. She is right.

"I'll let you take care of him, if you feel it is your duty," she continues. "But I'll spend the night too, like I always do each year."

As our group ascends the two steps of Doctor Kinney's porch, I open the door. Bern and Mitch haul the slurring doctor up the stairs to his bed. He collapses, but is still awake, trying to put two sentences together. He is disheveled and ridiculous. Oddly, I am more worried than upset. I did not expect this of him.

"Alright then?" Bern looks at me. I glance at the bed, where Doctor Kinney now mindlessly hums an Irish ditty.

"Widow Hawks and I will manage from here," I say, sounding more confident than I feel. He nods tightly and does not look at the older woman as he and Mitch leave the room and clamber down the stairs. Widow Hawks and I wait quietly until the screen door slams.

"That was kind of Bern," she mentions.

"Doesn't he typically help around town?"

She slides a glance my way. "No. Courting you has changed him."

"I see." I hope I do.

"I'll bring up a few cool cloths," she says into my uncomfortable shift. "In the meantime, why don't you take off his boots?"

I look at the doctor. The last time I was alone with a helpless man was when Henry lived. He was, in the end, too weak to manage much for himself, and I was a capable helper. I suppose I can draw on that strength, though for some reason, the alcohol is more unsettling than cancer. At least Henry had always had his wits about him, until sleep had become all he could manage.

182

Drawing up to the bed, I untie the laces and take off the heavy, dusty, well-worn shoes. He starts to sing again, watching with bleary eyes. It is a tune about a girl with lovely eyes and ample hips. I try not to listen. Then the song switches again, his voice slurring and thick.

I met a girl last summer
with beauty in her eyes
and in this song we call life
we seemed to harmonize
And though I didn't know it
my luck began to slide
it was getting closer to the day
when I'd be tied and dried

"Jane, here's towels. And some water, too." Widow Hawks returns. He quiets and closes his eyes. I wonder how much the room is spinning for him, or if he will even remember how we help him now. I hope he really only does this the one time a year, and I do not have to expect a repeat at Christmas.

Widow Hawks heads downstairs again to make tea. I turn to Doctor Kinney, now half-propped up in his rumpled bed, watching me with a small smile on his face. Well, at least he is not an angry or mean drunkard! It could be worse.

"Mrs. Weber," he says sluggishly, his brogue muddled. "Beautiful—"

"Drink this," I say, and hand him the water.

"Beautiful," he says again, and dutifully guzzles. "Kate. Kate seemed to enjoy dancin' with me."

"I noticed," I say shortly, and remove his stockings. I gently press his shoulder back. "Lay down now. How do you feel?"

"I feel fine," he says, slurring the last word. "How are you feelin', sweet mother?" His hand comes up, and he haphazardly rubs my arm.

I take his fingers and hold them in both of mine. "I am fine, Doctor. Don't you worry about me."

"But I do!" he insists, and he tries to sit up again. I can smell the booze reeking through his every pore. "I don't want you workin' too hard."

"I'm not working now. Lay down," I plead, squeezing his fingers. I free a hand from his and place a cool, damp towel on his sweating forehead. "Tell me about Kate. Did you like dancing with her, too?"

He gives a broad smile. "Oh, aye. Aye. She's just lovely, a special woman. Do you know I was a bit taken with her when I stayed with her parents? Before I had the house. I know some of the men around here won't look twice at her because she's half Sioux, and if she didn't have the general they'd probably want her out of town too … but I don't mind. I was an outcast in Boston as a child, bein' Irish. We're kindred spirits, Kate and I."

"Of course," I soothe. "A man would be lucky to have her as his wife."

"He would. A battle for his children, though, with native blood. And Mrs. Weber," he says, and twists to look up at me. "Always wanted to fill up the rooms with little ones." He gets a bit teary at this comment, so I think it's wise to have him drink a bit more water.

"You need something else to sober you up."

"I'm soberin'," he insists, but his words are still fuddled. I shake my head at him, and rise from the side of the bed, but he grips me close. "Mrs. Weber, are you leavin' already?"

"Just wait here, I'll be back in a moment."

"I'll wait." His eyes pierce mine, clear and blue. I frown, shaking the quiver of uncertainty flashing through my chest, and leave the room.

He is soundly asleep when I come back up with the water. Setting the glass on the table, I pull the chair closer to the bed to keep watch in case he needs something else, or, worse, wakes to empty his stomach. But I am well tired, and nod off almost immediately.

CHAPTER 12
5 July 1881

"Mrs. Weber."

I wake to a hand taking mine. The bandages are dirty. I've forgotten to re-wrap them after the activities of the Fourth, but at least the stinging is gone, and the blisters itch inside the linen. I'll take the itching over the pain.

Blinking in the early morning light, Doctor Kinney sits up on his bed, still in rumpled clothes, but looking rather well for his rough night. His lips are dry and he still smells like old booze, but he seems clearheaded enough.

"Are you alright?" I ask, relieved he appears somewhat recovered.

"Aye, I am, though a bit tired," he admits. "But I am appalled you stayed on."

"Widow Hawks is below. I think she slept on the floor in the kitchen," I say, but he shakes his head.

"Not that. Damn the properness. It's that you slept in the chair. You, pregnant." He pulls me up. "You must get some proper rest. I'd be a poor physician if I didn't insist. Here." He takes me across the hall to his aunt's room.

"But breakfast," I protest. "And at least the coffee."

"I managed before you came to Flats Junction. And though I prefer your brew over mine, I can take on the kitchen for a day," he says lightly. "Here you be."

He nearly forces me onto the bed, and draws the thin, patched curtain over the window. I sit and watch. I am exhausted, but also unsure about my employer's insistences.

"I can go down."

He gives me a stern look. "If you're so worried on my abilities in the kitchen, I'll ask Widow Hawks to help. Rest. You must. I couldn't let you work for me this mornin' after you stayed up until the early hours to manage my annual abandon. Please, Mrs. Weber."

It's no use arguing, and I am very tired. I lay down and close my eyes. The soft mattress feels like heaven. I have not been on a real mattress since Massachusetts. The doctor hasn't even left the room before I am asleep.

CHAPTER 13
5 July 1881

A plate rattles against cutlery, and I stir awake. It takes a moment to realize where I am. The light is bright and clean and yellow in his aunt's bedroom. The curtain does little to hide the midday sun.

"Widow Hawks made some jacks." The doctor balances a plate and a glass of milk on one of the slabs of wood I use for a tray.

"You've eaten, then?" I ask, sitting up. "I can certainly eat downstairs."

"Too late, brought it all up already." He hands me the plate piled high with the pancakes, cheese, bread, and tomatoes.

He goes to his room, comes back with the chair, and draws it next to me. I eat easily; it's good, more so because I did not have to make it. The bread is soft on the inside yet, and there is butter on some of the slices, which I eat first. There is sheep's milk cheese, soft and tangy.

188

"Mrs. Weber, I ..." He stops and gives me a hopeful look. "I hope I did not say anythin' last night that offended you."

I finish my bite and wave his comment away. Swallowing, I say, "You were a gentleman."

"I highly doubt that," he says, looking guilty. "I apologize you had to see me like that."

"You said it was your annual abandon," I remind him. "I cannot blame a man for indulging once or twice a year."

"You don't blame it on me because I'm Irish?" he asks candidly.

I frown. The thought had not occurred to me, and I shake my head. "I've lived among many Irish and most were not drunkards."

Am I unique in my lack of prejudice? Intolerance seems to always simmer beneath surfaces, but it's never been a thing to affect me directly. Henry had had opinions, and my father as well. But I'd always preferred to research before landing on a final decision. If pressed, I'd usually say I could not form an opinion without further inquiry. It had frustrated Henry to no end after we married. *Stop considering and just do! Decide! Do you not have a final opinion, Jane?* He'd say such things in frosty frustration when I'd debate over anything. I learned to hide my mind and questions from my husband, same as most of my society.

The doctor does not seem to immediately jump to conclusions or prejudice either. I suppose he had to handle many in the East who did not have a kindness for his heritage, just as the people in the West do not care for the natives.

"Doctor Kinney, I've been wondering about your accent," I tell him suddenly, the thought coming with my

189

reflections on the Irish of Boston. "You say you're Irish, and your name certainly is so. But you sound different."

"Aye. Scots-Irish," he agrees. "It's a reflection of my childhood. My great-aunt's employer, Andrew McClure, was from Ulster. You know the difference?"

I shake my head negative, and he gives me a small smile, leaning his elbows onto his knees and twirling a finger to remind me to keep eating as he talks.

"Many in Ulster have some Scottish blood. Back, oh … near three hundred years ago, the local chief in the north of Ireland, Conn O'Neill, gave large tracts of land to two Scotsmen in return for savin' his life. Over time, those Scotsmen brought over many of their kin to work the land of Ireland, bringin' with them their own version of Gaelic and customs. Of course, you can't stop a boy and girl from fallin' in love and many an Irishman married a Scottish lass, or the other way 'round, and there you have it. It didn't help when anyone comin' over from Ireland or Scotland in the Famine years were grouped together by the Americans who couldn't always tell the difference in accents, either."

I settle back against the headboard. "You're good at little history lessons."

He grins and sits up straight. "Anyway, you might say Mr. McClure rubbed off overmuch on me. I always did want to be like him when I was a wee boyo. I'm only sorry he never could be part of my adventure into the West." He grows pensive, then looks at me hard, his face suddenly unreadable.

"Mrs. Weber. Your husband. He died when?"

I gulp down the milk too quickly and cough. The doctor automatically thumps me on the back, and I straighten as best I can.

190

"Midwinter."

"Ah. And ... left you little money?"

Heat fills my cheeks. What does my financial position matter? "I sold the house to pay for the business debts he had left, and then closed the doors of the shipping company. I didn't know enough to keep it running and his business partner had passed already. I had enough for the train ticket here." And enough to live meanly in Rockport in early penury or with some charity, or to work in a great house with some leisure, or to purchase another ticket back to Massachusetts if I had to. But other than that, I have little to my name. And the bit of money I make whenever the doctor has the cash for my wages goes to Widow Hawks for my use of her home and bed. She takes it resignedly, but I'm glad to pay her.

He nods. "I know the way of it. When Mr. McClure died, after the debts were paid, there was little money left by the way of an inheritance."

I don't know what to say to his revelation, and bow my head over the last of the cheese.

"Well, I'm glad I did not say anythin' inappropriate last night," he says.

"You mainly talked about Kate and how beautiful she is, and how you liked dancing with her," I explain.

He looks boyishly sheepish, embarrassed at my words. "I did, eh?"

"You ought to formally court her," I recommend to him, though I find I do not have much zeal behind the words. I say it because I think it is what he desires, and I want him to have happiness. He is a kind man, and he deserves the children he says he dreams about. He is silent for a minute.

We hear Widow Hawks in the kitchen below us, tinkering with the cutlery.

Finally, he sighs. "I am glad you were here," he says quietly, taking the empty plate from my hands. "It was nice to wake to a friendly face."

I look up at him and smile. "I agree."

He stops at the door and glances at my bandages, visibly making a note in his mind, before nodding absently and clattering back downstairs.

CHAPTER 14
5 July 1881

I manage to make supper without any mishaps after my nap. Widow Hawks stays with me the whole day. She explains that it is to make sure I am not too tired, but she keeps an eye on Doctor Kinney as if she is waiting for him to relapse or collapse. He does neither, and he seems his usual self through the evening meal.

When I walk out the door with her, Bern is waiting. He is not surprised to see Widow Hawks, but tips his hat only at Doctor Kinney, who has followed us out.

"Thank you for your help last night, Bern," the doctor says. His voice is neutral.

Bern gives a brief nod. "Yes sir, Doc."

The three of us walk back through town. Widow Hawks hurries her pace until she is several feet ahead of us, leaving us alone, though we do not have much to say to each other today. I keep my eyes on her back so I do not need to meet Bern's. I am embarrassed on behalf of the doctor, and

193

nervous because I know Bern is not partial to Widow Hawks. As I gaze at her tall back, she stops suddenly, then almost breaks into a run. She stumbles once over one of the rail ties. The ungainly trip is so unlike her it scares me.

Bern actually crosses the tracks today. When we catch up with Widow Hawks, I see the windows of the house are wide open, the hides and calico ripped away, and the door itself is hacked to pieces, as if hundreds of hammers or a dozen small axes were used to utterly damage the wood. It is irreparable.

The entire outside of the house has been vandalized.

"Oh no," I breathe. Widow Hawks hurries inside to see if the vandals ventured inside, but I stand, flabbergasted, with a silent Bern.

"Did you know of this?" I ask him, thinking he might have a pulse on the townsfolk. Would he know who might do this cruelty? If he does, will he even tell me?

He looks away.

"Bern," I say again. He looks back, his dark eyes heavily shaded by the brim of his hat. "Who would do such a thing?"

He sighs. "Most of the town, and a lot of the cowboys, don't like her here. They want her to go back to her people, join the reservation, and leave us in peace."

"But she doesn't *do* anything disruptive!" I insist angrily. "Do you mean to say you agree with everyone?"

"Jane," he says, placating. "I know you are closer to her than most, since you have to live with her, but you don't know the history here. When she was staying with old Davies, they did what they pleased, and it was thrown in everyone's face. Even after the Crow raid of '74, when

194

everyone stopped feeling kindly toward the Indians, her kin came into town every summer to visit her when they stopped at their ancestral buffalo hunting grounds. They still do. If it weren't for their camp, the Crow would never have come or raided. People would still have their limbs. Heck, Franklin Jones was a cooper! Now you know he and his family lives mostly on charity. Nels Henderssen—Clara's husband? He was a farmer, and a damn good one. Because of the Sioux … and the Crow, he has no leg. They've had to move into town so he can scrape by with a small hobby farm and selling chickens. You just wait. The Sioux will be here soon again."

"Surely, she would ask them to stop doing anything bad," I protest. "Or at the very least, Percival Davies would have done so in the past."

"Never." He gives a hard, rueful chuckle and moves his eyes away from mine. "They are her family. I sometimes think he joined them at night around their bonfires up on the cliff."

"So?"

"So it ain't done, Jane." He is suddenly beyond irritable, tips his hat, and leaves me standing without anything more to go on.

I enter the home. Widow Hawks is kneeling by the fire. Sound travels through the thin wooden walls of the homes here, and I know she has overheard our conversation. Her head is bowed.

"I cannot leave town, you know," she says quietly. "Kate is my only family, my daughter, my little girl. I don't want to leave her."

I go to kneel next to her, and bite back an immediate response. Surely Widow Hawks sees that Kate wants nothing to do with her. Why hold on? I suppose I might understand these ties better once I am a mother. I reflect in the silence. When this babe is born, I will love it, of course. But will I do anything for it, and wish to care for it forever? I shake my head inwardly. I cannot fathom the deep love all say exists between parent and child. I must live it myself before I can judge.

"Perhaps we should tell Kate about this trouble?" I offer.

"She won't care," Widow Hawks says with finality and I know she is right. "No, let it be. We will mend the window papers and hides. The door will hold through the fall. I will see if Patrick can find us wood at the O'Donnell lumberyard. Since Percy died, he does these things for me. Now that my husband is gone, I find myself unwelcome most places otherwise."

"It's not right." My voice is defiant.

She reaches over to take my hand and gives a small laugh.

"Of course it is not right. Is prejudice ever so? But it is the way of people." She pauses. "Mine and yours, both."

CHAPTER 15
30 July 1881

As Bern predicted, the Sioux arrive in Flats Junction at the end of July. A ruckus careens through the streets, first an echo, then a whooping. I rush to the screen door while wiping my hands on my apron, trying to find the fuss. I cannot see anything at first, but as soon as I step outside, Mrs. Molhurst sniffs next door on her porch, shaking her head while peering down the corner of East Avenue, where it curves onto Main Street.

"What is it?" I ask her, my voice carrying easily across the yard, and jumping over the elderberry bushes she painstakingly tends.

She gives me a tight, appraising look. Mrs. Molhurst has consistently disapproved of me ever since I displayed my inability to handle that small nest of mice. Of all the neighbors on the doctor's street, in fact, she is the least welcoming. I am not sure if she had hoped for my job to carry her through her widowhood, or if she doesn't approve of my

197

boarding with an Indian, or if she simply does not like me. I will likely never really know.

"Blackfoot," she says. Then she scurries inside.

It must be Widow Hawks' family come to visit. I wait a moment longer, just as a large group comes jostling around, cutting through Sadie Fawcett's lawn. Some are on horses, an elderly woman reclines on a travois, and a few children dance around the edges. They are all dressed in buckskin, buffalo hides, and faded calico. Realizing I'm staring, I move back and stand inside the screen door to watch them pass. As I count the dark heads, I notice Widow Hawks among them. They head north on Second Avenue, taking Buffalo Jump Path past St. Aloysius. I'm both nervous and curious. But they are Widow Hawks' family! Well, when I am done with my chores I will go meet them. For now, I must harvest the second crop of beans for canning. Alice Brinkley has promised to show me how to preserve, and I need to work on the laundry. Doctor Kinney has kindly agreed to pull water during lunchtime.

He comes in from his rounds around noon and brings in the pails for soaking sheets. He works quickly regardless of the heat.

"The *Sihasapa* are here. Would you like to meet Widow Hawks' sisters, brother, and their kin?"

"I would love to," I say sincerely. I find I mean my sincerity, truly, and it surprises me. I care for Widow Hawks, and I wish to understand her family better. And maybe ... I feel a bit beholden to do so, as if I should help fill Kate's absence, though I should never presume I would ever replace a true blood daughter.

The doctor gives me a wide grin, turns to refill a pail, then swings back. "Perhaps you should give Widow Hawks time with them tonight. She'll likely camp up on the cliffs. Kate ought to be able to find a bunk for you in her back room."

I do not know how I feel about Kate anymore. She seems to think the incident of the cornbread over, and she talks to me like I am her dear friend, but I am troubled by her lack of regard for her mother. Perhaps there is still another piece to the story I do not know. Is it as simple as anger running deep? I nod in agreeance with the doctor anyway, turning back to the bread as he ambles to the well for more water.

"You're set," he says, bringing the last of the laundry down from his bedroom. We have a nice way of it now. He is not angry with me for trying to do too much, and I am grateful for the help. Though I am finally seasoning to the hardness of labor in the Territories, I am just now starting to thicken in the waist and I will soon be unable to do much lifting regardless of my desire to keep from being a bother. He seems to know this innately without me drawing attention to my widening size, and once again I'm grateful. Desperately, deeply grateful.

I pull a small cast iron skillet down from a hook and fry some eggs with dill weed to go with fresh bread. As he sits down to eat, I find the courage to ask my next round of questions.

"Bern seemed to think Widow Hawks isn't welcome here." I think of the animals at her doorstep, and the damage to her home. I find I do not trust the quiet of the town so much when it comes to the topic of the natives. I'm also

199

fearful for my own safety more than ever, even though no one has been unkind.

The doctor presses his lips together. He knows about the vandalism. He found a new door for Widow Hawks relatively quickly. I hurry on now that I have found a voice.

"Or more, the townsfolk don't like the natives coming to town. I shouldn't really pry, but I hope her family won't meet with much ... intolerance while they are here? I cannot expect they do harm to anyone."

"They don't," he says. "They don't bother to trade with Kate; she has explained she has no need for pelts or native arts. But one or two might find their way into the mess hall by the depot or the Golden Nail, and alcohol does not sit well with them. And they do their fires and dances, as usual, for it's a bit of a ... holiday for them to come through here."

"Bern mentioned they visit their ancestral grounds."

"Aye. The old buffalo jump." Doctor Kinney nods. "You can still find the bones of bison on the bottom of the cliff. The Blackfoot Sioux would drive the herds there for easier, safer huntin'. Hundreds and hundreds of years ago now. And then the wagon trail used to stop up there, too. Good view, safe place to camp."

"But they don't go wild in town?"

"No."

"That doesn't sound awful at all," I say.

The doctor takes a thoughtful bite of bread. "No. But it unnerves the conservatives." He gives a tight one-shoul-dered shrug. "And no one likes too much of a brush-in with the Blackfoot. They all still think about the war like it hap-pened yesterday. And I suppose ... well ... some lost kin in the skirmishes. Not too many from Flats Junction, but when even one man is lost here, everyone takes it personally."

I ask him to explain the viewpoint of the town to me. The news back East always cast Custer as a sensational hero after the Civil War and during the Reconstruction. Even I had been taken in by his wild and handsome face on the cover of *Harper's Weekly*. Only five years ago his last battle and death hit the papers. Everyone was shocked about the turn of the battles, appalled that the natives had killed a hero. Headlines had screamed about the indignity of it all. But my mother had tried very hard not to let us be completely mindless about written words. She'd always say there was more to any story. The compelling chance for more narrative and research surges through me.

"You know of the reservation?" he asks, mouth full with lunch.

I nod. I have heard tell of it, but of course I don't know much about it, or what it means, or even how it all came about.

"Well, before the Army arrived, the territory was mainly Cheyenne and Sioux tribes hereabouts. Widow Hawks' people pushed out the Cheyenne. But when Custer came out and found gold in the *Paha Sapa* back in '74, the subsequent rush created a lot of problems with the local tribes. And the government wanted the gold, too. So, they took more land for the Territories, the sacred *Paha*—" He stops and shakes his head. "The Black Hills, so they're called by us. Anyway, eventually many of the different peoples got together, lots of the Sioux and Cheyenne especially, and decided the only way to keep their way of life was to ... well ... start a war."

201

I listen hungrily. He is a good storyteller, and even though he lived through this war, he tells it so that I am not keen on either side, but can see the war dispassionately and carefully. I do not ask many questions, preferring to hear the whole of it first. We enjoy talking so much that he starts to help with the laundry so we can continue. I hear of the story of the Battle of Little Bighorn—or the Greasy Grass as the Sioux call it—and more of the Cheyenne and Arapaho nations. He speculates about the great leader called Sitting Bull, who is rumored to still be ensconced somewhere in the Canadian wilderness in the north, and he deftly lists the many inter-native wars that had crisscrossed the plains on top of the settlers coming in.

I am mesmerized. It is the best lesson I have had since I left school so many years ago, and it gives me more knowledge about the history out in the Territories than any newspaper would care to publish. I realize the railroad that goes past Flats Junction is incredibly new. Only two years ago, it was attacked by renegade Sioux who had still wished to keep whites out. I am glad I did not know all these stories when I agreed to come West. I might not have been courageous enough.

"How do you know all this history?" I ask, as he wipes his hands of talc and water casually on a corner of my apron.

"Percy Davies would talk about everythin' Indian with reverence over supper, and he made sure to give both sides of any tale for his wife's sake. Widow Hawks will tell stories too. I enjoy learning about the past, and so did my dear auntie. As for the wars ... well, old Henry Brinkley fought out of duty to the government, but had a pretty hard time of it afterwards, and sometimes I think it eased his mind to talk of it with me. Henry never seemed to get over the required ransackin' of Indian villages that the Army did. I used to wonder if it was because Percy loved and married a native girl, and Percy and Henry were close. I think Henry's hesitancy about hurtin' the Sioux rubbed off on some of his sons. The Brinkley boys are generally decent to Widow Hawks. Strange to see how our lives might affect any children we may have."

I agree with him, and I think over his words as I take my time over the last of the laundry.

The doctor paints a picture of a happy, loving Davies home. I rather like the way he makes Percy Davies sound. How could the banker and Widow Hawks be so blind to Kate's alienation by the town? They seemed to be attentive, at least to themselves and aware of the world around them. Or did Kate make it worse on herself somehow? Was she too proud, or overly smart? Those qualities are never becoming to any girl, let alone one who is struggling with prejudice from the start.

And then I think about how the doctor speaks of children, how he still plans very much to have some. I'm glad for him, if he thinks his future with Kate is possible. I know he holds her in high esteem, enough to get a bit bashful when I bring her up. I hope they are well suited. He, being a man of science, and Kate, with her hard independence and strong opinions about her mother, seem a strange match.

But perhaps opposites attract. Perhaps that is what makes a union fiery and passionate. Henry and I were both suitably muted, and we could only share a small bit of tenderness.

203

I should like to think a true romance, like the one between Percy Davies and Widow Hawks, had quite a bit of passion to keep them so happy for so long.

CHAPTER 16
30 July 1881

We eat a simple supper of bread and cheese, which I slice right off the crusts as we eat. Then the doctor and I head toward the cliff. The shade of the pine trees swarms with bodies in hides, furs, beads, and calico. I am nervous, but one glance at Doctor Kinney's happy eagerness puts me at ease. So far, I have not been remiss to trust him.

"Will they welcome me?" I ask.

He gives me a warm look. "I'm sure by now Widow Hawks has told them all about you, about the comin' baby, that you are like a daughter to her."

"She would say that?" I am taken back. While I find myself caring more and more for the older woman, I did not think she would so easily return the feelings.

"She's often said it in such a way to me."

"When do you see her so much?"

He shrugs. "Kate is often unable to drop off the goods Widow Hawks needs, so I take a box once or twice a week to her."

I fall silent. Does the doctor manage her household and needs as a son would? Is it because he is beholden to her for accepting him into town? Or simply because he is a good man, and believes her to be his adoptive family?

We arrive, and the doctor is quickly enveloped by some of the men. The ponies grazing nearby are decorated prettily, with beadwork on the blankets draped across their backs, and feathers in their manes. I recall the doctor mentioning horses as a sign of wealth. So then, Widow Hawks' family is well off. There are strange smells of things cooking over fires that I do not recognize. Small huddles of women, old and young, mingle with children of various ages, and the men circle with Doctor Kinney. He has started to pull unexpected things from his pockets: buttons, a spool of fishing line, and hard candy for the little ones. Around this group, though, it is obvious that many do not speak English. Even so, the doctor reveals he has some working knowledge of their language. He seems to be thrilled to review his vocabulary.

"Jane!" Widow Hawks comes over with a smile. She gives me her hand, and turns to the old woman sitting in a crumple of mismatched calico strips, deer hides, and even a bit of buffalo fur in the heat. She is brown, her skin a deeply lined almond, and her black eyes are buried in sunken sockets, but she smiles, showing missing teeth.

"My mother," Widow Hawks says, by way of introduction. Sinking to my knees, I give a little bob of a bow as the native language washes over me. I do not know what Widow Hawks says, but her mother continues to smile, then leans forward and takes my hand. Her grip is strong and bony and arthritic. Who would have ever expected me to be circled by a large number of Indians? I'm a bit apprehensive, but oddly I don't have a racing heart.

I try to stand once the older woman releases me, but Widow Hawks holds me down firmly. "My mother and sisters wish to get to know you."

But I do not speak their language, so at first, I sit quietly, almost reverently, next to the matriarch. There is high laughter and chatter among the women, and yet it is not out of control, and I am not frightened. I feel a tap on my shoulder. It is one of the younger women. She takes up my hand and draws into it with her finger. She does not look particularly pleased about what she is drawing. I do not want to offend, so I continue allowing the young woman to silently draw circles in my palm, though I'm unnerved. The grandmother leans in to watch, and gazes into my face before shaking her head and calling out. Widow Hawks appears again.

Crouching next to me, Widow Hawks watches, then sighs softly, glancing at her mother.

"My sister-in-law, *Hantaywee*, has a way with ... spirits. She draws a moon in your hand."

"She does not look very happy about it," I say worriedly. "Should I ask her to stop?"

"She will stop when she feels it is right. My mother says you will either have a very good pregnancy, or have need to be fertile again in your life. They know you are widowed, like me."

"Oh dear," I say. Because much of this is very blunt and open, I feel more than a bit exposed. Widow Hawks gives my arm a squeeze.

"You are doing well. I know it is a lot."

"Before I forget, I am to stay with Kate tonight. So, you needn't worry about me with your family here."

"I see." Her eyes flick over her kin.

"It's not that I do not want to meet them all," I explain. "It was Doctor Kinney, thinking I needed to sleep elsewhere so that you would not need to bother."

Her face softens, and she glances at the doctor before sinking to her knees beside me.

"Stay, *Dowanhowee*. The house is open for you. I'll stay here with my family tonight. It is our old place, a place of the ancestors, and they tell me it will be the last time. You will be able to sleep without interruption."

I am very relieved there is no need to ask Kate for charity tonight. "Thank you. Tell me, though, please, what was that you called me?"

Her eyes laugh, and she nods to her brother and nephews. "They've given you a *Sihasapa* name, Jane. You made an immediate impression when you spoke."

"I suppose I should thank them?"

"No need. Now, to serve the food."

The woman releases my hand, and I rise to help Widow Hawks and others serve a meal. We offer her family native cooking, and I do not know what I am doling out in mismatched cutlery, but it smells delicious. The doctor asks to have some too, even though we just recently finished supper.

"I did not know you liked this type of cooking," I say, as I ladle fragrant beans. He sits with the men in a separate circle.

"You forget, Mrs. Weber, that when I first arrived, this is all I was served in the Davies' home. It's a treat to get it now. Like this *agúyapi*." He lifts a piece of fried bread.

208

I cannot help but admit to him, a bit proudly, "They've apparently given me an Indian name."

"What is it?"

"Don't ask me to pronounce it!"

He glances around, announcing he will find out so he can call me by it, but I know he is teasing.

"Do they not have a name for you?" I ask. He nods around a mouthful.

"They do indeed, though I earned the most recent one only three or so years ago, when they figured I was not goin' to marry. I am called *Takoda* now. Friend-To-Everyone. Though before that I was simply *Peḣiŋ Akáŋ Lúta.* Red-On-The-Surface-Hair."

"Oh," I reply, glancing at his dark head. "But you're not much of a redhead."

He laughs. "That's what I said, too. I guess the sun hit it just right the first time I met them all."

Once everyone is served, I join Widow Hawks. She oversees the cornbread finishing in the fire.

As I watch the bread brown, I finally ask, "What is your full name?"

She gives me a sideways glance full of bewilderment, and I amend my question. "Everyone in town calls you Widow Hawks, but I know you did not marry Percy with such a name."

"My name, when I met Percy, was Flies-With-Hawks. Or just Čatán, for Hawk, because my mind always seemed to be soaring in the heavens with the birds, thinking up fanciful futures for myself. It was an apt name, and I keep it to this day. Now I will think of it as a way to watch over my family from a distance."

I frown, unable to catch her meaning. "Won't they come again next summer?"

She shakes her head, and I see sadness stretch across her broad features, strong and deep.

"No, Jane. This is the last of it. They will slowly make their way to Fort Buford in Montana, where they will join Sitting Bull's people. It has been said he is going into the reservation at last. There are no more free People. *Hečato weye*. It is so."

CHAPTER 17
31 July 1881

The next day, I am surprised when Bern meets me on my walk to the doctor's in the morning. If I see him in the early part of the day, he is usually busy with his morning chores at the livery before heading out to the Svendsen ranch.

"You stayed with the Indians last night?" He is almost accusatory. "I looked for you, but Sadie saw you and the doc leaving to visit with them after supper."

"I slept in my usual bed at Widow Hawks' house. They all slept outside in the hills." I hope I do not sound too defensive.

He shakes his head. "When are they leaving?"

"They didn't give me their plans. I do not speak their language, you know." I think guiltily of my newly minted Indian name, but I realize Bern will not think it extraordinary.

"Well, they should head off. People aren't happy about them in town to begin. The sooner they go, the less chance for trouble."

I lift my chin. "I was told they plan to live on the reservation now. They won't be back. At least, not next year." Truthfully, I have no idea what it means for the Sioux to go into the reservation, and I only know the idea inexplicably fills me with sadness. Bern, on the other hand, seems to relax at the news, though he does not respond to it.

He simply gives me his customary hat brim touch and leaves me at the entry of the doctor's house.

CHAPTER 18
8 August 1881

In the hot sweltering heat of August, I slave over the canning
jars. Alice wavers next to me, and her little Pete coos happily in
a pile of blankets. I have learned to can green beans, and now
we are making chutney. So far, with Alice's help, I am able to do
this task without much failure, and the larder is filling nicely for
fall. I take the time to write down her instructions as she gives
them, so I might do the same next summer too. Her gentle babe
gives me hope that I will have time to do this, even with a child
of my own to watch over. I harbor a little hope that I might be
able to join the Brinkley women for their annual can. If I can
get to know Alice's sisters-in-law, it is possible.

Alice is generous to give me some of her family jars
to use, as well as her time. My gooseberries, currants, and
raspberries will make good sauces for the winter. The harvest
is plenty already, and I plan to salt and dry most fresh foods.
As for the chutney, it will be a luxury to have sugary things
on hand. The doctor does have a sweet tooth.

She tells me how to boil each mix long enough without burning so the fruit will store without spoiling. While I did not have a very easy life in Boston, I did not have to worry over the food the same way that I do here. By some luck, kitchen duties come natural to me so that I am not daunted by food tasks, but rather enjoy them. As for everything else in the Dakotas, there is no guarantee I'll do right, or succeed, or even know the best action.

Yesterday I was supposed to help the doctor with an emergency bullet removal at the Main Inn. No one would say exactly how the farmer ended up with a lead ball in his leg, and the blood was horrible, dousing the linen on the operating table a deep, thick ruby. I had no idea what to do, and the doctor ended up nearly shouting at me. I'd handed him the wrong instruments most of the time, completely failed at keeping my stomach at the sight of all the blood and exposed meat of the man's leg, and couldn't even manage a proper dressing of the finished, sewed wound. Doctor Kinney had been very short with me last night. It seems he considered those activities basic nursing, and I failed even that.

"And then you do the rest of the steps once more," Alice explains, encouraging me with the simplicity of the task as we pack another jar nearly to the brim. "Just like the others."

She watches me put the jars in boiling water and nods with approval. I feel closer to her more and more, now that I reach the middle of my pregnancy. It's only just becoming obvious. No one has said anything to me directly, though I'm sure there's speculation, and I have no notion how to head it off. I do not think Kate will be very sympathetic. Alice, the dear that she is, has only been as encouraging about my situation as she

214

is about my canning ability. At least there is one person in Flats Junction who believes I can do something right.

"Alice," I ask, as we watch the jars heat underwater, "how are you getting along with Mitch's family since your birth?"

"Oh!" She smiles happily. "Fine, now that Mitch has been back at the fields all summer. I know they were not happy with us taking time away from planting, but it was so wonderful to have him around to help for a few days, and to have him bond with little Petey."

"I can only imagine how much Mitch enjoyed his time with his boy," I say, and try not to wonder at the man's strange behavior. It is an odd man who will put his child before the fields, even for a few days. I still cannot fathom his reasoning, but the little one is most definitely dear to me, too, if only because I treasure his mother's friendship deeply. There is not much time with the harvest coming to fondle and dandle babies on one's knee, but he's a smiley lad who is easily entertained. I wonder if all babes are so. Theodore's personality is very shadowy in my memory. I will not know if the child will be like him or no.

As we stand over the stove, I feel a twinge in my lower abdomen. It is light, fanciful, and I think, at first, I only imagine it. We eat a lunch of leftover gooseberries and plums Alice brought from her family's orchard, and continue with the canning. In the soft heat of the kitchen, little Pete falls peacefully asleep in his blankets.

I wince again. I have no way to know if there is pain as a child grows, or if it is how a babe moves in the womb. But the twist is sharp and low. I bend over a little as it pierces my stomach.

215

Alice looks at me strangely. "Jane. Are you alright?"

I start to nod yes, but then realize it is a lie. "No. I don't believe so. I'm sorry, Alice, but I need you to go ask for Doctor Kinney at the general, or have someone send him here. Just say ... if he can find time to stop between his patients ... it would be good. Or tell Kate—or Horeb and Gil—or possibly Nancy—she sees everyone at the post office—anyone who might chance to see him." I refrain from telling her how scared I feel. With all my rough, hard work, my body has yet to fail me. Will this change now too?

Alice's face is white. Without another word, she goes to gather up her sweetly sleeping child. Her eyes are big as she turns to me at the kitchen door.

"It's not good to have pains so early, Jane. Are you sure you'll be all right for a bit? Perhaps get off your feet."

I wave her away. Early? Indeed. Alice—*everyone*—thinks I am close to eight months pregnant, and I have taken to wearing the yellow dress with the seams out, so I look bigger than I am. What I am really? Not even a full seven months. I know exactly the week I conceived toward the end of January.

It is early to have cramps, this much I understand. It might be something normal, but in my ignorance, I cannot diagnose myself. And I only will trust the doctor's word. Trust? Since when have I started to trust a doctor so completely?

A stab of freezing doubt hits me hard, just as the throb turns into a constant ache. Every day, I battle the elements, the harsh work, the laboring chores. That alone is fearsome. This is different. I am *frightened*, desperately so, and all I want is the doctor to come home. I don't feel well. I feel dizzy, nauseated, and sweaty.

216

I decide, in the time to spare waiting for the doctor, to start on supper. Anything to help take my mind off the pulsing pushing inside my body. Using most of the vegetables we have not put in canning jars, I boil them, add herbs and butter, and then begin the soup.

It's no use distracting myself. The pains start to come regularly, and I feel fluid run through my clothes. I am afraid to look, but finally realize I will need to wear some rags.

In the laboratory, I find a few clean operating cloths. I take one and go to the upstairs washroom to take care of any little stain.

It is not a light smear of blood. Even in the dim light of the bathroom, I see it is quite dark, and there is more than I thought. I have already ruined my petticoats. Nothing can be done. I'll have to soak them a long time to try to remove the stains. I wrap the laboratory towel around my middle under my dress, and head back to the kitchen, where the haphazard soup is starting to simmer.

I do not know how long I stand at the stove. Time seems to lose meaning as I endure another contraction, sinking into my worries, afraid to sit lest I ruin one of my few dresses with the blood I can feel seeping through the cloths. I pray the rag holds the gushes in, and I am not such a disaster as I feel.

"Jesus, Mary, and Joseph!" The thick Irish swear booms through the kitchen. I turn around and see the doctor standing in the doorway. His eyes are wild, his hands hanging limply at his sides. He stares at the floor, and I look down hazily to see tiny pools of blood at my feet.

"Mrs. Weber!" He suddenly springs into action, striding across the room as he talks, bending swifter than I would have thought him capable, and picks me up as if I am not a grown woman with a mind of my own.

"The soup!" I manage lightly.

"To hell with the soup," he growls, and marches sideways up the stairs to his aunt's bedroom. I wrap my arms around his neck to keep from slipping from his arms. "How long have you been bleedin'?"

"I ..." I try to think. "Perhaps an hour or two. Three? Did Alice not send for you?"

"No! I was comin' home early. Thought to help you tonight and give you a bit of a rest as I know you're comin' into your time."

I try to answer, but I cannot because I must breathe through another bout of cramping.

"Did you lose the babe?" His brogue is more pronounced, and he is all business, lying me down, bunching up the sheets below my hips. I shake my head negative, though he is not looking, and is too busy removing my boots and socks. I finally register that he plans to half undress me for an examination.

"Wait!" I struggle to my elbows. "Surely there's no need ... a midwife?"

"I *am* the midwife," he says flatly.

"But—"

"Mrs. Weber." He looks at me finally, holding my stocking foot, and ignoring my protests. "Did you lose the child?"

"I don't know. I don't think so. Yet," I whisper. I expect to start to cry when I admit it, but I do not. This child is such an enigma, a babe who might grow up the spitting image of its father, to remind me always of my lusty moments of weakness and a man I barely know. It is a child unlooked for, unexpected, and brushed aside by my shame and my new daily hardships.

"I have to examine you. I'll gather instruments and send one of the neighbors for Widow Hawks to help you undress. Can you remove your petticoats?"

"I'll try."

He leaves the room. I sit up and hike up my skirts so I can shimmy out of the stockings. The rags I'd clipped to staunch the blood are drenched in hot, dark, red-black congealed tissue. I give a small gasp, realizing all my underskirts are, regardless of my efforts, destroyed. And the amount of blood makes me cry out.

The doctor must not have gone immediately for the neighbors. He bolts up the stairs and back into the room when I make a noise. He stops short, his eyes taking in the utterly soaked cloths at my feet. Another contraction seizes. I hold my breath, terrified about what I ought to let my body do, and double over against the effort of trying to stay upright. As the pain hits, a stream of blood pours out from under my dress, unstoppable, deep red, and sweltering. I have not yet let my skirt down, so my naked leg is scandalously in view. One look at Doctor Kinney tells me he does not care about my ankles, or the white flesh of my knee. He seems horrified about the blood, and that scares me more than anything else. My heart feels as though it will give out. It's pounding fast and strong, and I can't breathe without feeling like I will choke on my own spit.

"Sweet mother Mary," he swears again.

"Stop, please. The pains are not horrible. It cannot be so bad, can it?" I beg him to agree with me. And it is true.

219

While the contractions are strong and push hard in my belly and back, and my womb throbs, it is not unmanageable, and is not excruciating.

Instead, he reaches and eases me onto the bed, situating more rags beneath my body.

"I've got to look, Mrs. Weber, there's no waitin' for it. I'm sorry," he says. I mutely follow his instructions, uncomfortable and nervous. I did not truly think about what it would mean to birth a child here, let alone miscarry, only that I believe it is safer to try birthing than an abortion. Neither guarantee survival, but one has slightly better odds.

"There's still a chance, of course," he mutters. "It could just be a wee bit early."

"A chance?"

"You're what—eight months? A bit more?" He gazes over my stomach with a critical eye. "If I recall correctly?"

He's reciting the proper length of time, given what I told him when he'd first asked. But he's wrong, and I know it. There's no way this baby will live, if I'm truly giving birth. If the child still lives at all.

Strange, terrible, guilty relief surges through me, shocking and appalling and utterly wrong. I do not want a baby—*mine!*—to die! What kind of woman wishes for this? What kind of unfit mother would hope to lose a child? Is that what I am? A failure as a loving wife, a failure as a housekeeper, a hopeless trial of a nurse, and now unable to be a mother?

God save me.

But if this is a miscarriage, it will set me free from the constraints laced around my life. It's a repulsive notion,

220

horrifying in its own tantalizing and yet outrageously compelling way.

And if the child does not come, and lives?

Then I must endeavor not to fail at motherhood.

The doctor bends over my bare legs, and a new reality hits all too clear. Doctor Kinney, my employer, will be delivering my baby, and seeing me in all states of undress. How improper! I should have a different doctor! Another contraction hits, and I gasp through it, all thoughts fleeing.

He looks up in concern, then rustles at my midsection while I concentrate on the ceiling and at the Catholic cross on the wall, pretending to ignore his rummaging along my inner thigh and quick, thankfully gentle, probing. Then he is at my side, standing over me, wiping down his slick, bloody hands.

"You're deliverin' the babe," he says, all matter-of-fact. "It's early but there's a good chance you'll do fine and the child can live."

"Well, that's that, then." I try to stay light, because he still seems so upset. He shakes his head.

"It's a lot of blood for a delivery. I've got to watch it. But first, I'll go have someone fetch Widow Hawks."

CHAPTER 19

8 August 1881

Widow Hawks will arrive too late to undress me. I deliver the child quickly, while I am still clothed. Doctor Kinney is the only one in the room to manage the earthy muddiness of childbirth.

It is an easy birth, for the babe is tiny and my body is strong from all the heavy work of living here, but the doctor's face transforms as he gathers up the tiny limbs.

"A boy. But stillborn," he says softly, and then cradles the child into a clean sheet and reverently lays him on the sideboard. The news is not a surprise to me. I could not believe the child would live. While I wait for the relief of the release from pregnancy, I am amazed to realize I feel nothing. Not even a dull sorrow at the loss of the babe. There is nothing left. I'm stuck, drilled into the bedding, locked into a box of shock.

He looks to me after examining the baby's body, his cheeks and the lines around his mouth unreadable, but before he can speak, we hear Widow Hawks run up the stairs. She stops short in the doorway, taking in the bloody cloths, our wild eyes, and my state of dishevelment.

"Oh no, Patrick," she says softly, and then moves to me. "I'll get her comfortable, if I can. Is there still time?"

"No."

Her face falls. "The baby?"

"Stillborn."

When he says the word again, I wait to feel something: sorrow, pain, disappointment. Still nothing. I feel as though my body is starting to float.

Widow Hawks closes her eyes, then glances at the blood around the room again. "I'll clean her up. Jane. How are you feeling?"

"I'm not leavin' now," the doctor says intensely, giving me no chance to answer. "I want to make sure she finishes up well. The bleedin' was more than usual."

I am shuddering and shaking from the birth, so I need Widow Hawks to unbutton my overdress. She takes the yellow calico and lays it aside, then helps me ease under the sheets. Doctor Kinney has not been watching. Instead, he carefully re-wraps my dead son once more. Oh heavens. Will he know? Can he guess? Will he care?

I want to see the tiny child, to prove to myself this was not a dream. Then again, I do not. I want to forget.

Another contraction hits. It is a wave, still strong and long, and I feel more fluid flow out. I suppose it is normal for this to take its time slowing down.

"How are you feeling?" Widow Hawks smooths hair from my forehead and reaches back to unpin the braids.

"Rather tired and dizzy," I admit. Doctor Kinney swings around.

"Dizzy? How much so?"

I think, and as I do, another cramp seizes my middle. I breathe through it, feeling more blood run out between my thighs. To my embarrassment, I see the black-red liquid soak through the sheet.

"Pat." Widow Hawks' voice is low, and she puts a hand on my shoulder. "Jane is still having pains."

"What?"

"I can't seem to stop." I sigh through another small one, recalling how many of the women here are on their feet right after delivering. "Maybe I should walk around a bit to soothe the cramps?"

I move, my legs landing heavily on the floor, and stand before either of them can stop me. I think that if I am determined to go about more normally, perhaps it will all go away. I need to think clearly again. I must decide what I should do with myself now.

There is an emptiness in my womb, but by standing, another contraction hits, and blood streams down my leg, creating an instant puddle. I cry out and crouch, and as I do, a large piece of slimy matter slides down to the floor.

"I thought I'd delivered the babe!" I panic. The earthiness and bloodiness now seem unnatural. I do not recall hearing stories of birth like this. Should I bleed so much? No one talks about this! No one explains exactly what to expect! There are no books on this subject, no pamphlets to teach me! I had no way to prepare, to learn … I blame the lack of education on some obscure publisher, my mind wandering to the library in Boston.

"The placenta, perhaps." Doctor Kinney comes around and stops short at the side of the bed. "By God, Mrs. Weber! Back in bed now!"

He leaves the room abruptly. I look at the large puddle of blood and tissue at my wobbling feet. Is it so disgusting?

The doctor bounds back up the stairs as Widow Hawks helps me under the covers, replacing the red rags below me with new ones.

"We'll watch for a bit and make sure she delivers the afterbirth," he says, but he puts his medical bag nearby, and lays out syringes and several bottles of medicine.

They clean around me. I bear through the contractions without issue. They are not painful, just actively running through my middle and lower back, like waves hitting the shore. I know I bleed with each. The ocean. It is waves like the ocean. Like home ...

Will I go back to Massachusetts now? I can, without a need to worry, or hide, or face the implications of my weak moments. But ...

Why?

Why should I go? What would be the point?

Flats Junction has supported me, even with my newness, my pregnancy, my living with Widow Hawks. Would I find such companionship in Boston? Would I want to live with Mother and Father and see Anne and James at holidays again? Do I want to trade the freeness, casualness, and nosy teasing of the townsfolk for the luxuries of the city? It would be an easier life, surely ...

Ah ... it is too hard to think. My head hurts. I can't seem to raise it up.

Eventually, Doctor Kinney checks under the covers, and announces I have lost quite a bit of blood, but that all should end up well enough.

"Rest a bit, Mrs. Weber. It seems to have eased off, and your body will start to relax. We'll go grab some quick lunch and be right back."

"I might try to sleep," I say. "You take your time."

They walk out together, and I close my eyes against the dizziness. A fitful sleep comes at first, but then I realize I will not be able to sleep easily with the pains that continue, sometimes quickly and sometimes not. I wonder how much blood I have lost. Raising the sheet, I am astounded to see that I have soaked through everything. Black clots of tissue still run out of me with each pulse of my womb.

Sitting in bed makes me feel suddenly faint, so I lay back on the pillows. Time seems to float. I do not know how long I am alone.

A cool hand on my forehead rouses me. I open my eyes and find that I cannot see purely. A grey, soft haze touches everything, and I cannot focus, but I register Widow Hawks.

I feel lucid, and I truly think I can understand everything. There is movement around me, but I cannot tell if it is hurried or slow, worried or no. I can clearly hear words spoken around me. There are questions and I answer, believing my responses to be concise.

"Patrick! Patrick!" The shout is near, but it takes me a moment to realize that it is Doctor Kinney she calls for, and then suddenly he appears on the other side of the bed, tearing away the sheet.

"Jesus."

"Shall we pack her womb?"

226

"You know that never works. It doesn't stop anythin' if the body doesn't rest the pumpin' of blood. We need the uterus to contract, empty on its own accord. Mrs. Weber, are you awake?"

I think it is obvious I am, though I find I cannot really open my eyes. My body is riding contractions now, and each takes me further away. I am powerless.

"Jane, can you speak?" Widow Hawks bends over me, taking my face in her hands. Her strong fingers feel hot. I think my eyes are open, but my vision is narrowed. A pin-prick. My heartbeat feels very pure, as if I can sense every particle riding through my veins. I am sweating, little rivers sliding down the insides of my arms and along my neck, and yet I shiver without stop. I'm not cold, am I? Doctor Kinney measures my pulse, his hand firm over my wrist.

"Jane," Widow Hawks says again, and I shift, sigh, and answer lowly.

"I'm awake."

"Don't let her sleep. It'd be a coma, and I don't think I can wake her up after that." The doctor's voice has changed pitch. There is an acute note of anxiety under the schooled calm. I find I cannot rouse myself to have a reaction to this, as if I am under a spell, unable to feel fear or worry. My entire being is beyond all that is happening, as my body contracts and yanks, curling into itself and unwinding. My insides are not my own. Is this me? Is this my body? My moments?

Widow Hawks sits on the bed next to me while the doctor continues checking vital signs. She asks simple questions about my parents, my sister, my education. I answer her softly, breathing carefully, but I am drifting as I do it. What is she asking? What did she want to know? I understand her ... yes? The answer ... she wants an answer. What is it?

Who? Yes ... that's right. I'm a widow. Yes, my husband is Henry. Yes. He died at Christmas. Oh and yes ... yes, I have a sister named Anne. And my mother? Her name?

Ruby ... my mother is Ruby.

My father? Hobbs ... no. Rupert. Hobbs.

When? You want to know ... what?

The babe? How f ... Yes. Yes, six months.

Maybe less ...

Do not ask me to count.

I want to swat her away irritably and stop the questions. I can't see her. Where is she? I feed her my responses, sure that they are correct. Sure that they are true. Sure that she is speaking ...

Yes. Yes. I'm awake.

What? What does she want now? Another question ... another answer. Who?

`The doctor peels away the covers, a stethoscope pressed against my chest. I feel the cold metal of it. The cold seems to seep in everywhere.

"My arms are freezing," I suddenly say, interrupting Widow Hawks' line of questioning.

"Hypotension, dear God," the doctor mutters over me, but I am not really looking for him or Widow Hawks anymore. I close my eyes as the numbness fills my fingers, starts to creep up my feet, and into my arms and shoulders.

Heavy blankets tumble on, weighty and solid, and there is some warmth that immediately comes from them. It is suffocating, but I cannot seem to say anything to free my limbs. Besides, my teeth chatter, and I am shuddering beyond help. Through it all, the contractions continue, regular and strong and full.

"Jane." Widow Hawks is over me. "Can you hear us?"

"Mm."

"Mrs. Weber, I have to try ergot. I have a little. It's been banned for childbirth otherwise."

"Tea?"

"Like that, only—"

"Pat, explain later," Widow Hawks urges.

"I have to say somethin'. I've never used it. I acquired some last time Bobby MacHugh sent a trunk of medicines. They said it was a good hemorrhage drug. Good for emergencies, to make the cramps strong—like my homeopathic trainin'. Treat one illness with medicine that does the same thing, the two cancellin' each other out. I don't like that I have to try it on her first and I don't know what I'm doin'. She should know." I hear him fumbling along the sideboard, his words barely registering. "They said it should narrow the blood vessels and passages, to stem the flow of bleedin'."

It comes to me I should answer him. I want to tell him to do what he must, but my breathing is too hard, and my words are stuck. I am still incredibly cold.

Cold. I know I'm cold. I'm shaking.

I'm shuddering ...

Eventually, I feel the prick of a needle, the fluid flowing into my veins. He immediately checks my heartbeat.

"And?" Widow Hawks grips my hand. "*Wakantanka tunkasina*, please." There is more silence in the room, and she asks again. "Pat. Will it work?"

"I don't know yet." He is tight with her. "I wish we had thought about the plain tea from the first, if I'd even

229

realized she might bleed out. Or if I'd the proper tools for the new intravenous therapy from that doctor from Leith I read about in the *Lancet Gazette*." He is rambling. I cannot focus on each word. "... usin' saline to resuscitate after hemorrhage. It would have worked, I think. Damn. Damn!"

"She's so pale. Her lips are blue." Hands smooth back my hair, while Doctor Kinney busies himself with his stethoscope again. "It will be all right, Jane," Widow Hawks says.

Will it?

Yes. Now it will ... it will ...

I am tired, and without another memory, I fall asleep.

I dream. A man softly weeps, but the tears turn into Henry's death rattle. It takes a moment, even in my dreaming, to remember that he is dead. And then a baby's cry shoots out, and I think of a soft head, downy, with pale blonde hair.

When I wake, it is only briefly. I am finally warm, and almost comfortable. My head pounds with pain, and I am thankful it is now night. There are no lights and no questions. Without being able to help myself, I drift back into slumber.

The sun streams in when I wake again. My head is worse this time, and I immediately close my eyes, but someone is there. I feel weight on the bed.

"Are you warm enough, Jane?"

I nod. I am deadly tired.

"Can you eat? You really ought to." Widow Hawks' voice is soothing, hopeful, but I shake my head no, and fall asleep.

When my eyes flutter open the next time, the light is dim. It is either dusk, or early morning. This time, I think I can stay awake longer, but find I cannot. The room is quiet, empty, and I do not even bother to raise my head. Slumber comes fitfully now, as if my body is afraid to go back to sleep.

Sometime in the night, I hear soft voices.

"There's nothing much we can do but wait, Patrick. She'll wake up and eat soon."

"She needs to. She's gettin' weaker." His voice, even in half-whisper, is rough. Is it worry? Anger? Frustration?

"But the pains, and the bleeding, have mostly stopped," she reassures him. "The medicine worked."

"I don't know what else I can do."

"Care for her, as you do any patient. You're a good doctor, Pat. And you've saved her."

"Not yet."

They continue to talk softly, argumentatively, but I drift off, and sleep fitfully this night as well.

I wake again to the gentle brush of fingers on my thigh. It is a caress, a trail of touch. As the room wanders into focus, I feel hands lowering my knees, squeezing my ankles as if examining their strength, and I follow the sensations to where a sheet lowers onto my legs. Doctor Kinney covers me; his head is bowed. There are pale glimmers of early grey in his dark hair as the light hits it just so. I glance to the window and remember where I am. I am not at Widow Hawks' home, nor back in Massachusetts. I'm at the doctor's place, in his aunt's old bedroom.

He has not realized I am awake, and continues to sit at my feet, taking a moment to focus on something. I do not know if it is the pattern of the coverlet or the wood planks of the floor. His shoulders are slumped, and his cheeks are peppered with stubble. I have never seen him unshaven. He looks rough and tumble, as if he has not slept well. It comes

231

to me that perhaps it was my miscarriage, my bleeding, that has caused this. That it is my health he worries over so thoroughly. An enormous wave of affection washes over me when I think of this, and of him. It is an emotion much stronger than I am used to feeling, and I catch my breath and blink back unbidden tears.

At my intake of air, his head snaps up. His eyes are red-rimmed and bloodshot.

"Janie!"

He uses my front name as an endearment, as if somewhere during my episode I gave him permission. He rises and comes to me, touches my forehead, his fingers gentle.

"You're goin' to be alright. Everythin' is. I've made sure. Now, it's time for recovery."

Before my eyes, he transforms into a physician, though he is still haggard in appearance. He stands over me, listing off warnings to watch for: clots, blood color, fatigue, and fainting. I do not think I will remember all these things. He is unwavering and professional and clinical. I think I misjudged the tender way he just touched me. It is not especial care, but his bedside manner.

"Paddy."

The voice comes from the door. It is a gentle admonishment in a motherly tone. We both look at Widow Hawks, where she leans on the doorjamb, cloths tucked under her arm.

Doctor Kinney stops talking. She gives a small shake of her head.

"Let her rest a bit. She will hardly be able to remember all your direction now."

"It's important, Esther."

"I know. But let it be for a moment. Let me help her wash up. She'll be right and downstairs soon enough, now that the worst is over. And I'll stay here until the bleeding slows so she can come home with me."

He gives an angry little shake of his head in return; he does not like the interruption. His words to me are gruff.

"Don't overdo it now, Mrs. Weber. Just take it easy. Even standin' could make you dizzy."

I watch him walk out, stiff-backed and silent. I am confused. First he is kind, and then upset with me, and I have not even spoken. Widow Hawks—did he just call her Esther?—walks in and sets the clean rags down. The top one is lukewarm and wet, and she starts to wash down my legs and arms and torso. It feels lovely.

Finally, I find my voice. It sounds small even to my own ears.

"Is he angry?"

She stops her massage and looks me straight on. "Jane. No. He grieves for the loss of your little baby, as if it was his own flesh and blood. And you mean a great deal to him, you know. He finds your help indispensable. He thought he was going to lose you."

I frown at the description of his worries. "I'm sure he could advertise for another housekeeper."

And will he need to? Will I stay, now that I do not need to do so?

She resumes her washing, and gives a short *tut*.

"Maybe so, but what are his chances of finding another he gets along with so well, or who fits in with the town readily enough? Regardless, you think him heartless if you do not realize that he cares."

233

"I know he is not heartless. He is a good man," I placate, not wishing to delve further into the doctor's character in this moment. I am too tired. It is too many changes.

"He is," she says, and follows my lead, filling the room with her companionable silence.

CHAPTER 20
11 August 1881

I sit in the golden sunlight of the late afternoon. Widow Hawks tinkers loudly in the kitchen. She insists on cooking supper, that I am to stay off my feet and rest another few days, but I want to help. Maybe if I try my hand at being a housekeeper again, I will have my decision.

Stay, or go?

All I know is my time in the West has made me prefer less pampering. I am still bleeding, and I feel faint when I stand for too long. Widow Hawks hovers nervously each day. She says her people do not typically have such difficult births, and she is uncertain about what to do.

There is a rumble of a voice in the house; the doctor must be back from his rounds.

"Where is she?" I hear him through the open window. There is more muted chatter, and then he darkens the sunlight over me. I look up. I do not have a bonnet on, but I do not care, and he is unreadable and black against the sun.

"You're doin' all right?"

I shrug. "Just tired."

He crouches next to me, careful, as if I am breakable.

"You look awful pale. You're still bleedin'?"

I nod, and trace the pattern of the wood on the chair. His hand comes to cover mine to stop my half-hearted picking of the grain. The touch is unexpected, and fills me with a strange, fuzzy tightness. It is as if I am newly awakened. I have long realized he is a tactile man, very much because he is a doctor. But I also know I respond to his touch now, as if my being has readjusted to my world. Emotions course through me quicker, stronger. It is incredibly disconcerting. I've spent my life curbing my questions, my fascination with learning, my unfashionable passion, and now the flood surges through me, urging me to swim in feelings and to forget about logic and properness. As much as I don't like to admit it, I now delight in the doctor's touch, more so than I recall. But at what cost?

"Mrs. Weber, I'm very sorry about the child."

"It's not your fault." I do not like to think he blames himself. "Really, from what I understand, this is natural."

"No." He shakes his head. "You nearly died. I should not have let it go so far."

We are quiet. I reflect on this. He is right. I know I was close to death, and that the recovery might be longer than is typical. The thought of what I might have lost: my friendships to him, Widow Hawks, Alice, Anette, Sadie, and even Kate and the others ... it makes me weak to think of it.

Is that my answer?

There is so much I want to try and see and experience. I'm determined yet to thoroughly clean the house, to

236

grow and harvest the garden. I want to get better at nursing. When I miscarried, I was fading without thought. I did not understand how the loss of my life was so near, and what it would mean to lose it. But I think I might, now. And I know, as surely as I know I like his hand over mine, that Doctor Kinney is the first doctor I completely trust. Perhaps I did before this. In fact, I know I did. But it was never so acute, nor so obvious to me.

"I was thinkin' ..." he starts quietly, breaking into my reverie. "We need to bury the wee babby. It's too hot to wait. There is the small Catholic cemetery. My great-aunt Bonnie is buried there, along with a few others, and he could rest next to her. If you don't have a preference, that is."

I glance at him. "That's fine."

"You're not even Catholic, are you?"

"No."

He shrugs. "I'm impressed you've put aside your preferences for mine. What are you, then? Calvinist? Episcopalian?"

"Congregationalist."

He nods as if he was expecting something like that, and then presses his hand flat against mine, trapping my palm against the wood.

"Mrs. Weber. The babe. It was very small. At first, I thought it'd died in the womb a long time ago for the size, but then you should have had a fever, and it would have festered and killed you."

My heart stops, and my head jerks back, snapping a cord in my neck, agony shooting down my shoulder. I try to pull my hand out, but he has it trapped almost painfully against the wavy bark of the chair.

"You say Mr. Weber was ill. Often, and it was a lengthy illness. A weakness. And even if he was robust until his death ..."

I refuse to look at him, closing my eyes, willing the tears to stay put, my chest to pump air in and out. What now? He's asking the questions I feared. *If only!* If only I hadn't miscarried! Then perhaps the babe would only be late ... or small ... or ...

Damn this! Nothing works!

I thought to flee from prying eyes on my thickening waist. Now I face the same type of discovery, but for a different, inverted reason.

Which is worse?

Nothing—*nothing* good came of my damnable curiosity to try something. To live just for a few days with something a little brighter and happier than I'd ever had before.

He's waiting for an answer, or anything I can give him, and I search my mind for the words, coming up with nothing sustainable, nothing worth trying.

"I don't want to go back."

It's not what I meant to say, and he shifts a little, though his palm continues to smash mine.

"Go back?"

"I don't want to go back East."

"I'm not askin' about that. I'm askin' about your husband. Your babby."

My laugh is odd and bitter and tinny. "The child wasn't my husband's, if that's what you're getting at—as I'm sure you've figured."

The admittance is a trap in itself, binding me to the truth, and I can feel the doctor tremble with it once, briefly.

Perhaps he is only reacting to the shattering of my reputation, the crack of the shell of proper civility I wrapped around myself. Now will he send me East? I have given him his answer.

And I will go. I will go back and leave everyone else, and leave him, if he asks me to go. But I don't want to. Faced with it, I have *my* answer.

"Whose, then?"

That he asks at all is a surprise.

"A man."

"That much I can manage on my own," he says harshly. "But—was it somethin' else? A … an unwanted man?"

My other hand covers his, grasping it strongly. My chest feels tight, and my head still pounds and aches, but I know that I need to touch someone, and am desperately thankful for his sensitive ways. He is willing to continue looking for a way to save my character, to give me a reason beyond my wantonness to have come to such a low point. He still wishes to think well of me, and for a moment, I want to play along. I want to continue a lie, a charade of falseness that gives me the same quiet pity of the townsfolk. I could say it was a rape. I could ask him to tell everyone that it was Henry's child. I could still live here under the guise of the proper, respectable widow. I'd have the adventure, the work, and a kind man to care and cook for. I'd have the friends I've made—more friends here than I ever had in Boston, and no one would be wiser.

But I can't. I can't feel the strong pull to him while also holding tight to a story that isn't true. If I've ever flattered myself as one who liked to learn the root of a question, and searched for the answer to a problem, then I must stop pretending. I must give my own reality a voice.

239

"It wasn't a man who forced himself on me, Doctor Kinney," I tell him, my voice soft and muted. "And you're right. The babe was the child of a lover. The cousin of my brother-in-law."

"And you didn't want to marry him? He didn't care for you? Or the child?"

"He never knew," I admit. "It was a brief affair, only a few days of … of enjoyment." The word sticks in my throat, and I cough it out. "And it was mutual. We started and parted ways understanding that it was simply a … an exploration. I'd never had relations with anyone but Henry, and those were … ah. Few. I … I wanted to learn. And I didn't think I could conceive anyway, at least not well."

"And you didn't think to tell him?"

"I didn't love him. I didn't wish to marry him. What would it have served? He might have felt beholden to propose, and I might have been tempted to say yes. To bind myself to another plain, cold union … Anyway, I couldn't."

"And with Mr. Weber already gone, it would have been quite apparent what had happened. This—the job, this life. It was an escape."

He slips his fingers away from mine, and the air around my hand is cool and empty.

"So, you hid here to preserve your properness, your widowhood, and respectability."

I nod once, staring at the prairie dust flaking onto my boots. I know I am foolish and weak, and stupid for putting so much stock into appearing so perfectly refined.

"And why wouldn't you tell me this when you were bleedin' out? It could have meant your death. I would have known it was a miscarriage from the start, for how early it was!" His words are a lash and a question filled with sadness. "Couldn't you trust me even in your time of need?"

That he feels inadequate now, in the middle of my confession and revelations, jolts me hard, and I twist to look at him fully. He gazes over the garden, with its leafy, heavy, wide squash leaves, the maroon and green of the beet fronds, and the climbing, weeping beans. The slash of his mouth is set, and the trickle of small lines around his eyes are smooth in the light.

"I trust you. I did. I do. I asked for you from the start when I began to bleed." Why do I say this? Does my word even matter? Will he ever believe me? Will he understand that most of what holds my tongue is the properness of society, the careful cultivation of upright virtue I tried to emulate before and after my marriage?

He heaves a sigh and shifts so he's sitting on the ground next to the chair, his arms folded around a knee, looking almost forlorn.

"You told me all this, you know. Me and Esther. When we were tryin' to keep you awake. You answered the questions, but the answers didn't always match what you'd said before."

I want to bury my head in my skirts and settle for my hands. "Then why are you asking me now?"

"I wanted to hear you say it—*if* you'd say it—when you were aware. If you'd tell me the truth of it. But I still have a wonder ... I wonder why you didn't simply have it cut out when you were in Boston. Surely there are practitioners there who could have helped you. And you'd continue on, as if there never was a child or a lover. You'd have carried on as a modest, appropriate widow and no one would be wiser. Why here? Why this hard life?"

His questions are allowed, but I wish he wouldn't ask. Can he not just be satisfied with my answers, and my simple admittance? Why must he want to understand it all?

"I knew an abortion to be dangerous. And it's illegal."

The doctor gives a short nod. "I know. The American Medical Association was on a trail to illegalize it startin' in '57, well before I started my apprenticeship."

"And there's little information on it," I add, suddenly wishing to vindicate myself and my actions, explain my desperation. "The Comstock Act has banned the pamphlets on anything to do with ... with sex."

The doctor looks up sharply, but he doesn't frown. Instead he leans forward. "You understand the laws, then? How did you find—"

"The library. There are a few medical books there that hadn't been banned, or a librarian hadn't confiscated them yet, so I pieced together some of what could be done. And I asked my friend Lucille. She was always good for knowing things a lady shouldn't know. It sounded very dangerous. Worse than giving birth."

"It is, that," he agrees. "Dr. Ed Kellogg and his wife Delia are well-known over in Helena for handlin' abortions. I think he's on trial yet again for another woman's death. You truly did try to teach yourself such things? A woman, learnin' the trade?"

"Henry didn't like it," I say. "He didn't like when I tried to find answers to his illness, and he said I could only continue doing so if I didn't tell the doctors my theories. It embarrassed him, to have a wife who liked to learn so much. I tried to shut off my interest. I truly did. But then with his

242

sickness, and later, with the babe in my belly ... research seemed the only thing to do.

"And I know childbirth is just as dangerous, sometimes," I continue, surprised he is handling my revelations so pragmatically and quietly. Hope inexplicably rises in my blood, shoving away the tendrils of pain in my womb. "But I thought I'd take my chances with it. So, I couldn't stay. I had to ... hide. As you say."

"It might have worked," he says slowly. "Had you not miscarried. I might never have known."

"I know."

"And would you ever have said anythin'?"

"Would I need to?"

He shrugs, and shifts to look over the prairie. His deliberate movement, calculated to keep us separate and our eyes unlocked, slaps my chest. It is exactly what I feared: avoidance, judgment, disgust. Even here, I must face the consequences of allowing myself to be free with my feelings.

What a stupid woman I am. What a failure—even with all my learning.

"I suppose ... you had no reason to trust me with the truth," he says calmly, surprising me with his stoic comment. "And I ... I know what it is, to be in the city and try to fit in ... and what it means to be unable to do so."

"But—"

"Let me finish!" he says, with a touch of his Irish heat. "I cannot fault your reasons. I am perhaps more fascinated that you would choose this, that you would take it upon yourself to leave the ease of Boston to save your reputation. That you'd teach yourself about the science, and be careful. It is not what a properly bred woman would do."

"Does a proper woman take a lover in the weeks after her husband's death?" I ask bitterly.

"You were grievin'."

"Not in the way you think."

"Whether you were upset with the loss of Mr. Weber or the loss of the life you'd built and planned, it makes no difference."

"So …" I feel I must ask, and I worry I will beg him if I don't like his answer. "So, you'll keep me on?"

He finally looks up at me, the blue eyes bright against the yellow and brown of the prairie.

"Of course I will. Unless you've any other secrets? A penchant for killin' employers, for instance."

Relief rains in me, stealing my breath and my heartbeat all at the same time. "No, you've managed to discover everything." Except, perhaps, the way his nearness makes me flutter. That, however, seems completely irrelevant.

"About your babe." He spins the conversation back to the beginning without preamble, as if we have not just delved into the depths of my lacking character, enormous shortcomings, and mistakes. I'm not sure what to make of his attitude, but he continues as if the discussion is purely natural. "We'll bury him next to my auntie."

That he will do this, even knowing the child is illegitimate, collides together with the relief. How can I ever repay him such kindness?

"I'd be honored," I whisper, and then we are quiet together. I wonder if he too reflects on the strange way of life and death, as the prairie grasses undulate in ribbons against the hot August heat, spreading out before us like an endless sea.

244

CHAPTER 21
12 August 1881

Widow Hawks and the doctor decide I can finally have a bath, and I'm glad. The old blood on my skin is starting to stink badly. Doctor Kinney spends the evening hauling water up the stairs. I do not mind that it will be a cool bath, as the August heat is nearly unbearable today. The burial will be in the afternoon tomorrow, when the sun is lower.

We are all together at the doctor's house still; me, because he refuses to let me leave, and her, because she refuses to tarnish my reputation. It's laughable, now that they both know how disreputable I am, but they seem to be willing to shield all of Flats Junction about the truth of the stillborn child. I am grateful for them both.

Widow Hawks takes me into the washroom and helps me with my clothes. I am to bathe completely nude to wash away any remaining crusted blood. Dried, pale streaks of it still run down my thighs.

The dark curtain is drawn between the tin tub and the door, but she sits next to me, ever wary of me fainting. We are quiet but for the sloshing of water along the sides of the tub. I look at her, where she sits serenely and brushes down my cleaned dress. Below, the doctor putters in his lab, the echoes of his tinkering audible all the way up the stairs.

"Why are you called Esther?" I ask.

She looks up and smiles. "My husband was Welsh, and he liked the name. I was called Esther Davies until his death, though some called me Esther Flies-With-Hawks, back when this was Flats Town, before the rail. And then people started to use my old name, in a way."

"Which do you prefer?"

She shrugs indifferently. "I am all of them, so it is no matter."

I look again at her, at her lined face and gentle eyes, and I reach out a wet hand to touch hers.

"Thank you for being as a mother to me."

She nods, and I press on. "I'm sorry Kate does not seem to treasure you as a daughter should. I wish I could do or say something to change that."

She shakes her head, resigned and yet still content. I do not know how she manages the balance.

"Kate wishes to be seen as something she is not. I am proud of my daughter, and how she has made a strong life for herself. But she refuses to recognize her situation, that her half-native blood is both intimidating and sympathetic to the townsfolk. She's been a success. They see her as one of them as much as their prejudices allow. No one harasses her, nor tries to hurt her. Still she dislikes to have me in town, as a reminder of her ties to my people. I suppose someday I must

246

leave, must drop away to let her be. Maybe then one of the men might marry her, though I do not know if she wants to be married."

"I think Doctor Kinney might," I say softly, and am surprised at how difficult it is for me to say these words aloud, as if saying them makes them true.

And why should that matter? He has cared for Kate for many years. If she is what he wants, he ought to have her. And now, at least, I think I might understand why Widow Hawks and Percy Davies did not intervene on Kate's behalf in youth. They needed her to grow strong and defiant, half-breed that she is, so she might survive and even thrive.

Her head comes up at my notion on marriage for Kate, and she gives a rueful smile. I am reminded at how much of a mix she is, both Indian and white, and how beautifully she transitioned between the two worlds for the love of her man. I am still amazed at her strength to do so.

"You must see that my daughter's bitterness runs deep. She has no interest in affection, especially for her own family. Do you think that is a good match for the doctor, knowing his character?"

I look down at the water, pale and tinted a soft pink with my blood. No, Kate might not be a good match for Doctor Kinney. I would be saddened to see him tie to her. Still, it is not my choice, nor my place to give voice to my hesitations. And anything I say would be tainted with my own self-serving emotion.

I sense Widow Hawks watching me. She is, her eyes dark and opaque in the lamplight. Her hand comes to take mine.

247

"You'd suit him, Jane. More so than my daughter, who does not cherish history, and is filled with intolerance of her own race. If you'd let yourself, you might find you could love him."

"Me? I'm a soiled woman." I dismiss this at once, though the idea lodges in my mind as something I wouldn't mind at all. "And I'm nothing but a housekeeper."

"Soiled? How? Do you call me soiled?"

My head jerks up. "What? No!"

"But how are we so different? I was not married in the white man's way when I bore Percy's children."

"But … you loved one another. You were wedded to him in your people's way."

She shrugs. "And yet. Do you see the doctor shunning me for this? Do either of us judge you? For being a person, a woman with a desire to feel something? You were unmarried when you found this man—this Theodore—and he was unattached as well. How is this wrong? If you were a Sioux woman, you would not be dismissed."

"The doctor is not Sioux."

"But he is fair-minded. And he is a good match."

It must be the unbalance of the miscarriage making me so emotional, for her words fill my eyes with tears, though I do not know why. Is it because she is so kind, or because she speaks a truth long subdued within me? Or is it because I nearly died, and now, newly awakened, I see my world differently? Am I more apt to take a chance, even though I know it is foolish to allow myself to *be* myself? I do not know what it is, only that she has landed on something that makes me weep.

"Oh, Jane." Her arms caress my shoulders, and I

abandon myself to softly crying, as if I were a child and she truly my mother.

There is a step behind the curtain, and my head comes up with hers.

"Everythin' alright?" There is genuine worry in the doctor's voice. I wonder how much sound carries below, where he works in his laboratory. Has he heard us?

"Yes, Patrick," Widow Hawks answers for me. My own voice is still too soaked with tears.

"Good." I can tell he is still uncertain, and he does not leave immediately. "Do you need more water? How is the bleedin'?"

"It's nearly stopped." She peers into the water and makes a judgment. "I would say she could go home with me tomorrow."

"I—" He pauses. I can imagine him, standing in the greasy glow of light next to the wash bowl. His mind might be churning, his eyes on the floor, his long lips trembling a little as he decides what to say. There is a part of me, newly unbridled, wishing to see him, touch his mouth, tell him that he is fine to speak out to me. I will not mind whatever he says. I think of him tracing my legs and my thigh, of his fingers on my face, and I feel a surge of inexplicable emotion, full and tight. I am overpowered with these feelings, and it does not help when my head continues to pound every moment.

Perhaps it is all just my rebuilding health, and nothing more.

"I'd like you to stay on here another few days," he finally admits, and I know he is talking to Widow Hawks. "It's best if I can keep an eye on things."

He is kind to worry, but his generosity is unnecessary. He can certainly stop into Widow Hawks' home any time he wishes to check on me. I do not like to be an imposition. For all our candid discussions, I'm uncomfortable and exposed in his presence. He knows me, all of the pieces of my being, and he still looks at me over the dinner table with a clear, frank gaze. It is unnerving, yet it offers such a yawning freedom I don't know what to do with it.

It occurs to me that he might like a busy house, with things happening and voices chattering, even if it's just us womenfolk. He might have liked to have had a child tripping about the floors, regardless of whose it was, or why it was there.

I find my voice. "Tomorrow is the burial. We can go to Widow Hawks' house afterward. I don't like to outwear my welcome."

He does not rejoin this. Instead, he leaves, and I turn to Widow Hawks, who is looking at me with a sad sort of smile. We finish the bath, and later, for the first time in days, I fall into an easy sleep.

CHAPTER 22
13 August 1881

Kate doesn't speak about my miscarriage, but she knows. Everybody does. It's uncanny. Now, I am not only the object of speculation as a greenhorn and a pregnant widow, but I'm a widow who has lost the one piece remaining of a dead husband. I'm not sure what is worse: having undeserved pity because of a lie, or knowing how the truth would brand me.

It doesn't matter whether others in Flats Junction might have loose morals. Everyone knows what men visit which girls at Fortuna's Powdered Rose, and everyone knows Alan Lampton and Miss Lindsey the schoolteacher are sleeping under the same roof, unmarried. And people don't speak of the fact that for all Fortuna and Dell smack and yell at each other for having similar business names, they're obviously enamored with one another. They were spotted kissing behind the train depot a few weeks ago, and it's speculated that neither of them were even liquored up at the time.

But it's not my way. I'm supposed to be the proper widow, the doctor's upstanding housekeeper. I wish for this to continue. If not for me, for him. I don't want his delicate, still-fragile reputation with half the people in Flats Junction to disintegrate because of me.

My heart aches when many townsfolk show up at the burial. Anette left her children with her mother, and she stands near me with her solid and amiable Jacob. Sadie and Tom Fawcett are next in line. I am surprised to see the smith, too. Marie is impossible to miss with her wild black hair and singed dress.

Why are so many here? It is not as though it is uncommon to lose a babe. Is it because I am a widow woman, too? Or do these people actually care for me, for my empty heart and empty arms? The enormity of that notion is more overwhelming than the loss of my child, who is still a phantom in my mind.

After the words of Father Jonathon, everyone files back quickly to their chores. Life here does not lend itself to leisure, and the light doesn't keep. As Doctor Kinney ushers Widow Hawks out, I pause at the grave, wondering what kind of identity I should create for myself now. I was a widow and an expectant mother. Now I am only a widow.

"Jane."

I turn and meet Marie's frank gaze. She is the last person I expect to seek me out, and she glances down at the soft-churned dirt before meeting my eyes again.

"I'm sorry for your loss." Her voice is heavy. "I have lost two in such a way. If you ... I know you are alone here. I have been alone before, and if you need to come for a cup of tea, I can make some. To talk. Womanly things."

Her offer is awkward, but deeply meant, and I give a whisper of a smile.

"I'd like that very much."

It is one more friendship I want to grow, and one more that I'm glad I am staying for, and I smile a bit wider as I nod.

She nods back, twisting scarred hands into her skirts, and moves away down the back of the cemetery's hill where her husband waits. I watch him link his fingers with hers as they pray at what looks to be a family plot, with over a half-dozen small copper markers staking the ground. I feel as though I am intruding on a private moment of their own mourning now, and turn to leave, where Kate is waiting for me as well.

CHAPTER 23
25 September 1881

Over thick coffee while a soft September Sunday creeps along, Kate tells me there were whispers of the earliest sort in the weeks following my miscarriage, wondering if perhaps my child was the doctor's. It started in the Golden Nail when the cowboys, already disinclined toward the doctor for his affinity to the natives, among other things, and wary of me because I stay with Widow Hawks, thought such speculation valid.

The notion, the gossip, the possibility ... it makes me shiver.

Thankfully, the doctor's reputation is just upright enough that the idea didn't take full hold on the town's imagination. I also have both Kate and the Warren women at the Nail to thank for quenching those rumors from the first, else my time in Flats Junction might have come to an immediate, scandalous halt. It helped that Anette and Sadie alike refused to believe it, and they would also retort against the rumors hotly and loudly.

Kate tells it so that it sounds as if she was at the center of refuting the tales, that she's responsible for allowing me to stay without ruin. To lose the friends and life I have built here would have been more crushing than the miscarriage, and I feel indebted to all the women beyond measuring. Kate, as well as the others.

"So, you don't mind that you nearly died in childbed, then?" she asks after our coffee, as I buy a bit of precious brown sugar to go on squash. I am getting in the harvest slowly but surely, and while I still tire easily, Doctor Kinney will let me do most of the house chores again without fuss. Soon perhaps he will let me go back to hauling water, as I did before he knew of my condition.

I shake my head. "I don't. There is nothing I could do about it anyway. You know that."

Kate raises her eyes to the ceiling. "I'm glad I haven't had to worry about it."

"You might, someday," I tell her.

"The men here don't want to marry a half-breed," she says lightly, but there is weight to her words, and it draws me up. Therein lies the crux of her issue with anyone: herself, her mother, Doctor Kinney, the townsfolk. She must be so aware of her status as a part-Indian that she cannot see past her own skin. I am silent while I reflect on this. These types of revelations are swift and sudden now, as if nearly dying has let me see people clearer.

I find myself pushing the issue, just to hear her speak on it.

"I don't think Doctor Kinney cares much about your heritage. He might embrace it."

"Just what I need!" She gives a hard laugh, then stops, giving me a strange look. "Well, what if he does start to court me earnestly? He has not shown much interest."

I shrug, but I also wonder if I might repay her kindness about stopping those rumors. She is quiet as she wraps up my packages, perhaps thinking of my notion. I watch her long-fingered, strong-nailed hands tie string, and then she looks up at me. I cannot tell if the look in her eyes is shrewd or honest.

"Suppose he does want to court and marry me. Should I?"

He. She means the doctor. I do not know if the question is rhetorical, but I answer a bit sternly, as if she should not even consider saying anything but yes to him.

"I think he might, though I cannot speak for him." I think about what she is asking, and finish up decisively. "And if I were in your place, I'd choose him over any man in town."

He deserves whatever happiness Kate can bring him. He is kind and earnest, and he has shown depths of a tolerant character. I wonder if he could truly and eventually wear down her hardness. I hope so.

"What of your own beau?" She is fishing for information about Bern Masson. He walks me home again, though our words are stilted and careful. Our conversation now reminds me very much of my marriage with Henry. Cautious, sterile, ordinary, as if passion is not allowed because it is unseemly. I wonder if it has always been so, and I have never noticed it, or if my fresh views of the world make it hard to have trite conversation easily. How is it I've never felt the animosity he holds for Widow Hawks, or grasped the undercurrent of his preferences? Have I been so pleased with his attentions that I have, once again, let a man's failings slide?

256

"What of him?" I run my finger along a soft pink calico, newly arrived. It would look lovely on Kate should she wish to make it up for herself, and I say so, but she is not to be distracted.

"Bern's courting you, isn't he?"

I glance up at her. "That's what it's called, I suppose."

"Yes! Damnit, that's what it's called!" Horeb yells, looking up briefly from the checkerboard. I'd almost forgotten he and Gilroy were there. They're very quiet around me now.

She shrugs. "You're a widow. You can't expect much more, and you don't have a parlor to sit in on Sunday or a father to ask."

I frown. It paints a cold picture of love, and an uninspiring prequel to marriage.

"Well. He hasn't asked for anything formal yet. I'm not to worry, I should think," I say evasively. "What about you? What will you do when it's your turn?"

"You mean, should Pat ask if he might court me?"

I shake my head, pushing myself to ask the question. I need to know her mind. "No, Kate. Should he ask you to marry him."

"But the doc, he's poor. And the old sawbones hasn't done much lately. Not since the Army came through back in '76 and he tried to fix up those men," Horeb interjects, taking Kate's defense. "Do you want such a man, Kitty?"

She has the grace to blush, and she does it prettily, the high color making her eyes light up. I could not measure to her beauty ever, and I do not expect to, nor ever find the need. Her spirited, fiery personality is captivating. It is why I wish her to be my friend, and why I believe she is tolerated among the townsfolk beyond her running the general, even with her native heritage. It is probably why I believe the doctor has pined for her for so long, even when she is aloof to him and all the other men.

"I think I might say yes," she says slowly, almost bashfully. "He is handsome, and kind, and I should be accepted even more to the town."

Horeb snorts but makes no further comment.

"He would take care of your mother, too," I remind. "Take her the food she needs and manage the house."

Her smile shrinks, and she presses her mouth together.

"He wouldn't need to, I expect," she says. "I am sure once I am married, Widow Hawks would be able to get on with living elsewhere. Go back to her people." The idea is said slowly, thoughtfully, as if she has not realized this before.

"I should think she'd like to stay and see grandchildren," I reason.

Kate's mouth sours. "Anything else, Jane?"

I sigh. Her moodiness does not bother me any longer. Since feeling the coldness of death in my arms and legs, I find many things do not unsettle me quite as much as they used to, so I shake my head and leave.

Walking back to the doctor's house, I reflect. My pace is slow as I consider the dusty ground. September is dry on the prairie, though the trees on the old buffalo jump still are tall and green. I have actually grown to enjoy the land, and I don't miss the ocean as much as I had feared. Or maybe I just like the people.

I make a hearty stew with the early fall produce. It is difficult, because I have to pause often and wipe my eyes on my apron. Doctor Kinney ought to pursue Kate, to have his heart's desire. He deserves to have the family he wants, for all he hasn't said so explicitly. I should repay the doctor's kindness for the burial of my son and saving my life.

My thoughts turn over, and I start to think in steps. I will help Doctor Kinney see that he ought to woo Kate. It is not what I would wish for him, and I know Widow Hawks does not approve. But he softens when he talks of her, or with her, and he has no other prospects. And once I see he is earnest in courting her, I will leave. I need not return home to my elderly parents, worrying their minds about my status and my care. There is freedom in being a widow yet, and I have no child to burden me now. And I know hard work. I can carry on even if I'm not in the West.

"Smells divine, Mrs. Weber!"

I have been lost in musings, and I do not hear him come in until his voice is right over my shoulder, peering into the pot. I try to give my expected little response, and he leaves to wash up. The sunlight slants into the room just so, igniting the amber bottle of ointment he'd mixed for me. *Warm regards*, he'd written. My heart rises and jerks, like a bird when it flees from its perch, only to be shot in flight. When we sit for supper, the same sunlight filters in from the windows, casting shadows in the kitchen and along his face.

I wish to be his.

It is a selfish thought, and an improper one. And I have spent too many weeks as his sisterly housekeeper to ever ask him to love me differently than he does. It is not my place to expect or ask it of him, for all his acceptance of me and my flaws and my mistakes.

God forgive me. I love it here, and I want this to be my home. But I am not brash or outspoken, and I will not chase after a man who does not love me, nor need me to stay.

"You're quiet," he states around a mouth of stew.

I glance down at my spoon. There is no good time for my words. If I never push him, he may never have happiness. Without looking at him, I say, "You ought to court Kate, Doctor Kinney."

He is silent, staring at me strangely, as if my idea is utterly foreign.

"I think you should. And I think you'd find her very receptive."

"Mrs. Weber ..." He leans back. "You're a mite involved in our personal lives."

I cannot tell if he is angry or not. Then he leans forward and searches my face earnestly. "You really want me to do this?"

"I think it ... wise." I look back down at the food. I am not much hungry these days. My feelings for him have slowly built in my chest, tightening it so it is hard to breathe sometimes when I think about his large hands and his merry laugh. "A doctor should be married. And she seems fond of you."

"Hm." He does not say much more, and instead of helping me with the dishes as usual, he goes to his study. I fear I have unsettled or irritated him.

Or perhaps I have given him hope.

We do not say anything the rest of the night, and Bern is at the door for me at the usual hour. With the fall season, the light turns orange earlier, and the shadows grow blacker, and the wide, flat planks of each business and house look ashy and grey against the boldness of the sky. Tonight, Bern speaks of politics, though he does not ask my opinion. President Garfield was shot in the summer, but only died a week ago from the wounds. The countryside is still mourning and reeling from the news, which flew down the telegraph line as the announcement sped toward Fort Randall. Bern wonders if the new President Arthur will make the Dakotas part of the Union. I keep my eyes down and reflect on the conversations the doctor and I had when the bulletins came through occasionally, discussing President Garfield's condition. Doctor Kinney was frustrated and passionate about the likelihood of disease and infection. He believes few doctors use carbolic acid for disinfecting, and we had a strong discussion about surgical anesthesia. But Bern won't care about any of this. I let him speak of his own thoughts, and I hold mine tight and silent.

As we near Widow Hawks' door, he turns to me to bid me goodnight. I put out my hand.

"You do not need to come around anymore."

He drops his fingers from his hat. His black eyes are in shadow, but his grim mouth tightens. I cannot tell if I have made another man angry tonight. Bern is still a bit of a mystery to me. I do not understand why he has spent weeks courting me, and why he continued after my pregnancy became obvious, and then even after miscarriage. I'll likely never know.

We do not speak words of affection. And I know I do not love him.

"What are you saying, Jane?"

"I'm saying that I don't think we ought to continue on like this when I have no intention of marrying you."

My words are more confident than I feel, for he is not a laughing man. I suppose he will take my rejection to heart more so than he will let on.

"Do you think you'll get a better offer?" He is not rancorous, just curious, as if he wonders how someone else could have started to court me without his knowledge.

"No," I say. That is a truth, indeed.

"Then why not make some sort of a life here?" he wonders, and I put my hand on his arm lightly, to stop him from questioning further. It is the first time we have touched since the Independence Day celebration dance, and it feels odd to put fingers on the worn denim of his shirt.

"Because it would be a sad life, Bern. We would not find much to make our life together interesting, and we would eventually resign ourselves to misery. I have done it once before, and I do not want to do it again."

"How long have you felt this way?" he asks. He is right to ask, and he deserves an answer.

I sigh. "I don't know. I know I've not ever cared deeply for you, though I thought I might, someday. I tried." This is not entirely true. "But I don't. I am sorry."

He is quiet for a long time, looking at the ground. "I thank you for your honesty."

Touching his hat to me one last time, he turns around and walks away, a long black shadow in the setting sun. I think I should feel happy, but I am simply exhausted, and go into Widow Hawks' house, where it is dim and dark.

262

Mrs. Mary M. H. May
32 Pine Street
Gloucester, Mass.

Dear Aunt Mary,

I deeply apologize to so unexpectedly impose on you, but I find myself in need of introductions in Gloucester. If you've heard from Mother, you know I have tried my luck in the Dakota Territories, but find it to be unsuitable. While I hope to return to Massachusetts, I'd like to continue living, as you do, on my own.

However, Henry's estate has not left me enough to live on, especially after the expenses of travel, and I will need to find a situation to sustain me. My experiences as a wife include nursemaid and cook, and I have furthered my skills in housekeeping, cooking, and gardening since widowhood. I do not plan to trouble your domestic situation, but will need your expertise in finding a suitable cottage for rent.

I look forward to hearing from you as soon as you are able to reply, and I will be on the first train out after receiving your favorable letter. Thank you for your help. I am eager to spend time rekindling our relationship as it was when I was a child, visiting you at the seashore.

Until then, I am your loving niece,
Jane

CHAPTER 24
30 September 1881

I bring my laundry and a bit of Widow Hawks' to the doctor's house to start the washing routine. She has very little I can rinse out. Much of her fall wardrobe consists of buckskin, deer hides, and furs, which I do not dare try to clean myself. The doctor brings up water in the morning after breakfast, and I spend the better part of the day soaking, beating, and wringing out all our clothing, sheets, and blankets. I have decided to have Kate send out for some fabric for new sheets. My bleeding ruined an entire set of the doctor's. The cloth should arrive soon, and I can replenish his linen closet with a bit of cash I've saved from my wages.

The late September breeze is still warm in the afternoon. Everything here is yellow with light after lunch, and yet the evenings are colder every day.

The news in town has turned away from me and my miscarriage to guessing on whether Alan will marry Harriet. If so, the town will need to look for a new schoolteacher come spring. And Robert Brewer, the owner of the Main Inn is ill—Doctor Kinney has been over every day all week—so Elaine Warren is hovering near Tommy Winters' house, hoping the lawyer can draw up a new deed the minute Robert might pass away. It's said Joseph Greenman is offering extra prayers and candles at both St. Diana's *and* St. Aloysius for Robert to die so Elaine will stop eyeing up his own Prime Inn. It's also said that Doris Tucker is watching over Elaine, who she fears will try to make a move on Tommy Winters—Doris's target for matrimony—though anyone with eyes can see Elaine only has interest in making money and she won't trade her Trusty Willy for anyone. I don't blame her that. I've heard how Trusty Willy was knocked over by Elaine's apron string from the moment they met, and he's happily let her run the Golden Nail and anything else she wants to do as long as he can keep buying new inventions.

I will miss these people and their ways. I will miss how nearly anything is possible here. And I'll miss the doctor.

Doctor Kinney courts Kate most nights. I do not need to make him supper anymore, for he eats with her on the front porch of the general store. Many of the townsfolk stop to say howdy to them, and some evenings it is like they are setting court for all the bodies drawn to their cozy tableau.

I miss him desperately. He has breakfast with me and we are companionable, but I admit I try to hold myself apart, so that I am not pulled into his warmth overmuch. He is his usual lighthearted self, and sometimes I laugh because I cannot help it. And I am so happy during these moments of the day. I gaze at his face, delighting in the slant of his cheeks, the wrinkles around his eyes, and the languid brogue. His words wash over me, and I cannot help but finally be lost in what could be, if the world were different.

I do not admit this to anyone, but seeing the doctor with Kate hurts my heart, my stomach, and my head. It is not for me to choose what matter of a person he marries, or whether a pair will be well suited together in the years to come. It is not my place to speak up any further to my employer. He seems to now have a spring in his step, and he whistles when he leaves to see her at supper. His happiness is beautiful, regardless of how I am devastated by it. I'm glad I sent the letter to Aunt Mary. For all I want to stay—*had* decided to stay—I will not spend my years in Flats Junction watching them marry and build a life together. I am maybe stronger than most women I know back East, but I am not unemotional, and I have means of my own if I must use them. The small bit of leftover money from Henry's estate burns in my mind, winking and promising. I could go back. I could escape heartache here. I have just enough left for one ticket.

Some nights I lie awake and wonder why I survived, why against all odds I lived through my miscarriage, if only to live a life so alone. Perhaps it is my burden for trying to live a lie.

Listen to me, turning Catholic after attending Mass— another false thing I still do—with these thoughts of penance! The doctor doesn't say anything when I continue to attend St. Aloysius each Sunday, but I wonder if he has issue with the fact that I go, now that he knows I'm not his faith. How could I ever tell him that I pretend at those Masses? I imagine we are together, and I have turned to his religion for him, and we are pillars of Flats Junction society as Dr. and Mrs. Kinney.

It seems I am still as foolish as ever before.

266

Henry's ring twists around one of my soaked skirts. Pulling my hand out of the water, I inspect the band. It is dented with use now, and spins around my finger due to weight I have lost. I slip it off and set it beside me on one of the garden rocks so it won't come off in the suds.

Standing at the laundry, a secret part of me imagines that we are all family, living happily together. Widow Hawks lives with us at the house, and I pretend my son is alive, and he is not Theodore's child, but the doctor's. And all is well.

There is a shout on the street. I glance up, but do not stop my tasks until I hear yet another cry, and then a woman's scream, and then horses whinny, and I smell it on the breeze.

Smoke.

Wildfire.

Hay-fire.

Something hot and acrid. A fire now on the prairie will raze the town.

It is a death knell.

I spin, thinking to carry water to whatever it is, but then I realize I do not know enough to help, so I pick up my skirts and run, through the backyard, the kitchen, the hallway, and I let the screen door slam as I join the small groups of people sprinting down the streets.

The blaze is high, hot, and fast. Men already try to contain it by shoveling around the fire so that it cannot jump further onto the grasses around it, though there are not any homes nearby that might catch easily. There is far less damage than I had imagined at first, but it is enough for me to stop in the middle of the street in horror.

Once the men finish protecting the town, they stand back while Widow Hawks' home burns. It is this refusal to douse the house with dirt or sand spurring me into action again, and I run toward the building, and toward the bowed head standing apart from the group.

"Mrs. Weber!" There is a yank on my arm. It is the doctor, looking both aghast and furiously frantic. "Stop runnin'! There is nothin' you can do now. And you are weak enough as it is."

He holds my upper arm in a tight grip and marches us hurriedly down Main Street to join Widow Hawks. We are a line, braced against the iron rails of the train track, watching her life turn to black puffs of air, like charred snowflakes wafting toward the sky instead of away.

"Why is no one helping? Why are they not putting it out?" I ask her and the doctor together, appalled and frightened. The fire is lifelike, hungry, angry. The timber of the house, the dried baskets, herbs, and hides do not have a chance.

"They do not wish to do so." Her voice is resigned, but steady. "And they do not want me here anyway."

"Who did this?" The doctor leaves us, and paces in front of several of the men. They are bland, their faces streaked with soot, sweat, and dust. They don't appear to care about the home turning to charcoal. They are likely only satisfied that nothing else catches fire. The heat radiates off of the building. Waves of air are visible, wafting around us.

One of the men gives a crass shrug and spit. "Aww, Doc, we know you're soft on the Indians, whatever good it does ya. But now maybe there'll be no need for them to come back to town. No place t' stay, as it were."

"That doesn't answer my question, Tate."

Of course, none of the townsfolk—and the cowboys here in particular—would care to discover that the last of Widow Hawks' family is on the reservation for good. That they cannot leave it now, even if they wished to see her.

Had anyone thought to ask, perhaps her life would not be curling in smoke now. Bern knew. I'd told him, hadn't I? Where is he? These are his friends.

The doctor can't believe anyone will own up to this assault, this terrible action of anger and intolerance, can he? He can't expect them to admit and confess to him. Especially given that people are skeptical of his skill, and his affiliation with the natives is a black mark against his character. Even though the settlers have won the battles and the wars, it is as if they do not feel solid with their victory until all of the tribes are gone from sight. Some of the men standing about are mere overgrown boys. They could not possibly have fought in the war, and ought to have no real issue with Indians other than what their parents warned and prodded them to feel. I know prejudice exists everywhere, but where I come from in Massachusetts, it does not feel quite so blatant. It does not include such annihilation. At least, not anymore.

The afternoon grows older, and the flames are peach and orange and gold. The fire starts to roar less, slowly, as time stretches out and then contracts. Before long, it is night. Still I stand next to Widow Hawks, as she stares at it all burning to ruin. There were other things in that home: memories cherished from the man she loved for decades: love letters, a bridal veil, gifts and books. All gone to ash.

Mitch Brinkley arrives, finally, with his father, three brothers, and one brother-in-law. Their wagon is full of

269

sandy dirt, and they throw it on the small flames. The fire hisses, dying further, until the embers themselves are buried in blackness.

They swing their lanterns over us. The other cowboys melt away, assured the town is safe. I cannot think that one of them is responsible for this. Still ... what if they watched only to be sure their own handiwork did not do more damage than they wished?

How do I recover from such violence? What happens now? Who stands as the lawman?

It is a good thing I am looking to leave Flats Junction. I am not so sturdy as I thought. I cannot handle all of this chaos without feeling as though my world constantly crumbles. If it were my house, I would be sobbing. Instead, Widow Hawks says nothing.

"Will you be alright?" Mitch asks the doctor, who nods, taking one of their spare lights.

"I'll take the women to stay at Kate's for a bit while we sort out the mess."

Mitch glances over to us, and says casually, "We'll go with you. There's enough mischief afoot tonight."

The doctor does not bother to argue. We jump into the wagon bed and I wedge next to George and John Brinkley. I am numb with anger and shock and betrayal. This was hatred, with no purpose other than to cause pain on another. Will the people of Flats Junction even care to track down the perpetrators, to bring this to justice for the sake of an Indian woman? If not for her, at the very least for the memory of her husband, or her daughter?

Kate is standing on the porch. She has had a clear view of the flames this entire time, and I know why she has refused to come to her mother's side. It is her selfishness. Her fear.

"Kitty," Doctor Kinney pleads in a low voice. I hear it because I am out of the wagon at once, and on the stairs. "You've got some room. Can you make up a bed for Esther and Mrs. Weber?"

"Why? There's room with you." Her answer is clipped.

"Because it is your mother and she has suffered tonight. I expect she'd like to see her daughter, and you know Mrs. Weber cannot stay with me alone."

Kate gives a shake of her head, her lovely hair cascading in slight waves. Even in the dark, she is stunning and proud and unyielding.

"My *mother* should take herself to the reservation."

"You know she does not want that. Her home is where you are."

"I'll not take her in." Kate's voice is a whisper, angry and fierce. "I cannot have anyone thinking I am partial to her, that I would put my native birth first."

"That is not the point here, Kitty." His voice is soothing, but I cannot see his face in the oily lights from below. "Your mother needs your help."

"I will not help her. You should know better than to ask this of me. I'm sorry, Pat. I can't do it."

They stand there, as if measuring each other's mettle, and, finally, the doctor gives in.

"Kate is too tied up with goods this time to make room," he says generally to the Brinkleys in the wagon. "We'll make do at my place for now, and we can decide tomorrow what is next."

"We'll talk, certainly, Doc," old Henry agrees heavily.

The Brinkleys see us to the doctor's house. I light a lamp so we can see our way upstairs. It is unspoken, but I will share the bed with Widow Hawks so she does not need to rest her old bones on the floor. We all walk up the stairs in states of shock, and she goes immediately into the spare bedroom, where only weeks ago I nearly died. The doctor comes up the stairs after us, and in the dancing shadows, I notice he is downcast. It's likely he mourns for his adoptive family, for the loss of Widow Hawks' home, and for the evil of the arsonists, whoever they may be. I know I do, and I don't even have half of the history he does with the Davies family.

"Doctor Kinney," I say softly, laying a hand on his arm as he moves past to his bedroom. He pauses, and glances down at me, but does not meet my eyes. I wish I could touch his forehead and the plane of his cheek, and we could face this tragedy together. Instead, I try to soothe him. "I am sorry you had to quarrel with Kate on our behalf."

"It should never have been an argument. Good night, Mrs. Weber."

He pulls away, and I turn to the other bedroom, where I undress in the lantern light. Widow Hawks is already in the bed with her back to me. Tears tickle my eyes, and I wonder at her staunchness. How can I cry for her loss when she bears it so readily?

I put out the light, climb into bed, and put my arms about her shoulders. She is strong, with a boniness that comes with age. Her hands grasp mine, and the power in the hold speaks to me, and tells me she is hurting. Eventually, I fall asleep. I do not know if she does.

272

CHAPTER 25
1 October 1881

In the morning, at first I think it is a dream, that my hair does not really smell like smoke, that I am still simply recovering in the doctor's house, that time has not pushed forward. Widow Hawks is gone from her side of the bed, even though the light is watery and pale and early. There is a rattle of crockery below, and it is not Widow Hawks' gentle hand, but the doctor's tumbling way of making coffee. I listen to his steps, counting them from the kitchen to his study.

I go down to the kitchen, realizing that the clothes I had been washing the day before are still in the washbin in the yard. The soak probably did them more good than harm. Everything lies about the yard in a haphazard place, tasks unfinished. I sigh. Now is as good a time as any to wring things out and soap them up. I take out the tin of charcloth, flint, and steel from my pocket and light up some soft dry grass easily, the quick puff of fire a reminder of yesterday's fast blaze. I build the flames, and prepare the lye

273

with exceptional care, and start to haul up water from the well in small buckets to fill the bigger wash kettle.

As I wait for the water to heat, I pull the washboard toward me, swirling my hand in the chilly water and gaze at my garden. It has done well this year, and I wish I would be able to stay and cultivate it better in following years. But this will be Kate's realm soon enough, surely. It will be her green patch, and her washbin. It was never really mine to begin with, so it is not truly a loss for me. I commit these words to my mind, over and over: *it is not mine.* This is not my place. I am only a paid housekeeper.

"Stop." The doctor is behind me, holding steaming mugs full of coffee.

I sigh and take one of the cups from him. He does a decent job with the brew, and I sip it slowly, watching the bits of morning haze and fog shift on the grassland around us. He stands next to me, comfortable and at ease, while my body tenses. I fear if I am not on guard around him, I will give in. I will grab his hands and kiss his mouth, and he will be shocked and repulsed and will no longer wish to spend such moments in friendship together.

"Where did she go?" I ask instead.

"Esther? She went down to the rubble, to see if she can glean anythin' from the ashes. I doubt she will, but there's always a chance."

"What now?"

He gives me a sliding glance. "You mean, what happens to those who did this?"

I nod, and he gives a long, sorry sigh.

"I'm not the lawman, and even if I were, it would be hard to get people interested in talkin' if they knew somethin'

274

about it. She's Indian, pure and simple, and folks don't think our laws apply to them. It doesn't help that memories here are fresh of the wars and many think of natives as shirkin' the law anyway. It's a huge mess, is what it all is."

"We don't have a sheriff here, do we?"

"No. Old Henry Brinkley is as close as it comes, short of bringin' in someone from Fort Randall or Yankton. We prefer not to have that. So many are barely above the law as is. Usually anyone callin' himself a deputy or sheriff is mainly a hooligan lookin' for a payout."

I grow hot with anger. "So, nothing will be done?"

He shrugs and looks into his coffee. "I'd like to see somethin'. I'll be makin' general inquiries when I can, but I know my place here isn't quite so revered as all that, and you know it too. There's enough of the town still skeptical of me, and of doctorin' in general, so I can only ask carefully. Unless someone outright admits or brags of it in a moment of drunken pride, I doubt we will ever really know who did it. If old Davies were alive, there'd have been hell to pay. If Kitty wanted justice, some would probably listen."

"Then she must! For her mother's sake! You ought to talk to her about this. You're her beau." The word trips from my mouth and hangs between us. We have not discussed their relationship since the evening I forced the issue, even though it is obvious what has happened.

He gives a bemused smile as he looks down at me. "Speakin' of beaus, I noticed you walk home alone when you go by the general."

He's trying to be lighthearted, to deflect attention from his personal life, and I suppose he is in the right. As my employer, he does not need to answer to me about

275

Kate. I gulp down the rest of the coffee, nearly scalding my throat.

"Yes. I—that is to say, Bern and I decided it was not necessary to continue on."

He seems genuinely surprised, and a strange look passes across his brow.

"Why? Are you not interested in settlin' down? You're young yet, and could still even have children. I have made sure of that as best I can."

"I know, and I thank you for it," I say. "But no, I do not wish ... I've been married once before, and it was not easy. Henry and I had a decent marriage, but I could not tie myself down again simply to marry. I'd prefer a love match, though I think I might be too old."

"You never know," he reminds me. "Think of old Walter Salomon and his elderly bride, Berit. It might happen to you again."

"Well, unlikely," I say flatly, unable to look at him, swallowing the bit of boiling, suffocating nausea lifting in my lungs when I think how true the statement is. "Anyway, I knew Bern was not the man I wanted. For all that it would have been easy enough to wed him, I didn't think it right to do so."

"This is true. You're not one for takin' the easy way. I remember."

"Should I have allowed him to court me, knowing I do not love him?" I ask, feeling as though I can ask him such questions, considering how deeply he knows my story. "Why should I? I want a good marriage, whatever that is."

"I can understand that," he agrees, though I do not think he truly could, given how long he's been a bachelor. He

276

finishes his coffee before insisting on helping pull up more water. He does against my protestations that my strength is returning easily, then leaves for his rounds. There's a sharp sound from around the elderberry hedge. I glance up to see the quivering straw hat of Mrs. Emma Molhurst bouncing behind it. Has she been eavesdropping? I find I don't care a bit.

She disappears inside her own house soon after the doctor departs, though, and I stand in the quiet for a minute before bending back to the washboard. A winking in the sun reminds me of my wedding band. It is still on the garden rock. I bend to pick it up, inspecting it. It seems a shame to give it up, for it is a stout piece of jewelry and could be pawned if I ever fell into penury. Why do I wear it? It seems frivolous now, and there is no point in it. Henry's time in my life is over. Putting it in my pocket, I turn back to my chores.

CHAPTER 26
1 October 1881

Widow Hawks comes back soot-stained and weary. In her hands is a small wood box streaked black, one corner so charred it breaks away as she opens it.

"My wedding band, a hawk's feather, and the pearl buttons from the first pair—only pair—of gloves I ever owned," she says softly. "I would have taken the photo of Percy over any of this."

The box sits on the table between us at the doctor's house, forlorn, half empty, a strange collection of sentimental items that survived the flames by chance. It had been buried under the iron stove, which is blackened and choked, the tin piping twisted beyond use, but it is the only thing still standing. She is as emotional as I have ever seen her, more affected by her loss now than while it was happening in front of us.

"What will you do now?"

She sighs and sits, leaving the box open, and picks up the feather. "I know my daughter would have me go to the

278

reservation, west of here. Or perhaps even further west. I don't know how far my family made it before they settled for the season." She pauses, and then looks at me serenely. "I think I will stay here for a time, and help you and the doctor."

I look down at the well-worn grooves of the planks. I know the creases that collect the most dirt, the drafts around the doors, which stairs squeak particularly loud. I know where the mice like to hide, and I'm very fast at killing them now. I know where the doctor keeps all his files, and how to find a case at the moment it is needed for reflection. And I even know most of the patients personally. Everything in this house is mine. No! Not really mine. I cannot offer her the sanctuary she requests. It is for the doctor to decide.

But I will not stay. Even now, Doctor Kinney does not come home for supper, choosing instead to dine with Kate. Why should I stay and watch this unfold? Why should I wait for their wedding? He's known her for as long as he's known Widow Hawks. Why shouldn't he wed her? Men and women have married with less in common, and less history. He may not agree with Kate all the time, but a quarrel does not always end a romance.

And what will become of me when he marries? He will not need a housekeeper. He will have a wife.

Widow Hawks is watching me. I wonder how much conflict shows on my face. Slowly she reaches across the boards and grasps my fingers.

"I do not mind the loss of my house, Jane. Do not weep for me. The memories most dear are still in my mind, and that is all that matters."

"That is a lovely thing to say."

I turn to the stove to make us a light supper, mostly of squash from the garden. We eat in silence. My appetite is still diminished, and for the first time, she notices acutely.

"What troubles you? Do you not feel well?"

I choke down another bite of the simple meal, and then put my fork down. I push my fingers into my eyes, willing them to keep from crying, but it is no use. I am much too passionate. My miscarriage seems to have let loose torrents of feeling, and I do not have the language to explain it most times. I deserve little happiness for the choices I've made, and certainly don't deserve what my heart desires.

"Jane!" She stands and comes around to the bench where I sit, and her hands cover mine, pulling them away from my face so that I must look at her. "What is it?"

I sigh inwardly, then realize the truth is better than anything else I can say. This, at least, I have learned well.

"I will be leaving you, and I will miss you."

"What?" Her shock is genuine, perhaps even more so than when her house was on fire. "When will you go?"

"As soon as my aunt writes of a situation that will suffice. I expect her letter in a few weeks, I hope, and then I will take the next train out."

"But why?"

I give her a small smile. "It is as you said. I suit the doctor and I should love him."

Her eyes immediately grow warm, but she seems to innately understand my dilemma. As a mother would, she draws me near, embracing me lightly, whispering to my hair in her own language, and the undulation of the strange words rolls over me: "*Owákaȟniǧe ye*. I understand. *Wana wa⊠-eye'ye*. I am crying now. *Owákaȟniǧe ye*."

I try not to weep on her, because she has lost so much herself, but I cannot help it. My tears turn to sobs, and I cry for the future I have lost, the chances I wasted, and the words I'll never be able to say. Even with her arms around me, I feel empty and alone, as if crying forever would not make things right for either of us.

CHAPTER 27
2 November 1881

The sunset is golden today, and the weather unseasonably warm. The long grasses of the prairie are gold as well, and soft pale ivory, and brushed red. The colors are vibrant here too, in the tiny cemetery at the northern edge of Flats Junction. Grasses grow thick along every small stone and marker, except the clay-and-sand filled mound, freshly finished for my little son.

Wandering through the cemetery, I stare at the words stamped into the copper crosses, already turning green along the edges. It is the family section where Marie the tinsmith loitered after my son's funeral. Some grave markers are placed so close together I cannot see how so many bodies could fit in the earth below. *Tomasz Kotlarczyk. Wojciech Kotlarczyk.* Further away I read another last name: *Monika Salomon.* Several others. And the two stillborns she'd mentioned, unnamed but marked as well.

I've yet to make it to Marie's for tea. I'm too nervous. And now I'll never go.

I move to kneel next to the small cross of my son, and I absently pull young renegade weeds from his grave. No one will think to come here when I leave, and he will turn to dust without prayers over him. There is some comfort that his bones will not be lonely, as I have been, and at least he rests near a Kinney. The small stone next to his marker is young and fresh, placed in recent months. It reads: *Brónach Caera Kinney. Beloved Sister, Aunt & Wife. 1822—1880.*

I look back at the smaller grave.

"My boy," I whisper. The wind catches my voice and pulls it away from me. "I'm sorry I never was able to hold you, and that you left my body early, so you could not even breathe one puff of air. You might have loved it here."

Would he have grown to look like Theodore, with his brown hair and solid jaw? Would he have taken after my father, with his broad chest and stomach? I cannot imagine any of these visions.

Would I have loved him enough, for all he was unplanned?

I brush the dirt in swirls with a finger, and feel tears pressing against my eyes, but thankfully they do not fall. I'm quiet for a while. I hear a dog bark in the town and a wagon creaks by. But no one hails me. Perhaps it is an unwritten courtesy that one does not call out to someone mourning at a grave. Maybe the bulk of St. Aloysius blocks me from most eyes.

The wind slows, and in the silence of the grasses, I say, "And I will remember you, my little one, though I never met you, and though I know I could not have given you everything you deserved. Your father and I—well ... I'm sorry. I must leave you. Please forgive me."

"Where are you goin'?"

I nearly jump out of my skin with surprise. The graveyard, even in daylight, is a bit disconcerting.

It is the doctor, probably on his way to Kate's for supper, as it's about that time. He stands nearby, arms crossed, his broad mouth trembling with words, and the light shines into his face so his eyes are blue and pure. I do not have the energy to rise and tell him my news. The letter just arrived today. I've been stopping at the post office each day, hoping for news, unable to bear the heaviness in my chest each night the doctor dines with Kate. Douglas Ofsberger gave me an appraising look each time I asked, as if I was awaiting some scandalous news. Nancy would speculate, but she's guessed wrongly. News from home is simply news from home, I'd told her.

There is always a train heading east on Fridays at five in the morning. It feels hasty and too fast, but I'd written to my aunt that I would head straight out once receiving her letter. I wish to do something right for once. It is proper of me to keep such a promise.

"My Aunt Mary has found me work," I finally answer the doctor. "I'll need to leave on Friday to make sure I have time to set up a cottage before I start cooking for one of the great houses in Gloucester."

He drops his arms, gaping at me.

"And why would your Aunt Mary write you about a job when you've got a good one here?" He is indignant in his surprise. He is nearly angry, given the way his arms uncross and re-cross, but it seems he's more shocked than upset right now. I sigh, clear my dress, and slowly stand, careful so that I am not too dizzy when I do.

"Because I need to have a purpose, Doctor Kinney. And once you decide to stop courting Kate and marry her instead, I won't have a thing to do here. There will be no reason to stay. I need to make my own life."

"Aye, but there's no reason it can't be here. I've a practice here that could use help." His voice is low, and his gaze is locked with mine. "You know this. You've done much—and learned too. I thought you liked to learn."

"I do."

"Then ... why? How will I manage the patients? I've grown used to havin' you about for the smaller tasks. Keepin' my papers and the like."

"I'm easy to replace. I think you might find an avid helper in Widow Hawks. She is capable. She helped you save my life. She has nowhere to live. It works out right ... proper." The ill-put English slang slips out as I try to fend off my unease. This is not how I had planned to tell the doctor of my departure.

"If you are doin' this because you don't wish to impose on my charity, I have no issue with you both stayin' on with me."

"Doctor Kinney." I shake my head at him. "You know that it's an impractical arrangement, and eventually the town won't like it. You've enough against you already. And you know it will not work once you are married."

He gives me a hard look. "You seem so sure I'll marry."

"Won't you?"

I brush past him, heading back to his house, irritated I have nowhere to retreat from the argument. He follows me to East Avenue, though Kate's store is in the opposite direction.

"So where will you go?" he asks, badgering me, and obviously frustrated.

"My aunt has found me a cottage to let in Gloucester. I'll be on the seashore again." The idea gives me some small hope. Surely, only good can come of living by the ocean once more. It will be homey and I will be able to start over with the introductions Aunt Mary has found. I might forget the doctor, and find a beau.

"Gloucester. Jesus," I hear him swear lightly under his breath. We stand outside his door, facing one another. He stares at me, as if deciding whether an argument now is worth his time.

"It seems damn foolish," he bites out bluntly. "Here you are, all trained in the ways of country nursin', knowin' my patients and the pace of my days, and you're leavin'?"

"It's a good opportunity," I tell him, and that part is true.

"You've decided you don't need this now, is that it?" he asks, gesturing to the slope of his roof and the squat houses of the neighbors. "Now that you've lost the babe, you have no need to hide from your family and your fancy Eastern city. I thought you better than that. I thought you preferred it here. I … you can teach yourself here. I won't stop you from readin' my medical books. I won't question you furtherin' your education."

He speaks to my heart, my nature, while at the same time his accusation is the worst pain of all, for it is far from the reality. How I desire to tell him of my emotions! How I wish I could shove past the vestiges of learned respectability and take him up on his offer to stay! But stay as what? The housekeeper? When every particle in my blood screams to be his lover?

286

"You're very kind. Too kind to me," I say. "But it's for the best."

"Well, Mrs. Weber," he says after a long moment, and I cannot read the feeling behind his tone. "I did not expect this of you, though I suppose I can't force you to stay if you feel you truly must go."

"Then I'll get to packing tonight, so I might say some goodbyes tomorrow."

He does not meet my eyes, and walks away down the small yard into the street toward Kate's welcoming porch. The evening chill descends quickly as the sun sets, but I do not go in and pack. I watch him walk away from me, his lightly striped shirt sometimes grey in shadow, and other times washed a brilliant rose in the late sunset.

I hope I will have a memory of him always, regardless of what my future holds.

CHAPTER 28
3 November 1881

"But you could work out here," Alice Brinkley urges. "I'm sure Sadie Fawcett would love to be the only one in town with a live-in cook, and Tom can afford it."

"No." I shake my head, though I smile at her earnestness.

"Well, I still don't see why you should rush off when it's not even settled between the doc and Kate. Their courting could go on another year or more."

"I'd have to look elsewhere to find a job when they do wed. There is an opportunity now. You understand, Alice? I don't wish to be redundant."

She sighs and presses a small wrapped cheese for the journey into my palm. At least this time, I will not be with child on the train.

We give a teary goodbye to each other, and we promise to write. I will miss her cheery ways, even though I did not get to see her as often as I would have liked.

As I walk back to town, I look at Flats Junction, spread out in dun-colored sunlight. Many of the homes are familiar to me. I know the families and children who live in them. Most have been kind, welcoming, or at the very least, cordial. It is obvious that without even trying I have found a little place for myself. If I had a choice, I would set up a home of my own, where I might look after myself and the doctor, as would be fitting. I'd have Widow Hawks stay with me, if she wished. *Dreams.*

The edges of the town meet prairie suddenly, and the dusty land is pocketed by small holes filled with the little dogs. It's too soon in the day for coyotes, though I know now they are easy to scare. I think that it is a very lovely town. My nostalgia comes with my leaving it.

And yet ... I am still appalled no one searches out the arsonist who burned Widow Hawks' home. It is probably best that I go. I'd start asking questions, and get indignant at the lack of response. I'd stir trouble, which would be entirely inappropriate and unbecoming of a lady.

Kate is out on the general's porch, shooing Horeb and Gilroy off for their supper at the mess hall, though I notice Gilroy goes north to the Golden Nail instead today. I wonder if he's trying to make eyes at Toot. Everyone knows she'd be quite receptive. Or he's off to see the coffee mill Trusty Willy has just brought in, which is said to be so new there's no patent on it yet.

It is November, but the night is still warm enough that Kate and Doctor Kinney can court in the open air. She is setting the table. I find strange solace in the idea that he will be well looked after.

"Kate," I call. I stand at the bottom of her stairs, just like I did the first morning I arrived in Flats Junction. She gazes down at me, but her eyes are not shrewd this time. She seems in a good mood, and comes down to where I am waiting, taking my hand in hers. News has traveled already, and she knows I am leaving.

"I'll miss you." She gives a small laugh. "Who will help me run all the festivals in town now?"

"I should think that you'll manage splendidly." I cannot bring myself to speak more; she will eventually have Doctor Kinney at her side to help with whatever projects she undertakes.

"Well." She gives a shake of her head. "I'll make sure the doc is fed and cleaned up."

"I know you will."

"And you're likely glad to get out of here. We're just a small, ignorant town compared to Boston." The forced lightness of her voice hides a tight frustration I can hear anyway. "Aren't you just lucky to have the money and the ability to leave a place whenever it suits you?"

She smiles at me, but her eyes are cold, and there are no tears of sadness at my departure. For several months now, I have thought of her as a friend. One with whom I do not always agree, and sometimes her behavior appalls me, but a friend regardless. I believe now she has never really thought so highly of me. Perhaps she will be glad to have me go, if only to speed along the doctor's expected proposal. Without a housekeeper, he will likely take a wife, finally. Why wouldn't he?

"Mrs. Weber!" Doctor Kinney himself appears from inside the general, clambering down the stairs and interrupting us. Kate backs away from me. His hand comes up and touches her shoulder. They glance at each other in a comfortable, familiar way, and she starts back up the stairs.

"Supper is nearly ready."

"Spiced cornbread tonight?" he asks hopefully, and she gives him an exasperated look.

"You know I don't do any of that type of cooking, Pat. It'll be a stew."

I know she will never give him the type of food Widow Hawks makes, foods that I would have learned for him so he might have special meals sometimes. But that is his choice. He should understand his sweetheart has no intention of ever doing anything remotely Indian with her life.

"I was just giving my goodbye." I nod at him, indicating he can follow Kate, take a seat on the porch, and wait for her to serve him. For all that she scoffed at domesticity when I miscarried, she's fallen easily enough into the pattern of it.

He looks down at me and does not smile. "You really mean to leave tomorrow, just like that?"

"I must, Doctor Kinney." It is all I can say. Every time I think of leaving him, pain runs through my chest and stomach. Could I tell him I love him even if pressed? I doubt it. The rejection he would give me would be even worse than the relief of honesty on my part. There are times when it is good to hold things close.

I walk toward East Avenue, unable to glance backward to watch him sit with Kate. As I walk, Douglas and Nancy Ofsberger come out to bid me goodbye, with Douglas' father calling out from his perch on the post office's porch. Sadie rushes out for an embrace as well. I'd said farewell to Anette earlier when she left her mother's house, and I had raised my hand silently at Marie when she opened up her shop. For all my friendships, no one knows how lonely I really am, how much I hate to leave them all, how much I mourn. Our friendships, as tentative and new as they are, are one of the richest, loveliest things to ever happen to me.

Without caring, I let the screen door slam behind me. There are no smells from the kitchen. Widow Hawks is not inside. I can only imagine she is back at the burn pile of her house, or outside in the backyard tending the garden a bit. It is my last night in this place and I find myself wandering the rooms. They are silent, as if waiting for their next adventure, the next womanly hands to touch them. The spigot in the lab shines, the floors are swept and scrubbed without a flake of lye on them. Upstairs, my small trunk is packed and closed, the clothing carefully folded up. I do not expect to need a split skirt in Gloucester, but I will take it nevertheless. I'd asked the doc about repaying him for the clothing and he'd brushed it off, angrier than ever, and I did not dare offer the idea again. My small personal items are tucked in the carpet bag, with the medicine bottle from Doctor Kinney's prescription, with his dear note, curled inside my best handkerchief.

I wander into the doctor's bedroom. It is not so sacred a place to me now. I have washed the man's clothes, cleaned his bedding, and scrubbed the floors and window. His parents gaze serenely from the portrait on the wall. I know now I like the look of his mother's eyes because they remind me of his.

"I love him," I tell her softly. "I hope that he is truly happy." My voice falls into silence again.

In the kitchen, I debate making overnight oats or

292

starting a dough for the doctor's weekly bread. I should, as one of my final acts as his housekeeper.

The pantry door creaks slightly when I open it. As I reach for the flour, the grey shadow of yet another mouse streaks behind the sack, and disappears behind the goods. Without a thought, I grab the heavy skillet on the wall by the larder and yank the flour bag back with a violent jerk, giving no warning to the cowering creature. Blindly, I swing, arcing the iron over my head and smashing down with a reverberating force. The collision of the hit with the hardwood floor shoots up my arm, but with the first smack, the tears fall, and the snapping of tiny bones is lost in the aggression of my weeping.

I cannot manage it, but I must. I do not wish to go, but I will.

The ironware seems to live in my hand, thick and black and heavy. I bring it down again, harder and faster, unable to truly see in the dimness of the pantry or past the tears. Over and over, faster and fiercer, a relentless banging cacophony, the iron and my arm are one. Strength from hard labor, from a deep welling of remorse and loss, and the inability to understand it all pours from my skin and into the cookware.

My God! My life! It's shreds of what it could have been, might have been. Here, in Flats Junction. It is over, and I must start again.

And again! And again! *Again!*

I am so tired of this. So desperately tired of starting again. So lost. Alone. *Again.*

I don't want to leave. I don't want it.

I don't want this.

Please.

The mouse is demolished, a bony smear on the bottom of the skillet, and I've split the bag of flour, the seam an ugly, fat, hole pouring grainy globs onto the floorboards. And still I bring the iron down in brutal blows, striking without pause.

It is too much. It is too much to ask.

Too much! Not enough!

I want to scream. *Don't make me leave! Don't ask me to leave!*

My arm is rubbery, and my tears slow, my sight clearing, yet my blood congests in my head, making it feel as heavy as the iron in my palm.

The pantry floor is an utter mess, and the bottom of the skillet bumpy with bone and fur and pinky flour-and-blood. Standing slowly, my hands and apron cloudy with white, I inhale so shakily I think I might weep again just by drawing breath.

When I turn, my heart freezes.

Doctor Kinney stands at the side of the table, immobile and needle-straight. His face is slack with shock and he seems so appalled he's beyond language.

We stare at one another, and I try to dredge up something to say, some way to explain, but pain and embarrassment block my tongue.

I toss the filthy skillet onto the stovetop, and twitch my fingers along my skirt to flick away the drops of flour. Marching past the doctor, I hike up the stairs and into my bedroom, closing the door against him and his silent judgement, and go to bed early. I don't want to miss my train.

CHAPTER 29
4 November 1881

In the morning, I do not bother to make coffee or tea. Widow Hawks will do so. We did not speak much last night when she came into the bedroom, and we said our goodbyes simply. She pressed her forehead to mine, promised to write a bit, and held me tightly as we slept in the small bed. I've grown used to her next to me in the sheets, a surrogate mother.

As I dress, she wakes and watches. We do not speak. It is not a silence that makes me uncertain or uncomfortable, as it did those first few weeks together. Now we are quiet because nothing needs to be said. It is a trait I've learned from her without meaning to do so.

"I will write," I tell her again. "And I will miss you so much."

She smiles at me, accepting of this as well. I pick up my bag and trunk, and walk down the stairs, trying to keep my shoes from making too much noise. I do not wish to bother Doctor Kinney so early. My right arm is sore, but I can bear it. How amazing is it to have the strength to carry the small trunk? I have grown heartier to be sure.

The town is quiet, though I know it will pick up as soon as the train comes in. No one can really sleep through the whistle of the steam and the cracking of the tracks. Even now, I can hear the engine making its way through the prairie, though it is not quite in sight. The platform is empty, and Franklin Jones takes my money with his only arm, frowning and irritable. Wagons creak through the streets. Farmers are bringing fall produce to be sent down the rails and sold at the bigger towns along the way, some bring livestock.

There is a hoot and a whistle, and the black engine grows from the land, tiny and dark, looming bigger by the minute. I cannot believe how recently I came here, and yet I will leave Flats Junction already. Now that I am on the brink of the next journey, the time here seems both longer and shorter than the reality. So much has happened. I have learned the depths of my strength, of my abilities, and my tolerance. I am wiser, worldlier.

The train shrieks as it slows and then comes to a full halt, waking most of the town with this last, bone-crunching sound. There are shouts of men suddenly, and a general scurrying. I take a step toward the passenger car just as the brogue cuts through the noise.

"Mrs. Weber!"

I turn and watch the doctor hurry toward me. He does not even have his hat, so he must have sprinted out without pause, and has barely adjusted his clothes; the train's sound must have woken him moments ago. There is a moment of foolish, ridiculous hope. Has he come to stop me, to keep me here?

It doesn't matter. I could not do it, even if he asked. I could not watch him court Kate, and marry her. Heat floods my face when I think of him standing in the kitchen yesterday. How long had he watched me smash about his pantry? I'm glad I can leave, and don't have to hear his questions.

"Mrs. Weber." He comes in front of me, gazing down with something between confusion and hurt across his face. "Did you mean to leave without sayin' goodbye?"

"I didn't want to wake you, Doctor Kinney."

He runs an agitated hand through his dark hair, still tousled from sleep. "Are you sure you're well enough to travel? No more dizzy spells?"

"I can manage it," I say placidly. "I did before."

"I know it," he says resolutely, then stops fidgeting altogether and looks hard at me. I am too distraught to really glance up at him, though I feel him inch toward me, as if he wants to give me a hearty embrace. I wish he would, but there are too many people on the platform and below it, and such warmth would be unseemly in so public a place. Or maybe he wants to chastise me for my uncommonly vicious behavior. I jump into the conversation before he can.

"Well, then," I say. "I have told Esther I will write. You might learn of my adventures through her if you like."

"Mrs. Weber." He says my name again, then stops, and speaks so softly I can barely hear him over the steam and shuffle around us. "Jane."

My head comes up. I want to kiss him. I turn my face to look at the train instead.

The whistle blows, sharp and shrill and screeching.

It is my signal to leave Flats Junction.

297

"Goodbye, Doctor Kinney," I say, and I smile at him tightly, for my smile is not very sincere. "I wish you much happiness here." This I mean truthfully. "Thank you—for saving me, for giving me work when I needed it. Thank you."

I turn, going into the train and finding a seat among the many empty ones before he can catch me with another word. I choose a place on the opposite side of the car, so that I do not need to watch the platform. Slamming my trunk at my feet, I look out over the prairie, where Widow Hawks' house is a black wound.

I like to imagine him standing there, watching the train leave, when in all actuality, he probably walked away as soon as I boarded.

This way, I will never know.

Gloucester

CHAPTER 30
20 March 1882

I like the little cottage I live in, and my employers, though exacting, are kind. Time here in Massachusetts seems to slip by a little quicker each week. I eagerly wait for warmer spring days when the beaches will heat up, the ice floes will melt, and I can walk the sandy stretches and listen to the waves.

My Aunt Mary, while elderly, is thrilled to have family in Gloucester. I know all her friends, and I have met some of their granddaughters. Rose Albin, a lovely girl several years my junior, is not yet married, so we make time for tea once a week to discuss her coming wedding plans. It's not my favorite idea of chatter, but it's what's expected of me.

The Chesters are patient employers. Though I have cooked in their large, shiny, tiled kitchen for four months, I am still perfecting some of the fancier dishes. They are newly minted in their money, having inherited the estate from Mrs. Chester's father, and are desperate to make a go of it properly. Mrs. Chester hired a kitchen girl to help me with the cleaning, and they keep a small group of maids. I am glad when they hire an older woman as a housekeeper shortly after I start; I should not like to be in charge of such a large place, or a staff. Besides, I have enough on my hands now, as Mrs. Chester also wants to start having formal teas and pretty luncheons.

I go to the larder. It is always packed with things I still consider delicacies: candied ginger, unusual spices, fruits, and jellies. Will I ever get used to the finer things again?

But I enjoy making unique dishes with specialty ingredients. Monday is the first tea, and while I will have off on Sunday as I do every week, I want to make sure I am prepared.

As I reach through the bags of tea, cones of sugar, and sacks of flour, and pull what I need for a pastry, my hand knocks against the coffee and the bag splits open, enough for the smell of the pre-roasted beans to waft upwards. I pause. It smells so very much like the brew I would make for Doctor Kinney each morning after roasting the beans myself in the small tin roaster. What a luxury it is to buy them already browned!

Tears come without warning sometimes, and this is one of those times. I stand there, holding the coffee, and my shoulders tremble as I close my eyes and try to hold in my longing. I don't speak of him to anyone—my aunt, my new friends, or my acquaintances at the Chester house—as if by staying silent, he will disappear eventually from my memory. I will be able to think of him fondly without missing him quite so much, only recalling him during soft, faded moments in summer gloaming.

Does distance make my heart fonder? I wonder. I miss my friends too, almost as much as I do my days with Doctor Kinney. I wish I had had more time to laugh at Anette Zalenski's off-color jokes, to sit for tea with Marie the smith, to help Alice can more goods, and to hear Sadie's prattle. I even miss Kate. And Widow Hawks' absence from my nights is a constant ache.

"Mrs. Weber?" It is Beth, the kitchen girl. "Are you alright?"

I straighten, but am not able to turn quite yet.

"Yes, yes. Just planning out Monday's tea."

She leaves me be, and I go ahead with organizing the menu again.

I'm grateful I need only be in the great house from four-thirty in the morning to ten at night. From what I hear, many women are stuck in the kitchen for longer hours, or even live with the staff. I'm fortunate. Aunt Mary found a very fine arrangement for me.

My employers pay me well considering my shortened time, so I am able to afford a tiny cottage on the beach in Gloucester. One large room contains the kitchen and sitting space, all of which has a window overlooking the ocean, with a porch along the front facing the beach. There is a washroom leading into a bedroom, and that is it. The renters before me were a married pair and the bed is enough for two, so I sleep in the middle. Some nights, early on, I would wake, thinking Widow Hawks slept next to me, but those mild sleep-dreams have since stopped.

After lunch is served and then cleaned, I go to the market. The stalls are always open, come rain, shine, or snow. Tonight, I will be making a vegetable puree and potato soup to go with the meat, and I need end-of-season turnips and parsnips.

I walk the stalls. It did not take long for me to meet most of the keepers. Some are elderly sisters who know Aunt Mary, and know I am her niece. They offer me their chickens and eggs for a good price. The butcher is a round, happy man who reminds me a little of my father in a holiday mood. The dairyman has a son who is widowed like me, and while I have not talked to him much, I recognize in him a pain I never felt with the death of Henry. The dairyman's son truly loved his wife. Would I be distraught, had I married Doctor Kinney, and he died? Likely.

Ada Baker is waiting for me next to vegetables of all sizes. They tumble out of baskets in a green and pink medley. She and her daughter Jean have the best produce, and they do a roaring trade every week.

"Will we see you tomorrow?" she asks warmly. Sometimes Aunt Mary and I sit with them at church, and then Jean and Rose both come to my house for tea in the afternoon.

"Of course," I say, and place turnips into my basket. Jean comes around the corner with parsnips and smiles at me. The ladies in this city are usually cold to outsiders, but Aunt Mary paved the way before my arrival. She hinted at my miscarriage as if it was a strange illness, and alluded to my time out West as wild and mysterious. I think some of the women assume I still miss my husband.

"We've got in the first spring asparagus," Jean announces. "I'll bring a bit for tea tomorrow."

"Thank you," I murmur, and move on to the dairy stall for cream. My employer, Mr. Chester, likes his food full of flavor. I think a bit of cream in the puree might be an unlooked-for treat tonight, and I wish to please Mr. Chester as well as his wife.

"Here you are, Mrs. Weber." The dairyman reaches under his stall with my request, where an icebox keeps things chilled even though it is not very warm outside yet. Andrew, the son, comes around the corner hauling a large cheese. He sets it down carefully and gives his head a shake to the little hands reaching up from below the counter to pick at a curd. His wife left him a son and a daughter to care for; the daughter is at school, but the little boy is still at home with the men and his grandmother.

"On the Chester tab, as usual?"

I nod, give a small smile to Andrew, and head back up to the house. The roads are winding, twisted, and cobbled in places, though a few are still dirt and mud. Everything leads away from the wharves, where the inky water is home to fishing boats. My path is up the hill, with the ocean to my back and the wind in my face. Everything here feels heavier, older, wetter. I am not sure which I like more: the coolness of Gloucester, or the dustiness of the Territories. Nostalgia always hits when I am away from either. Granted, I will not return West, so I suppose I will always feel nostalgic about it. It is strange to hold with genteel traditions, such as a Congregational sermon every Sunday. It's odd to wear lighter boots and put on gloves when I go out. The life I had out in the Dakotas seems so much more colorful than what I have now. But I do love the winds off the ocean, the salt in the air, the crying of gulls midday, and the white of the houses and the sky and the salt marshes.

Beth is waiting for me at the trestle table in the big house. She has heated the stove for supper and set water to boil. She learns quickly, and I am pleased with her. I will have to say so to Mrs. Chester when I next get a chance. My new tendency to daydream is always cut short when I enter the kitchen. Always so much to do, so many things to attend. It is a good, busy life.

"Mrs. Weber, I was hoping I might help with the tea on Monday," Beth asks breathlessly. I see her eyeing up the jam I have put out and give a laugh.

"You can taste it when it's all set. If there is enough pastry dough, we can make petites for all the staff to try. I don't think Mrs. Chester will mind."

She comes over to help me unload the basket, and then starts to clean the turnips. I pull out the mill to grind the puree once the vegetables are soft. It is a luxurious, fantastic kitchen to be sure, with plenty of space, many surfaces, and the stocked larder, but I miss the simplicity of the doctor's. I am sure it is, once again, just nostalgia.

"Mrs. Weber?" Beth breaks into my thoughts. "Where did you learn to cook?"

"I'm mainly self-taught," I say, concentrating on putting the mill together. "I cooked for my husband, and then for a doctor in the Dakotas, and now here. Time helps us all learn."

"I'd like to be a fine cook like you, someday," she says wistfully.

"We'll make sure you have an education," I tell her, and find myself warm at the idea. I could find purpose in that, teaching a young orphan a skill so she might always find work. It is not unlike having a daughter for a few hours in a kitchen, teaching her how to make her way as a wife. I smile fully at her. "You will be making the main dishes in no time."

306

"Really?" Her soft, violet eyes sparkle. "I've only just started, but you think I might do so well?"

"It's a bit of an art, but not a difficult one."

She is so happy with this idea she falls to scrubbing the vegetables with renewed care. I smile at her young, narrow back. Yes, I will find a life here. It is possible.

CHAPTER 31
22 March 1882

Aunt Mary sings off-key, but she does it with gusto. I look
down at her in the middle of the church hymn and smile. She
is tiny, like a delicate bird, and she wears overlarge pearls in
her ears: her one glory from my uncle long since passed in
the War Between the States. The wide-brimmed hat trembles
with her warbling, and she has her eyes nearly closed, as if
singing is an utter delight. I envy her abandon, her freedom
in her age. Like me, she has no children, so my appearance in
Gloucester gives her new life and vigor, and she is blooming
with activities and notions.

My mother is disappointed, but she understands my
plain reasons for refusing to go home. I did not wish to return
to Rockport, and live under a roof where I am a dependent
again. Mother always did give my nature some encouragement, and she swayed my father in line with my preference.
Anne, of course, thinks I am rash, and foolish, for remaining
unmarried and taking on work.

308

But Aunt Mary likes the simple method of life, the undulating of the sea, the quaintness of the village affairs, and she understands me well. I have only fond memories of her during my youth. She does not pry into my past much, and seems to surmise enough on her own with my sparse responses.

The tune finishes, and we all file out of church. Ada and Jean Baker slide out before us, chatting happily with Mr. Baker and Jean's beau, Clark. Rose is on the arm of her betrothed, their heads bent, still planning a wedding that has been the talk of Gloucester for months. Her grandmother, a close friend of Aunt Mary's, is not helping matters by continuously adding new ideas and frills to the day.

My eyes pass over the crowd. These are good people and they are more welcoming than I was expecting. I am lucky.

And if I do not think about Doctor Kinney, I am that much better.

As I nod about and follow my aunt, I catch the dairyman's son watching me.

He has his young boy on his hip and the girl in his grasp, and he is staring, as if measuring my strength. I have not spoken to him much, as his father runs the business ably, and I never met his young wife before she died, but he seems a gentle man.

As he catches my eye, he gives a grave nod of his head, acknowledging that I caught him, then follows his parents out of the church.

I frown. I do not think I want attention from any man just yet. But would Andrew's interest give me a chance to move ahead, and perhaps have a baby of my own? Perhaps. Else I will dwell on my dusty past forever.

309

CHAPTER 32
22 March 1882

At my little cottage, I prepare the tea for Rose and Jean, who arrive soon after church, flushed with spring chill and giggling over their menfolk.

They are pretty things. Rose is slim and tall, and Jean is robust and also quite tall, and they make merry friends. I will be sad when they are each married and unable to come around quite so easily.

"Come in, come in!" I open the door wide, and they walk into the kitchen, where the window gives a beautiful, wide view of the water. "You know where to put your wraps."

They trip in and out of the bedroom, then help with tea, chattering away as if they do not need to breathe. I enjoy their talking. It is refreshing to have it wash over me, so I do not need to think. It is my Sunday evenings, alone and quiet, that are the hardest to fill.

"Did you see Andrew Angus making eyes at you?"

I look up from my cup, surprised. I did not think anyone had noticed.

"I don't think it was quite like that," I say carefully.

"Andrew has kept his head down with his children for nearly a year now. I'm glad you caught his attention. He needs a nice woman to make him happy again," Jean states.

"Does he? I thought he was still grieving his wife."

"Oh, Janie, you ought to consider it!" Rose puts in.

The two of them are love matches, so they think everyone else might be as well, and they dive into speculation of my future with gusto.

"I've decided I am not meant to be a wife," I say, and offer the biscuits in hopes of changing the subject. Jean takes one and bites off a corner.

"You'd be grand at it, and you know it. Are you really happy being a cook at the Chester house? That's what you want?"

"I don't think it is really about what I want, but what is. This is my life, and I'll find happiness. I've found you two."

Rose hums. "I still say you should at least consider him. I've known him all my life, and he's a very dear soul."

My silence prompts them to tackle the latest of Rose's wedding decisions.

They know me enough to understand I won't speak if I don't wish to divulge anything further. I've finally been able to master my easy emotions by not talking much to anyone, especially on topics like these.

The glint of amber catches my eye, where the bottle and Doctor Kinney's handwritten prescription sparkles on the fireplace mantle, half-hidden behind my new handful of secondhand books.

Warm regards, he'd written.

He doesn't write me at all, now.

311

CHAPTER 33
23 April 1882

Andrew Angus, the dairyman's son, asks Aunt Mary if he might court me formally a month later. I do not see why, and I ask him so bluntly at our first uncomfortable sitting in her parlor on Sunday afternoon. Aunt Mary, my chaperone in Gloucester, is with us. As we are both widowed, she does not see the need to actually sit in the same room, and graciously excuses herself at my bald question. Through the narrow doors, she is a shadow in the adjoining room.

He has the grace to flush at my question, the high color turning his blond hair almost pink, the dusting of freckles disappearing for an instant. He leans forward, the starch in his shirt crinkling and crackling.

"I suppose because I realize there is no other way to really get to know you, Mrs. Weber. And whether or not we decide to marry, I'd rather see for myself first if we'd be a good match and go from there."

His honest answer makes me smile. It is much like how Doctor Kinney would respond, and a tiny seed of wonder wells in me. Maybe I am not destined to be alone after all, though it is too soon to hopefully speculate.

CHAPTER 34
16 June 1882

I learn his children's names: Anna and David. Suddenly I have two surrogate daughters: Beth in the kitchen who has a knack for bread like I do, and Anna who shadows me whenever she can. I like that I can mold her a bit, that she is eager to please. School goes out in May and she comes with me several mornings of each week to sit in the kitchen at the Chester house, learn some basic cooking, and watch. It is a gift to Andrew, who otherwise has his hands full helping his father run the dairy farm and the market, and keeping an eye on little Dave.

As I drop off Anna at the dairy stall, she scampers off to help her grandmother in the back with the cheese wrappings. Andrew brings me my order instead of his father.

"I must thank you for your time with Anna," he says, handing me the milk and eggs. "She speaks about you nearly every night, and what you show her and tell her about the world, even beyond the kitchen."

"She is a good girl," I say with a smile. I hold my words tightly to my chest, just to keep myself in check. Still, I do not think Andrew would judge me for the love I hold for Doctor Kinney. In fact, I think he would understand my story completely. It is one of the reasons I am slowly taking a shine to the man.

"She is a good girl, and much like her mother." Even after a full year, Andrew still gets a bit emotional when he speaks of his wife. I know he stops by her grave every Sunday before church. I've seen him there, his head bowed and his children close.

"I wish I could have met her."

"You would have liked her well enough, I suppose."

I raise my eyebrows and wonder if the hold his wife has in his memory finally wanes. It would be a step toward building a life with me, if he can be more stoic about her.

"Well, anyway, she has a lovely little daughter," I say, and put the rest of the cold goods in my basket.

"Perhaps you might still have a daughter," he says, and I stop short. He plunges on, and does not even flush at his romancing. "I think you'd make a very good mother, anyway."

Now I am the one blushing, so I move away before his father comes back out and sees us standing there, like two young ones falling in the first flushes of love.

CHAPTER 35
21 August 1882

My mother smiles across the tray and cups. I try to spend a Sunday afternoon here and there with my parents in Rockport. It is not so far a distance from Gloucester, so I might accomplish it when the weather is fine and stay for tea before going back to my cottage.

"So, your aunt is still well?" she asks. It is a routine question. Aunt Mary is one of Father's relations, and Mother is always careful to be proper and ask about her. Father himself would care to hear, though he continues to busy himself in his study this Sunday instead of joining us.

"She is, of course. I don't think she'll ever change," I say, and take the offered cup.

My mother pours herself the brew and daintily adds a small sliver of lemon and lump of sugar. She still has the prettiest manners. Anne and I always tried to emulate her as we grew older and entered society. She led by example rather than harsh forcefulness, which was a good practice for willful young daughters.

316

"And how is Anne?" I return the question.

Mother sighs, but not unhappily. "She is busy, of course. I'm sure she would love to see you sometime, now that you're back in the States."

"Perhaps at Christmas," I reason, hoping to delay the visit. My sister and I were never very close, which was exacerbated when she married James. To this day, I am not sure if she really knew I had cared for him. That I had hoped, once, to be Mrs. Miller. I do believe, now that time has passed and I am older and widowed, that she and James truly care for one another. It was a better match.

And then there is the other reality. Anne and I view life very differently, and I'm vastly fortunate Mother has always seemed to understand and nurture her daughters accordingly. She is the type of mother I hope to be, should I ever have children. Tolerant. Perhaps that is why I am tolerant of others, too.

My thoughts are on children and family, so I offer up a tidbit of gossip on my own life.

"I have a beau, now."

My mother's cup comes down with alarming speed, though she has the presence of mind to set it on the china saucer with care. Her eyes widen.

"You do. For how long?"

I think back. "He began to court me in the later spring. It is very proper, and Aunt Mary is a good chaperone."

My mother sits forward. She is not overly eager for details, but wishes to know as much as I offer, and I find myself staggering to say more, now that I have let out the secret.

"Is he well off?"

"He is a merchant," I explain slowly, choosing how to describe Andrew. If I were to talk about Doctor Kinney, I might be able to paint a vibrant picture of broad brogue, generosity, and kind manners, but truthfully, I know so little about Andrew. Our stilted, careful, public conversations are usually overheard by several people, and I have only known him in the privacy of Aunt Mary's parlor for a handful of hours over the weeks.

"He is a dairyman," I elaborate.

"Ah."

I know it is not so prestigious as a lawyer or a businessman. Mother might not even tell Father unless my courtship becomes more serious in nature. He will frown a bit at my marrying a dairyman and becoming a farmer's wife, but he cannot stop me at this point in life.

"He is kind," I reason. "And he has been widowed, like me. And it would be the type of active life I like."

"That is true. My Janie, who never does the expected or easy way of it," she says gently. Her tone carries both an acceptance of my nature, and a soft wish that I was a bit more complacent with my lot, instead of seeking some sort of unique situation. But she does love me, and does support me, and of this I am grateful. If there is something good from leaving the Dakotas, it is that I am nearer to her. No matter where I am, I have a mother to whom I can speak. That is a comfort in itself.

CHAPTER 36
16 October 1882

I wave goodbye to Andrew as he leaves my aunt's home. He gives me a little smile, lighting up his green eyes, more brilliant because of the cloudy day.

Summer in Gloucester has been busy. Now it is fall, and I finally feel that I have found some peace. October storms roll in often. The sea is churning, the waves are soothing, and I have a little romance with the dairyman's son.

I like him. His children are sweet, his parents welcoming. Aunt Mary is beside herself, hoping for a wedding to plan with her friends. We have courted nearly a full six months and he is, as my friend Rose once said, a dear soul. We do not touch, and we are quite proper as is expected. I miss the easy, tactile way I had with Doctor Kinney, but that was something altogether different. I shouldn't compare.

Andrew rounds the corner as the wind picks up, and then disappears up the hill. The sky fills with clouds and darkens to a pale purple and grey. I think I will go walk the stretch of beach in front of my little cottage, as I like to do before the rain hits. I love the smell of the sea when it is cleansed with new water from the rains, as if the beach itself is washed. It is a pure, salty scent, free of fish and grit.

"All is well?" Aunt Mary gives me a hopeful grin as I go into her kitchen, where she knits for the ladies' group at church.

"As always." I bend down and give her skinny shoulders a little hug. She absently pats my hand.

"When do you suppose you might fix to marry that nice man?"

I sigh. She asks the question at least twice a week. It is her age that makes her eager, too, as I know she'd like to have a wee one to hold before time takes her away.

"I don't know. That is to say, we've discussed what I'd do, how I might leave the Chester house and work at the Angus family farm. I wouldn't mind the work. It sounds rewarding. But he hasn't asked me, anyway."

"Well, he's asked me."

My heart stops. "He has? When?"

"After church, two weeks ago."

"Well, why so long ago?"

She arches her eyebrow at me. "So eager for him to ask? Because he's still not certain you'd say yes, Janie."

I inhale. She's right. I don't know what answer I'd give Andrew. I like to think I would be grateful for another chance at happiness, even if it is a quiet marriage. I might grow to be very fond of him, even though I do not ache for his touch, or feel overwhelmed with his nearness.

Never mind. I will reach the moment of truth soon enough when he asks me to share a future with him, however

320

long or short it might be. He would be a gentle husband, likely more sensitive than Henry had been.

"My dear, it's time you let go of whoever you are pining away for." Aunt Mary's words pull me away from reflection.

I give her a careful look. "I have not ever said I pined for anyone."

She chuckles and puts down the knitting needles. "You don't have to. I've seen a lot in my time, and it's always apparent when someone is worrying over someone else. Besides, there's no other reason for you to hesitate over Andrew Angus. Someone from out West, then?"

"Well, no matter. Mr. Angus might ask me next week," I say, and then bend to kiss her dry cheek before heading home.

Rose is married now, and Jean is in the throes of her own wedding planning to young Clark. I have a good rhythm to my weeks: teaching, cooking, courting. And I am near the ocean. There is little for me to want. This is a peaceful, fulfilling life. If I put the words in my head often enough, surely I will start to believe them.

Aunt Mary wants me to stop pining away. In the quiet of the cottage, I sigh. I do not dwell anymore on the fact that I haven't heard from Doctor Kinney. Widow Hawks writes in her halting letters about town life, and I receive the gossip from Alice Brinkley. My friends in the Territory do not yet know of my beau, as I have only just admitted to it on paper, and it takes a week or two for the mail to reach the West. Soon I will be able to write my own happy tidings, should I accept Andrew.

I should stop pining. I know this.

Glancing up at the mantle, I gaze at the little glass bottle, long empty and kept only for my own silly sentiment.

Pulling it down, I run my nail along the handwritten note. A groove bites the paper where I often have caressed the words, as if willing any emotion to leak out of them and into me.

Slipping my finger pad over his signature, something bear-like and black crushes my breath. Enough. *Enough!* The power swells through my arm and shimmies down my elbow, bleeding into my hand until the bottle flies out of my palm to smash against the edge of the hearth. The crinkle of glass shards is so loud in my tiny, lonely house that I wince, and the tears of surrender gurgle in my stomach. Weeping, I fall to my knees, heedless of the glass, and pick up the label. It is still whole, but that seems wrong. It shouldn't be whole.

I grasp the top to split it down the middle in one, long, agonizing pull.

It is much like ripping open a seam. Or peeling off an old skin. Or tearing out one's heart.

The second tear is easier, and then the third. By the fourth, I cannot find enough room for my fingers, and the paper falls like white ash to the floor, scattering about the broken bottle. The ink against the white paper still peeks at me, mocking me.

Enough.

The beach is a solace today, so I go to walk it with a ponderous stride. Sand finds its way into the black shoes. The boots I used in the Dakotas sit forlorn and unused next to the split saddle skirt in my closet. It is too soon to part with those relics, but I suspect I will dispose of them when I permanently plant my roots in Gloucester. After nearly a year back in Massachusetts, once again I am used to the grittiness of sand, of the heavy air, and the salt that seems to sit in my hair. There is mud instead of dust, and the oldness and stone of the buildings are so different from the newer planked wood of the houses out West. Everything here is sharp angles and soft fog at all times, a strange mix of elements I find both familiar and tiring.

The wind is strong, almost horizontal, and the clouds streak purple and blue and grey across the sky, skittering over the black water and white-capped waves crashing onto the beach. I stop walking and hug the shawl over my shoulders, my hair whipping around my head. I do not need to wear bonnets against the dust here. Some Sundays, I keep my braids loose and soft when I see Andrew, so he can notice the dark luster of my locks against the pale, muted colors I wear. It's my way of flirting, I suppose.

I think on him. I do not desire him, but there is a stirring of romance when I remember his kind ways and gentle heart. If I think about Doctor Kinney too much, I will feel all the weight of my sadness, so I focus instead on my real possibilities.

I could marry, and move to the Angus farm, and help a new family with their way of life. I needn't stay in service all my days, and perhaps Andrew and I might have children. The thought of lying in bed next to him does not thrill me. I do not hold any lust for him, but I have had a marriage bed like that before, where passion is put aside for expected convenience. It's nothing new. It's not what I'd hoped for, but it holds some merit against the solitude. I see that, now. I'd been so sure I would never marry for anything but love. I was too proud of my newly minted widowhood.

Of course, I could always rebuff Andrew if he does ask for my hand. I have earned the right to stay single forever. But then I will always be lonely. With Andrew, I won't be alone.

Yes, I will marry him. The decision is made slowly, but decisively. The mind can wander without actually thinking while the pound of the waves lulls, and then a final choice can be picked up without the brain being too crowded with thoughts. The same small seed of wonder unfurls again within me: I might find some happiness yet with another.

There is a pale, pink calico at the mercantile. It reminds me of the pattern and color I saw at Kate's a year ago, and I decide I will buy it and make it up for my wedding dress. We can marry in the spring when things are new and fresh, and I will move forward with as good a resolution for my life as ever.

As I walk carefully, balancing around the wind and my skirts, I see the gait of the passerby on the road along the beach, and I pause.

Is it Andrew, coming to find me after our Sunday sit in, unable to wait to ask for my hand? My throat goes dry and scratchy. It is time to accept my future. I don't want to. God knows, I don't wish for it. I shouldn't. I cannot. *I will not.*

I say such things to myself while knowing, deep in my spirit, that I will accept him. When Andrew asks, I will tell him yes, no matter what I want.

There must be some hope, and I will hope to learn to love him. It is hope, or smashing everything I own before going into a madhouse.

The dark clothes are unfamiliar in the dim light. At first, I think I have misjudged.

But no.

It is Doctor Kinney himself walking down the dunes toward me. His stride is single-minded and quick. This is not possible. Perhaps I am still harboring my old fantasy. Surely, I would have had word that he was on his way.

As my steps halt, I wait, and when he is at arm's length, I look at him intently. All I think to do is reach out. My arms loop about his neck, and suddenly his are holding me, too, so tightly that I am lifted off my feet. There is the smell of him: his medicines, the carbolic acid, and old dust cling to his suit, and I bury my face into his shoulder.

"Janie!" His voice sounds smaller than I remember in my daydreams, or because the wind captures it, and throws it against the roar of the surf. I refuse, at first, to even speak, in case doing so will break the spell. I fear that I will find I am not in this embrace, and am alone near my little cottage, bearing the ache of an unrequited love.

"Doctor Kinney. Is it you?" I wonder, still holding to him tightly. His arms are strong, but he sets me down, so I need to release him or risk looking clingy and improper. The space between us yawns open.

"It's me," he says happily, as if no time at all has passed, as if it has not been a year since I've last spoken to him or touched him. "But as I am no longer your employer, you could call me Patrick."

I shake my head in disbelief. "What are you doing here?"

"I'm pickin' up medicines in Boston over the week and attendin' a short lecture at Cambridge on new laboratory tests. It is close enough to Gloucester."

My heart might fly out of my chest. But before I say more, the rain arrives in sharp pellets, driving with the wind. We race up the beach to my cottage in a rather undignified manner, and we get in just before the big droplets begin in earnest. It is a hearty, late afternoon storm, so I put the heavy iron kettle on the stove and light the lamps. The rain is loud and comforting against the window, and Doctor Kinney goes to the glass to watch.

He gives a low whistle. "Now that's a view worth leavin' Flats Junction for! Look at those waves! It's been a long time since I've been here on these beaches, and I've never seen it storm."

I am speechless. It is as if I have suddenly entered my own daydreams. I'm overwhelmed, desperately wishing he might confess an affection for me, or that he will say something wildly romantic. Am I foolish to hope so? Likely. But I am hardly able to fathom his appearance. He fills my rooms, and I am utterly aware of his nearness. I can smell the same medicinal scent on his clothes, and I notice the way his hair waves back. I want to touch him again, though there is no excuse I can make to do so. The silence fills the kitchen, but it is as comfortable as always. Finally, I find my voice.

"Have you already been to Boston?"

"No." He turns from the window to me. "First I thought I might see you. And then, yes, tomorrow I'll head into the city and take in the lectures and get the medicines."

"So, you're only here for today?" I am moved he goes so far out of his way to see me, but I tell myself not to expect it means much more than friendship. "I am so glad you came."

His eyes are warm, a clear blue, and his face looks the same as I remember. He gazes down at me, so near I could simply reach out and run my hand along his shoulder. Time has done nothing to cool how I feel when I am close to him. It is undeniable.

"I had to come, Jane."

"You did?" The kettle whistles, and I turn from him to take it off the stove. "You are lucky to find me here."

"You're leavin' again?" There is surprise in his voice, and I find I cannot face him while I admit my future plans.

"No, I'll stay in Gloucester. But Aunt Mary just informed me that the man who has been courting me has officially asked permission for my hand."

"Mrs. Weber!" He is immediately at my side, turning me to look up at him, his urgency unexplainable at first. "Jane. You haven't said yes?"

"Andrew hasn't asked me yet, so no, I have not given an answer."

"Well, you'll have to tell him no," he determines, his tone final. "You're comin' back with me as soon as you can resettle things here."

I laugh a little at him. "You think it's so easy? I've built a life. I'm not thinking of leaving it."

He sighs and looks back out at the window.

"Esther said you might need convincin', but I didn't think it might come to this, that you might be marryin', and so soon."

"Widow Hawks spoke to you of me?"

"Oh aye. We read your letters together over supper. Or that is, we did." His forehead creases. "She's gone off, you see. To the reservation to find her mother. She said it did not matter how I think of her as my own family. She's decided her place now is with her people as her daughter won't have her at all and you left her, too. Kate won't even speak to her own mother, and …"

"Then who received my last letter?" I ask, already knowing the answer. I wrote of my courtship with Andrew most recently. Doctor Kinney admits to it without preamble or excuse.

"I didn't think you'd mind. You said I might get news of you through Esther's letters."

"You certainly did."

"You're not upset about that, are you?"

I could not be truly angry with him if I had wanted to be.

"No, Patrick. I'm not." His name falls out of my mouth with effort, and it is a bit foreign to say it. I look over his dear, familiar face and recognize the fatigue lines there. "But the tea will keep. I can reheat it again. You ought to take a rest from your journey. Will the sofa suffice?"

His eyes travel over my simple cushions. "You know me too well. Will you wake me in time to get to the inn for supper?"

"I'll wake you for supper, but you'll eat with me. I want to hear all the news from Flats Junction."

"You'll make me one of your meals?" He takes a seat and stretches out with a groan. "I hadn't hoped I'd be so fortunate."

"I'm glad my cooking still pleases you."

"It never didn't."

I plump a pillow and hand it to him, and he stuffs it behind his head, staring up at me. There is a change in his face, as if he sees something he did not notice before.

"My word, Jane. Do you have any idea how pretty you are?"

His words fill my spirit, but he says them plainly, and without a twinkle of affection. He has been too long in the company of men on the train car. I shake my head.

328

"You are flattering me just so I agree to return to the Dakotas with you to keep house. I'm no old maid yet, but I know beauty when I see it. Kate, not me."

His eyes are already closing. As he drifts off to soft slumber at once, I hear him mutter Kate's name, as if the reminder of her made him dream of her loveliness from the start. How can I compete with that?

It is not even worth a try.

CHAPTER 37
16 October 1882

I sneak glances at him as he sleeps while I pour myself some tea and quietly warm up leftover soup I brought from the Chesters. There is enough for two, especially when I add in some bread and put a squash in the tiny oven.

The storm howls. It will get dark quickly due to the time of year and the rain clouds stretch across the sky. I wonder when he made the arrangements at the inn and when he'd decided to make the trip east. There grows in me a bit of hope, even while I push against it, that he came to see me, to stop Andrew from marrying me, to whisk me back to the Dakotas so that I am with him always.

I sit at my little table and look out over the black waves and angry sky. Doctor Kinney's arrival sets loose my heart, which has not stopped pounding since he walked across the beach toward me. When, for a fleeting, wild moment, I thought he was coming to claim me. I'm flattered he wants me back to cook and clean for him, but I don't know if it is the right thing for my own mind. It would be torturous. And then there is Andrew, who has courted me so prettily, and who I have grown to care for as a very kind friend.

The problem is being near Doctor Kinney again has reminded me how passionate I feel. I cannot help myself wanting to be with him, wanting to touch him and be touched by him. It is an almost violent desire I thought I'd never find, and to deny myself that and turn to a quieter type of marriage is much harder to do. Now that I remember how such a love feels in the flesh, how can I say yes to Andrew, knowing I will be living a lie?

I think I've had my fill of such half-truths and hidden feelings.

I weep just a little and bury my face in my hands, willing myself to stop this silly emotion and be strong. It will be fine. He will leave and I will not see him again, and I can go back to trying to forget. The thought is not comforting, but it is true, and the sooner I set my mind to the reality, the better.

"Mrs. Weber." I hear him sit up on the couch. "Jane."

"Yes." I raise my head. "Would you like some tea?" Anything, so he doesn't see my red eyes.

He swiftly rises, his movements quick and precise, so unlike Andrew's simple, slower ways, and his hand is on my shoulder.

"Are you alright? It's been so long, but you've recovered well?"

I smile a little. I do not think of my little boy buried so far away in that Catholic cemetery half as much as I dream about Doctor Kinney, and I do not think of my health at all. "Oh yes, I have. Thank you."

I push off from the chair, keeping my back to him, and pour him tea. The soup is nearly heated, and he clatters about setting the table, as he did when we ate together in his home. I try to keep myself from thinking how wonderful the arrangement is, and how easily we move around each other in a house.

"Jane's cookin'. I can't wait." He pulls around the edge of the table, catching my eye. "What is it? You've been weepin'!"

"Seeing you brings back so many memories of my friends in Flats Junction."

"Good!" He plants himself in front of me. "Then you'll come back."

"Doctor Kinney," I sigh. "You cannot ask me to leave this life I've built. It was hard enough to start over. Tell me instead of Alice and Mitch. They're well and little Pete is still growing?"

He pulls out our chairs and we sit. After giving me a long look, he dives into the food and the news. "Aye, and Alice's just confirmin' she's pregnant with the second, so Mitch is hoverin'. And Sadie is expectin' again and even Marie, so I've been told."

We talk about everyone: the postmaster died of a heart attack, but Nancy is happily managing the office without Douglas while her elderly father-in-law watches the little ones. The Brinkleys have added a hundred head of cattle to their farm and Danny Svendsen had another successful steer run. A bison was found wandering the street one morning this past summer, and there were no fireworks on Independence Day. One of the Salomon boys had severe burns from hot steam while working with Thaddeus in the forge, though the doctor wasn't called to treat the child, and Tim the far-rier has a new apprentice who has all the single girls making moon eyes. I drink in the news, more colorful and funny than when it arrives in a letter. I watch his face, trying to commit his words to memory. The news feels never-ending, brilliant and exciting and comfortable. I miss everyone with a painful, tearing pull, but I don't know truly if I fit there. How can I, now? If I went back, what would I do? What would be the point?

We do the dishes companionably as we used to do, and he asks me about my work at the Chester house, and Aunt Mary, and the townsfolk, and how I fill my days, and who my friends are in Gloucester. He grows quieter as I tell him about Rose, Jean, my aunt's dear friends, tea parties, the Chester pantry, Beth's lessons in the kitchen, and then of the Angus farm, and Andrew's kindness, and his sweet children.

As we finish the last of the tea with a few biscuits I find in the back of my larder, he looks out into the deepening sky. A heaviness sits inside my chest as I look at his profile. I have missed him so desperately, and this will likely be the last time I see him.

"It's been long since I've been back. It feels good."

"Back to Boston?" I ask, running my finger along the rim of the teacup.

"That." He nods. "And Gloucester. I was here, once, in my youth with my auntie and her employer. You recall what I told you of Mr. McClure? In fact, my old friend, Bobby MacHugh, the one who placed my ad, and sent your letter, used to live here in his childhood."

"He's a doctor too, isn't he?"

He smiles a little, thinking back. "Aye. It was a peculiar set of days, to be sure, the time I spent here. Hot. His father was ill. It's how I got my first real start as a doctor, in truth."

I want to ask him more, but as he is not the man courting me, I don't wish to pry into his past unless he offers it on his own. Instead I just sneak looks at him from behind my tea. How do I memorize him? How do I settle him into my past without losing a piece of myself?

"What happened?" I forget myself and ask anyway.

He rewards me with a sideways grin. "Oh, Bobby's father had an episode. Lookin' back, I'm sure it was some sort of heart condition, somethin' acute. When it happened, I was only a small boyo, just learnin' the early ways of bein' a vet. But when Mr. MacHugh fell on the beach, gaspin' for breath, well ... I just knew I wanted to help. I had a knack for it. And Mr. McClure agreed."

"Where's Mr. McClure now?"

Doctor Kinney's shoulders sink an inch and I know his answer before he gives it, remembering he told me once, more than a year ago.

"He passed—oh, a while ago now. His death is the reason I headed West with Aunt Bonnie. It was my turn to support her, and there wasn't much room in Boston for yet another physician, especially an Irish one. Granted, it took me many years to settle and find a place that could support me. As much as Flats Junction supports me as a doc," he finishes ruefully.

I'm glad he doesn't dwell on his time in Gloucester. I would learn what streets he walked, and what he did when he was last here, and every time I walk there I would think on this. I do not need more reminders of him.

334

He rises with his empty cup. "So, you've given up your proper ways then, have you, Mrs. Weber?"

I stand with him, frowning. "My proper ways?"

His arm circles carefully, balancing the teacup in the saucer as he does. "Havin' a man here, unchaperoned. It's unseemly, isn't it? Will you be branded a brazen widow now?"

Is he teasing me? Trying to be lighthearted? Or is he blaming me—accusing me of my forward ways with Theodore, and now him? My head buzzes, but I settle on his eyes, and they are gentle and kind.

I smile slightly at him.

"I'm afraid I've given up all those ways where you're concerned. It's worth dashing my respectability to see an old friend. And besides, it was raining too hard for you to leave."

He smiles back, then puts his cup on the sideboard. "Speakin' of rain and weather, let's put up your fire."

Turning to the hearth, he bends for the wood box and pauses. The chink and chirp of glass crunches slightly as his boots find purchase against the broken amber bottle I'd left, and he slowly straightens, toeing the fragments and swirling the torn label. A piece flits up half-heartedly in a puff of air as he scuffs, his scrawled name obvious on the white of the paper, and a painful stillness chokes the kitchen. My face feels bloodless, and the old tears claw up my throat.

Doctor Kinney clears his own, methodically adds the log to the fire, and then another, bending and tossing fluidly. He watches the fire build itself back up for a long moment, then spins to find me, where I've been glued to the floor. What will he think? My eyes fall to the busted bottle, the purposefully ripped note, and my heart rattles and cracks.

Sighing, he takes up his hat. "It's early, but I ought to leave for the inn. Good night, Jane." His voice is flat.

I am both relieved and dismayed. He does not press his case by continuing to ask me to return to Flats Junction. I suppose he is too much a gentleman to do so, though a part of me wishes he would vehemently protest about my staying in Gloucester. He could demand I go back with him because he needed me, for myself. But that is a silly girl's hope, and nothing more. And I know it. Now, more than ever.

"What time is your train?" I ask, as he clatters down the two steps onto the path leading to the road. "I'd like to see you off in the morning if I might, before I need to be at the Chester's kitchen."

He looks up at me, where I stand on the porch. The rain has ended, but the wind is still strong, and I can just see him in the lantern light.

"The early one, at four."

"Good."

He turns, and melts into the darkness toward the town's brighter lights. I go inside; I do not sleep all night.

336

CHAPTER 38
17 October 1882

We meet on the platform at a few minutes to four. The air is chilly, damp, and cool, and the fog lays so heavy the train is a few minutes late. He wears his Stetson, a hat that looks so out of place in the East, but it makes him look as I remember him.

If I'd never been bold in my past, I might speak out against the properness suffocating me. I would not have qualms about breaching propriety and telling him how I feel. But, why should I? He has not offered me affection, and I'd be even more a fool if I put voice to my own. It's best if I stay aloof and calm. But oh! My heart feels heavy and silences me at first, until I find words.

"Please give my best to Esther, whenever you see her next. And tell Alice hello. And Kate too, of course," I say, the usual niceties falling heedlessly. "And ... all the others. All of them."

He turns to me. I hear the train coming, and there are more people on the platform than I would have liked, because I want him all to myself when I say farewell for always.

"Will you really stay? And marry the man who courts you?" His eyes are grey this morning, as if he is tired, too.

The train comes in, loud, obnoxiously so, and I wait for the noise to clear, and the bustle of bodies to start.

"I don't know if I can marry him," I say carefully. "But I can't go home with you."

The whistle blows. He must board now, but still he loiters. This goodbye is even harder than the first one. It removes the hope I carried that he would come after me. He has, but not in the fashion I dreamed about. It is wonderful to see him, but it's devastating to realize that my fantasy is just that.

"So, thank you for coming," I tell him, as the whistle blows again. "I know you want me to go to Flats Junction with you, Doctor, but I won't." For one, brief, moment, I find more strength inside than I thought I had. I look at him, and I do not weep. "You have to board."

"You won't come with me, Janie?" He sounds resigned.

"I won't go, only to watch you finish courting Kate," I say in a rush. "You cannot ask me to help you woo her, to dance at your wedding, and bounce her children on my knee as if my loneliness would be filled simply by watching your happiness. I can't do it."

"All aboard, sir!" The conductor is behind him, shuffling him along. Doctor Kinney pauses, his face raw and unreadable. I do not believe the situation is as dire as all that. He will find another housekeeper if he truly needs one.

I am dispensable. I always have been. He is edged closer to the train as the last few people rush by to swing into the car.

"Jane—" He shakes his head slightly, and shrugs with a shoulder. "Goodbye, then."

The whistle shrieks the final call, and the steam rushes out in an angry hiss. He boards, and when his back is turned, my eyes finally fill, and I don't bother to brush away the tears. He takes a seat near the window, his face disjointed through the wavering, watering glass, looking down at me, then away.

The train pulls out and rushes off, and he is gone.

CHAPTER 39
17 October 1882

I pull the pastries out of the oven for Mrs. Chester's latest tea party. I must concentrate carefully. I feel as if I am in a half-dream. Did I really say goodbye to Doctor Kinney only hours ago? How could I have let him go without telling him of my heart? I know the answer: it is because I could not bear it when he would pat my shoulder, and be sorry, because he loves Kate and she loves him. I am the unrequited woman, and I know I am not alone in such a situation. Knowing so does not make the pain in my chest go away.

"Can I fill them?" Beth asks.

She is too young to realize I am troubled, and I am grateful I do not have to explain myself. Just as I lay out the different preserves and spoons, Beth shrieks so loudly my ear feels as though it bursts.

"What is it?" I whirl, following her eyes, and spy the small grey shadow flickering along the perimeter of the kitchen.

"A mouse!" Beth breathes unnecessarily.

Grabbing one of the skillets, making sure I take one without feet, I stalk the mouse, hoping to catch it before it hides behind the wide stove. The animal pauses behind the great, plumped barrel of brown sugar and I plant myself so it cannot pass without running over my shoe.

Beth screams again as the rodent makes a dash for the pantry, running over my foot in the process. But my aim is still good, and I smash the mouse hard, feeling the sickening splatter under the iron.

I straighten, take up the broom from the corner to sweep the mouse outside, and then put the soiled skillet into the big pot of hot soapy water we keep on the edge of the oven. When I turn around, Beth has her skirts still bunched to her knees and she's staring at me with something like worship.

"That was amazing, Mrs. Weber," she breathes. "How did you learn to do that?"

"Practice," I say crisply. "You'll learn too."

I pretend the action doesn't fill me with dread and sorrow. Beth would not understand how the thwack of the skillet against bone and wood reminds me of my regret and the torment of my own weakness and loss. Of the doctor, staring at me with shock and, quite possibly, disdain. Or his quiet discovery of the broken bottle, and, most horribly, the obvious clutter of his note, written in kindness, which I tore apart as if it was so worthless it could not even be burned. If only he'd known. Would he understand?

I'll never know. Will the unknown ever stop eating my soul?

We make salad with fresh whitefish from the market. Beth walks to the stalls to get lettuce, though it's slim pickings in October. There are raspberries on top of the pastries, and I arrange a plate of quickbreads made with pumpkin and cherry.

When the food goes upstairs, I sit at the table and think over the rest of the week's menus. The fall produce is bountiful, so I will be able to make hearty food. There were recipes I used last year when I'd first arrived that did not go over well, but others were good, and Mr. Chester requested them again, so I pull those out and set to writing down the lists.

It does me good to keep busy like this. I suppose I would be just as busy if I married Andrew Angus.

But can I, now? I still don't *want* to. I truly do not.

It is not comforting to know I cannot move forward, even though I have been trying.

CHAPTER 40
21 October 1882

The week slips away. I realize, surprised, that tomorrow is Sunday and Andrew will find me at Aunt Mary's parlor again. Will he ask me to wed him? I was so certain of my answer a week ago. I was sure I would be happy enough.

Ada Baker and Jean are busy in their market stall. They have many different squashes out, eggplants, late blackberries and root vegetables. I will make a soup for the Chester' lunch and supper for tomorrow. I pick up the meaty beets and zucchinis, weighing them in my hands.

I glance up, my eyes wandering through the market. Andrew is at the dairy stall, but he looks surly. I ought to stop by and try to liven up his day, but as usual I am never quite sure what to say to him. Our rapport is still shy as it ever was.

It is harvest, and the market is busier than usual. My sleepless nights and daydreams of the doctor have me imagining him everywhere out of the corner of my eye. Every man in a dark traveling suit might be him, but I know it is not.

I turn to Ada, who watches me shrewdly, her hands on her hips. I am pressed close to her. The swell of people in the walkways is thick. She shakes her head at me.

"Was he the man you've pined for all these months?"

"What?"

She juts her strong chin. "You were seen on the beach last week in the arms of a stranger. From the sound of it, I'd guess he was the one you've been remembering so desperately."

I close my eyes briefly. So that is perhaps why Andrew looks angry. I am suddenly grateful it is busy today, that holiday groups and families are out strolling, filling the market so my voice is not audible.

"Yes."

"Who was it?"

"A doctor, from the Dakota Territories."

"He came to take you away?"

"Not like that," I say, shaking my head. Jean comes out and stands behind her mother, listening hard, a small smile on her face. I do not mind finally explaining to her either, and I wonder how much Aunt Mary has already heard. Surely, she will be able to put it all together. She'll know I have fallen for my employer out West.

"He … he is wooing another woman in Flats Junction, and he wants me back as a housekeeper. I decided not to go."

Jean leans forward. "What about you? Don't you want to be near him?"

"Of course I do!" I am surprised at how vehement I sound, and take a breath. "But I could not do it, could not watch him marry another. What kind of life would that be?"

"So you won't be saying yes to Andrew when he asks for your hand?" Jean asks.

"I'm destined for a life apart, maybe."

Ada's eyes grow soft. "I doubt that, Janie."

Her kindness threatens to make me weep. Jean comes over, the small smile still on her face. She is trying her best to cheer me up.

"I'm sure it will all work out, Jane." It is an easy and trite thing to say, especially by one who is heady in love with a man who has asked for her hand. She weds Clark in a few months, so I turn the conversation to that wedding, deflecting talk away from the workings of my heart.

CHAPTER 41
22 October 1882

Andrew visits Aunt Mary's parlor as expected. His hat in hand, he sits on the edge of the plush chair with sharp elbows on broad knees. He is tall and strong, and his blond hair is combed back from church. We are quiet, and I pour some tea out for us, but we don't touch it.

He sighs, and then looks up at me.

"As you know, I have been courting you, hoping we might grow fond of each other, and maybe decide to marry."

It is this fairness that draws me to him, the way he speaks as if we would decide everything together.

I smile sadly at him. I've ruined it all without having to refuse him. His tone gives away his mind, but he plunges on.

"I thought we might reach a reasonable understanding. I like you, Jane, and I was thinking you felt the same."

I put out a hand, but stop halfway. As is proper, we rarely touch, and to put my hand in his now would be misleading.

346

"I do like you, Andrew."

He nods, as if expecting that. "But we are not in love, are we?"

I am surprised he includes himself in the comment, and I agree. "No, you're right. We are not. I don't think you should ever love me the way you loved Elizabeth."

He gives a little smile. "You're right, too. I was hoping I might learn to love you, though. Or at least, be happy together so that I am not alone, and my children have a mother."

"Your children are dear."

"And you still want the man you left out West," he states, and straightens up to look at me fully. The gossip has indeed reached him, then. "I don't think it's fair to ask you to care for me when you are still pining away for another. You are only luckier, in that your heart's desire still lives."

"Is that easier?" I ask painfully. "When he is as good as dead to me? I doubt I will see him again. Besides, he is off to marry another."

Andrew gives a rueful laugh. "He is a fool to have even looked at another woman if you were offering yourself."

His compliment clatters through my mind, then breaks apart and dies. Then he stands, and I go with him.

"I should like us to be friends," I tell him.

"That would be very nice, Jane. I don't think we ought to hold out hope for anything else."

We walk to the door, and he leaves after giving a little bow. I turn around. Aunt Mary stands on the threshold of the kitchen. She knows we will not be marrying, and gives me a sad little smile, understanding all.

CHAPTER 42
22 October 1882

My Sunday afternoon is quiet. Jean was supposed to come for tea, but that time has passed, and I decide she must be with family, discussing wedding details or making bows. Weddings here are prettily done. I enjoyed Rose's nuptials, and I look forward to Jean's as best I might. As much as I wish I could join their ranks and marry as well, I've made my choices. Do I really think I should have happiness after all the ridiculousness of my past?

Another October storm is rolling in from the east. The clouds swell, slowly stalking the beach, which turns grey and tan and black. It smells wet, heavy, and salty, like tears and rain mixed. As it picks up, I close my eyes, thinking about what I can do to keep some semblance of reason in my life.

I will be a good cook, and perhaps I might take in some classes to learn more delicacies. There are places Mrs. Chester could send me should she wish for fancier dishes. I'd like that. I'd like the challenge and the education. And I will teach Beth, and be like a little mother to her. I will have lonely days, I'm sure, but my cottage is cozy, and it is really all I need.

As the afternoon darkens, I go in to light the lamps so I can see when it is time to make supper. Finally, I'm used to cooking for one person. It is a talent in itself. But I am glad I have had time alone; not many women have this type of freedom. Instead, they go, like me, from parents to husband. I might regret this freeness someday, when I am old and wish for a partner or children or grandchildren, but if I am still employed by the Chester family or some other great house, I will be busy enough.

I heat tea water and go to the window, watching the storm scurry into the bay.

It will have to be enough.

Oh God. It won't be.

I know it, as much as I pretend otherwise.

How will I manage?

Will my insides stop shriveling?

I will write to Alice Brinkley and tell her goodbye. To hear from her will become too painful, and I do not think I can get any more letters to Widow Hawks now that she is gone to the reservation. Kate must be so pleased to have the last obvious token of her heritage gone, and to have a man who adores her.

The tea is not yet done and the storm has not yet hit, and my body thrums with some unexplained pulse. If this is heartbreak, I think it might slowly destroy me.

I suppose I can pretend, sometimes, that I was married to Doctor Kinney, and we had years of memories and passionate embraces. I close my eyes again to remember his arms

349

around me on the beach, and his rough, large hands holding mine after my miscarriage. I can build on these memories. Many women do, and I am not unique among them. It'll have to be enough.

Enough.

I'm still as foolish as ever I was. Such memories will never, ever be enough.

I sigh and bite back the convulsions in my chest and burrowing into my marrow. If I had more glass to break, I would.

There is the split skirt, I recall suddenly.

Destruction seems to live inside my muscles, giving me strength and power. Yanking out the clothing, I grip the long seam and pull, weeping as intensely as I tear the fabric. Though it is wasteful and nearly insane, I feel I must do this, must lash out this way, or go wild.

What woman can bury her sadness, her resignation, her futile hopes and efforts forever? It is too much to ask, and yet it must be. Will I rail against my lot more and more as time marches on? Will I finally descend into some unending spiral of madness, huddled in the corners of my own mind where I can find happiness?

If I were brave enough, I like to think I'd walk into the ocean and never come out.

The stitches screech and snap, breaking apart with agony and resistance, but my hands do not let go.

Tear. Rip. Lash.

When the skirt is in pieces, the threads floating about my bedroom floor like whispers, I go outside for a moment to cool my blood. The sound of the surf worms into my hearing, dampening my emotions, drying the fine slick of sweat on my brow. There is a small measure of peace in looking out over the waves, taking in the slate color of them. I have the ocean, at least.

Soon it is time to go inside, even though the rain has not yet hit, but I am too sorrowful to stand here any longer, like a sailor's wife wishing a husband home safely.

At first, I swing by the porch entry, knowing it is just my tiredness and my fantasy that he might come back, but I stop short.

He is there, in his dark suit, with one foot on the step, staring at me. How long has he been there? I was so caught up in the wind and my own thoughts that I did not even hear him.

I do not think I can manage this all over again.

I cannot say goodbye to him one more time. How strong does he think I am?

He comes toward me, solid and real and unstoppable. My first inclination is to touch him, reach out and hold him.

Instead, I grip the porch railing to keep from buckling. "You came back?"

How many times must I refuse him?

He stops in front of me, smiling slightly, as if we had not just parted ways a week ago. I cannot understand him. The doctor is usually so patient and accepting of people's choices. He must leave me be, must let me gather the shreds of happiness left to me.

"I had to come back. I had reason. What you said gave me hope."

I think back to our conversation at the train station. I'm certain I didn't tell him anything he might misconstrue to believe I would accompany him to Flats Junction.

351

I shake my head. "I think you've come all this way for nothing. My answer still stands."

He takes another step forward, frowning, and I try very hard to hold my ground.

"I realized you did not know. Kate and I have parted ways. I am not courtin' her—I have not been for many weeks. You need to know that."

The wind gusts and his hair blows with mine. I forget to school myself with my practiced detachment. I reach up to brush the hair out of his face, but I stop the action halfway, and tuck my hand back in the folds of my skirt. I'm nearly certain this conversation is a dream. *He is not here.* This is a nightmare, slamming into the daytime. I will wake, and find myself on my bedroom floor, covered in scraps of cloth and thread, my destroyed Western skirt about my ankles.

It must be I *am* going mad.

"You should not have stopped courting her. You've cared for her a long time, Doctor. She was accepting your suit. You always wanted that."

He reaches across the porch and captures my hand, holding it solidly in both of his. The touch is hard and true, and convinces me of the reality of this moment. I notice how his eyes are a cerulean blue against the softness of the clouds, the black and grey of the water, and the dullness of the sand behind him.

"No. Not always." His lips tremble, the way they do when he wishes to say more, when he is intensely zealous about something. He hesitates, then brings my fingers to his lips, the way a gentleman would bid a lady farewell.

I rip my hand out of his, a physical tearing and an

GLOUCESTER

emotional one, too. I have gone months without his touch, and now the easy manner we have makes me desire him, even after such a small, simple show of affection, however innocent he means it.

"Please." His voice is low, rough, his face lined with apprehension. "Come back with me. I will bring you here as often as I can manage it, I promise you. But I need you home. It is ... it is not even home without you there."

"You miss my cooking and cleaning? That makes it a home?"

"Confound it, Jane," he says irritably, shaking his head at my caustic attitude. "I am tryin' to explain to you that I love you."

The words come out, catch in the rising wind, and ring through my ears.

I am mistaken.

Surely, he does not love me like that.

His Irish eyes meet mine and I see he is in all seriousness. He seems to expect me to devastate him with rejection. When—*how*? How has he grown to care for me so strongly?

"You love me," I repeat, daring him to confirm it. Because I do not resist him with words, the doctor takes my elbows, drawing me up against his body.

"Love of my life," he says quietly, sincerely, and then he kisses me. It is—oh! It is what I have always dreamed of, and yet it is so much more than I had hoped for. The kiss is not tentative. It is full and heady and alive. His mouth tastes like a man, but more a man than I've ever known. I feel the strength in his hands as he squeezes my waist and captures my face. I do not realize I'm crying through our first kiss until his thumbs brush against my cheeks.

353

Finally, our lips break apart. He is flushed and smiling widely.

"I think you cry out of happiness, Janie?" he teases lightly, giving me a swift soft kiss on the lips again before resting his cheek on my hair.

I pull away to look up at him. Does he really mean this? That he loves me? Loves me enough to come, yet again, to fetch me? It is impossible. Improbable. *This is a dream.* I say it over and over to myself, if only to protect my swirling spirit. The questions pour from me, as if by asking them, I will know my reality.

"How did you think to return?"

He smiles again. "When you said goodbye last Sunday. You told me you couldn't go back to watch me marry Kate. I realized you didn't know—how could you?—that I had decided not to wed her. I had to come back, to see if you were truly pained with the idea of me marryin' another. It may have been a hypothesis made of my own desires, but I believed the answer to be logical. If so, and my theory was correct, then likely the only reason my marryin' could hurt you is if you cared for me yourself. Finally, I thought I knew your heart."

"Then you didn't know?"

"How could I? You left the Territory, in quite a storm of flour, if you recall. And then last week, when I saw how you'd torn into my wee attempt at a soft-hearted note, I lost all hope."

"That was a love letter?" This conversation is ever more unbelievable, and my veins pump so hard I can't focus well.

"Rather." He shrugs, looking slightly uncomfortable. "It seemed a bit presumptuous to write more than I did, and then shortly after that, you pressed for me to dance with

354

Kate. I started to wonder if I had a chance. I've near given up. *Had* given up."

"I should have said something," I tell him quietly, thinking of my blinding sorrow, and how I'd let it consume me when I was alone. Perhaps I should have let my passion spill out. "Then you might have known."

"Known what?"

I blush, and admit to it all. "You didn't know I loved you? That I *do* love you?" The admittance scatters the last sadness from my chest, leaving me empty and full at the same time. What is this? Is it acceptance? Love? Joy?

He looks pleased. Triumphant. "I have hoped for many months that you might, someday. I can hardly believe it's true as it is."

The rain suddenly hits, pelting the beach before it smacks the wood of my roof, and we turn as one to walk into the cottage, though the doctor—*Patrick*—does not release my hand. Inside, in the warm, dim glow of the lanterns, we sit side by side on the couch. Above, and at the windows, the hard rainwater drums, encasing us in a cave of privacy. It is highly improper we are, yet again, alone in my house with no chaperone. A beachside twirl, and now the same man in my home once more? It would be enough to damage my reputation. Still, I find I do not care. I won't care. It doesn't matter.

"So you've come in today?" The small talk feels safest for the moment. I think if we dive into anything more romantic than that, I will shatter.

"Aye. This mornin'."

"And you waited all day?" Was he searching himself when he arrived, wondering if he loved me enough to return to my door?

He gives a little sigh and smiles sheepishly. "My mind had been playin' our conversation many times over while I was at the lectures. I borrowed a bit of money from a colleague—from Bobby MacHugh—and came back as soon as I could. But I wasn't sure your work—if you had to work today. I went up to the Chesters to ask the help there, and was told you were home."

I put a hand on his cheek, battling my old hopes, still not completely believing this all comes together now.

"How long have you loved me?"

"I don't know," he says. "A long time."

"But you didn't want to court me," I tell him, trying to sort out his actions from his words. He places his hand on my shoulder and looks at me directly.

"Jane. Believe me when I tell you that you took my breath away the first time I saw you, standin' at my door. I could not believe you were to be my housekeeper, that you would be in my home, at my table, every day."

I take his fingers, wishing to get more of his earnest honesty. "But you still pined for Kate, Patrick."

"Ah, aye," he sighs honestly, and drops his hand. "Yes, I did in a way. I had spent so long rememberin' her for the spirited young woman she was when I first met her that I think I refused to see how hardened she had become to her own roots. She would turn her back so entirely on the mother who loves her ... She will do most anythin' to be seen as non-native, even at the cost of her family ... It is a fundamental difference I cannot overlook." His eyes meet mine. "I cannot love a woman who will do such a thing, who will be so intolerant."

"So, I was next best?" I offer, needing every ounce of truth from him.

356

"Janie," he admonishes. "There is no contest. It was different with you. You must believe me."

"But—"

"You were more real to me than any woman I've ever known. Tangible, reachable," he vows. "Kate was a phantom, an untouchable woman of my past. I got along well with her from the start, yes. But I only considered her because I thought you were interested in Bern Masson. You … you *insisted* I court her, when all I wished was time with you."

"You mean to say you pined for me too?" I am incredulous.

He nods, and brings my fingers to his lips again. I close my eyes against the sensations. When I open them, he leans in.

"I thought you were quite wonderful from the start. I expect I will always think so."

"Patrick." I battle my practiced, simple ways with words. My sweetheart is eloquent enough, and I must try to communicate in kind. "I hope you might. I know I will."

We stare at the floor as one. I know what I want, but am afraid to let it loose. I know my own passions and my penchant for the extreme when I allow my heart to take the lead. I suppose I should confess to such a character flaw.

"Will you let me explain why I was so very violent the last night in Flats Junction?" I ask him. To even put the question out is terribly intimate.

I still cannot look at him, but I feel him shift toward me on the couch.

"If you feel you must," he says slowly.

"You don't care?"

357

"You know I'm always hankerin' for answers, but I won't press. I figure it came from grief. At least, now knowin' what I do of your heart, that's my best guess."

Covering my eyes with my hands, I bend forward toward my knees, thankful, grateful, and relieved I need to say so little. "You don't condemn me, then?"

"Am I right?"

I nod, and his arms slip about my waist and tug me to his side. I go, willingly. He kisses me hard and long, and I find myself overcome with desire, lust, want. I have lain in bed for months thinking of and wishing for this moment, but the heat I feel is many times deeper and more overwhelming now that he is here in reality. He fumbles with the buttons on my dress, blindly trying to expose some of my flesh, even if it is only the inches of my neck. His obvious need for me is wonderful, and I help him with the tiny hooks and bands of a bodice's neckline. He seems a man enraptured. His breath comes short, and he captures my face in both of his hands, kissing me softly, tenderly.

"Marry me," he whispers. "Please. Marry me."

"When?"

He pulls away, his blue eyes searching mine, as if incredulous again. "You mean you will?"

I give a little laugh. "Of course I will. I have never been so ..." I stop and blush, for this emotional disclosure is still new. "I have never felt so much passion."

"What about ... the other? The man after Mr. Weber?"

Strangely, I feel no shame when he brings up the phantom of Theodore. I think he does it to settle his own research and questions, and I cannot blame him for that. And the fact that he knows this weakness, this unsavory bit of my life, and still wants me? I can tell him whatever he wants to know in these moments.

"Passion and love are very different than wanting to escape, Patrick. I wish to marry you, love you, help you. Just you, and no other. The man after Mr. Weber was ... no more than an experiment. I cannot recall his face, though your features are burned into my heart ..." I trail off, thinking of how I had fallen in love with him once I'd woken from my shivering, bloody bed. How do I put all that into words?

I suddenly realize how exposed I am with my neck open to his eyes, and demurely put a hand to my throat. The heat between us certainly makes me less prim than I expect of myself. But no one has ever lusted after me so that I would be so eager like this.

"Why are you hidin'? Your bosom is legendary, Jane." Patrick takes my hand and pulls it away.

"Indeed?" I give a nervous laugh.

"Oh, aye!" He drinks me in, as if thrilled he can now look at me openly. "The cowboys always gave me tease that I should have a housekeeper with a bosom enough for two men to lay their heads. They wonder why I did not try to court you myself from the start. Then Bern had the guts to try to woo you."

"He didn't manage it. Nor did Andrew. I realized I loved you, and a commitment to any other man was pointless," I say honestly.

My admission grants me another hard kiss, passionate and titillating.

He breaks away and mutters, "Sweet Jesus," before curling his face in the crick of my neck. The faint tickle of his cheek and hair is delightfully sensual. I am amazed at how stimulating this is, how I utterly desire his nearness. I want him to continue touching me. This is what I missed in my marriage: this heat, this conversation, this need. I will not mind tying myself to this man with a promise and a ring. My hands come up unwittingly and stroke his face and hair, hugging him nearer.

We sit like this a long time. Are we calm enough so our passion cools? We ought not devour each other in any unseemlier a fashion than we already have, though just thinking about his hands on me is enough for lust to course through my body all over again. How long did he hold this hearty yearning inside? How silly of me not to notice it earlier, how ridiculous that I felt so alone in my love for him, so blinded by Kate's beauty to think myself not enough. Clearly, he says I am.

His head comes up, tousled and flushed. I think he has mastered his desire so I might get up and make some supper. Instead, he bends down and runs his lips along my neck before releasing me entirely.

"How did you learn to make a puddle of a woman?" I gasp. His eyes are clouded, but his unmasked craving makes them a brighter blue.

"I have dreamed of what I would do, if I had you alone and you'd let me, by some miracle, touch you."

"Patrick," I breathe. "You've thought a long time then."

"Nearly since the first day I saw you. I've been buildin' ideas since then." He gives a wicked grin.

Now that we are not so near each other, the windy chill of the storm outside seeps in, and Patrick kneels to fix the fire without another word. At least the glass is gone.

As I heat the water for turnip and potato soup, he comes over to the small stove, takes one look at me, and shakes his head. Snaking an arm around my waist, he pulls me tight to him.

"You'll not get much supper done, I'm afraid," he admits. "I'm too distracted, and I won't be able to stop kissing you." He bends down to plant a kiss at my temple.

I give a soft sigh. If I let myself go, I could be entirely scandalous, and I want to do this right by him.

"So, you really will marry me?" he asks again. He seems genuinely amazed at his good luck, when it seems to me it is I who is the lucky one.

"Yes," I say, and smile at him. "Gladly and with a full heart."

"Then you'll wear this." He dips his hand into his pocket and pulls out a simple band.

I stare. "When did you think to get that?"

"This mornin'. I had hope," he explains. "Will you wear it?"

"Of course."

He picks up my hand and slides the cold metal on. It instantly warms. I look at my fingers clasped in his. It is amazing. I will be able to hold onto him whenever I want.

"Kiss me again," he requests, and I drop the spoon and turn into his embrace.

I kiss him, but behind me I can hear the soup bubbling. I pull away, though he leaves his arm about my shoulders, and watches me scrape the bottom of the cast iron pot to turn over the vegetables.

As we eat, the fire crackles in the hearth and shoves heat into the far corners of the room. I look out at the rain and ocean. Doctor Kinney seems attuned to me, reaching across the table to finger the band of gold.

"I meant what I said, Janie. I'll bring you back here as often as we can manage it, whenever we can afford it ..." He trails off and looks at me strangely. His voice is suddenly rougher. "I would think we should let our children know the sea, as you did."

"What is it?" I wait as he struggles to keep a casual composure. I've forgotten how expressive he is. It is this empathy that makes him a fine doctor, and a tolerant man. His strong hand pulls at mine, grasping it tightly. Finally, he clears his throat.

"You don't know how much I worried when you miscarried. There's only so much medicine can do at times like that. I was scared, more so than I'd ever been before. You were dyin' in front of me, and there was nothin' I could do but wait. I did not realize how much I loved you, even then. Only, your death would have brought me to my knees. It was the most difficult day and night of my life."

I thought I'd heard a man sobbing. Had that been him, at my bedside? The thought is too dear and too sweet to ask.

"I lived, though. And yes, Patrick. I'd like to have children."

He is quiet again for a moment, gazing at my hand, rubbing it with his thumb. Why had he waited so long to profess his love? Maybe he kept his heart locked because he believed I did not love him. I try to map my past. I suppose I was not interested at first, and then I was too shy, and too proper, to show any feeling. What man would reach for that coldness?

He sighs and meets my eyes. "You know, when I first discovered you were expectin', I thought it would be nice

362

to have a babe in the house, someone to watch grow." He pauses, then plunges ahead. "I began to think of that babby as mine, or my kin, anyway. It was imaginary, I know."

"We'll have that," I promise, reeling a bit myself. He says he daydreamed as I did?!

"What do we need to do to get you gone from here?" he suddenly asks pragmatically. "Do you need to give notice?"

"Yes, traditionally I do. Several weeks, to let them find another cook. But I've been teaching my kitchen girl for months. She possibly could do well enough until they find another."

He glances at the clock on my small mantel. It is late on a Sunday evening; not exactly the time to go calling on my employers. I know what he is thinking. He wants to take me home to Flats Junction as soon as possible. My thoughts fly to the split skirt I shredded. It'll have to be mended, now. But I don't want to admit to another fit of weakness.

"I can stay at the inn another night, but that's all." He hints to how he will run out of borrowed funds, but he is matter-of-fact about the next. "Still, I'm not leavin' until you're on the train with me. No more goodbyes like that. I think the next one might kill me."

I laugh a bit tremulously. "I think Aunt Mary might be very happy to fill her guest room for as many days as needed to get things settled."

He laughs, a deep, sweet-sounding rumble. "I can't wait to meet your Aunt Mary."

CHAPTER 43
23 October 1882

I visit Mrs. Chester first thing as the sun rises. Today it is not stormy. The sun is crystal, white, and bright. I smell briny saltwater on the breeze, refreshed by last night's rain, as I walk into the great house. Mrs. Chester is in her morning gown, writing a note, her hair pinned up prettily and her toes folded over daintily. She is a very lovely woman, and kind, and I have been fortunate she is so easy a mistress, willing to take me on with such little experience and no real reference. It was probably helpful I did not make many wage demands.

My hands twist nervously. I have not mastered the easy stance of people seasoned in service.

"What is it, Mrs. Weber?"

I instinctively pause at the title. It is the first realization that soon I will have a new name. I look at the floor, and then into her clear face. "I am ... I've been offered marriage, ma'am."

Her gaze flicks to my fingers. The new gold of Patrick's ring glimmers in the early, soft light. She gives a delighted smile.

"Why Mrs. Weber! How splendid for you! I am glad you've found someone to make you happy." She stops and squints at my face. "You do, indeed, seem very happy. Love becomes you."

"You're not very cross, then?"

"How soon do you have to go?"

"In a few days. I have been teaching young Beth. I thought if you might be able to find someone in a fortnight or so, you'd be fine with her."

"You'd like to be married so soon?" She arches her eyebrow, and I flush. Yes, I cannot wait to marry him. Perhaps she thinks there is another reason for the speed, but I find I don't care a bit if she has suspicions on my virtue.

"He's a doctor, ma'am, and needs to get back out West. I'd like to go with him when he leaves."

She gives a small sigh. "Well, I don't like the speed of your departure, but I have no hold over you. It's a good reason to be a little relaxed with the rules, anyway." Then she laughs. "You will have to be sure Beth has all of Mr. Chester's favorite recipes. He might faint if he thinks he won't get your creamy soups ever again."

"I will. Thank you, ma'am, truly. I'll have her settled in a few days."

She nods, and then turns back to her desk.

That was easier than I thought it might be, and I head to the kitchen with a light step. Beth is waiting there for the morning's list, and I break the news. Her eyes well with tears.

"Oh no, Mrs. Weber! But I'll miss you so much!"

I hug her shoulder with an arm. "I know, and I will miss you, too. But we have gone over so much, and this may be your chance. Please Mr. Chester and his wife. They may not hire a new cook at all and give the post to you."

Her face pops up. She is a bright and ambitious girl. It would be grand for her to land the position so young.

"See?" I soothe. "Let's plan to do that for you."

CHAPTER 44
23 October 1882

Doctor Kinney is waiting for me at Jean and Ada's stall in the market. His face lights up when he sees me, and I feel myself blossom in return.

"How did it go?" he asks, as I loop an arm through his. I feel I'm bursting with love, but am unable to even glance over at the dairyman's stall. For all that Andrew and I parted on good terms, I feel badly for flaunting any of my joy where he might see it.

"Wonderfully so. We can leave together."

"Now that is good news," he says contently, then looks around the marketplace. "Do you have time to go to your aunt's now?"

Jean gives me a little wink. She has been listening, and I'm sure Patrick has not been shy about our story. "Go. This order will take quite a while to fill."

I smile thankfully at her. Oh, how I will miss her, too! It seems no matter where I go, I will leave pieces of friendships behind. Patrick and I walk the short distance to Aunt Mary's little house quickly.

When she opens the door, her narrow, bird-like face erupts in wrinkles and a huge smile.

"There you are! Finally, you've come for her!" It is a classic greeting.

Patrick has the presence of mind to take off his hat and give a half-bow of his head.

"Doctor Patrick Kinney, at your service."

"Are you really? What fortune." My aunt gives him a hard eye, then smiles again. "Come in, then." She opens the door wider, and we file into the small foyer. I am happy to introduce her to my love, as I know she won't wrongly judge him. I'm still spinning with happiness that he is here, that he loves me, that I can leave with him in a few short days.

"Tea?" she asks, as she sits in front of her service in the parlor. Only yesterday did I sit here and dismiss Andrew's suit. Now, I am an engaged woman, and it is Patrick whom I sit with as Aunt Mary considers the match. There is an odd space between him and me until he swallows, gives up, and takes my hand. She glances at us as she pours but says nothing about his physical touch.

"I am sorry I did not have the presence of mind to ask your permission," he starts. I know these formalities must be a bit beyond him, and he is nervous. "I was uncertain Jane would even say yes, and I admit I was distracted with worry about the whole business. I've never married, and things are less involved in the Territories."

"Oh yes, the Dakotas. I've heard tell." Aunt Mary sips her tea carefully, but her eyes are very bright.

"I ..." He looks at me. I know he wants to pull me

368

closer, but he doesn't dare in front of my aunt. He takes a breath and turns back. "I love your niece, and I have for some time."

"Why'd you let her get away from you, then?" she asks shrewdly.

He smiles a little, as if the memory is painful. "Because I was a fool. And because, as you may know, Jane does not express herself overtly. I never had so much as an inklin' she might care for me as well."

"Oh, I'll give you that," she agrees, and shakes her head gently at me. "You'd do well to remember this man will want for your attentions and nurture."

"Yes, of course, Aunt Mary," I say, and blush like a silly schoolgirl.

"And be sure you say to him how you feel, so he doesn't wonder."

"Listen to your aunt. She gives good advice," he teases me, and I laugh tremulously.

He seems to see an ally in her and leans forward. "We'd like to marry."

"Of course you do." She looks at me. "And what will you do about the Chesters?"

"I've already asked to leave."

She spreads her hands. I can tell she is excited. "Well, when can we have the wedding?"

"As soon as we might." Doctor Kinney pleads with her, though I know he doesn't need to do so. She will humor us, no matter the speed. "Perhaps on Friday."

"So soon? There will hardly be time for a cake."

I look at him. We've discussed this. He does not care one whit about a cake, or flowers, or bows. In truth, neither do I. My first marriage was heralded with a bit of fanfare and it did nothing to help find love and happiness.

"Aunt Mary, we just care about the logistics. Keeping Patrick here in Gloucester until we are wed and can travel together, for instance, and settling up my cottage. Getting the license."

He gives me a grateful glance and squeezes my fingers.

She frowns a little. I know she wants to enjoy a bit more fuss, just like her friends do, and I have a suspicion they will throw just as much compacted energy into this quick affair as they can anyway. Then her face clears and she smiles.

"I'm sure we can make it work. In the meantime, you'll stay here with me." She directs this to Doctor Kinney.

"Thank you kindly ... Aunt Mary," he says, and the title makes her chuckle.

"You'll want to wire her father," she instructs. "And we'll want to go to Essex for a dress for you, dear." She looks at me and I shake my head.

"I don't need a dress, and there won't be time to make one up."

"Nonsense," she scoffs. "I do not have any children, and I've always wanted a little family wedding. I've enough to do something for my favorite niece."

"Thank you again," Doctor Kinney says, speaking for me. I can tell he is as touched by her generosity as I am.

"I don't know what to say," I pipe up. "I feel so fortunate on all corners."

We stand. I need to get back to the house for the meals. Now that things are settling, I find I am eager for the week to move forward so I can finish my time in service and marry. I *want* to be married. Apparently, I was very wrong when I'd sworn off the idea of it.

"Stay back, Doctor. Patrick." Aunt Mary puts a hand on his arm and looks up at him merrily. She says his front name with more comfort than I expect. "You can help me open up the bedroom, and then go get your things from the inn. Jane can come tonight for a spell to see you."

I smile at them. They look like two kindred spirits already, but as I move to open the door and head back to the market, he breaks from her arm and moves to me. Unapologetically, he puts a hand about my waist and presses his forehead to mine before releasing me.

"Have a good afternoon, Janie," he says, his voice deep and soft. I want to melt into him.

"I'll see you tonight, Paddy," I say softly, using his nickname. Out of the corner of my eye, I can see that Aunt Mary looks very pleased. And as he goes back to her as I leave, I hear them plotting his stay. She will be in her element this week, and I'm so glad I can share this happiness with her.

CABLE MESSAGE.
THE WESTERN UNION TELEGRAPH COMPANY.

All CABLE MESSAGES received for transmission must be written on the Message Blanks
provided by this Company for that purpose, under and subject to the conditions printed thereon,
and on the back hereof, which conditions have been agreed to by the sender of the following Message.

A. R. BREWER, Secretary.   WILLIAM ORTON, President.

To *Ruth Hobbs*

Received at _____

October 24 1882

*Getting married on October 27 in Gloucester 11 AM – St. Anne's
Very happy. Hope to see you and Father.
More in letter. J. Weber*

CHAPTER 45
25 October 1882

Wednesday, my last day at the Chester house, I write my sister and my mother letters beyond the wire I send to Mother about the wedding. I tell them about Doctor Kinney's two arrivals in Gloucester and his proposal. My letter to Mother is long. I finally confess what I have held so close to my heart, and I know she will understand, though she will be sad I thought to keep such heartache from her. I do not bother to wire Anne. She will only disapprove of how quickly it all is happening, and she won't make time to come up from Boston anyway. But still, I want to share my news. I want to tell her I have found deep happiness.

The caretaker of the cottage comes in the afternoon to discuss taking my key and what furniture needs to be covered with sheets. Then I head to my aunt's home. Aunt Mary and I will go into Essex to look for a dress today.

When I let myself in, I hear her and Doctor Kinney chatting in the kitchen. The voices echo, and I pause, taking delight in hearing how well they get on. I will miss my aunt greatly, and have thought to ask her to come out West with us, but I know she would miss the sea and her friends. It would be too much to ask of her.

"Oh, yes, of course I know all about the Eclectics. My husband, may he rest in peace, was very much interested in the workings of the physicians. It was one of his hobbies. He liked how the Eclectics took a bit from each school of thought in medicine and created their own version of practicing. It felt the most thorough branch to him."

"He was a kind of doctor too, then?"

"Heavens no! He was just very curious and the science of the profession drew him in. Jane is like him, though she's not his blood."

"I had a good apprenticeship under a homeopathic doc, though he leaned Eclectic," Doctor Kinney explains, the excitement rattling in his voice. "And good trainin' before that too, in animals. I think most successful docs beyond the coast must manage both beast and man."

"And Jane, too, knows something of doctoring, as I'm sure you've known."

"She does," he agrees. There is a slight pause, and then he dives into a personal question, his low voice carrying through the doorway. "But ... you're certain she really cared all this time? That she was unhappy away from the West?"

I shake my head. I doubt either of us can believe our luck.

"I really couldn't figure it," he continues. "If I'd known she cared, I would have stopped her from leavin' Flats Junction. I nearly did try anyway, but she held herself together so well I didn't think my beggin' would amount to much."

"Well, you were courting another." My aunt's voice is reasonable.

"True. I only … I was cut to the quick that she left. It was my … a surrogate mother who made it all a bit clearer. Later. When I was inclined to listen."

"How so?"

I wait, too. I want to know how he came to his decision to chase after me, and I don't know if he will reveal all this if I were to ask.

"Well, she decided to take herself to a reservation. She's Sioux."

My aunt is silent. I know she is digesting this. The idea of savages is one that is well-documented, usually incorrectly, here in the East. The notion of a native woman who is genteel enough for a doctor takes time for her to understand, and I know it only paints a more vivid picture of the wild West where I choose to live.

"What does that matter?" she finally manages. "How did the woman help you see your choices?"

"Esther asked me if I cared for Janie, and I admitted I thought of her often. And she accused me of bein' a fool for not seein' how Jane was a far better match for me than any woman in Flats Junction or beyond, and I ought to fetch her. And she was right."

"You'll find many women are right," Aunt Mary says cheekily, and he chuckles.

374

I take this as a cue to come around the corner. "Who's always right?"

"Women," she announces. "Something a doctor should remember."

"Oh, I'm quite aware of the wiles and minds of ladies." He smiles at me as I take the empty space next to him. Handling the pot, I pour a cup of tea from the service on the table.

"Warm up." Doctor Kinney reaches and briefly rubs my shoulder. "We're off to Essex."

"You're coming?" I am surprised. "I didn't think that was done."

"I've got some shoppin' to do," he says. "And now that you're free of the Chester house, I plan to spend as much time with you as Aunt Mary allows."

"You'd think you're not planning to marry and spend years in each other's company," my aunt laughs, and we join her. "Well then, you finish your tea, Jane, and I'll go get my hat." She leaves without ceremony, giving us time alone again, which she does artfully, but so often it's plain and obvious.

She is not even out of the room before I take his hand. How will I show him that I really do care for him as he does me? He doubted me so fully. Thank God he thought to brave the uncertainty and ask me for my heart anyway.

"Oh, Janie," he breathes. "Friday does not come fast enough."

"I can't wait to marry you," I agree, looking up at him and smiling. "I want to go West."

He squeezes my fingers tightly. "I'm a bit excited to travel with my wife, and to show you off on the train as mine."

I laugh again. "I'm rather excited for that, too, and also to have you completely to myself." I blush, but plunge ahead, determined to take my aunt's words to heart and tell him how I feel. "I am desperately wanting to have you in my bed, my love." It is an inelegant thing to say, and vulgar, but it is the truth. And really, I'm no shy, blushing bride. If anyone knows how true that is, it is Patrick.

His reaction to my words is immediate. He bends down for a devastatingly long kiss, as if my admittance means much to him. Then he looks at me pensively, as if debating to speak, before saying quietly, "I'm a bit nervous about that myself, Janie."

"I'm all healed," I say, dismissing the notion quickly. I am disconcerted we are talking about these bodily compulsions. I must constantly remind myself that he is a doctor and is open about the science of it all. He saw my own limbs in near nakedness, and he was not overcome with anything but how to cure my ailment. He is not lewd, at least.

"It's not that. It's the act itself. I'm afraid I'll ... well, you've been married before. I haven't."

"Don't men visit establishments to ... um." My cheeks are on fire. "Learn?"

His own face burns, but his eyes are merry and trained on me. "I didn't. It could be the old Catholicism in my blood, but mostly it's that all the girls in the bordellos are my patients. It would have been highly uncomfortable. But you ... Jane. You know what I'm tryin' to say?"

"Paddy." I touch his cheek. "You must understand what we have already shared pales anything from my first marriage ... and beyond it. I'm nervous, too."

His honest face breaks into a grin. "Thank the saints!"

376

"And what are we thanking for now?" Aunt Mary comes around the corner finishing up her hat. She has taken her time on purpose.

"For my Janie." Patrick flashes me a devilish grin behind my aunt's back as we leave the house. He makes me feel desirable and young with his unabashed happiness. I mirror it, for I feel the same joy flooding my marrow. How can I ever repay those saints for my good fortune?

CHAPTER 46
27 October 1882

The pale, dove-grey dress has lace on the bodice and along the hem. My aunt and her friends pulled together a few late-fall flowers for my hair and a little posy for my bouquet. They cooked a small spread of food, now waiting for us at Aunt Mary's parlor. Jean, Rose, and their menfolk join my aunt and parents as witnesses. It is not much, and I almost feel guilty that Doctor Kinney does not get to experience the whole wedding extravagance I know Aunt Mary would have liked to do for us. Though as I stand next to him, and he holds my hand, staring down at me while we echo the vows, he seems to only care that I am marrying him, and happily forgets about ribbons and bows.

My mother and father arrive for the nuptials as well. It was a breathless surprise. She can see I am beyond happiness, so she is mollified for the moment, though likely she aches to know more. My father says little, his dark eyes taking in the tableaux, but he is placated knowing I wed a doctor who has proven he can support me.

When the priest says we are wed, I am filled with so much happiness I do not know what to do with the emotion. Doctor Kinney is smiling at me with glittering eyes, so I reach up and kiss him. My family and friends follow us over to the little luncheon, where more of my aunt's friends are waiting. The Angus family was invited, but they do not attend, and I do not blame them. A part of me is sorry to not have a chance to say goodbye to Andrew and his children.

Doctor Kinney does not know the people here, so Aunt Mary is gracious enough to keep the party small. He keeps a hand on my elbow as much as he might, and it is all I can do to remember how the older ladies would not take kindly to me kissing the groom whenever I like. Are all newlyweds in love matches so happy and bursting? I feel as though I might wake to find this all a dream.

I'd thought we would take the evening train out, but Aunt Mary had other plans. She will stay with Ada and Jean Baker tonight, and Patrick and I will have her little house to ourselves. I want everyone to leave now, but instead the usual conversation swirls. Doctor Kinney discusses the West with Jean and Rose's men, who seem genuinely interested in the gold often discovered in the Dakotas.

"Jane." Jean is at my elbow, balancing a glass of champagne. "I'll miss you so much."

"You ought to visit," I tell her warmly. "We'd love to have you."

"Clark and I should honeymoon there in the spring." She smiles and takes my hand. "You know I'm very happy for you."

"Thank you. We will write," I say.

As the afternoon wanes, people depart in groups. Mother comes and embraces me, her eyes wet. This wedding means I am leaving. A wide distance will spread open between us again. I share her sadness, but I am too excited about my future to dwell on it.

"I'm very glad for you, Janie," she says quietly, as she and Father prepare to return to Rockport. "I expect you will explain everything in your letter."

"Everything," I promise her, and hug her again. In a way, spilling my heart in a letter to her is best. I was more eloquent on paper than if I were to tell her over tea.

Aunt Mary and her friends tidy up, and both Doctor Kinney and I help. They think he is only drying dishes to hurry them, though I know he genuinely enjoys people and conversation. So much of that happens in the kitchen. But maybe he is helping to hurry them just the same.

"I'll see you off at the train tomorrow, my dears," Aunt Mary says, picking up her satchel at the door. "And there is cold chicken for supper in the larder."

The moment she shuts the door, my new husband comes up behind me, wrapping his arms around my waist. "You look perfect and lovely," he murmurs into my hair. "But I want to see less lace and more of you."

I turn in his embrace and cock my head at him. "You've seen plenty of me, you know."

He knows innately what I reference. "That was different."

We kiss, as if reaffirming life. I find I'm nervous and yet utterly desirous. The sun has not even set, but the door of Patrick's room beckons us.

My aunt is not a flowery person, so the bedroom is

decorated as most austere, proper New England homes ought to be: pale blue walls, painted wood, bare furniture, and an iron bedstead. Patrick pulls the curtains, though no one can see in through the garden and trees in the backyard. I gaze at him; his loose frame, strong arms, and vivacious health. Need drops down through my shoulders, stomach, and loins. He is mine, not Kate's, and he says he loves me.

"What is it, Mrs. Kinney?" He comes to me, grinning.

I laugh. "I am indeed Mrs. Kinney. Jane Kinney. My heavens. I never thought it would happen."

"And I'm a married man, now," he says happily. "It was worth the wait."

He falls to kissing me again, and we press tightly together, the hardness of his body against the softness of mine.

After a long while, when my lips are swollen, he pulls away, his eagerness barely masked. "Might I see more of you, Janie? I have been achin' ..." He pauses, and restarts. "I have spent many nights dreamin' about seeing you just so, even when I didn't think you'd ever be mine. And now to have you like this, I'm afraid I've become even needier."

"Well, it's a bit early in the evening to think of this, but yes," I say with more confidence than I feel. "Yes, please."

The stays loosen, with the camisole and petticoats falling to the floor. His eyes feast on the sight of my skin, the lines of my form hazy and muted through the watery paleness of my chemise. Henry and I only ever had intercourse in the dark, and Theodore and I never used more than a candle, so to have someone see me in this half-golden shadow of lamplight is disconcerting. I forget briefly that my love is a doctor, has seen many a body, even my own, in the most intimate way.

"You are … well. Glorious. Is that too much to say?"

"It's romantic," I admit, my heart hammering.

"Good." He frees my flesh completely but for my shift, eventually picking me up and reclining next to me on the bed to help peel off my stockings. I am unable to stop touching him, and I am suddenly glad we do not wait for full night to begin.

He reaches up and unties my hair, slowly withdrawing the pins. When it falls out and down my back, he rakes his fingers through the strands, pulling my head up and kissing me as if he never plans to stop. I hope he does not, until I find myself unable to end it here, and I am untucking his shirt and loosening his tie. I've seen a naked man before, but not a man I desire so entirely. I want such closeness with him, and I say so, forcing myself to be emotionally vulnerable. He complies without a word of protest, stripping down so quickly my breath disappears.

He has a light dusting of brown hair across his chest, and his skin is pale, as I would expect of the Irish in him. I lean forward and kiss his shoulder, where it rounds into his arm, and taste his cheek while running the back of my hands along his skin, amazed at his vitality. I drink in the strength of his thighs, the broadness of his chest, and the sinewy lengths of his arms. We intertwine our legs, all while I marvel that he is mine, that he desires me, that his hands are everywhere, tugging off the last of my clothing.

"Patrick, I never want to leave you," I say playfully, running a finger along his jaw and down his neck.

"No. You'll stay with me always." He loops his hands low on my waist, pressing his palms into my hips. "No more leavin' after supper, no Bern to take you off for an evenin' walk."

"Did that bother you?" I ask, burying my face into his skin, our bareness rubbing deliciously together. I never knew the act of love could be prefaced with so much passion!

He nods. "It was very difficult to say nothin'. I wanted you to stay as my housekeeper, not go off and marry some cowboy because he was the only one who made a pass. And then I wanted you for myself in an entirely different way."

"What way?" I know the answer, but gasp a little as he flips me under him, melting us into the mattress.

"I wanted you this way, here in my bed, in my arms." He bends down and kisses me hard. We stop talking so we can focus on each other. Soon enough he is holding me, and I can hardly breathe. I must have him. I ache for him so much that when we finally join, I flow up and down, unable to stop from crying out. It is no matter that I am quite lusty, because I feel his body responding likewise, and we lay panting in short order.

"Sweet mother," he lightly swears, burying his face in my bosom. His voice is muffled. "Is it always like that?"

"I wouldn't know," I say, clasping him. "It has never been like that. I would hope so."

His head comes up and he chuckles. "Me too."

CHAPTER 47

28 October 1882

We walk to the station, with my belongings smashed with his in my brass-cornered, battered trunk, his new medicines balanced on top, and the rest of our things in the small carpet bag. I wonder if everyone who sees us can tell we are new-lyweds. A few who know me call out, some using my new married name.

Aunt Mary waits for us at the depot. She is too old to cry over our departure, but she tucks a lace hanky in my pocket and gives Patrick a little kiss on the cheek. She is glowing, as if she is the one who was married.

"My sweet niece," she says fondly. "I am so happy for you. Many blessings!"

She turns to Patrick and gives him a strange, shrewd, appraising look. Then she nods, once, and says off-handedly, "It was a good choice."

His eyebrows go up, and I jump in. "I think so too, Aunt Mary."

She smiles, and the moment is gone, as if she has made her final judgment on our entire situation, clasping Patrick's hands in goodwill, telling him to take care of me and our future children, that she will write.

I cannot stop thanking her and she waves me off, as if I am the one who gave her a gift. I will miss her very much and know there is a good chance I will not be with her again in this life. So, I am weeping as the train pulls out, and I wave until I cannot see her any more.

CHAPTER 48
31 October 1882

We arrive in Flats Junction on the five o'clock train. There is snow on the ground. Patrick says it can come in October sometimes, but nothing is frozen yet, and the road and platform are mucky.

The minute I step off, I hear a voice shout. "Jane! You're back?" Swinging around, I find Jacob Zalenski driving a wagon of corn and waving a hat in my direction.

"I am!"

"I'll tell Anette. She'll be glad!"

Patrick bumps down the stairs, just as Horeb Harvey ambles by. "The sawbones is back, is he?"

"Aye. You're still alive, are you?"

Horeb smirks, then notices me. His tiny green eyes widen. "And you too?" His narrow shoulders hunch, and he scurries up the road toward the general store.

We follow Horeb's footsteps at a more leisurely pace, and as we pass the mercantile, another voice rings out.

"Mrs. Weber! Jane! You've come back!"

It is Kate. She comes down the general's stairs toward us, her eyes bright. Patrick tenses next to me, and his steps falter. To avoid her innocent smile, I twist the box of medicinal vials, my gold wedding band clanking against the wood.

"And Pat." Her voice is guarded. "You've returned as well."

"I have."

"Then you've found Jane and convinced her to come and keep house for you again? Good! I've missed my friend."

She seems to not mind he has stopped courting her, and for a brief, wildly unclear moment, I wonder if he misspoke to me. Suppose he never ended their courtship?

"Let me help you." She relieves him of the satchel, slinging it over her shoulder.

Patrick and I glance at one another, but our tongues seem stuck. I can understand his hesitancy. There doesn't seem to be a good way to explain we are married. Many of the townsfolk thought the doc would wed Kate. Will people take sides? Mine versus hers?

"Jane! You're back!" Sadie Fawcett waves heartily from her family's wagon. Mitch Brinkley is in town, but he is juggling Petey while Alice is in the post office. Old George Ofsberger tips his fingers from his rocker. Clara Henderssen, walking with her elderly mother-in-law, breaks away from her children to embrace me. The familiar, pungent scent of Alan Lampton's pig farm hits my nose. The only difference is that Harriet Lindsey is obviously living with him now, given the bloomers hanging on the line. There are so many dear, friendly faces here that I am suddenly overwhelmed with happiness. Who cares about all the dust, grime, and fatigue of travel?

Yes. I'm indeed back. It is enough.

Kate runs commentary on the past weeks, full of her usual news and gossip. "Some Indians were seen passing nearby, but none came to town. Shouldn't wonder, there's no reason for them to make a stop, they'd be reported fast enough for being off reservation. It wouldn't be Widow Hawks' family anyway. Might have even been Crow. And Alice thinks she's having twins. And one of your neighbors, Anna Pavlock, has gout."

We walk, stiffly formal, regardless of her chatter. As we turn onto East Avenue and approach Doctor Kinney's house, I am only half listening to Kate. To think his house will be my home for always! The permanence is deeply satisfying. We pass the Wu brothers as they trek out for a long day in one of the Brinkley fields. Mrs. Molhurst glares from her kitchen window as we march toward the porch.

Kate opens the screen door. It creaks a bit now. She places the bag inside and turns to us, her face blooming. I wonder if she thinks Patrick left only for lectures, and perhaps thought about her romantically with the distance. Her entire body quivers with this energy. She is just as beautiful as I remember.

My husband does not seem to notice Kate's obvious intention. He is too busy peering into the rain barrel and checking on the garden. I peek at what's visible and cringe. It is mostly a tangled mess of old weeds and vegetables gone to seed or rot.

"So," Kate says to me. "I am not sure if you know, but Widow Hawks has left town for the reservation."

"I know it. I wish she'd consider coming back."

Kate gives a swift laugh and flicks her hand. "Why? She has no home now, and you're here to replace any work she might have. I *am* glad to see you, Jane."

"I'm glad I am so welcome," I say carefully. Kate stands for a minute. She sneaks glances at the doctor as he comes up the stairs, opens the screen, and takes the trunk in. He disappears into the dimness of the house. Kate suddenly looks a bit nervous. I do not blame her. Patrick's attitude is one of indifference. I am sure part of that is because he is no longer pining for her, and the other because her disregard for her family so disgusts him. Still, his reaction must be disconcerting, and Kate is more sensitive than most.

"Janie." He comes back to the door, opens it slightly, and holds out his hand, smiling a little at me. "Give me the medicines and your little bag. I'll take it up to the bedroom."

"Oh!" Kate's exclamation makes him pause. "Jane doesn't need to stay here, Pat. I'm sure I can find room. I mean, there's nowhere else other than one of the inns now, and that is expensive after a while." She turns to me with a friendly air, as if offering a favor. "We don't need your reputation turning right away."

She says this easily enough, but she barely hides the glowering inside. She is reminding me how it would not take much to start tongues wagging if I were to stay at this house, unmarried and unattached, with no chaperone. She alludes to her power in this place, even though she herself never really seems to do much with it. Suddenly, my welcome to Flats Junction doesn't feel quite so wonderful.

"Well," I say carefully, moving so I am on the same step on the porch, though she still towers over me. "I thank you, Kate, for the offer."

"Yes," Patrick interrupts, and gives her a smile, but I can tell he wishes her to be gone. "Yes, that is very good of you, Kitty, but no need. Mrs. Kinney and I are perfectly happy sharin' the house and a room."

"Of—" She stops halfway through her nod. Her gaze swings wildly to me and then to Patrick still standing in the darkness in the house. Empathy rains into me.

I'm sorry for her.

Her bitterness is a loneliness she is starting to wear. I watch as her face registers sadness and anger.

"That is ... Jane?" Her eyes find my finger, where the gold glints in the afternoon light.

"Yes, Kate. We've married," I say gently. I will not apologize for my marriage, and even though she has proven herself a flighty and unreliable friend, I also don't wish to hold a grudge. Flats Junction is too small a place for such resentment on my part.

There is a moment of silence. Then her old shine comes back, and she tosses her hair.

"So that's how you brought her back, Pat? You bought her off with a ring?"

"Oh! Aye." I can tell his next remark will be cuttingly, damagingly sarcastic, and I jump in, placing a hand on the screen to silence him.

"Yes, you're right. He brought me back as his wife, as I'd come no other way. But it was not a compromise."

She snorts, a delicate sound, but one of disbelief anyway. "Distance made the heart grow fond, I suppose?"

"Jane is the reason I went east, Kitty. I need her—love her." His admittance is unexpected. A joy glows deep in the bottom of my stomach.

She scoffs again, and then looks between us. Her shoulders harden, and she seems more hurt than angry. Without another word, she walks off, and I know her feelings will likely be vented on anyone unlucky enough to walk into the general this morning.

"Come in, Janie." Patrick's voice is gentle, and he opens the door wider. "Come home."

His words make me close my eyes for a moment. Then I follow him in, and the familiar sights and smells of the house fill me. I have missed the occasional drip of the spigot in the surgery, the smell of prairie grass, the creaks of the wood.

He does not give me much time for remembering before he picks me up as a bride and carries me up to his—*our*—bedroom. We devour each other as I have so desperately wished to do the entire train ride out.

Afterward, he draws a bath and we take turns washing the travel grime away before falling to the mattress again for well-needed rest. It is a wasted day, without much housework done, but Patrick does not seem to mind, so I will not, either.

At night, I stay awake a bit longer. My return is too surreal. I will wake and find it is not the doctor's arms around me, or his leg between mine. I am almost too afraid to really sleep well.

But sleep comes. I drift off just before we are awakened in the wee hours of the morning by a pounding on the door.

It is one of the cowboys. Manny, it sounds like. One of the best horses is sick at the Svendsen ranch, so my husband ruefully pulls on his clothes and heads out after a quick, hard kiss.

CHAPTER 49
1 November 1882

He does not come back to bed, so I rise with the morning light, pull on a serviceable blue calico from the East, and make the coffee. The kitchen—*my* kitchen—is just as I remember it.

"Mrs. Kinney." He comes in, cheerful as the sun, no matter how exhausted he looks, and I can tell he is delighted to call me such. His eyes are intense and happy, and his arms come out on their own accord to grab me around the waist, pulling me in for kisses and a squeeze.

"Paddy," I laugh. "Breakfast is ready."

"I'd like to say forget breakfast, I'll have you instead," he quips gamely. "But I'm half starved. What'll it be?"

"I've got flapjacks started. First batch is in the oven."

He pulls them out eagerly. "It's like the first mornin' all over again. Flapjacks!"

I pour out coffee. "Is it very cold out, yet?"

"No," he says, shaking his head and placing the hot food on the table. "Yesterday's snow's mostly gone already, but winter will come quick enough. Soon we will have many a cozy night while stayin' in around a fire. Good weather for makin' babies."

"Patrick!" I swat him with the dish towel. He grabs it as he used to do before, and brings me close, planting a kiss on me.

"I thought you wanted children."

I close my eyes against his nearness.

"Oh, yes."

"Well, we ought to get started," he says. "But first I need to eat, and those look delicious."

We sit down and he tells me about the horse that had to be shot. Danny Svendsen is stewing on what ailed the animal. Patrick himself needs to look up the beast's symptoms in one of his old veterinary books. And we need to head out to the Brinkley's this morning to check on Alice's condition. I am very eager to see my friend.

"What about Marie? You said she was expecting?"

"Aye." He sighs. "But I won't go unless she or her husband asks me to stop by."

We discuss how to best help Sadie manage her pregnancy, and talk about the lack of vandalism in town since Widow Hawks left. The notion that her presence spins violent acts gives me pause. I have a hope for her to still be part of our lives, but I need to be aware of all the pieces. As he guzzles down the coffee, he asks me to check on old Mrs. Pavlock's gout.

"She likes the chatter, and today I'm too busy for it. You don't mind?"

I don't, glad to help him right away. My role as house-keeper and part-time nursemaid falls completely back on my shoulders, and I find I am more than ready for all the tasks. It will be worth the hard hands, the calloused feet, the dusty hair, and the back-breaking hauling if only to do all of it with my husband.

Suddenly, he reaches for my hand. I stop eating and look up at him. His eyes are bright.

"This is how it will always be now, Jane. You and me, and God willin', children. Together at this table. And in our home. How did this happen?"

"Well, you chose my letter when you advertised for a housekeeper. And then we fell in love."

He chuckles. "You make it sound simple."

"All ended well, Paddy."

"It did," he agrees, and then smiles at me. "I don't know if it can get better than this."

I know how it might, for all the trouble it may bring. "I was thinking … We ought to go fetch Widow Hawks. Esther. I don't like the notion of her at the reservation. She's our family. Whether we build her a new little place, or have her come live with us, I feel as though we should bring her home to Flats Junction."

Patrick sits back, relaxed and considering. "Well, there isn't much room here. Perhaps we could have a little side room off the kitchen, or a cottage in the yard. Or yes, figure on a way to build her somethin'."

He obviously likes the idea, and I plunge in further, dreaming aloud. "It would help when the babies start arriv-ing, to have an extra set of hands around. Then I can still cook and clean and help you with the office and the patients.

Neither of us have family around to help as it were, and we'll need it."

He's nodding, agreeing. "We'll make plans to set right off to get her before the weather turns nasty, though it'll be tight. We can leave as soon as I finish all my rounds in the next few days."

"Kate won't be pleased with us," I warn, and he gives a half-contrite grin.

"I don't think she's a mite pleased with us anyway, gettin' married and all. But she's cast off her own family. We're adoptin' Esther as grandmother for our babes. It's a grand idea, Janie." He smiles again, and then sets out for another trip to visit patients so he might catch up on the town's long list of ailments.

I watch him leave, his bag in hand, to help ease discomfort and fix what he might. He is mine, and we have created a life, a family, and a purpose here. *It is enough.*

CHAPTER 50
9 November 1882

I am painfully tense as we make our way to Fort Randall.
Though renegade Sioux are no longer roaming the plains
and picking off travelers at a whim, the journey is still
tight with danger. There are wild animals, from wolves to
the rare bison, the uneasy fall weather, and of course, the
occasional group of self-named cowboys who are more like
pirates.

We have joined a small wagon train that will continue
further west. Flats Junction is still on one of the old trails,
the buffalo jump always doubling as a traditional stop. We
joined with the freighters going to the fort and the handful
of settlers hoping to get to the Black Hills before winter. It is
safest to go in such a group, and we are thankful for the men
and women in the wagons around us. The grass undulates,
reminding me once again of the ocean, though I do not long
for it as desperately anymore. The afternoon light is rich
with golden color, even as the days are cooling and nights are

colder. The people call to each other, hailing one another's children or shouting at horses or cattle.

Our own group is silent. Kate has joined Patrick and me and she is stonily quiet, which keeps us from having our own light chatter.

I did not expect her to come with us. Swallowing my discomfort in her presence, I had asked her to accompany the doctor and me to Fort Randall, where we are told Sitting Bull is kept captive. We hope to hear word of Widow Hawks there from the Sioux who scratch a living around the edges of the Army location. I thought Esther might actually agree to return to Flats Junction more readily if she could see Kate still held some sort of affection for her mother. And I wanted Kate to prove to me, and to Patrick, that she is not without redemption.

Her immediate response was to shut her door in my face. She is angry with me, of course, for marrying Patrick, for settling back into Flats Junction as if I'd never left, for wanting her mother to come back.

I waited until I was in the general to buy goods to ask once more. She will not refuse to serve anyone, regardless of her feelings or mood swings, and when I had dallied long enough until we were alone, I had begged her to reconsider.

"You're asking too much of me," she had snapped.

"No, I'm not," I'd retorted, knowing I was still pushing my luck. She would be swallowing her pride, facing her half-native heritage, and thereby reliving all of the ridicule she'd endured as a child. I could not imagine what emotions she wrestled with as she and I had bartered back and forth for a half hour.

In the end, I had left the general store with her resounding negative in my ears.

But as we hitched up a borrowed wagon, Kate arrived with a tight bundle and an even tighter look about her eyes. She didn't speak, and jumped into the back, her spine straight and her face away from us.

It has been three days on the journey to the reservation, and still she does not offer a single word to Patrick or me. I can only imagine the tempest in her heart. She is traveling with me—once a friend, and then a betrayer—and the man she'd thought would wed her.

And she is going against the independent nature she spent so long cultivating in defiance of the way some in Flats Junction treated her. She is, in her own eyes, a non-native, willful woman who has no need of family, especially the side that is Sioux. Oddly, considering what I've gathered from Widow Hawks, Kate would be welcomed wholeheartedly into the Blackfoot Sioux community, whereas she has had to fight constantly in Flats Junction to remind people of her preferred status.

Like me, Kate does not always choose the easy way.

I spend many hours musing over Kate's motives for joining us. I wonder if I will ever have a chance to ask her, or if she and I will ever have kind words between us again. Patrick doesn't seem to have half of my worries. He is merely glad she has decided to come. He seems to think she will have a change of heart when she sees her mother, but I do not have quite as much faith in Kate as that.

CHAPTER 51
12 November 1882

The Sioux village is dirty. It is the first word I think of as I look at the huts huddled near Fort Randall. Though this is not a reservation, it is nearly like one, with slapped-together shacks, so thin and ridiculously flimsy against the elements, never mind the winter weather that will arrive soon in the Territories. In the haphazard cluster of dwellings, I see some traditional tipis, a few *wetus* with smoke curling from the cracks, and a number of open campfires, rowdy children, and gaunt dogs. There is a lot of mud mixed with human debris. It is as if the tribes are trying to straddle two things; their community, and the way of the white settlers, and in doing so are failing in both respects. My heart aches with sadness and shame.

I am appalled that Widow Hawks, the neat, precise, graceful woman I remember, resides in a place like this. Surely, the real reservation will be better. But suppose it is not? I am once again thankful for my husband, who agreed with me that she must return to us.

Ignoring most of the Army soldiers milling around, Patrick makes inquiries with the Sioux as best he can. A few can capture the English words, and he knows just a little of their tongue. I am useless, so Kate and I sit in the wagon, watching Patrick gesture and pantomime. The man he is talking with finally shrugs, his face never once showing a flicker of emotion, and turns to give a guttural call: "*Mačsaŋni ki!*"

Eventually a woman pokes her head out of the nearby shack. She approaches and listens to Patrick inquire again. I think perhaps he has finally remembered Widow Hawk's name in *Sihasapa*. There is a nod.

He leads her to the wagon and helps her up. Behind her, the husband hands up two of the smallest children and goes back to the shack, his tall, lean body bending against the breeze, a gaggle of young ones still around his knees.

The woman turns to us, her black, beady gaze passing over me and landing on Kate. She stares, completely unabashed, at Kate's broad cheekbones and glossy locks. Finally, she puts one of the children next to me and says, brokenly, "To Čatán."

Čatán! I recall it is Widow Hawks' name. I nod, eager and hopeful. She knows of Esther? Where to go next?

Then Patrick says, "*Dowanhowee.*"

The woman pauses, looking between my husband and me. He nods, still holding the reins and watching the horses. The woman gives a shrug, acknowledging me.

"*Dowanhowee.*" Her voice makes the word sound earthy and rich.

Patrick offers a little smile. It seems he has remembered the name Widow Hawks' family gave me so long ago. I am touched and delighted.

We follow the line of the choppy road, around the meandering huts hugging the side of the fort walls. I am shocked at how many people live here, and the conditions they endure. Several men sit outside in the cold, looking worse for wear with drink, and the women seem worn and rough. It is as if they were placed here haphazardly, told to make a living from nothing, and perhaps that is what really happened. I find my lack of understanding frustrating and a bit frightening.

When we arrive at a very large tipi, the woman juts her chin toward a nearby *wetu*. Strange chanting filters out.

She says gravely, "*Inipi.*"

I do not know what she means until Patrick has the presence of mind to say to me, "Sweat lodge, for healing." I realize our new acquaintance has decided to show us the sights as we are obviously rather ignorant white travelers. I wonder how Patrick knows this, but maybe he often asked Widow Hawks what her people did for medicine.

As we sit in the wagon, Widow Hawks herself comes out of the nearest tipi. My heart stops. She's here!? Patrick gives a short, happy whoop, and swings down to her.

"Esther!"

She gives him a warm smile, the light of it chasing away the questions. He gives up all propriety and pulls her into an embrace. I climb down as well, and when Patrick is done with her, I take a turn. She feels the same in my arms, and I want to weep with relief. We'd thought we would have to inquire at Fort Randall, and then return to Flats Junction until spring allowed us a chance to travel further for her. My joy is a palpable thing in my chest.

"You came back, then, Jane?" she asks, though the answer is plain. "And married him? I am so glad."

401

"Now, it's your turn," I say, stepping back. "You must return, too."

She pauses, and doubt wrinkles her forehead. She gazes past me, to the wagon, where Kate still sits. As one, Patrick and I turn to watch. Kate is not moving, not looking at our trio, her head turned away to gaze out across the prairie.

"*Aŋgpétu!*"

The word is odd, and at first I do not realize it is a name. Kate's head whips around at the sound of it. She stares at Widow Hawks, her face unreadable and her jaw set. Intense wonderment strikes me. Why make this journey, in silence, in anger, if only to reject her mother again in the end? Did she wish to see Fort Randall only? See what the Sioux looked like when crowded together and their culture cracking? Where her mother would perhaps die and be buried? I could not even start to ask all the questions.

Widow Hawks calls again: "*Aŋgpétu!*" And then she moves toward Kate, who is frozen. As Widow Hawks draws up with the wagon, Kate stiffly clambers down until they are face to face. Their resemblance is immediately apparent, from the straight nose and cheekbones, to the carriage of their shoulders.

They do not embrace, and I suppose I do not expect it. Kate is likely too angry, and Widow Hawks too proud to ask what her daughter will not willingly give. But suddenly Kate gives a tight jerk of her head, an affirmation of some sort. With that, Widow Hawks turns and comes back to us, Kate following, and the other Indian woman clambers down with her children, chattering away to Widow Hawks as if a spell has been broken.

I am confused, but before I can start to ask Patrick questions, he is smiling and nodding.

"I think she will come back with us."

"I might have gathered that, but I don't know what decided her."

He begins to explain his theory but is interrupted by several bodies pouring out of the tipi. I recognize Widow Hawks' sister-in-law *Hantaywee*, and a few of the adolescent girls. We are ushered inside the tent flaps and I'm assailed with the scents of tobacco, urine, fur, smoke, and corn. Seated in a corner is the crumpled but smiling form of Widow Hawks' mother, and four men lounge near the central fire. They all sit up when we enter and scrutinize us, as so many have since our arrival.

We are served food and someone passes Patrick a pipe. Widow Hawks' mother smokes one behind us, and Widow Hawks herself is lively, chattering in a mix of native language and English. I stare at everything, from the mixed clothing to the oddly prepared food, even more unusual than what Widow Hawks used to make.

Kate sits next to me and refuses to eat or to join in any conversation. How does she stay so silent? Isn't she hungry? I do not think, even in my quieter days, that I could abstain so long from speaking to another person. She keeps her head down and her mouth tight, but I see Widow Hawks looking at her fondly, happily. It is as if Kate broke a barrier with arriving here, as if that was all Widow Hawks needed.

I smile at everyone, bobbing my head, and Patrick is talking with the men as best he can with their jumble of words. One of them, a strong handsome man, continues to gaze at me, and I wonder why. It ought to be apparent that I belong with Patrick. And then I realize he is not looking at me, but at Kate. She does not notice this, and I do not think she would like me taking liberties, telling her how a man has taken interest in her, especially a Blackfoot Sioux. Or maybe he is a similar Sioux tribe. *Hunkpapa*, like Sitting Bull.

The language washes over us, and every once in a while, Patrick gives my shoulder a squeeze. The men eventually take him out, and he explains briefly as he goes.

"One of the family is ill. They want me to take a look and see if I can do anythin'. We'll be spendin' a night or two here, Jane, and will catch others headin' toward Flats Junction so we aren't alone. I'll inquire about when the Army plans to head in for supplies. That will be a good escort."

"We'll all sleep together?" I ask incredulously, looking around the tipi. It is the first full conversation I've had in English since we've arrived, and I'm grateful he thinks to talk to me about all this. At least I will not be surprised.

"Yes, to keep warm, as it is. It will be alright; Esther is here and so is Kate."

"Will you be back quickly?"

"I don't know," he admits. "But they say it is not far, and if the illness is what I think, there will be little I can do."

"What is it?"

"Liver issue. Comes from too much of the drink. They'd do better with their beloved *pejute sapa* than liquor."

"The *what*?" I try not to let my sheer annoyance with all the language barriers show. It has been a trying day to say the least.

"Sorry. Coffee. They love it. In fact, why don't you pull ours out of the wagon to share around? Least we can do for their hospitality."

"But Patrick—I don't know what anyone is saying!" It's all I can do to keep from venting my frustration at him.

404

"Ask Esther to translate for you, she doesn't mind. Kate knows Lakota too. Or at least, she did in her youth. I won't be long."

With a brief peck on my forehead, he is gone into the late, chilly afternoon with the men.

I turn back to see Widow Hawks smiling at me. "What?"

She shakes her head. "It is so good to see you, Jane." There is much emotion in that comment, but I wonder if she cannot say more with Kate sitting nearby.

Instead, I try to talk of lighter things. "It seems my husband has the presence of mind to remember bits of your language, though I do not even know how to pronounce my own name."

Widow Hawks blinks, as if trying to remember it, and then translates. "It is *Dowanhowee*. Singing Voice."

"Oh." It does not seem a fitting name for me. I have never been praised for my voice, though perhaps to the Sioux it is different enough. I sound it out, and several of the children clamber over to help me say it. In the clutter of their voices, with soft hands on my knees and shoulders leaning into my body, I notice Widow Hawks smiling again at me, as if it is a vision she enjoys. I try not to wrinkle my nose at the pungent odors of fur and food hanging tightly around the little writhing bodies. This is her family, after all, and I do not want to offend anyone.

"So, then, what do you call Kate?" I ask, trying belatedly to bring her into the circle of conversation. She swings around to look at me, but her expression remains neutral. She will not offer me her name.

"She is *Aŋgpétu*. Part of her always will be." Widow Hawks looks directly at her daughter, as if memorizing her face, reminding herself of the girl and woman before her. "Radiant. Or simply, Day. That is what her name means, and to me, she will be so until she returns to the ancestors."

I almost expect a rejoinder to that, but Kate remains silent, as if willing herself to be separate. It is all I can do to not shake her, to beg her once again to consider her mother. But it is enough that she is here. I cannot ask more of her, and by the softness around Widow Hawks' face, I know she feels the same.

CHAPTER 52
21 November 1882

We will arrive back in Flats Junction late in the afternoon just before the tendrils of the next snowstorm of the season creep over the horizon, following an empty Army freighter and surrounded by a handful of men from Fort Randall. Kate and Widow Hawks sit side by side in the back of the wagon. I often sneak glances at them both. I have not seen or heard them speak a single word between them. Is it the Sioux way to say so little, to have an understanding with a simple nod of the head? Are they resolved to live near each other? Does Kate have any forgiveness in her for her mother's choices, and does Widow Hawks readily forgive Kate for her anger and rudeness?

Once I look back and I see their hands clutched, old and young fingers together, but the same shade of brown. I am relieved and heartened by this. I am sure my questions will be answered in time. That is the way of life, I suppose: to seek answers slowly, in a long revealing meandering, instead of having it all wrapped up neatly and easily.

"Esther will stay with me until she has a place of her own," Kate announces as we stop the horses near our home. It is shocking to hear her voice, and it is slightly hoarse from misuse, but most strange is the declaration.

"Stay with you?" Patrick is the first to recover.

Kate gives him a defiant look. I wonder when they discussed this, or if Widow Hawks is only hearing of it now. She is on the other side of the wagon, and I cannot see her face.

"Whatever you wish, Kate," I say. Perhaps this is the way to reconciliation after all: stilted, angry, and yet not without merit.

She pauses, gives a curt nod, and turns away. I give Patrick an incredulous glance, and he offers a cheeky grin and slight shrug in response. I'm not sure if any of us are truly vindicated by the past few weeks' actions, but I feel as if we might all be on a better footing now. That is comforting.

"Well, then, Janie." Patrick is at my shoulder as we both watch the two silent, straight backs of Kate and Esther walk away from us without another word. "Before we return the wagon to Sadie, and the extra horse to the Brinkleys, we ought to take a moment. I know you're no longer my housekeeper, but might you make up some flapjacks for your hungry husband? And before that, give him a kiss?"

I laugh with him, and willingly oblige.

The End

Notes for the Reader

Widow is set in the fictional town of Flats Junction in a very real historical backdrop of the Dakota Territories in the late 1800s. The map of the territory in the beginning is correct, as are the rail lines shown on it. I placed Flats Junction at a cross in the rails, where a junction made sense, but also added a historic Sioux hunting ground, where later wagon trains chose to stop. There are many prehistoric buffalo jump sites in South Dakota that simply do not have the funding for excavation. If you find one, you might even find old bison bones piled up at the bottom.

Jane's experiences in Gloucester are also steeped in history, and the references to the living experiences Esther/ Widow Hawks and her family experienced outside Fort Randall are true. In fact, today the only reservation where there is still her specific branch of Sioux—the Blackfoot Sioux, or *Sihasapa*—is Standing Rock Reservation, where Sitting Bull was taken in 1883 after captivity at Fort Randall.

Many tidbits dropped into the story are fact. For instance, by the 1880s, nearly all the bison were gone from the prairie, which is why one spotted was a rarity. The railroad building in the Dakotas had jumped back into action after the recovery from the economic depression of the early 1870s, and almost all of the local First Nation members were on reservations after Sitting Bull turned himself in during the summer of 1881. The newspaper article on the first page lists true advertisements from the time that I've cobbled together from various newspapers of the era—all except the one Jane answers, as it were.

In the 1880s, doctors were just starting to gain a solid foothold as a profession, and their reputation and belief in the science they practiced was a struggle the further west one traveled. Doctor Kinney may have found his footing seven years into living in Flats Junction, but would just as often hit resistance. People did not yet fully understand the concept of microbes or the dangers of childbirth, though doctors who kept themselves informed would be learning quickly of all the ongoing changes in the medical field. Jane's husband Henry would have, with the right type of doctor, been diagnosed correctly to have cancer, but the medical communities in America had no real way to test for multiple cancer types, and were only just starting to think about how to treat it. Surgery was still very rife with risk, even with the existence of carbolic acid for disinfectant and the use of crude anesthesia—and that assumes the doctor operating believed in the use of disinfectant to begin with! The dangers of abortion were whispered, as the Comstock law made information about the body—not just abortion, but contraceptives and anatomy as well—illegal, for their "lewd" instruction. An informed woman would have to take a risk of abortion or childbirth, but both were likely to end in death. The self-abortion written on the patient sheet of EvaRose the prostitute was a common antidote to an unwanted pregnancy in the 1800s.

It would have been two years of mourning for Jane after Henry Weber died, and those years would have been spent in black and grey, purple and lavender, so her change to colorful clothes in less than six months would have felt highly improper to an Eastern woman. Plus, her pregnancy would have been quite a huge scandal considering the timing. Jane's miscarriage and subsequent hemorrhage is correctly portrayed.

The Irish really did have a huge hand in creating the West, and America, as we know it. With their ability to assimilate, as well as the lack of a social hierarchy in Western towns, the Irish typically found little resistance in finding success, but not always.

All the food and kitchen tools used in Jane's kitchens, and the "new inventions" Trusty Willy bought, are period correct, and while it was not common, women could and did run general stores and tinsmith shops and post offices. The West was very much a place of new freedom, for all that it also could hold with typical prejudices and intolerances. Living for that freedom, and for love and family, was intensely important to all the pioneers. It's a theme, I think, that is still important today.

With joy—Sara Dahmen
overlooking the fields, Wisconsin

Acknowledgements

It truly takes an army to get a book off the ground, and I've been fortunate to have a ridiculous amount of support and mentors throughout the years as well as family members who understand my need to write. First, thank you to Ben and all the folks at Promontory Press for giving this book its second life. I am incredibly appreciative of the support of the series and Ben's deep, sincere ability to see the big picture. Thank you to Lenore for creating the media around Flats Junction so it roars. I must also thank my editor, Craig Andersen, for the nudging on a variety of corners to prod *Widow 1881* into the form it takes today. And thank you to Bonnie Nadell and her associates at the Hill Nadell Agency for loving *Widow 1881*!

A shout goes to Leanne Yarrow, for the brainstorming session out of which Jane's agony arose. Without the guidance of Lesley Kagen, I likely would still be foundering in the early wanderings of a newly minted author. Thanks to Kathy and Daine for believing in the series. And without my parents and my in-laws, I'd probably never get two seconds to write, as they help corral my children as needed—children who I hope will read this someday or become authors themselves.

And of course, this book owes its lifeblood to John. My husband. My *wičaȟča mihigna*. My "other skin."

Historical References

Steele, Volney, M.D. *Bleed, Blister, and Purge: A History of Medicine on the American Frontier*. Missoula: Mountain Press Publishing Company, 2005.

Utley, Robert M. *The Indian Frontier of the American West, 1846–1890*. Albuquerque: University of New Mexico Pres, 1984.

Mueller, James E. *Shooting Arrows and Slinging Mud: Custer, the Press, and the Little Bighorn*. Norman: University of Oklahoma Press, 2013.

Bynum. W. F. *Science and the Practice of Medicine in the Nineteenth Century*. Cambridge, UK: Cambridge University Press, 1994.

Tyler, John. *Early American Cast Iron Holloware 1645–1900*. Atglen: Schiffer Publishing, Ltd., 2013.

Hyslop, Stephen G. *The Old West*. Washington D.C.: National Geographic Society, 2015.

Wright, John Hardy. *Images of America: Gloucester and Rockport*. Charleston: Arcadia Publishing, 2000.

Frontier America: The Far West. Boston: Museum of Fine Arts, 1974.

Erbsen, Wayne. *Manners and Morals of Victorian America*. Ashville: Native Ground Books & Music, 2009.

Cosentino, Geraldine and Regina Stewart. *Kitchenware: A Guide for the Beginning Collector.* New York: Golden Press, 1977.

St. Germain, Paul. *Cape Ann Granite.* Charleston: Arcadia Publishing, 2015.

Wright, Carroll D. *The Working Girls of Boston.* Boston: Fifteenth Annual Report of the Massachusetts Bureau of Statistics of Labor, 1884.

White Hat, Albert, Sr. *Reading and Writing the Lakota Language.* Salt Lake City: University of Utah Press, 1999.

Dungan, Myles. *How the Irish Won the West.* New York: Skyhorse Publishing, 2011.

Wilbur, C. Keith, M.D. *Antique Medical Instruments.* West Chester: Schiffer Publishing Ltd., 1987.

Broom County Historical Society. *The American Hearth.* Exhibition Brochure.

Webb, Jim. *Born Fighting: How the Scots-Irish Shaped America.* New York: Broadway Books, 2004.

Barnes, Ian. *The Historical Atlas of Native Americans.* New York: Chartwell Books, 2015.

Book Club Questions

1. Jane is rightfully nervous about moving to the western Territories. Are there ways in which you would contrast the physical hardships of Western daily life to the new kinds of expectations and hardships modern women manage?

2. The idea of staying with a Sioux Indian would be frightening at the least to an Eastern woman who has been taught that all Indians are savage. What character traits does Jane show by staying with Widow Hawks anyway?

3. Widow Hawks and her family are often referred to with fear, but her behavior is never nefarious. Are there ways you would consider Widow Hawks to still be uncivilized?

4. Did you feel Kate's attitude toward her mother was justified? How is her behavior similar to what we see in mother/daughter relationships today?

5. Were you surprised at Widow Hawks' resigned attitude toward her living situation? Would you have stayed and suffered violence to be near family?

6. Did you find Jane's lack of attachment to her child or deceased husband shocking or surprising?

7. How is Jane a product of her time?

8.   Do you think Jane was particularly obtuse about the budding romantic interest of the doctor? Do you think she loved him before she articulated it? Why do you suppose she did not act on her growing attachment to him and instead pushed him toward Kate?

9.   Compare your concept of romantic love and married love to Jane's other romances. What did you think about her marriage to Henry? Her courtship with Bern and Andrew? Do you think these types of marriages and relationships still exist in our society? Do you think they end similarly? That is, do people still marry for some convenience and plan to stick together?

10.   Jane's behavior with Theodore during her early widowhood would have been considered exceptionally scandalous for her time. Today, unmarried or unattached pregnant women do not suffer such extreme stigma in general; how do you think behaviors and prejudices have changed? Stayed the same?

11.   Were you surprised by the violence done to Widow Hawks and the lack of response to it by the town? How you do feel about her role as the banker's mistress for many decades?

12.   What do you think is the biggest turning point in the book? Why?

13.   Were you surprised at the depiction of the Native American situation along the walls of Fort Randall when Jane and Patrick go to get Widow Hawks?

14. Flats Junction is populated by many different people. Did you have a reaction to any of the other peripheral characters? Why?

15. Do you think Kate was a relatable character? Do you feel she imbues parts of your personality in some respects, in terms of her independence? Is she a redemptive character?

The Flats Junction Series

Tinsmith 1865
Medicineman 1876
Widow 1881
Outcast 1883
Trader 1884
Stranger 1886

For more information,
visit www.flatsjunction.com.

To connect with Sara,
visit www.saradahmen.com.
Find her on Twitter at @saradahmenbooks,
on Facebook, or Instagram at @sara_dahmen.

To learn about Sara's cookware line
inspired by her research for Flats Junction,
visit www.housecopper.com.